Lizzie Enfield is a journalist and regular contributor to national newspapers and magazines. She is married with three children and lives in Brighton.

Praise for Lizzie Enfield:

'Wonderfully funny and warm but also thought-provoking, we loved this' *Closer*

'A clever, witty read' *Best* magazine

'You'll love debating the questions raised by this deliciously witty, thought-provoking novel' *Weightwatchers* magazine

'A warm-hearted and engaging insight into many a marriage' *Take A Break*

'Picking up this book is like meeting a dear friend . . . This is her first novel and we can only hope for more' *Red* Online

'A funny, warm debut' *Bella*

'Wonderfully funny and warm but also thought-provoking, we loved this' *Closer*

'For the Allison Pearson market and a sophisticated cut above the orm' *Bookseller*

D1579627

By Lizzie Enfield and available from Headline Review

WHAT YOU DON'T KNOW
UNCOUPLED

Uncoupled

LIZZIE ENFIELD

headline
review

Copyright © 2012 Lizzie Enfield

The right of Lizzie Enfield to be identified as the Author of
the Work has been asserted by her in accordance with the
Copyright, Designs and Patents Act 1988.

First published in 2012
by HEADLINE REVIEW
An imprint of HEADLINE PUBLISHING GROUP

First published in paperback in 2012 by HEADLINE REVIEW

1

Apart from any use permitted under UK copyright law, this
publication may only be reproduced, stored, or transmitted, in
any form, or by any means, with prior permission in writing of
the publishers or, in the case of reprographic production, in
accordance with the terms of licences issued by the
Copyright Licensing Agency.

All characters in this publication are fictitious
and any resemblance to real persons, living or dead,
is purely coincidental.

ISBN 978 0 7553 7790 9

Typeset in Bembo Book MT Std by
Palimpsest Book Production Limited, Falkirk, Stirlingshire
Printed and bound by CPI Group (UK) Ltd, Croydon, CR0 4YY

Headline's policy is to use papers that are natural, renewable and
recyclable products and made from wood grown in sustainable
forests. The logging and manufacturing processes are expected
to conform to the environmental regulations of the country of origin.

HEADLINE PUBLISHING GROUP
An Hachette UK Company
338 Euston Road
London NW1 3BH

www.headline.co.uk
www.hachette.co.uk

To Chrissie, Kitty and Lucas
(you shouldn't be reading this yet)

Chapter One

BBC Radio 4
12 April
9 a.m.
The news is read by Charlotte Green.
We are getting very early reports of a train crash on the Brighton to London line. Part of the Southern train appears to have derailed inside the Balcombe tunnel between Haywards Heath and Gatwick Airport. Passengers on board say the vehicle was going into the tunnel, when there was a loud crash and it jolted to a halt.

Emergency services are on the way to the scene . . .

Holly knew that by staying with her he was putting himself at risk. But, as he held her in the darkness, she didn't want him to let go.

He squeezed her hand, as if he knew what she was thinking, and said, 'It'll be OK.'

It was eerily quiet in the tunnel and Holly suspected he was as scared as she was. The initial cries of surprise, when the train had lurched from standstill and ricocheted off the walls on to its side, had quickly given way to a quieter sense of shock and then a unanimous flurry of activity.

'We ought to get out,' several voices had said at once.

'We'll need to break the windows,' a chorus of others responded.

Then there was the sound of windows breaking and people scrambling up over the upturned floor of the carriage, desperate to escape.

No one actually said, 'Do you think it was a bomb?' or 'There could be another.'

And, with a perverse sense of logic, Holly thought that as long as she didn't say it either then it might make it untrue.

But that didn't stop her from being terrified, especially when people began to struggle up from wherever they'd been thrown and edge themselves towards the broken carriage windows. Then she realised that she was trapped beneath the twisted metal of her seat and couldn't move.

'We need to get out,' a soft voice said somewhere near her.

In the weak light, emanating from mobile phones and laptop screens, Holly could just about make out the outline of the young man who'd been sitting opposite her.

'I can't move,' she told him, surprising herself by sounding remarkably calm and matter-of-fact. 'I don't think I'm hurt but I can't get out from under the seat.'

He bent down to investigate and felt for her in the semi-darkness, brushing her torso with his hands without apology.

'It's twisted.' He tried to move the seat but it was firmly lodged against the wall of the carriage and over Holly's prone body.

Holly saw him turn and look towards the other passengers who were now climbing through the broken windows.

'Please don't leave me,' she heard herself say, although she wished she hadn't.

He ought to get out too, whoever he was. He might have a wife and family of his own who needed him more than she did.

But he was already settling down beside her, reaching out for her hand and taking hold of it.

Holly felt strangely detached from what was going on, as if she was watching it happen to someone else. She urged herself to think of Mark and the children, to try to see their faces and hear their chatter. She was physically unable to do anything, but at least she could stay focused on the people she needed to get out for.

As if he too was thinking the same thing, he began asking questions.

'Are you married?'

'Yes.' Holly felt the reassuring warmth of his hand in hers. 'And I've got two children.'

'Tell me about them,' he said.

Holly wished he'd been more specific, asked her what her name was or how long she'd been married or what she did or how old she was. His question was too general.

'Mark, my husband . . .' She considered this, thinking it was important to describe him accurately now. 'He's kind and clever and funny and good looking. And he's very compelling. If you met him, you would like him. Everybody does.'

Holly never prayed but she hoped hard now that Mark knew this was how she thought of him. He'd been a bit down recently, his energy diminished, and slightly less himself. She knew he was worried about work but hadn't asked if anything else was bothering him.

'And the children?' he asked, squeezing her hand again. 'Are they boys or girls?'

'A girl and a boy,' she said. 'They are both gorgeous.'

Saying this helped her sense them more keenly.

Chloe seemed to be emerging from the moody phase of

adolescence, beautiful, clever and enjoying Holly's company again, while Jake still filled her with wonder every time she looked at him. Even though his beautiful fresh face was peppered with spots and his hair was beginning to smell of wet PE kit, he still seemed impossibly perfect.

Chloe had been in the shower when she'd left the house and Holly had shouted goodbye through the sound of running water, but her daughter hadn't answered.

'Bye, Jakey,' Holly had said, trying to force something muttered out of him, when he left for school.

A group of his friends had called and when Holly opened the door and Jake had snuck past, his adolescent body language screamed: Don't try to kiss or hug me in front of my friends!

'I didn't say goodbye properly to any of them this morning,' she said, as if confessing this to a stranger would ease the burden of not having done so.

'We'll be out of here soon enough,' he tried to reassure her, but she could hear the fear in his voice.

Holly thought of her late grandmother, Mary, whose mantra had been: 'Never leave the house without saying goodbye properly, you never know when you might be hit by a bus.'

Mary had been Irish and her life was governed by superstitions. She was for ever crossing herself, calling upon various saints or shouting, 'Get those shoes off the table, before something terrible occurs!'

The saying goodbye properly was founded on a terrible reality. Her husband Bob had been knocked down and killed by a 5A bus, as he went to buy a paper. It had happened on the same morning Mary had turned on him in an uncharacteristic fit of anger when he'd asked, innocently enough, 'What's it like out? Will I need a coat?'

'How do I know if you need your coat or not? Are you not

old enough to decide for yourself?' she had shouted at him across the breakfast table. 'I've enough children without you wanting to become one of them yourself.'

'I'm sure he was fretting about it and not concentrating,' Mary said later, referring to the moment when Bob stepped into the path of the oncoming double-decker. 'Perhaps that's why he wasn't looking properly.'

Mary came to live with them, shortly after her husband's death. So Holly spent the last years of her teenage life unable to leave the house without an elaborate ritual of goodbyes. It had made her anxious at the time, never leaving to go to school without being reminded she might meet an untimely end.

As an adult, she'd happily shut the door on her family and gone wherever she was going without saying any fond farewells first.

But now, as her grandmother's face swam into the forefront of her mind, Holly wished she'd opened the door of the bathroom and said goodbye to Chloe through the steam of the shower, and that, instead of respecting Jake's pre-pubescent angst, she'd ruffled his hair as he left for school.

To Mark her goodbye had been a slightly mocking, 'Are you going to wear that hat to work?'

She'd said it in a tone that people who have been married for a long time reserve for each other. It wasn't outright rude but it implied that she didn't think it suited him. Twenty years ago Holly thought Mark utterly gorgeous, no matter what he put on or took off.

'Mark bought a hat at the weekend,' Holly told the man with her now.

'Yes?' He sounded unsure how to react to this.

'The children liked it but I didn't really.'

It was a grey pork-pie style with blue-spotted ribbon trim. A very pretty girl had been selling them in an outside stall in the North Laine. Holly thought Mark had stopped to look at the hats so that he could get a better look at the pretty girl and had been surprised when he had begun trying them on.

'How much was it?' she asked him as they continued their walk through the North Laine to the seafront.

'It was only eight pounds,' he said, and Holly presumed he'd thought this a price worth paying not to have the pretty girl think him a time-waster.

He had put the hat on when they'd got home.

'I love it.' Chloe had run her finger around the ribbon. 'Is it vintage? Can I borrow it?'

'You look like one of the Specials,' Jake had said, and Mark had done a little ska dance in the sitting room.

'When have you come across the Specials?' Holly asked.

'Chloe bought a vinyl album in the market.'

'But we don't have anything to play records on.'

'I know,' Chloe interjected. 'I want to get a turntable for my birthday. They're cool.'

'We should go to a gig sometime, Hol,' Mark had said, singing the first few lines of *Too Much Too Young* and taking her hands so she had to join him in the sitting-room dance.

Chloe had laughed but Jake had rolled his eyes in embarrassment and then done an impression of his parents' generation's dance routines.

'This is how middle-aged people dance.' He had stood up and, with his feet firmly rooted to the floor, twisted slightly at the waist and moved his arms a fraction. 'And then, when they get drunk, they do this!'

Jake had raised one leg off the floor, continued the slight twisting of the waist and begun rotating the lifted foot around in the same direction.

It was a good impression and they'd all laughed.

'It was worth eight pounds, just for that,' Holly had said, when Mark took the hat off.

Later, when she was brushing her teeth and she'd looked at Mark, lying naked in the bath, his hair plastered against the sides of his face, she had wondered if he was becoming sensitive about his receding hairline and the tiny coin-shaped patch of baldness which was new to the top of his head.

She'd bent over the side of the bath and kissed him and he'd slipped his hand under her dressing gown and stroked her breast, saying, 'I'll be out in a minute.'

Holly tried to keep hold of that moment now, and the evening which preceded it, not think about what might happen next.

'You should go,' she said, suddenly resolute that she shouldn't rob this stranger of his chance to get out of danger and near-stifling darkness.

'Is there anybody in here?' a voice rang out through the carriage.

'Here!' he called back. 'There's a woman over here. Her leg's trapped under the luggage rack and she can't get out.'

'It's OK now, love.' The voice came closer. 'We'll try and get you moved as soon as possible. Are you hurt, sir?'

Torches flashed through the carriage and Holly saw clearly again the face of the man who'd been sitting opposite her before it all happened.

He was bending towards her, and kissing her on the forehead.

'Good luck,' he whispered.

'Thank you.' Holly heard her own voice say this quietly. As she let go of his hand he disappeared into a blur of fluorescent jackets.

Chapter Two

People asked Holly afterwards if her life had flashed before her and she said, 'No, not exactly.'

She had suddenly recalled certain scenes from her life so vividly that they seemed almost real, like the last time the family had been on holiday in Cornwall. She wondered afterwards if she'd thought of this because they were going again to the same part of the country in a week's time. By recalling the past in such detail, she was probably subconsciously trying to cling to the future.

'Dad bought a wetsuit!' Chloe and Jake looked flushed and healthy from the two hours they'd spent chasing waves. They were beside themselves with laughter at Mark's new buy.

Holly had no idea why this was so funny but their laughter was infectious and she began giggling too, as she waited to find out what the joke was.

'Where is Dad now?' she asked them, as they queued to buy hot chocolate at the café next to the surf-hire shop. 'Does he want a drink too?'

'He's waiting in the car.' This was enough to start Chloe off again.

'He won't be joining us,' Jake snorted. 'He said we can have the drinks in the car. He wants to go straight back to the cottage.'

'Yes,' Chloe spluttered. 'He wants to go straight back!'

It was early May and Holly had the tail end of a cold and had not wanted to go in the sea, with or without a wetsuit. So Mark had spent the last couple of hours body-boarding on the beach at Polzeath, while Holly had walked across the cliffs to Daymer Bay and back. She'd hoped they'd all have a drink or lunch in the café together and wondered why he was so anxious to get back.

Perhaps he was cold, she thought. The children were rosy with exertion but when she'd kissed them their cheeks were freezing.

'Two hot chocolates, please, and a cup of tea,' she said, when she reached the front of the queue. 'And should I get something for Dad? Did he say?'

'Why don't you get him a hot chocolate and I'll have two if he doesn't want it?' Jake suggested hopefully, and looked surprised when Holly said that was a good idea.

They walked the short distance across the sand to where Mark was waiting in the car. He was sitting on a towel, still wearing his wetsuit. He looked up and smiled when Holly knocked on the window with the lid of the cup.

'Hot chocolate?' she asked as he wound the window down.

'Thank you, gorgeous.' He took it from her and winked.

'Chloe and Jake can't tell me for laughing how you came to buy a wetsuit,' she said, before walking round to the passenger seat and getting in. 'I take it it's the one you are modelling right now?'

'Does my paunch look big in it?' Mark asked, sitting up straighter and breathing in as she sat next to him.

Holly glanced down at his stomach. Wetsuits flattered only the very shapely. For all that they held bits of you in, they seemed to dislodge other bits and made you bulge in places where you hadn't previously. Mark now had a strange tyre slightly higher than where his, only recently acquired, excess flesh usually protruded.

'You've hardly got a paunch.' She leaned over and ran her hand across the black material of the wetsuit. She hadn't thought she had a thing for clammy Neoprene but felt slightly turned on by the feel of Mark's belly beneath it. If the children had not been climbing into the back of the car, she would have been tempted to undo the zip and stick her hand beneath it.

'I've got enough of a paunch that I may never be able to get out of this bloody thing.' Mark glanced over his shoulder at Chloe and Jake. 'You might have to cut me out of it when we get home, Holly.'

'That's why he bought it,' Chloe said triumphantly, doing up her seatbelt. 'It took him about half an hour to get it on, and when we'd finished he said he couldn't face trying to get out of it on the beach . . .'

'So he told the guys at the shop he wanted to buy it and wear it home!' Jake finished off the story for her.

'Really?' Holly looked at Mark.

'Really.' He looked sideways at her and shrugged. 'Thirty quid to save myself the embarrassment of being a fat bloke on a beach, trying to get out of a wetsuit. I need to lose some weight. I've had too many business lunches this year.'

'You look good to me.' Holly reached her hand over the gear stick and rubbed his stomach beneath the suit material again. It was true he had put on a bit of weight recently, but she thought it suited him. He was tall enough to carry off a bit of extra flesh around his midriff and, perversely, she found the flaw made him more attractive to her anyway. It was as if the slight imperfection of middle-aged spread and the few grey hairs that were appearing in his otherwise full head of dark hair gave him a kind of vulnerability which had previously been lacking.

Mark had always seemed too physically perfect to her. He was tall and dark and lean, but with a kindness to his face that softened his otherwise almost intimidating good looks. The stretches and scars of childbirth and the tell-tale signs of middle age had left a definite impression on Holly herself and, in moments of self-doubt, she felt inferior by comparison. So Mark's tiny bit of extra belly and his obvious embarrassment about it made her feel less vulnerable herself and more protective towards him.

'It was that trip to Finland that did it,' he said, starting the engine of the car. 'They fed us every five minutes.'

'Only when they weren't whipping you,' Chloe sang from the back of the car.

'Birching.' Mark grinned over his shoulder at her. 'There's a difference, you know.'

'It's all part and parcel of selling whisky to the Finns,' Holly said. 'Or so I'm told.'

'It's true.' Mark began reversing out of the parking space. 'Most of the business on that trip was conducted in the sauna or the snow, with a little light birching in between. I still have the scars to show for it.'

'Don't I know it!' Holly grinned.

Mark's business partner, Chris, had corroborated his version of discussing whisky sales in the sauna, before being led naked into the snow and handed twigs for tapping away impurities.

'I started tapping Mark and wondering how we would ever face each other in the office again,' Chris had told her, 'when Iivarim, who was six foot six and had the most enormous balls I've ever seen, said we weren't doing it hard enough and took over!'

'I've never been so scared in a professional capacity,' Mark had told Holly, as she rubbed Sudocrem on to the welt marks. 'But it was worth it. They're going to start selling Red Ptarmigan in several Finnish hotel chains.'

'Did they get a good deal?' Holly asked as Mark winced when she came across a wound that looked slightly raw.

'Yes. As you can see, they put me under pressure, Holly,' he laughed back and then inhaled sharply as her hands moved down his back.

'The wetsuit wasn't the only humiliation I've been subjected to today,' Mark said as he drove between the lines of cars parked on the beach. Their boots served as changing rooms for hard-core surfers, all of whom, Holly noted and hoped Mark hadn't, seemed to be peeling off wetsuits with ease and revealing perfectly honed torsos.

'You know that deli in St James' Street at home?' Mark looked ahead.

'Yes?' Holly caught sight of a man who had taken off his wetsuit and was wearing nothing underneath it. 'Wow!'

'What?' Mark glanced in the surfer's direction but he'd stepped around the side of a camper van.

'Nothing.' Holly smiled to herself. 'You were saying about the deli in St James' Street?'

'Yes. There's a very pretty girl who works in there. We had a conversation about Cornwall once and I told her we often went to Polzeath and went surfing.' Mark paused as he checked the traffic before pulling on to the road. 'She looked suitably impressed when I said it.'

'Do you mean you gave her the impression you were like someone out of *Endless Summer*?' Holly eyed him quizzically.

'Not quite, but maybe one of the penguins in *Surf's Up*.' Mark shrugged.

'How does she come into your humiliating day?' Holly asked.

'We got one really good wave that took us right to the shore and as I was floundering around in the shallows, trying to get up and looking like a beached whale, I heard this voice say, "Aren't you from Brighton?"' Mark pulled out into the road. 'I looked up to see this vision in a wetsuit, with a proper standing-up surfboard tucked under her arm, looking at me as if to say, "I never believed you could really surf."'

'I'm sure she was looking at you as if to say, "Wow, he looks hot in that wetsuit!"' Holly laughed.

'Err Mum, pl-ease,' Jake and Chloe had chorused from the back seat.

They'd have pl-eased some more if they hadn't gone downstairs to make more hot chocolate and slump in front of the television the moment they got back to the holiday cottage.

It had a huge wet room just by the front door and Mark had gone in there to try to get out of his new wetsuit and take a shower.

'Can you help me undo the bloody thing?' he'd called to Holly, as the kids disappeared downstairs, and after she'd managed slowly to unroll the suit as far as his waist, she'd found middle-aged spread wasn't the only bulge that was making it difficult to get off.

'That's not helping.'

She'd looked up at Mark and he'd looked at her and said, 'You're looking a bit salty after your walk, Holly. Why don't you have a shower too?'

I watched the news, because I couldn't think what else to do. I'd cried all afternoon, after I got the call. Then, when I was exhausted from the tears, I cleaned the kitchen; scrubbed it from top to bottom. I had to do something and cleaning has a certain reassuring rhythm and effect.

'Call someone,' Julia had said, when she left. 'Do you want me to call someone? You shouldn't be on your own.'

'No,' I snapped at her, partly because it wasn't her place to call anyone. It wasn't her who had lost her husband and I couldn't bear her concern. It seemed to make it worse, Julia thinking she might help if she called someone else to come and be with me. I didn't want to give her the satisfaction of saying, 'I made sure she had someone with her, just in case.' I wanted her to worry about me.

Besides, I couldn't think who else to call. I don't have that many friends here. Julia had to go and pick up her children from school and nursery; Toby and Gemma, her perfect offspring, one dark like her ex-husband and one blonde, like herself.

'Blessed,' my mother would have said, of her children, if she were still alive to see them. 'She's blessed with two beautiful children.'

My mother was only blessed with the one. 'A gift from God,' she used to tell me and anyone else who cared to listen. She was forty-four when I was born. Mum thought she couldn't have children. She'd resigned herself to a life without them and then suddenly 'a gift from God'.

Geoff and I hadn't been blessed either but I didn't want to think about that, not today. It was too much, on top of everything else. I'd lost my husband and with him my chance to have a child.

Julia, Toby and Gemma would be the perfect family, except that Andrew, her ex, left her not long after Gemma was born.

'He said it wasn't what he wanted,' she told me once, when I was having coffee in her kitchen. She threw out her arm in a broad sweep as she said it, as if it was the kitchen and the dining room and the lounge beyond that Andrew hadn't wanted, rather than Julia and the children and the domesticity.

'Do you think you'll ever get back together again?' I asked her once, over another coffee. That seemed to be the extent of our friendship really, the odd coffee, but in the absence of any others, I valued that. I thought of her as my best friend, at this stage of my life, because really there weren't any others.

I thought Andrew might regret it later, that one rash moment, triggered by something probably insignificant that made him decide to leave behind his life to date. I know my mother regretted not being at home with me when I was a teenager, even though she said she couldn't help the way she felt at the time.

'I should have been there for you then,' she said to me, when I visited her in hospital the week before she died.

'I was OK, Mum,' I said, lying to protect her. There was no point her knowing then how much I had hated the new life her absence forced upon me. And it was behind me now. I had Geoff and I was looking forward, not back.

Now I found myself looking backward again, to my time with him, because I couldn't bring myself to think forward, to the time without him.

So I put on BBC News 24 and watched their coverage of the crash, giving it my full time and attention, hoping maybe I'd catch a glimpse of Geoff, see him again in the moments while he was still mine. It seemed possible while I was watching. I almost believed that, if I caught sight of him on the television, then perhaps I'd be able to turn the clock back and make it all go away.

But I didn't see Geoff. By the time I turned the television on, the emergency services had been there for several hours and the reporter was saying that they were still working to free people stuck in the wreckage.

Then they cut to footage, filmed earlier, showing ambulance workers carrying a woman on a stretcher away from the mouth of the tunnel. There was a close-up of her face and I thought I recognised her from the train.

I've definitely seen her before. She's a striking-looking woman, with dark hair and dark eyes, not young but beautiful. I was sure as I watched her being carried on the stretcher that I'd sat opposite her a few weeks ago and she had smiled when I sat down, acknowledging my presence with an openness that a lot of commuters don't have.

They didn't say, on the news, what had happened to her or whether she was seriously injured or not, but when I saw her face she looked haunted, as if she'd seen something she wished she had never seen.

I recognised the look immediately, because it was the same look my mother wore when she'd realised exactly what we'd been a part of: a look that sets you apart from the rest of the world. The look of someone who has witnessed something they wish they'd never had to.

The woman on the news had been trapped in that tunnel God knows how long. Minutes? Hours? The reporter didn't say. But however long it was, it must have been long enough for her to question whether she'd ever get out. I wondered then, as I looked at her moving off the screen into a waiting ambulance, if she'd seen Geoff.

Had he passed her in the carriage, and had she smiled at him when he noticed her while looking for a seat?

The TV camera cut back to the mouth of the tunnel, where the back end of the train was being slowly pulled back, and the reporter was saying it might take days to clear the wreckage from the line, but it would take everyone caught up in the accident much longer to get their lives back on track.

I felt as if he was talking directly to me, as if he knew that without Geoff I had no idea how I was going to carry on. There are only so many times you can keep on picking up the pieces and carrying on. I didn't know if I could do it again, but I knew that in a few weeks' time, when people stopped being sympathetic and understanding and asking how I was, that was what I was going to have to do.

And so was she, the women on the stretcher. She was going to have to carry on too.

Chapter Three

BBC Radio 4
14 April
4 p.m.
The news is read by Corrie Corfield.
Another person has died in hospital following a train crash in Sussex earlier this week. Greg Simpson was travelling in one of the carriages of the commuter train, which came uncoupled and was hit by another train in the Balcombe tunnel near Haywards Heath. His death brings the total number killed to five. Several others involved in the crash are still being treated for their injuries, though none are thought to be life-threatening. The line between Haywards Heath and Gatwick Airport remains closed while accident investigators try to find out how the carriages from the Brighton train became detached . . .

'Your mother's here.' Mark didn't usually curtain twitch when either of Holly's parents was expected, but today he seemed eager for her mum to arrive. 'She's never going to get the car in that space.'

'Don't watch her.' Holly could hear a car moving backwards

and forwards, snail-like. 'You'll put her off. She hates parking at the best of times.'

'I'll put the kettle on,' Mark said.

He'd been doing this more or less constantly for the past two days. Holly wished she'd been able to go straight back to work, but people kept saying it was too soon: Mark, the counsellor he'd arranged for her to see tomorrow, the paramedics who had checked her over after she was cut free from the train, and her mother when she'd spoken to her on the phone.

'It feels odd, us both being at home with the children at school and nothing to do,' Holly kept saying to Mark, who had taken time off to look after her.

'Do you want a cup of tea?' was his usual reply.

Holly was glad of her mother's visit. Susan didn't really do fussing, a fact Jake became aware of when he was about five years old and she had looked after him for the day.

'If I fall over,' he told Holly on her return from wherever it was she had been, 'you stop whatever you are doing and say, "Oh, dear, darling, are you all right?" But Granny just carries on whatever she is doing and says, "Bad luck!"'

Holly suspected that if Susan mentioned the train crash at all it would be obliquely: 'How are you, really?' rather than just 'How are you?' or 'Have you been eating properly?'

She wondered what her mother would make of the fact she was booked to see a counsellor tomorrow. Neither of her parents believed in going over things.

'In my day,' her father, Patrick, would say if the subject arose, 'people just built the Burma railway and got on with it.'

Holly realised she was more like her parents than she had previously thought.

Even as Mark was phoning the counsellor to book an appointment, she was thinking that she didn't need it.

'I was lucky to get out alive and unhurt, when so many others were not,' she told him. 'I'd rather go back to work or do something than sit around talking about it.'

'It's too soon,' he had said. 'And anyway, it's only a few days. We're going on holiday on Friday. Shall I put the kettle on?'

The Easter holidays began on Friday and they were going to Cornwall again. The memory of their last holiday there, which had seemed so vivid to Holly on the train, now seemed distant. Holly felt as if that holiday had been taken by someone else, not the person who in a couple of days would be packing up the car and driving five hours to Polzeath with her husband and rapidly growing children.

The doorbell rang with a brisk 'ping', which suggested her mother was the caller. Susan was always keen not to disturb anyone or put them out. Rather than ringing the bell with the insistence of someone who wanted to come in, she brushed it with her fingertips, as if she might go away again, if no one heard.

'I'll pop in quickly on my way back from the funeral,' she had told Holly on the phone, with the emphasis on popping. She wasn't one to outstay her welcome.

'I'm sorry about Hugh,' Holly had said. 'Where is the funeral being held?'

'Forest Row,' Susan replied. 'I'll see you on Wednesday then.'

Her parents' lives seemed to be punctuated by funerals at the moment. Patrick was five years older than Susan, but friends of both of them seemed to keep passing on. They read the Obituaries every day after lunch and usually found someone they had known buried in the column inches.

'Darling.' Her mother stood on the doorstep, taking Holly in as if she expected to see some sign of physical change. 'How are you, really?'

'Hello, Mum.' Holly held the door wide open. 'I'm fine. How was it?'

'Oh, well, you know how these things are,' Susan replied, neither of them asking and neither of them answering the questions they wanted to ask and answer. 'I was quite glad to be able to get away.'

She put her bag down and hugged Holly, closer and for slightly longer than was normal. Holly suspected this might be her mother's only reference to what had happened.

'Susan, I didn't hear you arrive.' Mark appeared in the hallway now, lying. 'Did you manage to park all right?'

'It took me a while to find a space,' she replied. 'I'm in the street around the corner.'

'Oh.' Mark's voice registered surprise mixed with a hint of knowingness, as if he'd suspected all along that she would never be able to get into the space he'd watched her navigating.

He stepped forward now and kissed his mother-in-law.

'Would you like a drink, Susan?' he asked. 'Or a cup of tea? I've just boiled the kettle.'

'I'd love a cup of tea.' She was more appreciative of Mark's offer than Holly. 'I've been wanting one all afternoon. There was tea at the funeral but not enough cups to go round.'

'It was good of you to come on and see us.' Mark was boiling the kettle again and clattering around with cups. 'You've had rather a lot of driving today.'

'I wanted to come and see you all,' she said, looking around. 'Where are the children?'

'Jake's in his room, I think, I'll call him in a minute,' Mark told her. 'And Chloe isn't back from school yet. They'll be pleased to see you. It's a shame Patrick couldn't come too.'

'I know and he sends his love,' Susan addressed this to Holly, 'but he promised to stay and help Jean clear up afterwards. He helped her a lot with the arrangements, so I think he wants to see the thing through. It was terrible the way Hugh died. He had a stroke while they were on holiday in Petra.'

'Yes, Holly told me,' Mark said. 'It must have made it all seem much worse, being away from home.'

'I wish I could have come, Mum,' Holly said. 'I liked Hugh.'

Her parents had known Hugh and his wife Jean long before Holly and her sister Fay were born. They had moved around a lot and ended up living in Northampton, but often went to stay for long weekends with their old friends in Sussex.

'I liked him too,' Susan acknowledged. 'But there was no need for you to come too. Fay was there.'

'Jean is Fay's godmother,' Holly said as if explaining to Mark why her sister's presence at the funeral was deemed more necessary than hers.

'I can't remember meeting either of them,' Mark said, bringing a teapot over to the table where Susan and Holly were now sitting. 'Did they come to our wedding?'

'No,' Susan smiled thankfully at the sight of the tea. 'They were Patrick's friends really.'

'Were they?' Holly had never heard her mother describe them this way before.

She thought of most of her parents' friends as being her mother's primarily and that on social occasions her father, often grudgingly, simply tagged along. Patrick used to have a few colleagues he would mention from time to time, but not friends.

'Patrick was at university with Jean,' her mother said, pulling the teapot across the table and pouring herself a cup. 'He's known her since they were twenty, long before she met Hugh.'

'So were there many people you knew at the funeral?' Mark put a tin of biscuits on to the table.

'There were a few, but Patrick seemed to know quite a lot. I left him there, with old university friends, reminiscing.'

She rolled the last word around her tongue as if it were slightly distasteful to her.

'So, darling,' she changed the subject, 'you've been through the wars. How are you?'

'I'll go and see what Jake is up to,' Mark said, getting up. 'He can't have heard you come in.'

'I'm OK, Mum,' Holly said, adding a 'really' before her mother could say one with a question mark attached.

'But you've had such a shock. It must have been awful for you.' Susan paused, looking for the right words. 'Terrifying.'

'I was scared at the time, Mum,' Holly admitted. 'And frustrated. It seemed ridiculous that I wasn't hurt, but I couldn't get out and I was worried about what might happen next.'

'I heard about the crash on the news,' her mother told her. 'But I told myself there were so many trains going up and down to London that it was unlikely to be yours.'

'You never think something like that is going to happen to you, do you?' Holly replied. 'And now, I feel already as if it didn't.'

'What do you mean?' Susan asked.

'Like I said, I was scared at the time. But now I realise how lucky I've been. There were people killed, and I haven't even got a scratch to show for it.' Holly glanced down at her legs which were slightly bruised beneath the jeans she was wearing. 'I was very lucky. It could have been worse, but it wasn't.'

'Hi, Gran.' Jake ambled in and over to where they were

sitting, taking a biscuit from the tin with one hand as he bent over and lightly kissed his grandmother. 'I didn't hear you come in.'

'Gosh, look how tall you are!' Jake had had another growth spurt recently but the rest of his body was on catch up. He kept putting on inches upwards but never out, rendering him well and truly lanky. 'Were you plugged into some piece of equipment in your room?'

Susan and Patrick were perpetually bemused by the technology of the twenty-first century. At home they had a television, a 'wireless' and a 'gramophone record player'.

Holly had once bought them an iPod and dock for Christmas, planning to convert their records into sound files and load it for them, but even the sight of the box had reduced her mother to tears.

'I know it seems terribly ungrateful,' she had sobbed, 'but I really don't want to have to use it. Can you take it back?'

'I was on my Xbox.' Jake sat down at the table.

'Is that a reality TV programme?' Susan asked.

'No, it's a games console,' Jake told her.

'Hugh and Jean's daughter lives in France,' Susan told them all. 'She's got a five-year-old boy who hardly speaks any English. I thought it must be hard for them, not being able to communicate with him, but now I don't often know what my own grandchildren are talking about either!'

'I'll show you, if you like,' Jake said. 'I've got a Monopoly game on it.'

'Thank you, Jake.' Susan smiled at him. 'But I ought to get going really. I don't like driving in the dark.'

'When will Dad get back?' Holly asked, as her mother drained her tea.

'Actually, he was going to stay over with Jean.' Her mother

looked away as she said this. 'Her daughter's going back to France tonight and she didn't want to be alone in the house.'

'Oh.' Holly wasn't sure what else to say.

'Look after yourself, darling.' Susan stood up and gave her a hug. 'Such a shock.'

'I'm OK, Mum,' Holly told her again.

'Life goes on, I suppose,' Susan said.

Her mother had always been stoical, but as Holly looked at her now, she thought she saw tears starting to form in her eyes.

'Life goes on,' she repeated, blinking them away.

Chapter Four

BBC Radio 4
3 May
7 a.m.
The news is read by Charlotte Green.
Salvage teams have finished clearing the wreckage of a train from the Balcombe tunnel, in Sussex, and the line has reopened.

The carriages were stuck in the tunnel, when they became detached from the rest of the train and were then hit by another, travelling on the route between London and Brighton.

Five people were killed and scores of others were injured in the incident.

An investigation has been launched into the cause of the uncoupling . . .

I T WAS HIM. Holly was sure of it. He was sitting across the aisle a few rows ahead of her, facing in the direction the train was moving. Holly couldn't see his face but she recognised the slight wave of his mousey-blond hair and the way his shoulders hunched as he bent over a laptop.

Holly had hoped she'd encounter him again, at some point,

but she hadn't expected it to be so soon, or for her stomach to flip like it did when she looked across the carriage and set eyes on him.

She studied the back of his neck where a recent haircut exposed a white line above a level of suntan. He raised his hand and ran it through the thick crown of hair down to the newly styled nape, as if he could sense he was being watched. Holly saw he was wearing a wedding ring. Perhaps he was newly married.

She wondered if there was a word for how she felt now. She could only liken it to the way she had felt when she first set eyes on Chloe after she was born. It was not as intense, but it was the unexpectedness of feeling anything at all for someone you knew so little about.

It was a relief, as well as a surprise, when she clapped eyes on her newborn daughter and was overwhelmed by an all-consuming something for her.

It hadn't been love, not at first. But there had been a connection, and the initial fear had been replaced by a sense of wonder at what their joint futures might hold.

As Holly looked across the crowded railway carriage she felt a mixture of anticipation and relief coupled with a strange sense of recognition, not just of his profile from this angle, but of him. Even though she knew almost nothing about him.

Perhaps, she thought to herself, there is German word to describe what I'm feeling, like *schadenfreude* or *ersatz* or that Finnish word that Mark kept telling her meant leaving one last biscuit on the plate. It was the sort of thing he knew and liked to tell anyone who cared to listen.

'The French have a word for singing and crying at the same time,' he would say. '*Chantepleurer*. We don't have a word for that.'

'That's because English people don't do it,' Holly had replied.

'There's probably also a word in French for smoking Gauloises while wandering around your apartment, after having sex with your lover in the afternoon.'

Mark had laughed, a little oddly.

'It's *Latterkrampe* – the Norwegian word for convulsive laughter,' he informed her.

'Oh, I see. I thought you were spluttering because you suddenly felt guilty at the mention of an afternoon lover!' Holly had joked.

'*Freir Bunuelos*, darling.' Mark used one of his favourite Spanish expressions for 'get lost'.

'And fry doughnuts to you to!' Holly had replied, kissing him to show no offence had been taken.

She thought of Chloe again now, and how when her daughter had looked up at her for the first time she'd realised that they already knew each other, because for the past nine months they'd been sharing the same body. She felt as if she knew *him* because of the time they'd spent together.

The fat man sitting next to her shifted in his seat, nudging Holly back to the present.

The train was always busy at this time in the morning but she'd got on early enough at Brighton to find a window seat, facing forward, in the middle of the train. This, she told herself, was a safe seat.

Holly had taken her newspaper from her bag and tried to muster interest in a by-election for a hitherto Tory safe seat in London. She'd meant to bring her book, which might have absorbed her more than column inches of newsprint, but had forgotten it.

She blamed Mark for this. He'd been fussing so much that she'd just wanted to get out of the house. In her haste she'd forgotten half the stuff she would normally have taken to London.

By the time she'd read how Labour thought they had a real

chance of winning this particular election, the train had reached Haywards Heath and a man she was sure fell into the clinically obese category was inching down the aisle towards her.

Please don't sit here, she had thought to herself, knowing that he would. She was one of the few people on the train who actually fitted into the allocated seat space. The carriages were new but the measurements had obviously been drawn up by an anorexic dwarf.

There was a spare seat opposite but the newcomer had shifted his weight towards her now, and signalled his intent to sit next to her with a slight nod of the head. Holly reasoned that her instinctive recoiling was not because she was fattist, but rather slightly claustrophobic. The blubbery slab of thigh, which had overlapped on to her side of the seat, felt warm and sweaty and she felt the panic beginning to rise inside her.

She'd given the fat man a big smile, hoping this gave the impression that she welcomed his bulky presence. Then she'd felt her stomach lurch as she'd noticed the back of *his* head, bending over a laptop a few seats up the aisle.

Holly crossed her legs but kicked a woman who had just taken the seat opposite as she did so.

'Sorry,' she said.

The woman was filing her nails. Holly didn't think a train was the place for this. It was too personal, like brushing your teeth or shaving your legs, but the woman obviously thought the carriage as good a space as any to get ready for the day ahead. She put her file in a small make-up bag on her lap, took out a compact, snapped it open and began applying blusher to her cheeks with a brush.

This isn't a bathroom, you know! Holly wanted to snap, but she knew she'd be directing her irritation at the wrong person.

She smiled at the woman, in apology for what she'd been

thinking and the woman smiled back and took out a small compact from the make-up bag and began applying eye shadow. Holly noticed that her eyes looked slightly red, as if she'd been crying or maybe not sleeping properly. Had she been on that train, too, and was this her first day back? Holly wondered. Perhaps she'd been up all night, worrying about getting on it this morning, and that was why she looked tired.

Holly smiled at her again and the woman smiled back, a more decided smile this time, the kind you wore when you were putting on a brave face. Perhaps she was feeling some of what Holly was feeling. Holly relaxed a little now that she no longer felt annoyance towards this woman but instead a strange rapport.

She was still annoyed, though, with Mark for insisting on coming with her to the station and trying to keep her buoyant with jokes that she'd heard too often before.

He obviously thought his presence would be reassuring, but it had the opposite effect. His forced humour made it difficult for her to focus on staying calm. She knew she was being ungracious, but she couldn't help it.

If he makes the Hastings-and-or-where? joke, Holly had thought to herself, as a disembodied voice began announcing the arrival of a train on platform seven, I might just hit him.

Holly usually tolerated Mark making the same jokes over and over again. Every time she asked if they should go next door, meaning from the kitchen to the living room, and he answered 'Hadn't we better ask the neighbours if they mind?' she would smile indulgently. Mark had no idea she actually found the joke extremely irritating.

Today she was having trouble masking this irritation.

'The train on platform seven,' said the announcer, 'is the 8.58 service to Hastings, calling at . . .'

'You don't have to wait,' Holly had said abruptly to Mark. 'You'll be late for work.'

'Only a few minutes.' He failed to pick up on the fact she didn't want him there. 'I'd rather be here.'

'Bexhill-on-Sea, St Leonard's Warrior Square . . .' the announcer had been reeling out station names during their brief exchange '. . . Hastings and Ore.'

Ore, once a small village, was now a large suburb of Hastings.

'And or where?' said Mark, on cue and as expected.

'I *knew* you were going to say that,' Holly snapped.

'Can't teach an old dog new . . .' he began but stopped, realising she was annoyed. 'Sorry.'

'What for?' Holly scanned the departures board, hoping the London Victoria platform would appear and she could get away from him.

'I don't know.' It was true, Mark obviously didn't know but he was sorry anyway. That was typical of him, understanding, even when he didn't quite understand. And he *didn't* understand what she was feeling right now. Holly didn't really understand herself. She just wanted to get on with things, the first one being boarding the train.

'Platform four,' she said as the indicator flicked round to reveal that the train that had been standing at the platform for the past ten minutes was indeed the train everyone thought it was.

'Will you be OK?' Mark asked, tentatively, aware now he might be saying the wrong thing.

'I think so.' Holly was apprehensive but she knew she had to get on the train; delaying the moment wouldn't make it any easier. 'Goodbye.'

She turned to kiss him, hoping this would serve as an apology. 'See you tonight,' she said, turning towards the ticket barrier. 'Thanks for coming with me.'

'Holly . . .' he called after her.

She didn't answer, but looked over her shoulder as she fumbled her ticket into the barrier.

Mark shrugged and smiled.

Holly smiled back and waved the ticket at him before placing it between her teeth and making her way on to the platform.

Now, on the train, she felt bad, realising how her irritation with her husband contrasted with what she felt on seeing 'the man'. He hadn't seen her. He was too engrossed in whatever he was doing on his laptop.

Holly's phone rang, with the embarrassing ringtone that Chloe had put in for her. She answered it quickly, before the recognisable strains of Paulo Nutini disturbed everyone in the carriage. She knew it would be Mark, even before she saw his name and number on the caller display.

'Hi,' she answered quietly, not wishing to draw any more attention to herself.

'Hi.' Mark sounded concerned by her quietness. 'Are you OK?'

'Yes, I'm fine.'

You don't have to keep checking up on me, she wanted to say, but knew it would be churlish.

'We've just gone past Gatwick Airport,' she added, as if this might interest him.

'Is the train busy?' Mark asked.

'It's not too bad,' she answered, wanting him to hang up soon.

'Not squashed up with a sixteen-stoner then?' Mark joked.

Holly hoped the fat man could not hear him.

'I'm in a quiet carriage,' she lied. 'I ought to go.'

'Ok, I just wanted to make sure you were all right,' Mark said. 'I love you.'

'You too,' said Holly. She wasn't going to say 'I love you too' in a crowded train carriage on a Monday morning. Anyone within earshot would probably guess what she was 'you too-ing' to anyway, if they were taking any notice of her conversation.

Holly glanced around her as she said it and saw the man was no longer looking at his laptop but straight at her.

He smiled when she glanced in his direction, a half-smile that Holly was unsure whether to interpret as a gesture of recognition. She held his gaze and he smiled again. This time definitely in acknowledgement, she hoped, of what had passed between them. She looked away, busied herself with putting her phone away, and when she dared to look in his direction again he was back on his computer.

Was that it? Holly wondered. After everything, would a quick smile one morning be all that ever passed between them again?

Chapter Five

'I saw you flirting with the Home Secretary!' said a voice behind her as Holly stepped into the lifts of Broadcasting House.

'Oh, God! Was *that* who it was?' She turned round to find Dimitri, a fellow producer of *Antennae*, entering the lift behind her.

Seconds before, after she'd pressed the button to call it, a man in a suit had emerged, someone she'd recognised but could not quite place.

'Oh, hello,' Holly had said to him, finding that increasingly her memory was failing her when it came to names and faces – a sure sign of middle age.

'Hello,' the man had replied, and smiled before heading out of the building.

'Like you didn't know who he was!' Dimitri was saying now as he moved closer to kiss her in a friendly 'welcome back' way that acknowledged her temporary absence.

'Well, I wasn't *sure* who he was,' she replied. 'But I never pass up the chance to flirt with a man in a lift.'

Holly was strangely reassured that already she was having this type of banter with her colleague. She'd felt as if she had been away for ages when she'd first walked through the doors of Broadcasting House.

She expected the receptionist to look up and ask how she was or the security guard to remark on her slightly prolonged absence. Neither of these things happened.

The only reminder that she had been in a train crash was the card, which she felt for in her pocket.

He'd been waiting for her on the platform, when she got off the train.

'Hi,' he'd said. 'I don't know if you'll remember me . . .'

'I do.' Holly wondered how he thought she could forget. 'Of course I do. I didn't know if you'd be back.'

'Afraid so.' He'd smiled reassuringly, as if to say that everything was all right. Here he was on the train, living proof of that.

'I'm glad,' Holly said thoughtfully. 'I wanted to see you again.'

She paused to fumble with her ticket and push it through the barrier before turning to face him again. 'I don't even know your name.'

'Daniel,' he'd said, smiling and extending his hand. She shook it and smiled back.

'Holly,' she offered.

'Nice to see you again, Holly,' he'd said, still holding her hand and looking at her in a way that was at odds with the normality of his 'nice to see you again'.

For a moment Holly felt transported back to the last time she had seen Daniel, and she shivered slightly. As if sensing this he dropped her hand and took a card out of his pocket.

'I have to dash,' he'd said, pressing it into her hand. 'We should talk, though. Are you getting the tube?'

Holly shook her head. She wasn't quite ready to but she wasn't going to tell Daniel that.

'I usually walk,' she lied. If she'd left enough time or the weather was particularly nice, she did sometimes walk. And if she walked fast it didn't take much longer than getting the Underground.

'Oh.' Daniel had looked at her as if he knew this wasn't true, but understood. 'Well, I'll see you again some time, won't I?'

'Yes.' Holly slowed her pace, allowing him to put some distance between them, and looked at the card again.

'You look well,' Dimitri smiled at her now. 'You've aged, of course! But you look well.'

It was actually only three weeks that she'd been off work. She had planned to spend the last two of them in Cornwall with Mark and the children, but they'd come home early to escape the perpetual rain.

'The weather's generally nice at Easter.' Mark had tried to stay optimistic even as it rained hard for the fifth day running.

'Can't we just go home?' Chloe and Jake had asked hopefully.

In the event they did, though Mark tried to keep up the pretence that they were still on holiday by arranging local outings.

Holly knew he was doing his best to make up for the fact they could not afford to go abroad this year, but she wished he'd realise the kids would be perfectly happy to stay at home and have unrestricted internet access.

'It's good to have you back, Holly,' Dimitri said. 'How are you? Apart from having developed a bit of thing for the Home Secretary, that is.'

'I'm not sure he's really my type.' This much was true. Holly had what her children described as 'beard phobia'. She denied this, saying merely that she preferred her chins clean shaven, but Chloe and Jake insisted she was petrified of them.

'What about that man on *Masterchef*?' Jake would say if ever the subject came up. 'You didn't want him to win just because he had a beard.'

'I couldn't stomach the thought of all that hair so near the food,' Holly had protested. 'It's not the beard *per se*.'

'You are a beardist,' Chloe added, 'and a moustachist,' pleased to have two 'ists' to add to their growing list of things they believed Holly was prejudiced against. If they'd been here now they'd have backed her up about the Home Secretary definitely not being her type.

'So you say,' Dimitri went on. 'But I saw the way you were looking at him.'

Holly laughed.

She liked Dimitri. He was fun. He was in his early thirties but retained a certain cheeky boyish charm. A lot of men his age were full of their own self-importance, especially at the BBC, but Dimitri, though very good at his job, gave the impression of only being there for the pleasure of the office banter. He was an Alpha-male who gave the outward impression of being an Omega, if there was such a thing.

'Talking of which,' he added, 'a very pretty producer has been filling in for you while you were away.'

'Well, I'm very sorry for coming back then,' Holly said, thinking her temporary replacement would have been deployed elsewhere.

'Actually,' Dimitri corrected this impression, 'she's going to stay. Sarah got the job on *Woman's Hour*. Starts this week. So it's the old team plus the gorgeous Rebecca.'

The old team consisted of Katherine Murray, the programme's editor, Natalie the assistant editor, and a team of three producers: Holly, Dimitri and Sarah, who had now been replaced by the gorgeous Rebecca. They all worked on *Antennae*, a programme broadcast on BBC Radio 4. Their remit was to pick up on anything which might be of interest to listeners and was not specifically covered in any of the other programmes.

'So essentially,' Holly would tell her friends, 'it's a mish-mash of stuff that doesn't really fit anywhere else, or whatever we can come up with when there's a hole in the programme to fill.'

Antennae was presented by James Darling, the BBC's roving news correspondent.

James Darling's voice was his calling card. It was deep but soft and had a slightly hypnotic quality. Holly had heard him on the radio frequently before he came to present the programme, and from his voice had imagined a cross between George Clooney and Sean Connery; someone dark and tall. She'd imagined height and physical presence were prerequisites for anyone with a deep, brooding voice. She was not sure that she'd hidden her disappointment well enough when Natalie, who had known Darling since they'd worked together at Radio Hull twenty years ago, had introduced her.

In the flesh he was small. He couldn't be more than five foot seven, and without much of a frame to carry excess flesh he appeared rather overweight. He had obviously once been blond but had now lost most of the hair on his head and, as if to compensate, sported a large wiry beard.

He had, as they say, a perfect face for radio.

Dimitri Georgiades, by contrast, had a perfect face for life. He was tall, dark, olive skinned, hazel eyed – striking by anyone's standards. He was also very well spoken. Holly suspected he had been to an English public school but, with a name like Georgiades, imagined his parents were Greek.

They took the lift together to the sixth floor where a very pretty young woman was keying a security code into the doors that led to *Antennae*'s offices.

'The gorgeous Rebecca,' Dimitri whispered to Holly in a loud stage whisper, which Rebecca clearly heard.

She spun round, smiling.

'Hello,' she said to Dimitri, her tone of voice suggesting she found him equally gorgeous. 'Hi,' she said to Holly, more tentatively.

'Hi. I'm Holly.'

'Oh! Right.' Rebecca became instantly friendlier. 'Hi, I'm Rebecca. Nice to meet you. Great that you're back.'

A slight look of panic crossed her face, as if it occurred to her that she shouldn't have mentioned the fact Holly had been away.

'Nice to be back,' Holly said, wondering if others would keep reminding her why she'd been away with the things they said or didn't say.

She inwardly cursed Rebecca for the look on her face, which served as a reminder of the exact thing she was trying not to think about.

'I suppose I'd better report to Katherine before I do anything else,' Holly said briskly, to show she meant business.

She walked down the narrow corridor between the open-plan parts of the office to the editor's office. She peered through the glass walls and could see Katherine's immaculate dark bob bent over a stack of paperwork. 'Holly!' she cried, seeing her and opening the door. 'How lovely! Come in. Have a seat. It's great to have you back.'

This, Holly suspected, was a lie. Katherine didn't really like women, especially ones who had children and took maternity leave and holidays plus time off when they'd been in a train crash. She was of the generation who didn't have it all and were expected not to allow anything from their private lives to interfere with their work.

Holly had worked at BBC Radio 4 for nearly eighteen years; full-time at first, then part-time when the children were young. She'd started full-time again the previous September, prompted partly by the fact that Mark's business wasn't bringing in much and they needed the extra money.

'How are you?' Katherine said, wheeling a chair away from the wall for Holly to sit on.

'I'm pretty good.' She gave the response she knew was wanted, which was also fairly accurate.

'Good,' said Katherine. She seemed relieved. 'So you'll be able to cope with everything?'

Holly nodded.

'Excellent.' Katherine was already turning her chair back to face her desk, signalling their brief exchange was at an end. 'The morning meeting is at nine-thirty upstairs in the mezzanine. See you there.'

'OK. I'll go and get a coffee first then. See you in a bit,' she said to her boss's back and walked out of the office and straight into Natalie.

'Holly Holt!' Natalie said, smiling and dropping her bag where she stood in order to give Holly the biggest and most welcoming hug. 'I am *so* pleased that you're back. You look fantastic. Come into my office, I want to hear how you are.'

Katherine looked up as this exchange took place. 'Were you coming to see me?' she asked, looking slightly peeved.

'No,' Natalie replied. 'Well, yes, but it can wait. See you at the morning meeting.'

She closed the door of Katherine's office and showed Holly into her own opposite.

'It's really good to see you,' Natalie said. 'It felt like longer than three weeks that you were off. Everyone here seems to be getting younger and younger . . . except Katherine, who is getting older and more bitter by the day.'

Holly laughed.

'Dimitri told me I looked older,' she said.

'Untactful cheeky monkey!' Natalie replied. 'Tea?'

She pushed a polystyrene cup across the table. 'I bought two cups just in case you got here early – oh, and desk!'

Natalie pointed at a desk on the other side of the room from hers. 'No more open-planning it amongst the twenty-somethings. You'll have to put up with me.'

'Really? How come?' Holly rather liked the camaraderie of the open-plan bit of the office.

'Rebecca was at your desk while you were away and Katherine decided she should stay put,' Natalie told her.

'Great.' Holly tried to sound a bit more upbeat about sharing an office with Natalie.

In fact, it unsettled her. She'd wanted everything to be the same; to have her surroundings mask the fact that something in her had changed. And besides, she liked the company of the twenty-somethings.

Natalie was in her early forties, only a couple of years younger than Holly, but they were both well aware that they were both considered oldies who led dull boring lives with their husbands and children. Natalie had young twins.

'And,' she added, 'I think it pissed Katherine off, my having an office to myself. I think she thinks I do fuck all all day and now you will be able to keep me on my toes.'

'It'll be great,' Holly said, trying to emphasise the great.

She had first met Natalie when they were both in their twenties and worked briefly at Radio Northampton. Later Holly moved to Brighton and Natalie to Hull. Then, they'd spent a brief period on *Woman's Hour* together before Holly switched to a part-time job in Central Planning. When she'd started working full-time again, it was on *Antennae* and she was glad to be back with Natalie.

Holly knew her well enough to be relaxed around her, and

Natalie now had children too so they could compare notes on trying to have it all.

'How was the train journey?' Natalie asked, as Holly sat down at her new desk. 'Was that the first time you've been on one since . . .'

'I had a few practice runs with Mark.' Holly flipped the lid of the plastic cup and took a sip of the tepid liquid. 'We came back from holiday a bit early and he decided we'd keep up the holiday spirit by going on day trips to coastal retirement towns. We had lunch in Eastbourne, Littlehampton and Worthing last week.'

'The glamorous life you lead!' Natalie feigned envy. 'And was it OK? On the train?'

'I think Mark thought I'd be terrified of ever going on one again but actually it feels strangely normal. It's almost as if I've done my train crash now, so I'm pretty unlikely to be in another one.' Holly paused, wondering how much to tell Natalie about the journey. 'In fact, there was a man on the train . . .'

'Bloody hell, quick work,' Natalie interjected. 'First day back and you meet a man on the way to work. Who is he?'

'Daniel Harrison,' Holly told her.

This was the name on the card he had given her as they disembarked from the train and walked towards the ticket barrier. Daniel Harrison, Systems Analyst. And there were details of his office addresses and phone numbers. She'd stared at it as she walked through Green Park, as if by absorbing the stark typeface she would somehow be able to glean more details from it.

'And?' Natalie was looking at her expectantly.

'And what?' Holly wasn't stalling.

'Who is he? This Daniel Harrison?'

'He was on the train when the accident happened.' Holly suddenly found saying this out loud took her back to the scene of the crash and she didn't want to go there. Not now. 'He stayed with me until the fire brigade arrived.'

'Oh, I see,' Natalie adopted a slightly hushed reverential tone which annoyed Holly more than it should have. 'So, are you going to see him again?'

'I don't know,' Holly said, putting her hand in her pocket to feel Daniel Harrison's card again. It made her feel safe just touching it, representing as it did the man who had assured her that everything would be all right. 'I expect I'll bump into him again at some point.'

I've started to write things down again. The counsellor I saw before, after Mum went into hospital, told me it might be useful at the time.

'It might help you clarify your feelings,' she had said to me, during one of the sessions, and it did in a way. Any rate, I preferred writing things down to talking to her. That's why I stopped the sessions – that and Lisa telling everyone at school that I was a nutter too.

'Anne-Marie is seeing a shrink,' she told our friends, challenging me to deny it. 'Aren't you?'

'She's not a shrink, she's a counsellor,' I protested.

'Same difference,' Lisa had said, smirking, and even though it had helped, having someone to talk to, I stopped going. But I kept on writing the diary the counsellor encouraged me to begin. I still have them all, somewhere in the attic, with other stuff from Mum and Dad's house.

And now I've started another. I started this diary on the day of the crash, because I wanted to talk about it and the one person I really wanted to talk to was Geoff and he was no longer there. So I started writing instead.

I thought about the counsellor I'd seen as a teenager, too. She was nice. Helen, I think her name was. I did like talking to her and I often wished I hadn't stopped going. I still told her things, in the months and years that followed, but the conversations were only ever imagined, in my head, and then I moved on and forgot about her.

Now, I've started thinking about her again and I found myself telling a vacant chair in the living room that I'd started writing a diary. I imagined Helen was in the chair, listening, trying to understand.

'That's good,' she said. 'You won't feel like this for ever but it will help if you articulate your thoughts, rather than bottling them up.'

I wonder what she'd think if I was talking to her now, if she'd remember the conversations we had after my mother went into the psychiatric hospital, which made people realise that what we'd seen that day wasn't just a bad memory, it was something much more.

If she were here now, would she bring it up again? Or would she just ask me about Geoff and how I was coping; whether there was anyone else I could talk to about what had happened – friends, for example, or family?

She wouldn't know that my mum and dad had both died a few years ago, my mother from cancer and my father from heart failure.

'They just said it was old age,' I imagined telling her. It didn't seem relevant which particular bits of my parents' bodies had packed up or why. They knew death was coming eventually and preferred dying of old age to anything more medically accurate.

'And friends?' she might ask.

Would she already know about Julia, by this point in the session?

'Apart from Julia, I don't really know that many people where we live,' I would tell her. 'We only moved in the last year, from London, and we both commuted a lot of the time. So we didn't really have much chance to meet anyone new.'

We'd never have met Julia if it hadn't been for the postman leaving her mail-order shoes in our porch by mistake. She insisted I come in for coffee when I took them round. And then Geoff insisted she come in to ours for coffee when she stopped to chat to him, as he was weeding the front garden.

'I'm the shoe lady,' she had said, by way of introduction, but I hadn't told Geoff about the shoes so he'd had no idea what she was on about. To be honest, if I had told him he'd probably have forgotten and been none the wiser. So she'd explained and something in her rendition of the postman mistakenly taking her parcel to number sixty-eight instead of one hundred and sixty-eight had made Geoff laugh and he'd insisted she come and have coffee with us.

'What about your old friends from London?' the counsellor might ask. 'Or university? Or before even?'

But she would already know about my oldest friend, Lisa Woodward. Even if she'd forgotten, it would be in my notes.

'My best friend from university, Laura, went back to New Zealand.' I would fill Helen in on the years since she last saw me. 'And we seem to have lost touch.'

'Why was that?' she'd ask.

And I would probably say something about time and distance. But really I think now that it was because we'd become linked by something other than being outsiders and we both wanted to forget that.

She felt she'd escaped the earthquake by being in the UK and she didn't think she deserved to. Her parents were devastated by the loss of her younger sister, so she felt she had to go back. I told her before she left about my mother, about what had happened to us. I thought it might help her, but she didn't really want to know.

'What's happened in New Zealand is different,' she'd said.

We emailed regularly at first when she went back, and I still think of her as a good friend even though we've lost touch.

I've thought about calling Laura several times over the past few weeks, but the time never seems right. She's eleven hours ahead in New Zealand and, whenever I think I'd like to talk to her, I realise it would be the middle of the night there.

And then I wonder what I would say to her anyway when she picked up the phone.

It would be a bit of a shock for her, hearing from me after all this time and then me telling her about Geoff.

But now that I was thinking about her, it struck me that that was who the woman I'd seen on the news reminded me of. I'd thought she seemed *familiar because I'd seen her on the train, but now that I've been thinking about Laura, I realise she also reminds me of her. Maybe that's why I felt compelled to talk to her when I saw her on the train this morning.*

I didn't realise it was her when I sat down. She was reading a newspaper and I couldn't see her face properly, but then she put it down and I knew it was the same person. She looked nervous and I wondered if it was her first day back at work too.

I wanted to tell her that I'd seen her on the news and ask if she was OK. I don't know if it was because she reminded me of Laura or because of the way she smiled, but I had a feeling that I might be able to tell her about Geoff. Not immediately, of course, but at some point.

Her phone rang and she looked away while she took the call. I tried to catch her eye and smile again but she was looking across the carriage at someone. She had that look on her face again, the same look she had when I saw her on the news.

I waited for her to get off the train and I walked down the platform behind her. I imagined I might say hello or something, once we'd gone through the barriers.

But there was a man already there, waiting for her.

I couldn't really go up to her then, not with him there.

I wanted to tell her that I knew she'd been alone in the tunnel, and that I knew what it felt to be involved in something like that and to feel utterly alone. But I couldn't tell her because she was talking to him.

Chapter Six

M ARK WAS MAKING dinner when Holly got home that evening and, when Mark cooked, it was to demonstrate his abilities rather than to satisfy his family's hunger. He liked to use two or three TV cookbooks at a time, creating a main dish and at least two accompaniments. These never seemed to be ready simultaneously and only ever well past the point when everyone was hungry.

They did usually look and taste good but Holly could have done without the aesthetics and the painstakingly sourced ingredients. She would have preferred something on the table when she got home, rather than several hours later.

Mark also liked to use every single kitchen implement and pan they possessed. So, having waited several hours to eat, it would then take several hours to clear up afterwards. Holly thought this clattering of pans was the twenty-first-century equivalent to the hunter-gatherer's big kill. It was as if, by producing several options to eat, and using twenty different knives in the process, Mark was saying, 'Look what a man I am. I ripped a chicken carcass apart with my bare hands, beheaded butternut squash and had garlic cloves begging for mercy, just to bring you this meal.'

'Hello,' she said, trying not to think about the clear-up operation afterwards, as she surveyed the kitchen. There were already three different empty but dirty baking trays cluttering up the dining table.

'Hi.' Mark's tone had all the triumph of a man who had just headed up a mammoth hunt. 'Rack of lamb, with Moroccan parsnip mash and roasted vegetables, followed by almond oranges.'

'That sounds wonderful,' said Holly, wondering if cavewomen had felt the same feeling of dread when their menfolk triumphantly dragged back the carcass of a mammal. Were they hugely relieved that they would eat for months to come or secretly peeved that the cave would be full of drying skins, bloodied rocks and male triumphalism for the foreseeable future?

'How was your day?' said Mark, wiping his hands on an already bloodied tea towel.

Holly made a mental note to stick it in the washing machine, as soon his back was turned, and before they all got salmonella.

'It was fine,' she said, kissing him.

'Were they all pleased to have you back then?' He poured a large glass of wine and handed it to her. He had his concerned expression on.

'Yes.' Holly didn't think there was any point in telling him that her absence had barely been noted.

'And the train?' Mark looked at her closely as he asked this.

'It was fine,' she said again. 'I was a little nervous when I first got on, but as soon as it started crawling up the track, I felt OK.'

'Really?' Mark was adding wine to a pan of something that was bubbling on the stove, but still watching her.

'Yes, really.'

Holly hadn't said this to anyone, not even the counsellor, but she suspected that a small part of Mark wanted her to be more traumatised by the train crash than she was, so that he could step up and look after her.

He'd told her he was terrified when he heard the news that

morning that she might have been killed. And he was fearful, after she was cut free from the wreckage, that it would leave her nervous and reluctant to start commuting again. He didn't seem prepared for the fact that she felt as if she'd had a lucky escape and was carrying on as if nothing had happened.

Holly couldn't help thinking that rather than being relieved that she was OK, he'd found himself robbed of the opportunity to show he was still an Alpha-male.

'The Iceman cometh!' was how Mark had introduced himself to Holly, twenty years ago.

Lydia, a friend Holly then worked with, had decided to throw a party in the garden off her ground-floor flat, because the weather had been unusually hot. She'd invited a lot of people but done little else. Among the things she hadn't done was clearing her fridge. So, when people began arriving with wine and beer, there was nowhere for it to go where it would stay chilled.

Cue Mark who, as Holly arrived, walked up the steps to the front door behind her, shouldering a dustbin full of ice.

'Lydia's fridge is full of rotting meat!' he had said, as if by way of explanation after the Iceman comment. Then he put out his free hand to shake hers. 'I'm Mark.'

Holly immediately liked his openness and the casual way in which he was carrying what must undoubtedly have been a heavy load. And he was good looking too, tanned and dark-haired with eyes that looked almost black.

'Holly,' she said, taking his hand, which was cold from the ice. 'Bloody hell, you're freezing!'

'Cold hands, warm heart.' Mark had shrugged in acknowledgement of the cliché and the fact that he couldn't come up with anything better. 'Hurry up, Lydia,' he'd added as they waited for the door to be answered, and Holly had wondered if he was her boyfriend and if so why he didn't have a key.

'Were your parents *Breakfast at Tiffany's* fans?' he asked, putting down the bin and looking at Holly as if he needed to take her in properly.

'Yes.' Holly had indeed been named after Holly Golightly because her mother had watched the film, starring Audrey Hepburn, nearly every afternoon in the last few months of her pregnancy. If anyone ever thought to ask about her name, they usually asked if she was born at Christmas. Mark was possibly the first person who had instantly made the right connection.

'How did you know?' she asked, looking at him with renewed admiration.

'I thought you looked like Audrey Hepburn when I saw you walking down the road,' he'd replied. 'And then when you said your name was Holly, it seemed to fit.'

'Oh, thank you.' She wasn't usually good at taking compliments, but even though she'd only exchanged a few words with him so far she already felt relaxed enough in Mark's company to accept this one.

'How do you know Lydia?' she'd asked as he rapped on the door again.

'I live in the flat upstairs.' He'd nodded towards a wooden Venetian blind above the door, which was suddenly flung open by Mandy, another work colleague.

'Hi, Holly!' She had stopped to take in Mark. 'Hello, Holly's friend . . .'

Holly had expected Mark to say something about them only having just met, but he simply smiled and said, 'Hello, another of Holly's friends. I'll talk to you in a minute, but first I need to get this bucket of ice out the back.'

There had been something so masculine and confident about

Mark back then. It was this, as much as his dark handsome looks, which captivated Holly, first at the party and then during the subsequent months when he swept her along with his conviction that they must swim in the sea . . . walk on Beachy Head . . . watch the sunrise over the downs . . . move in together and eventually get married.

It wasn't that he was domineering or forceful in any way; rather there was something about him which was so self-assured and compelling that Holly found it hard to resist whatever he happened to suggest.

'Shall I get you another drink and then we can find somewhere to sit and talk properly?' he had asked her a few hours into the party as Holly made her way to Lydia's kitchen, hoping she might bump into him en route.

They'd chatted briefly to begin with, then Lydia had pulled her away to meet her old university roommate.

'Actually, I was going to see if I could make myself a cup of tea.' Holly smiled, sensing it was a bit middle-aged of her to be wanting a cuppa just as a party got into full swing.

But she'd had enough to drink for the time being and it was getting cold in the garden. She felt as if she needed something to warm her up.

'It's pretty crowded in there.' Mark gestured towards the kitchen. 'Why don't you come up to my flat and I'll make you a cup?'

'OK,' Holly had replied, even though her natural instinct would not have been to disappear from a party with a man she'd only just met.

She had the strange sensation, as they walked out of Lydia's flat and up the stairs, of having known him for some time. There was the usual nervous anticipation, but this meeting felt right.

'Sorry, it's a bit of a mess,' Mark said as he opened the door to his flat and indicated the living room. 'I've been away for a few days and haven't got round to clearing up.'

Holly looked through the door to the living room. It *was* a mess. There were newspapers and magazines strewn across the floor, clothes slung across the backs of chairs, and half-empty coffee cups and plates on just about every surface.

'Where've you been?' she asked, alluding to the days away and wondering if he'd been with anyone. Despite the mess, she did like the fact that Mark's living room appeared to be entirely free from any feminine influence. She hoped he lived on his own and did not have a girlfriend.

'My flatmate never tidies up,' Mark said, pulling clothes off a large leather armchair and gesturing for her to sit in it. 'Tim. Big guy with a beard. He was at the party too. Did you talk to him?'

'No.' Holly sank into the chair. She'd seen a man who fitted that description and hoped he wouldn't be coming home any time soon. She wanted more time with Mark, on his own.

'Paris.' He carried on tidying. 'In answer to your earlier question.'

'That's nice.' Holly couldn't help but feel disappointed. Paris was not the sort of city he'd be likely to have visited on his own.

'For work,' Mark told her, as if he could tell what she was thinking. He already seemed to have scooped all the clothes into a pile that he was putting on a stool, and picked up a large tray from the floor together with some dirty crockery. The room already looked a whole lot better.

'What do you do?' Holly had asked, and Mark had told her that he worked for the marketing department of a big American conglomerate, and though it was dull at times it was good experience. Ultimately he wanted to set up on his own.

'Are you a reporter or a producer?' he asked her as he brought a pint-sized mug of tea and a plate of biscuits in from the kitchen. He'd obviously talked to Lydia about the local radio station where they both worked.

'Reporter,' Holly had said, accepting the tea and looking around her at the walls, which were hung with several paintings of windswept coastlines. 'I like these. Are they of Cornwall?'

'Yes.' Mark had smiled as if pleased she'd recognised the scenes. 'My dad painted them.'

'Is he an artist?' Holly had been impressed.

'No, a local government officer. Or at least he was.' Mark paused. 'He died a few years ago, from bowel cancer.'

Mark must have been in his mid-twenties then. She suspected his father's death had come too early.

'I'm sorry. How old was he?'

'Sixty. I was at university, doing my finals. They didn't find the cancer until it had spread so there wasn't much they could do, but he gave up his job and did as much painting as he could before he died. He loved painting.'

'And he was very good.' Holly looked at the paintings again. 'Is that Sennen Cove?'

'Yes.' Mark glanced up at the painting. 'Do you know it?'

'We used to go there when I was a child, for family holidays,' Holly told him. 'I love Cornwall but I haven't been for years.'

'We'll have to go,' Mark said, sipping his own tea, as if what he suggested was the most natural thing in the world, despite the fact that they had only just met. He didn't seem cocky to Holly, just accepting of the fact that there was something between them. And not, like most men of his age, afraid of that.

'So, Reporter Holly,' he had said. 'Are you going to stay in local radio for a while or will you be disappearing off to London before we've had time to go Cornwall or anywhere else?'

'I like my job here,' she had told him. 'But I suppose eventually London will be the next step.'

She'd been right. Not long after they were married, she began commuting to London to work for BBC Radio 4 and Mark had set up his own marketing and PR company. Business boomed and when Holly had Chloe she went back to work part-time, to keep her hand in.

But then Mark's successful company began to struggle, slowly at first.

'I've lost two holiday company contracts,' he told her one evening when she'd asked why he seemed a bit down. 'Bookings are slow after 9/11 and they can't afford to use me any more. People are still nervous of flying, even though it's the safest form of transport.'

'I can understand why,' Holly had said, watching as he poured them both a large glass of wine. 'The world no longer seems safe.'

The twin towers had come down on their son Jake's first day at infant school.

It was a warm sunny day in Brighton and Holly had picked him up and brought him home for lunch. She put the television on so that he could watch *Teletubbies* before they went to get Chloe from school. Instead of being greeted by the cheery 'eh-oh' of Tinky Winky they saw the image of a plane hitting one of the towers, being repeated over and again.

Jake had thought the spectacle wonderful and almost immediately began building Lego towers and Lego aeroplanes with which he could destroy them, but Holly had felt as if something had been taken away from her personally, even though they were not directly affected.

'I think it was because it was Jake's first day at school,' she had said to Mark a few weeks later when he told her he'd lost the contracts. 'It should have been a day that was full of promise, but instead it seemed as if something had been taken away from us all.'

'Sorry, Hol, now I'm making you morose,' Mark had said, upbeat again, pulling her to him and kissing her. 'I didn't mean to, and I'm not really worried about these contracts. If people aren't going abroad they'll holiday at home, so perhaps I'll get something local to replace them.'

Holly had smiled, admiring his eternal optimism, but latterly she'd discovered it wasn't eternal after all.

'Best Homes has gone bust.' He had been despondent when he'd told her this news several months before. 'Another victim of the credit crunch. They owed us a few thousand. We'll never see it now.'

'Shit.' Holly knew that Best Homes was Mark's last remaining big client although he'd put in a bid for a job with a new chain of bars. 'Have you heard anything about the tender for Cosy Corner?'

'We didn't get it,' he'd said, refusing to meet her eyes as he spoke. 'It went to a new company which has just been set up by a couple of twenty-somethings.'

That was when Holly first noticed that the energy and drive that always used to keep Mark going were diminishing.

'I could go back to work full-time, now that Jake's at secondary school,' she had said, expecting him to say, as he always did, that she didn't need to.

'Do you think you could?' He'd glanced down with a look of defeat as he spoke.

'I'll speak to Personnel,' Holly had replied, trying to sound upbeat herself. 'I'd like to. It might mean I could work on a programme again, and I'd prefer that. I'm bored in Central Planning, but most of the part-time jobs are there.'

Holly knew there was a bit of Mark that still wanted to be the main breadwinner. The part of him that shouldered the bin full of ice with such ease would have liked to provide for all his family's needs.

He didn't like the fact he got home from work before Holly and was forced to fill the time with knife-wielding in the kitchen. He'd lost some of that initial sense of purpose she'd first found so attractive in him. He was no longer so confident and compelling.

And, although he'd never said it in so many words, Holly knew Mark hated the fact that he had not been the one to talk her through the minutes before the fire crews arrived to cut her free from the wreckage of the train crash.

So when he asked now how her train journey had been, she couldn't quite bring herself to tell him that Daniel Harrison, the man who had been there with her at the crash, was also on it.

Chapter Seven

'HI, MUM!' HOLLY heard Jake shouting from the sitting room in his newly deepened voice.

It still took her by surprise every time he opened his mouth – this new husky-sounding Jake, with his downy top lip, thicker hair and ever-increasing height. He had only just turned thirteen but already her little boy seemed to be disappearing before her eyes, to be replaced by a continuously growing young man.

'Hello, Jakey!' she said, going into the sitting room and finding him lying prone across the floor, apparently contemplating the ceiling. He'd obviously heard her come in but couldn't be bothered to move.

Jake grimaced as she was about to bend down and kiss him, something he still, thankfully, allowed her to do as long as his friends weren't looking. He put up his hand in warning.

'Ed's here.' He indicated the sofa, where a floppy-haired friend was also lying in a languid pose.

'All right, Holly?' Ed's sing-song, higher voice asked.

'Yes, good thanks, Ed.' Holly marvelled at the number of hours her son could spend doing nothing companionably with one of his friends.

Chloe was constantly talking, texting, listening to music or posting photos of herself and her friends on Facebook. She was more like her father. Mark had never been able just to be some-where without doing anything.

In the days immediately after the train crash, Holly had found it easier to be with Jake than anyone else in the family. He never asked her to talk or tell him how she was feeling, he'd just be in the same space as her, a reassuring presence.

'Are you two inspecting the ceiling for cobwebs?' she asked now, knowing that she wouldn't be able to stare at it for long without noticing some corner that needed dusting or a crack that warranted a builder.

There was an alarming-looking one over the bay window. When they'd moved in it was on Holly and Mark's list of things to do something about, but after about six months of painting and decorating during evenings and weekends they had lost enthu-siasm for home improvements.

'Are we going to get a new fireplace put in?' Mark had asked one autumn evening when the sitting room was feeling chilly.

'It would be nice,' Holly had replied. 'But I don't think I can face sharing the house with builders any more.'

'I thought you had a bit of crush on Vaclav?' Mark had teased her, referring to the Czech who had helped convert the attic.

'Familiarity breeds contempt,' Holly had said, putting her hand on Mark's knee.

'Thank you very much!' He'd looked mock-affronted.

'I meant Vaclav, not you!'

The house was in a quiet residential part of Brighton. Holly hadn't liked it at first. Looking out of the windows at the other large Edwardian red-brick houses opposite, she'd felt it could be in any city.

'I miss the sea views,' she told people. 'We could see the sea from our bedroom in the old house. And there were always lots of drunks around. It felt more like Brighton.'

'You can see the sea, if you're prepared to risk breaking your neck,' Mark said, demonstrating that if you stood on a ledge in the attic and stuck your entire torso out of the window and leaned, you could catch sight of a strip of silvery grey. 'And if it's drunks you miss, we can always open another bottle of wine ourselves!'

'Ed's not staying for dinner,' Jake said, looking up. 'His dad's coming soon.'

'That's lucky,' Holly said. 'Because Dad's cooking, so it probably won't be ready until midnight anyway.'

'We're just waiting for him,' Ed volunteered, as if this explained the torpor in the living room. 'Did you have a good day at work?'

'Yes, thank you, Ed.' Holly smiled at the innocence of his question. Ed was endearingly polite. Jake and he had been friends since infant school, and even aged five he'd always thanked her for 'delicious fish fingers' or 'a really fun day'.

'How was yours?' she asked both boys, but the ceiling appeared to be absorbing all their thoughts and energy and neither of them answered.

'Where's Chloe?' she asked this time, noticing that her laptop was not on the desk by the French windows and wondering if her daughter had it.

'I think she's in her room with Ruaridh,' Jake said.

Ruaridh was a close friend of her daughter's. Holly was beginning to wonder just how close. They'd met when they started secondary school and always been friends, but lately they seemed never to be apart.

Holly thought Chloe was looking particularly beautiful at the moment. Her awkward adolescent skin had cleared, and she was now all long limbs, shiny hair and very engaging smile. Holly wouldn't be at all surprised if Ruaridh had stopped thinking of her simply as a friend.

He was one of six children. His parents were Irish Catholics, which Holly supposed accounted for the six of them.

Mark almost always referred to Ruaridh as 'Scrabble Boy'. This was a joke he made nearly every time Ruaridh's name came up. The first time he had spelled it out for them, Mark had said Irish names must have been created during a game of Scrabble.

'Rory?' he'd said in his best Irish accent. 'How should we spell that?' Then proceeded to act out an imaginary scenario in which a family sat around a table pulling Scrabble letters randomly from a bag and deciding that that was how their names should be spelled.

'Niamh. Shall we spell that N-E-E-V-E?' Mark had lilted, before answering himself, 'No. I've got an "m" and an "h". We need to fit those in too.'

Holly had worried Ruaridh would think him horribly patronising, but he seemed to think it was funny.

'I'm here,' said Chloe, breaking into Holly's thoughts as she padded down the stairs.

'Hello.' Holly turned and bit back the temptation to ask if she'd worn that strip of material masquerading as a skirt to school today. 'Hello, Ruaridh.'

'Hello, Mrs Constantine.' Ruaridh grinned.

He had recently taken to calling Holly this, although she never actually used her married name. Holly's maiden name was Holt and she thought it suited her better. Constantine, the name of a Roman Emperor, suited Mark perfectly.

Holly suspected that Ruaridh was being ironic. This was one of Chloe's favourite current pastimes. She frequently used irony to explain why she was doing something that could be construed as childish. Like lining up all the soft toys she'd had as a child on the end of her bed, or creating sculptures out of Lego. It was as if she didn't quite want to relinquish her childhood but was embarrassed about playing with childish things. So she would explain, if anything was commented on, that it was ironic.

That would cue Mark to make his ironic joke.

'Ironic is getting your newly ironed shirt crumpled when you try to fold the ironing board.'

Holly sighed inwardly, thinking of her husband's tired jokes.

'How was school?' she asked Chloe.

'Fine.' Her standard response to most questions.

'Did you get your test results?' Holly had managed to extract the information from her earlier in the week that she was having a Spanish test.

'Yeah.'

'And?' Holly waited for a bit more information. 'What did you get?'

'I got a level six.'

This didn't really mean anything to Holly. The whole school system seemed to be structured towards making all pupils think they were doing fine, even if they weren't. And it seemed to exclude parents from knowing if their offspring were doing anything at all.

Chloe would be taking her GCSEs the following year and Holly had no idea if she was going to pass them with flying colours or fail miserably.

'Is that good?' she asked.

'It's the average level expected.' Chloe seemed satisfied with her marks.

Holly thought she ought to aspire to better than average. She'd said as much at one of the rare parents evenings their school held. The teacher had looked at her in disbelief, as if wanting your child to do better was outrageous.

'Well done,' she said, wondering if her words sounded as

hollow as they felt. 'That's really good, Chloe. By the way, have you got my laptop?'

'It's in my room.' Chloe seemed to distance herself from any involvement with the laptop, trying to make out it had somehow got there by itself. 'Do you want it?'

'I might need to send an email before dinner. Are you staying for dinner, Ruaridh?'

'No, I need to go home.'

Holly jumped as the doorbell rang.

'That'll be my dad.' Ed had suddenly sprung into action and was twitching back the living-room curtain to see who was outside. He slipped on his shoes.

'Thanks for the . . .' he said to Holly, and smiled, realising that the extent of their hospitality had been to allow him to lie on the sofa undisturbed.

'Any time, Ed!' She gave him a half-wave. 'Are you going to say goodbye, Jake?'

By this she meant get up and go to the door with him.

'I already have,' he replied, unmoving.

'Here it is.' Chloe had been up to her room and come down again with the laptop. She plonked it on the desk. 'Shall I leave it on?'

'Yes, please,' Holly said.

'I'm off too.' Ruaridh waved vaguely in everyone's direction and headed for the door.

'When's dinner? I'm starving,' Chloe asked.

'Me, too. Ravenous!' Jake had always liked hyperbole. 'Can I get a sandwich?'

'It might spoil your dinner,' Holly said, knowing this was unlikely. Jake seemed to be eating as much as the rest of the family put together these days, without it making much of a dent in his appetite.

'Dad says it's going to be at least half an hour.' Chloe came out of the kitchen, scowling.

'Go on then, Jakey.' Holly directed her son to get himself something to stave off impending death by hunger. 'I'm just going to email someone before dinner.'

'I'm going back to my room then,' said Chloe as Holly sat at the desk and tapped a key to wake the computer.

'Can you not call me Jakey when there are other people here?' he said from across the room.

'Sorry.' Holly knew he didn't like being called this in front of friends, but found it hard to kick the habit.

'It's embarrassing,' Jake muttered as he left the room.

Holly was glad to have the room to herself, as she needed space to think exactly what she was going to write.

Dear Daniel, she began, putting his card back in her bag after writing the email address. *I'm glad I met you on the train today. I wasn't sure if you travelled regularly. I also wondered who you were! It was my first day back at work today and I felt very reassured to see you there. Who knows if I would have been on the train today if you hadn't been where you were and done what you did then? Perhaps we can talk sometime.*

She began reading it to herself but was startled to find Jake standing behind her.

'I've brought your wine in.' He was holding the glass in one hand and a doorstep of a sandwich in the other. 'Shall I put it next to the sofa?'

'Yes, thank you,' she replied, hastily adding *Very best, Holly*, and pressing the Send button. 'I'm done here.'

Holly moved to sit next to her son.

She took a sip of wine as Jake stretched out and put his feet in her lap, balancing his plate on his stomach. He was still a very tactile and affectionate boy in private, despite the onslaught of puberty.

'How was it back at work?' he asked. The question when he voiced it didn't seem as loaded as when Mark had. 'Did the sanctimonious bitch give you hell?'

Holly laughed.

'Don't call my beloved boss that,' she said, squeezing his foot.

'That's what you call her.' Jake had heard her referring to Katherine in less than glowing terms once too often to be able to resist joining in.

'Yes, but I have to call her names as a way of releasing the pressure built up by working for her.' Holly watched him putting nearly an entire sandwich into his mouth. 'Don't eat so quickly. You'll get indigestion.'

Jake's mouth was too full to protest, so he made a noise which was accompanied by a ping from the other side of the room. This indicated Holly had an email.

She had to resist an unusually strong desire to jump up and open it as Mark came into the room announcing that dinner was ready, with a flourish of the oven gloves.

Chapter Eight

'THERE SHE IS.' Dimitri nodded towards a sofa in the lobby of Broadcasting House. Holly's mother was leafing through a magazine.

'Oh, yes.' Holly could see Susan now. 'How did you know it was my mother?'

'She looks just like you,' he said, crossing towards her.

'Hello!' Holly greeted her mother.

'Darling.' Susan looked up and began gathering her things. 'How are you?'

'Good, thanks.' Holly kissed her.

Dimitiri had told Holly he was popping out to buy a sandwich but appeared to be waiting for an introduction. She did the honours.

'Nice to meet you, Mrs Holt. I knew you were Holly's mother as soon as I saw you. Either that or her sister. You look just like her,' Dimitri said, shaking Susan's hand and holding it for rather longer than was necessary.

Is there no one he doesn't flirt with? Holly thought to herself.

'Oh, call me me Susan, please,' she said, smiling in a way which Holly could only think to describe as coquettish. 'Nice to meet you too, Dimitri. Have you been working on *Antennae* long?'

'It feels like that sometimes,' he replied. 'But only about a year. Do you listen to the programme ever?'

'No, she doesn't,' Holly answered for her. 'They tuned in once, decided James Darling was too full of himself and never listened again.'

'That's not entirely true,' her mother protested, embarrassed in front of one of Holly's colleagues by how little interest she took in what her daughter did for a living.

'Very wise. He is full of himself,' Dimitri responded.

'Shall we go?' Holly said to her mother.

'Holly says you're taking her out to lunch,' Dimitri said, failing to take his cue to leave. 'Are you going anywhere nice?'

'We're going to John Lewis. I want to buy a computer and I need Holly's help,' Susan said, revealing the purpose of her trip to London.

'Oh, really? Do you know what sort of thing you're looking for?' He sounded like a salesman, Holly thought.

'She has absolutely no idea,' Holly answered for Susan again, slightly embarrassed by the way she was so obviously flirting back with her colleague.

They had walked through the doors of Broadcasting House and were outside on the pavement now.

'We're going this way,' Holly said.

'And I'm heading in the opposite direction,' Dimitri replied, taking the hint now. 'See you later, Holly. Very nice to meet you, Susan.'

She stared after him as he turned into Mortimer Street. 'What an exceedingly nice young man. I'm surprised you've never mentioned him before.'

'I'm sure I have,' Holly replied. 'Let's cross, shall we?'

They walked down Margaret Street to the back entrance of John Lewis. It was her mother's favourite shop, and working so near meant Holly often met her there for lunch when she was up looking for socks or sheets or something.

Both Susan and Patrick were computer averse, and called Holly quite often to ask if she could look up something on the internet for them, because even the prospect of going down to their local library and being shown by the kindly librarian how to navigate in cyberspace filled them with dread.

'The place is full of mice,' Patrick had said when Holly suggested this. 'It terrifies me.'

'I did try to use one,' Susan had admitted, 'but I couldn't get it to work. The pointer thing kept disappearing altogether.'

Holly's sister Fay had once suggested getting them both a laptop as a joint present.

'You'd better ask them first,' Holly had told her, thinking back to the Christmas iPod that she'd had to take back untouched.

'They said it was a very kind thought but they'd absolutely hate it!' Fay had reported back, after asking them.

So it was a total surprise to Holly when her mother had announced she was coming to London to buy herself a computer from John Lewis.

'What on earth has brought about this transformation?' Holly asked her now, as they stood outside the lifts.

'Oh, I just felt as if I was getting a bit left behind. Lots of our friends have email addresses and I suppose it's a good way of keeping in touch with the ones who are still alive,' Susan said, before adding, 'Your father's even bought himself a mobile phone.'

'Has he?' Holly exclaimed. She found this hard to believe. She had lent him hers once when her parents had been to stay. Patrick had set off on a long walk, and Holly had given him the phone in case he got lost. It took her about an hour to show him how to make a call if he did. Then, when it got late and the rest of the family were starting to worry about him, she called but found the phone switched off.

'I didn't want to waste the battery,' her father had said when he eventually got back, unperturbed that they had been anxious on his behalf.

'What's he going to do with a mobile phone?' Holly asked her mother now.

'I'm not entirely sure,' Susan replied. 'And I've tried calling him on it a couple of times but he never seems to answer.'

'Perhaps you could get a phone of your own and then you could text him?' Holly suggested.

'Oh, I don't imagine he'll want me bothering him when he's busy,' Susan said as they stepped into the lift. 'Which floor was it?'

'Fifth,' Holly said, feeling slightly uneasy about whatever it was her father was busy with.

Holly noticed for the second time that day that her mother seemed to light up when there was a young man about.

Dean, according to his nametag, had asked if he could help.

'I want to buy a computer.' Susan smiled at him.

Dean led her to the laptop section and Holly trailed after them feeling like a spare part.

She smiled at a woman who was browsing digital radios. She looked familiar but Holly could not place her. She thought it was probably someone from the BBC.

'What is it you want to use it for?' Dean was asking Susan.

'I'm sure once I have it, I might want to do all sorts of things,' she told him, with an air that suggested she might even be able to. Holly doubted this.

'But initially I just want to stay in touch with friends . . . maybe even make new ones.'

Holly could see why her mother wanted to stay in touch

with friends, especially as those she had kept dying, but she wondered where this sudden urge to make new ones had come from.

'I'm not very technically competent, though,' Susan was telling Dean, who had already assumed this and began giving her a rough guide to the desktop.

'Why won't the arrow move?' Susan asked, exasperated, when he tried to show her how easy it was to shop online.

'That's the hardest part,' Dean said gently, and it wasn't long before she was clicking her way through online stores.

'It's a bit like returning library books.' She smiled gleefully, having managed to add some passion fruit to a virtual supermarket basket.

Half an hour later, she was marching Holly to the in-store café, with a netbook tucked under her arm.

'I'll ask Fay to help me set it all up. She's coming over with V and the girls at the weekend,' Susan said, settling down with a slice of quiche and plate of salad.

Vanessa or V was Fay's partner and the natural mother of their children, Kate and Lucy. Peter, a close gay friend of them both, was the father.

Holly and Fay's parents, especially their father, found it hard to accept this domestic set up completely. They did their best to give the impression that they found everything perfectly normal, but the effect was comic rather than genuine.

'Dad said he liked the new décor in Lucy's bedroom,' Fay had told Holly after a visit. 'He described it as: "What we used to be able to call gay!" Then Mum tried to make up for the gaffe by telling V she'd made a lovely job of painting the walls and how clever she was to "do all the man's jobs as well".'

'Have you spoken to Fay recently?' Susan asked now.

'Not since we got back from holiday,' Holly told her.

Her sister had called, concerned, after the train crash but hadn't been in touch again since.

'She said she was going to call you,' Susan said. 'I think she's coming up to London next week. She said she would try to meet up with you.'

'I'll email her,' Holly promised, taking a spoonful of soup. 'I suppose I'll be able to email you soon, too, once you've got it all set up. Will you get a joint email with Dad?'

Holly and Mark had their own separate work email addresses but at home they shared one.

'No, I don't think so.' Susan sounded appalled at the very suggestion. 'Anyway I don't suppose Patrick will have time to get to grips with it.'

Holly wondered again what Patrick was so busy doing but something stopped her from asking. She took another mouthful of soup instead.

'So how are you, Holly?' her mother asked. 'Really?'

'Fine.' Holly trotted out her standard response. 'And the children are well and Mark's fine too.'

'And how has it been going back to work?' Her mother looked at her more closely now. 'How are you finding the train journey?'

'It's OK, Mum,' Holly said truthfully. 'I was a bit nervous at first, but once I was on it was fine.'

'It must be strange though,' Susan persisted. 'I mean, are some of the people who were injured still travelling on the train?'

'I haven't noticed anyone,' Holly said truthfully. She'd not encountered anyone with any visible signs of having been hurt when the train crashed. But it was still early days. She presumed the people who had been seriously injured would not be back for a few weeks yet, if at all.

'And have you seen . . .' Susan paused and began toying with the salad on her plate, as if unsure whether to ask or not. 'The man who stayed with you, when it all happened?'

'I've bumped into him a couple of times,' Holly said, and looked at her watch, as her mother put a sizeable piece of quiche into her mouth.

'I ought to be getting back to work soon, Mum.' She had finished her soup, and although she didn't need to get back to work immediately, found herself not wanting to talk to her mother about Daniel Harrison – or to tell her that she was having a drink with him that evening.

'OK. Sorry, darling. I don't want to hold you up.' Susan had now finished her quiche. 'I might stay and have a cup of coffee but you go on back to work. I don't want to make you late.'

'It was lovely to see you anyway.' Holly kissed her mother goodbye. 'Good luck with the laptop. And send my love to Dad.'

'I expect he'll let you know his mobile number. Then you can text him yourself,' Susan replied. 'And tell that nice Greek chap my mission was successful, won't you?'

I saw the woman from the train again today, out of context, and I couldn't place her at first. I went to John Lewis in my lunch hour to buy a digital radio. The house is too quiet without Geoff. It's as if the silence in every room is a reminder that he's gone.

I wanted to get a decent radio. A cheap one would have made him seem easily replaceable, and it's not easy, not easy at all. I still switch off the alarm every morning and turn over to ask if he wants a cup of tea. I walk through the door at the end of the day and shout 'Hello', expecting someone to reply. I wanted something to fill that awful silence of the no reply.

I was looking a Roberts leather-covered radio, a modern version of the one my parents used to have, when I looked up and there she was. I recognised her but I couldn't think where I knew her from, and then I realised and smiled. She smiled back, as if she knew exactly who I was. And I thought that I could have talked to her then, said something, introduced myself, told her I knew what had happened to her, but she was with an older woman.

The assistant was showing them laptops. I kept looking over, thinking she might catch my eye and smile again. But she didn't. She seemed wrapped up in the discussions they were having. So I just watched them from behind the stack of radios.

I thought the older woman was probably her mother and that made me feel resentful. I know that's unreasonable. I should be pleased that she has

73

someone who is there for her. But when I first saw her on the news, she looked so alone and I thought she might be someone who could understand what I was going through. I thought maybe we could be there for each other.

Now, I am discovering she has people all around her; first that man on the train and now her mother. I told myself not to be silly; not to be cross with her. It's not her fault that I have no one, is it?

I keep imagining that I'm talking to the counsellor again, mentally explaining to her why I might be feeling a certain way.

'I think I felt resentful because I was already thinking about my mother,' I ran the imagined conversation in my head afterwards. 'Because I bought an exact replica of the radio my parents used to have in their front room and because I was in a department store.'

That always makes me think about my mother. For years, I never went into a department store and my mother stayed away from them until she died. But I realised I was letting events dictate my actions and decided to take control. I think Helen, the counsellor, must have told me that I needed to 'take control'. I don't think I would have put it like that myself, but it did gradually begin to dawn on me that avoiding department stores for the rest of my life was pointless.

'Do you want to tell me about what happened?' Helen asked me when I first started going to see her.

'It was because I needed a new coat,' I told her. 'We got there early because my mother thought there would be a queue, what with it being a closing down sale and that.'

And then I ran through the story about the crowd building up, so that by the time the store was due to open its doors, people were pushing against us and I felt myself being crushed against those around me. I was ten at the time, small for my age, so my face was being pressed into coat tails and I found it hard to breathe.

There was a small wall by the steps that led up to the shop doors and my mother managed to lift me up and place me on it, so that I was above *the crowd which still appeared to be growing and pushing forward with an intensity that made the people at the front start to panic.*

'You ought to open the doors,' my mother said to the security guard. 'I know it's not time, but someone might get hurt. All these people and nowhere for them to go.'

She smiled when she said this, as if it was just a suggestion. But the people around her became more agitated and began chanting, 'Open the doors. Open the doors!' And because they were chanting, the pushing seemed to get worse and the security guard, who my mother told me afterwards 'couldn't have been more than eighteen', looked unsure what to do.

'Stand back a bit,' he said, and began fumbling with keys. 'The doors open outwards.'

And those were the last words he ever spoke. We didn't know that at the time. We never knew when we surged inside the store and took the escalators up to the children's clothing section, that he'd lost his footing as the crowd began flooding in and over him, trampling him to death in their anxiety to secure cheap goods.

My mother wouldn't let me wear the coat when we heard the news. It was navy blue with silver buttons, a bit too big for me because she wanted it 'to last', but beautiful. I only wore it that once, on the way back home. After she'd switched on the Roberts radio in the living room and found out what had happened she wrapped it up again and put it back in the bag, then put the bag on top of the wardrobe in their bedroom, where she knew I wouldn't be able to reach it.

'It wouldn't be right to wear it,' she said, as I watched her. 'Not now.'

I wonder if my mother would forgive me today for using a department store. 'It's not as if there's a lot of choice,' I would tell her, if she was here to hear. 'The radio shop in the village closed years ago. It's here or the internet.'

'It just doesn't feel right, Anne-Marie,' I can almost hear her replying. 'But I suppose these are exceptional circumstances.'

She'd have tried not to mind that I'd broken her rule because she'd be so worried about me.

Part of me is glad that she's not here, that she doesn't have one more thing to worry about. It's the sort of thing that might push her over the edge again and she was OK, towards the end. She seemed to have stopped thinking about it, stopped blaming herself so much, started nodding when my dad said, 'It wasn't your fault my love. You have to believe that.'

If she was still alive now, I imagine my mother would have asked me to stay, cooked for me, looked after me. I could have really let go and maybe that would have helped. But I'm on my own and the only way I know how to cope is to try and carry on.

Perhaps that's what she's doing too, the woman from the train. Sometimes, even when you have people around, you can't always tell them what's happened, can you? You can't explain.

'I could never really explain to your father what it felt like,' Mum used to say to me. I wonder if this woman I saw today has explained to her own mother how it felt when she was trapped in that tunnel.

Perhaps not. Perhaps she can't. Perhaps she wants to spare her mother's feelings. But she could tell me, if she wanted to, because I would understand what it's like to feel alone, what it's like to worry that no one is looking out for you any more.

I bought the radio and it's on now in the living room, switched to BBC Radio 4, mocking me with idle chatter. I was wrong. It doesn't make the house seem less empty. If anything, it feels more so.

There are three people talking about global warming and I know that if Geoff were here he'd say something about it being a conspiracy. I don't agree with him and it always annoyed me when he started going on about the effects of burning fossil fuels being over-exaggerated. When they were talking about it on the radio I expected him to pipe up with his conspiracy theory. But of course he didn't.

I wanted to cry then, but didn't because if I started I'm not sure when I would stop and I'm tired of crying. There comes a point when you can't even summon up the energy to cry any more and I seem to have reached that point.

So, I got up and switched the radio over to BBC Radio 6. They were playing Arctic Monkeys' 'Don't Sit Down, 'Cause I've Moved Your Chair'.

I thought, Too right, you moved my chair. You pulled it and the rug it was on right out from under my feet.

Then I started to dance.

Chapter Nine

HOLLY OPENED THE door of the Lebanese brasserie tentatively and was immediately greeted by a waiter.

'I'm meeting someone,' she said, scanning the muted beige-and-grey interior. 'But I don't think he's here yet.'

'Holly.' She felt a hand touch her shoulder lightly and turned to find Daniel coming in the door.

'I've been walking up the road behind you,' he said, smiling at the waiter as if they were fairly familiar with each other. 'I tried to catch up but you walk very fast!'

'It's the only exercise I get, and I've been sitting at a desk all day,' she told him, although she always walked everywhere fast. Thankfully, so did Mark. She was not sure she could have married a dawdler.

'I would have called out but I wasn't sure it was you.' Daniel allowed the waiter to usher them to a small table in the window, with a low armchair set either side.

'This looks nice.' Holly looked around at the sleek curved lines of the restaurant. It reminded her of an ocean liner. 'I've never noticed it before but I must have walked past nearly every day.'

'A friend who's a recovering alcoholic told me about it.' Daniel picked up the wine list and shrugged as if in apology to his absent friend. 'He always orders mint tea, but I could do with a large glass of red wine. How about you?'

'Same,' said Holly, realising she'd felt in need of one ever since saying goodbye to her mother. 'I could definitely do with a drink.'

'What train do you need to get?' Daniel asked. 'Shall we share a half-carafe or do you want something else?'

'Sounds good to me,' said Holly, relaxing back into her chair, knowing that alcohol would soon be coming her way. 'I was going to aim for the seven-fifteen, but if you need to go earlier . . .'

'No.' Daniel was looking towards the bar, trying to catch the waiter's attention. 'I'll get that too.'

He had replied immediately to Holly's email, earlier in the week, and suggested they meet in a place he knew close to Victoria station. She was thankful to him for this. She had feared he would suggest simply sitting together on the train and she knew she couldn't talk to him in that setting.

Now she looked at Daniel as he pointed out the wine they wanted to the waiter.

'Do you want any olives?' he asked her. 'Or we could share a mezze plate?'

'Why not?' Holly was peckish and the food looked good. 'I'm getting hungry and it will be hours before I get to eat at home.'

The bowl of soup she'd had with her mother hadn't been very filling.

'No dinner waiting on the table for you back home then,' said Daniel, and then to the waiter, 'Can we get the mezze plate too, please?'

'It certainly won't be ready.' Holly thought back to the last few nights spent waiting for Mark's offerings to be brought to the table. 'My husband likes to cook. But he likes to take his time.'

'What does he do?' Daniel asked as the waiter returned and began pouring a half-inch of wine into his glass.

He gave a brief cursory swig and nodded, going through the rigmarole of tasting so that the waiter could then pour them both a glass.

Mark had mentioned he might have a drink with some former colleagues after work this evening. 'Networking,' he'd said, and Holly suspected he hoped it might yield more work.

'He's in marketing.' She raised her glass. 'Cheers! And thank you.'

'What for?' said Daniel, clinking her glass.

Holly sat back in her chair and looked at him. She must have seen him on the train hundreds of times before the crash but had never really taken in any detail about him. He was just another familiar face, to be ignored in a crowded carriage or occasionally smile at apologetically as she'd moved around him to get to a seat or reached up to take a bag from the overhead luggage rack. His face was becoming more familiar since she'd seen him again, last week, but this was the first time she'd had the chance to take him in properly.

She'd initially thought he was roughly the same age as her but now she realised he must be at least ten years younger. He was attractive in an irregular way. It was hard to make out whether his salt-and-pepper hair veered towards blond or brown, if his eyes were green or blue. He had the sort of face which she imagined would not photograph particularly well, but which in the flesh was strangely attractive.

'For staying with me,' Holly said, knowing that much was understood between them and didn't really need saying.

'It helped me, having something to do,' Daniel said, stretching his arm across the table and covering her hand briefly with his. The gesture didn't seem flirtatious, it seemed right.

'Daisy was angry with me afterwards,' he went on. 'She'd heard about the crash on the radio and had been trying to call me. When I didn't answer, she thought I might have been killed.'

'That's understandable,' Holly, said, presuming Daisy was his wife. 'She was angry that I stayed.' Daniel took another sip of wine. 'She told me I should have got myself out as soon as I could, let the rescue workers deal with everyone else.'

'That's understandable too,' Holly told him. 'I'm not sure how I would have felt if Mark had been on the train and he'd stayed to help someone, rather than getting himself out. It sounds selfish but I wouldn't have wanted him to have risked his life for some stranger.'

'It felt like the right thing to do.' Daniel looked at her. 'I didn't think about whether to stay with you or not. I couldn't have left.'

Holly was sure that if Mark had been in Daniel's position he would have stayed too.

Soon after she had first met him they'd been lying on the beach one day, dozing off a bedroom-induced lethargy. A boy who couldn't have been more than six had caught their attention as he walked along the groyne out to sea. He was holding his arms out like an aeroplane to balance himself, but wobbling precariously nevertheless.

'He's gone!' Mark said suddenly, jumping up from the towel they were lying on and running towards the beach before Holly had time to ask what had happened.

Then she saw what Mark had already seen. The boy had fallen into the sea, was out of his depth and being pushed under by waves that were rough for the time of year.

Mark swam straight out. He was a strong swimmer but Holly still worried when he dived under the water and disappeared.

He emerged, what seemed a long time later but could only have been seconds, with the boy under one arm and swam back to shore with him.

The boy's mother, whose attention had been focused on her new boyfriend's licking of her nipples, had seen none of this and seemed irritated when Mark brought him to her.

Holly had marvelled at the fact Mark hadn't even stopped to think but had gone straight after the boy. She dreaded to think what might have happened if he hadn't.

When the train was hit, they'd been as much in the dark about what had happened as they had been in the blackness of the tunnel. Only later would it emerge that their portion of the train had come uncoupled and the back been hit by another train.

As the smell of smoke began to filter through the carriage, Holly had wondered if there had been some sort of terrorist attack. She'd thought then, as people rushed to get out of the wreckage, that perhaps there would be another, nearer explosion. Daniel must have thought the same, and yet he'd stayed with her.

Holly pulled the elastic band she wore around her wrist so that, pinged against her skin just hard enough, if would distract her from thinking about what had happened. It was a trick she'd heard mentioned somewhere, she wasn't sure where, and it seemed to work. If anyone commented on the band, she'd say she was keeping it for Jake who was growing a rubber-band ball.

'I'm so grateful that you stayed,' she said, looking directly at Daniel. 'Things might have been different if you hadn't.'

'The fire crews would have got to you anyway.' He shrugged off his part in it all.

'I know,' Holly said. 'But I'd have been on my own.'

Daniel poured some more wine into her glass. 'Staying with you made me feel as if I'd at least done something.'

The waiter returned to the table, bearing a plate of mezze which he set in the middle.

Holly smiled in thanks.

'Everyone keeps telling me I need to talk, ought to see a counsellor, and that I need to deal with what happened . . . but it doesn't feel right to keep going over things, because I'm OK,' she told him. 'Counselling should be for people who were injured . . .'

Holly paused and Daniel said what she was thinking out loud.

'Or the relatives of the people who died.' He took a deep-fried aubergine from the plate between them.

'I went back to work immediately, even though it meant getting a bus from Gatwick to East Croydon,' he said. 'Daisy kept saying I needed time to get over the shock and the trauma, but I just wanted to get on with things.'

'Me too.' Holly took an aubergine herself. 'It's funny how people always seem to think it odd if you do, though. My husband's father died when he was at university. He had a football match that day. Everyone told him he should pull out but Mark played in it because he said he needed to do something.'

'Did he win?' Daniel asked.

'I don't know.' Holly considered this. 'I never actually asked. He told me about it when Harold Shipman was convicted. Apparently he went running after his mother died and all the pundits said this pointed to him being a serial killer.'

'Is your husband a serial killer yet?' Daniel raised his eyebrows.

Holly laughed again. She liked him.

'The wife is always the last to know,' she said. 'Or is that with adultery?'

'Probably both.' Daniel smiled. 'Does he keep himself to himself?'

'I'm not with you?' Holly looked at him questioningly.

'Serial killers,' Daniel said, and then explained further. 'On the news, they always say they kept themselves to themselves. If your husband is gregarious, you'll probably be OK.'

'Well, he's fairly sociable,' Holly told him, and then reverted to the conversation they'd been having before Harold Shipman somehow came into it.

'Have you talked to anyone?' she asked. 'About the crash, I mean?'

'No.' Daniel shook his head. 'You?'

'My husband made an appointment for me with a counsellor,' she said. 'I went, to shut him up, but I felt fraudulent. I hadn't got any scars to show.'

The counsellor had urged Holly to go over exactly what had happened that day. But she hadn't wanted to talk to him about it, or to Mark when he'd asked her gently what it had been like. The only person she thought she might be able to talk to was the man whose name she hadn't known until last week. The man who was sitting opposite her now, making her laugh for what felt the first time in ages.

'Is Daisy your wife?' Holly asked.

'Yes.' Daniel looked a his wedding ring as if to confirm the fact to himself.

'Children?' Holly asked, knowing the question was slightly impudent but wanting to get a fuller picture of him.

'We've been trying.' Daniel appeared not to mind the question. 'But none yet.'

Holly wondered how long they'd been trying for and whether other people had started trying for babies since the accident. She knew the birth rate had soared after 9/11, as people felt the need to take life-affirming action after such large numbers had died. Or perhaps it was just that they valued their own lives more and needed to get on with them, stop putting off families or marriage or whatever it was they'd been waiting for the right moment to begin. After 9/11 Holly had felt a strong desire to have another baby herself, but Mark had resisted and once Jake settled into school she found herself enjoying the extra time she had.

But the train crash seemed to have had the opposite effect on her, making her feel slightly detached from the life that she had and less willing to embrace it.

Daniel looked at his watch.

'We should get going,' he said. 'If we're still aiming for the seven-fifteen?'

'OK.' Holly reached for her bag, getting up slowly, in no particular hurry to get home.

They walked the short distance to the station together and Holly wondered if Daniel always walked slowly or if he was dawdling because she was.

'*Pagad*,' she said to herself, a word which Mark had told her was a Filipino expression, meaning to walk slowly so that a slow walker could keep up.

It implied, Mark had told her, that the person slowing their pace was considerate. She glanced at Daniel now, knowing this much already, and smiled to herself. The slight anxiety she had felt about meeting him had disappeared. She hoped she'd see more of him.

Chapter Ten

Tʜᴇ ʙʟɪɴᴅs ᴏғ the office Holly now shared with Natalie were still drawn and when she tried the handle it was locked. She took her key from her bag and was just putting it in the lock when the door swung open from the inside. Holly fell forward slightly and stumbled into the office and the arms of James Darling.

'Oh, sorry, I thought the door was locked.' She backed off a bit and stepped past James towards Natalie, who was leaning against her desk. 'Hi, Natalie. James.'

Holly was probably the only person on the programme who didn't call James 'Darling'. It felt too forward given that she didn't particularly like him, plus she suspected that, having had at least fifty years of people calling him Darling, he was probably getting a bit sick of it. He must have heard all the jokes a million times, if not more.

As if to underline her thoughts, Natalie piped up a well-worn line.

'Move over, Darling,' she said, noticing that James appeared temporarily frozen and was blocking Holly's access to her desk.

'Oh, sorry, Holly.' He stood aside.

Holly sat in her chair and swivelled round to face both of them.

Natalie was still leaning against her desk with an air of nonchalance. James looked as if he was not quite sure what to do with himself.

'So, have I interrupted something?' Holly presumed they'd been discussing some of the items under consideration for this week's programme.

'No.' James's negative came only a split second before Natalie's.

'No,' she said, picking up a sheaf of papers from her desk. 'We were about to go through a couple of possible interviews for this Friday, that's all.'

Natalie had known James Darling for longer than anyone else on the programme. They'd worked in local radio together and then in the Broadcasting House newsroom in their twenties.

In Holly's opinion Natalie was cleverer, sharper and more intuitive than James, but he had had the more glittering career. James had become a correspondent and spent his thirties reporting from Rome, Berlin, Prague and Kiev before returning to take up the new position of breaking news correspondent. Natalie had stayed in London, become a news producer and then moved into programme production.

'What's on the cards then?' he asked, nodding towards the sheaf of papers Natalie was shuffling in front of her.

'You're not going to like this but Katherine is very keen on it.' Natalie had the job of running though all the potential items in the programme with James early in the week. She had a knack for bringing him round to things he didn't like at first. They worked well together, possibly because of the longevity of their relationship. Natalie shifted up the desk a little, allowing James to rest his backside against it, next to hers, and read the piece of A4 she was holding.

'Global warming linked to snails?' he asked, nudging her conspiratorially as he did.

Holly couldn't help finding James Darling physically repellent. She found the way he peered through his ridiculous big square glasses rather creepy. Plus, he was slightly sweaty and his stripy shirt was stretched too tight around his spreading middle. If he wasn't careful he would end up like the fat man on the train whom she had deliberately avoided this morning.

Holly felt she had skipped a generation, and instead of turning into her mother was turning into her grandmother and becoming superstitious about all sorts of things. One was keeping Daniel Harrison's card in her bag whenever she took the train, treating it as a lucky charm to protect her against any future dangers. Another was trying to sit in the same place; window seat, facing forward, not too near the doors and in the middle of the train. Although the train crash had been a completely random occurrence and it was luck that saw her come out of it alive and in one piece, she also knew that if she'd been sitting further back she could have been injured or worse. So she'd stuck to the same carriage and the same seat as much as possible, since then.

The very overweight man appeared to be doing the same.

He'd sat next to her three times this week already and it wasn't only the way he seemed to spread over from his side of the seat and into hers that annoyed her. It was his personal habits too.

He'd had a cold and would shift around in their joint seat as he fumbled to get tissues from his pocket; tissues which, after a great deal of blowing, he deposited on his lap. Holly was sure she would come down with whatever virus he had. By mid-week the cold appeared to have affected his breathing and, although there were fewer dirty tissues around, her thoughts were disturbed by the heavy rasping of his breath.

So this morning Holly decided she'd had enough and sat in another carriage, further up the train.

There was a leaflet on the seat she found, giving details of the Balcombe tunnel survivors group's meeting. Holly skimmed the agenda. ALL WELCOME was written across the bottom in large bold letters as if, Holly thought, to emphasise that even people like her, with nothing to show for having been on the train that day, could attend.

If you were not a victim then you were a survivor.

Holly folded the leaflet and put it on the half-table by the window. She wasn't going to be either.

'Do you mind if I sit here?' said a voice she recognised.

She looked up and saw Daniel, smiling but looking hesitant.

'Of course not.' She smiled back at him.

'You looked as if you didn't want to be disturbed.' He sat down and put his cup of coffee by the leaflet on her table. 'I won't talk all the way to London or anything.'

He eased himself out of his coat and hung it over the armrest.

'I don't mind if you do,' Holly replied. Then, joking, 'I might not listen, but I won't mind.'

Daniel shrugged a quiet acceptance of the joke.

'You don't usually sit in this carriage?' he said questioningly.

'No,' she told him. 'I usually sit further back. I was getting into the habit of sitting in the same place but I thought I'd try to make a change.'

'I try to avoid the part of the train we were sitting in,' Daniel said.

'I was doing the opposite,' Holly told him.

'Why?' He reached across her to pick up his coffee cup.

'A sort of silly superstition.' She watched as he flicked the plastic lid off and took a sip. 'I got out in one piece, sitting in that particular carriage. I told myself I'd probably be OK there if anything happened again.'

'I try to sit anywhere but where we were,' Daniel said, licking a line of milky froth from his upper lip. 'Your routine makes more sense, though.'

'I don't know if any of it makes any sense,' Holly said, reaching for the leaflet which she had been trying to ignore. 'Have you seen this? Will you go?'

'I'm not sure,' he said, studying it. 'Will you?'

'I don't know,' Holly replied. 'It probably doesn't make sense but I think I'd feel a bit fraudulent.'

'It makes perfect sense.' Daniel handed the leaflet back to her. 'Sometimes I feel saying I was on the train when it crashed is a bit like saying I was on the roller coaster on the Palace Pier when in fact I was only on the bumper cars. I might have been in the same place, but I didn't have the same experience as others.'

Holly laughed.

'We had the same experience,' she said.

'I know.' Daniel briefly caught her eye and then looked away. 'We could go together? And leave if we don't feel comfortable?'

He'd stopped talking and shifted in his seat slightly, allowing a woman who had got on the train at Hawyards Heath to sit in the seat opposite them.

Holly recognised her as the woman she'd seen applying make-up on her first day back at work. She smiled and the woman smiled in return, as if she recognised her too. Today her make-up was fully applied and she sat still and stared out of the window for the rest of the journey.

Holly began reading her newspaper and Daniel took out his laptop and opened it, their conversation ended by the slightly uncomfortable presence of a third person in their quadrangle of seats.

Natalie obviously did feel comfortable with James Darling firmly planted in their office, his backside taking up most of her desk.

'That's all we've got for now,' she said, picking up a few more documents from her desk. 'Plus the ones we've already talked about.'

James put his hand out to take them from her, without looking up, and Natalie put the wad of papers in it, and then forced his fingers closed with her hand.

That made him look up and smile.

Uggh! Holly thought.

'By the way,' Natalie added, 'did you hear Liam Hicks has been having an affair with the singer from Ecstatic?'

Liam Hicks was a TV news reporter. He'd worked with Natalie and James in the radio newsroom but was always destined for television. He looked like a film star. Tall, dark, penetrating green eyes, six o'clock shadow – the works!

'Isn't he married?' Holly asked.

'Yes, to Maria Goulding.' Darling reeled off the name of another TV reporter. Maria was brilliant; clever, incisive and dogged. Her reports had won her numerous awards, but compared to her handsome husband she was mousey and unprepossessing-looking.

'Honestly!' Holly felt exasperated by the cliché of the affair. 'He's married to a very bright woman and yet he goes off with a beautiful airhead.'

'She is *very* beautiful,' James said, as if this justified Liam Hicks' dalliance.

'It must be a terrible curse, having a good-looking husband,' Natalie said.

Holly laughed out loud.

'What?' Natalie and James said together.

'Well, you sound as if you don't think you have a good-looking husband.' Holly watched Natalie's half-smile as she realised what she'd said. 'Or me, for that matter.'

'Oh, well. You know what I mean.' Natalie shrugged. 'Mark is gorgeous, of course.'

'And so is Guy,' Holly prompted, wondering if Natalie really thought Mark was gorgeous or if she was just being polite.

Holly seemed to have stopped seeing Mark as the almost unbelievably good-looking man she had thought he was for so long, but did others still view him like that?

'Cue my exit,' James said, standing up. 'I'll leave you to discuss the various merits of your husbands. See you later.'

'So,' Natalie rolled her chair over to Holly's desk and sat down, 'talking of which, how was the tall, dark and handsome stranger?'

Holly wondered what she was talking about and then realised it must be her drink with Daniel Harrison.

'Quite small and sandy-haired. He works with computers,' Holly told her, trying to give Natalie the impression that Daniel was ordinary. She didn't want her to probe any further.

'How disappointing,' she said. 'I'd imagined he would be like Dimitri.'

'Not like Dimitri at all,' she told Natalie. 'But nice. He was very nice.'

'Nice?' Natalie was unimpressed. 'This cup of coffee is very nice. What was he *like*?'

'I'm not sure how to describe him,' Holly said slowly. She felt protective of Daniel Harrison. She owed him that much. Natalie said nothing, sensing her mood.

'We only had a quick drink really.' Holly eased up a little towards her friend. 'But I felt as if I knew him quite well.'

'How so?' Natalie asked.

'It was a bit like meeting an old school friend,' she tried to explain. 'Someone you knew quite well, but haven't seen for years.'

'A bit like James Darling then?' Natalie nodded towards the outer office where he was presumably now hovering somewhere.

They were interrupted by a knock at the door.

Sharon, Katherine's PA, peered cautiously around the office, as if she expected someone else to be there.

'Katherine says can we have a meeting in fifteen minutes, in her office?'

'Yes,' Natalie answered for both of them. 'We'll be there.'

The interruption meant Holly never answered her question. In her mind she had formed a reply. No, he's nothing like James Darling. He's not like anyone I've ever met before. He's not like anyone I would usually be friends with, and yet I feel completely at ease with him and compelled to see more of him.

She kept these thoughts to herself.

Chapter Eleven

THERE WAS A time when Holly would have been pleased that
Mark had taken it upon himself to clean the fridge. But
when she got home from work and found its entire contents
strewn across the floor, she was annoyed – and not just because
it meant she had to step across bags of frozen vegetables to get
into the kitchen.

No, Holly was annoyed that Mark had nothing better to do.
'Be careful what you wish for,' she said quietly to herself, thinking
how it used to drive her mad that he never attempted the household jobs. He had always been too busy, dealing with clients or
bits of work that had to be tackled there and then.

'Hi.' Mark was crouching down, examining the contents of
the bottom drawer of the freezer. 'How was your day?'

'Fine.' Holly had long since given up filling him in on the
details. 'What are you doing?'

'A lot of this stuff is past its sell-by-date,' Mark explained,
brandishing a packet of frozen fish fingers in one hand to illustrate
his point.

'Does it matter?' Holly asked. She had always been of the mind
that sell-by-dates were manipulation by supermarkets, designed to
make you chuck out perfectly good food and buy more, rather
than to protect you from salmonella. 'This looks OK.'

She picked up a packet of soft cheese, which Mark had consigned to the kitchen table. Holly suspected the table was a staging post between the fridge and the bin. She looked at the packaging and then sniffed the cheese. It was a few days past its sell-by-date but it looked and smelled fine.

'You can't be too careful,' he said, taking the cheese from her and extending his foot to open the aluminium pedal bin.

'Well, it seems like a waste to me,' Holly said, doubly annoyed now that Mark was fussing around in the kitchen and also that what appeared to be perfectly good cheese was being chucked out.

Holly knew that she and Mark did not qualify as hard up, but with two teenage children to feed and a mortgage to pay, they weren't so flush that they didn't have to be careful. She felt, perhaps irrationally, that as she was the one bringing in most of the money at the moment, she should be the one who decided if it was spent on replacing items they might well have been able to eat.

'Blimey, look at this!' Mark appeared not to notice Holly's irritation and carried on rejecting packets of food. 'This bacon's going green.'

He held it up to show her before chucking it. 'And this butter looks a bit rancid, although the sell-by-date says it's still OK.'

Holly thought to herself, meanly, that it was not the food but Mark who was getting past his sell-by-date. Again, there was a time when she might have said this to him in jest and Mark would have laughed at the joke. Now she was not sure how he would take such a comment.

'Hi, Mum,' Chloe came down the stairs with Ruaridh in tow.

'Evening, Mrs Constantine,' he said.

'Evening, Mr O'Connor,' Holly replied. 'Hello, Chloe love. How was school today?'

'Good and bad.' She shot a sidelong glance at Ruaridh, as if seeking his corroboration that the day had had its ups and downs. 'I've got a couple of notes for you.'

She handed Holly a piece of paper and an envelope and Holly tried to clear a small space on the kitchen table. She sat down and opened the envelope.

'"Dear Mr and Mrs Constantine,"' Holly read out loud so Mark, who was included in the addressees, could hear what it was about.

'"It has come to our attention,"' she carried on reading, '"that CHLOE CONSTANTINE . . ."' her name had been inserted into what must have been a standard letter in bold capitals '". . . has been coming to school wearing a skirt which does not meet the school uniform criteria."'

Holly looked at Chloe. There was a tiny thin black strip, visible just below the end of her school jumper. It certainly didn't resemble a skirt.

'Did you wear that to school?' Holly asked. 'I've never even seen that skirt before. It looks like a boob tube you've stuck on your bum!'

'Everyone does,' Chloe replied. 'It's a long vest.'

She lifted her jumper and shirt to reveal that what was masquerading as a skirt was indeed just a long vest.

'Well, this letter says,' Holly speed-read the rest of the note, 'that you will now have to buy a regulation school skirt and wear that to school, which is a nuisance, Chloe, because I gave you money to buy a skirt you could wear to school only a few weeks ago.'

'We don't have to get one.' Chloe shrugged. 'Everyone gets sent that letter. They won't take any notice if I don't get a school skirt.'

'I think she looks nice,' Mark said, deciding to add his opinion.

'We're not allowed to wear skirts,' Ruaridh chipped in. 'Which is sex discrimination.'

'Would you want to wear a skirt to school, Ruaridh?' Holly said, looking up at him questioningly.

'I wouldn't want to wear one, personally,' he laughed. 'But there might be boys who do. So it's still sex discrimination. We could probably take the school to the European Court of Human Rights.'

'I wish you luck with that,' Holly told him.

'Ugh, what's this?' Chloe had picked up a tub of mouldy spread, which Mark had unearthed from the back of the fridge.

'Some sort of vegan pâté.' Holly glanced at the label. 'I bought it when that friend of yours who doesn't eat dairy came to stay.'

'Freya,' Chloe told her.

'Do you remember when you used to think virgins didn't eat dairy products?' Mark asked, landing a load more yoghurt pots on the table.

'Did I?' Chloe obviously didn't.

'You got virgins and vegans confused,' he explained, as she peeled the lid off one of the yoghurt pots and began licking it.

'Well, Chloe obviously eats dairy,' Ruaridh commented, and Holly looked up from the other letter she was reading and wondered what exactly Ruaridh meant by that.

She decided to ignore the comment and carried on reading the next letter from school.

'Botswana?' The letter was about a proposed school trip which would take place next summer, after Chloe had finished her GCSE's. It cost a fortune.

'I can't believe they are planning a school trip to Botswana!' Holly exclaimed, looking at Mark who was now putting things back in the fridge. 'That's a gap-year destination, not somewhere you go on a school trip. It costs fifteen hundred pounds! I can't imagine they'll have any takers.'

'I *really* want to go, Mum,' Chloe said. 'They showed us a film today of a trip from another year. It looked amazing.'

'I'm sure it did.' Holly hadn't imagined Chloe really thought she would be able to go. 'But we can't afford it, love. Can we, Mark?'

She looked to him to back her up but he appeared not to be listening.

'Do we still want these magnets?' He had closed the door of the fridge and was indicating the random magnetic words that had been on the door since Chloe and Jake were little. Holly had bought them to help them learn to read.

'It's much harder being a parent these days,' Holly remembered her mother saying, at the time. 'We never had to put magnets on fridges to get you to read!'

Or fork out for school trips to Botswana, Holly thought to herself now. The furthest she had ever been on a school trip was a day trip to the Isle of Wight.

'I don't care. Throw them away if you want,' Holly said to Mark. 'Did you hear *any* of what's just been said?'

'About Chloe's skirt?' He had obviously not been listening to the latter part of the conversation.

'No, about the school trip,' Ruaridh interjected.

'Are you wanting to go, Ruaridh?' Holly wondered if this was why Chloe was keen to go.

'No way would I be allowed,' he replied, and Holly realised this was true. If Ruaridh wanted to go on a school trip to Botswana, then the O'Connors might have to let all six of their children follow and she didn't imagine they could afford that.

'There's a meeting in the hall next week,' Chloe persisted. 'For parents to find out more about it. Why don't you go to that?'

'We could do that, I suppose.' Mark now appeared to be joining in this conversation. 'Couldn't we?'

'Maybe. Where's Jake?' Holly wanted Chloe and Ruaridh to leave them now to discuss the trip alone. Not that they could suddenly find an extra £1500 from anywhere.

'I think he's in his room.' Chloe took her cue. 'Shall we tell him you're home?'

'Yes, tell him to come down in a bit.' Holly smiled at Chloe, hoping she wouldn't be too disappointed to miss out on the trip.

'We could go to the meeting and see what we think.' Mark was reading the letter from school over Holly's shoulder.

'But have you seen the price?' She nodded towards the bottom of the page. 'Is there any point in going when we can't afford it anyway?'

'We could see,' he replied, and Holly wondered what he might have in mind.

'Anyway,' she continued, 'I'm not sure I can go. There's another meeting that evening that I said I might go to.'

'Oh, yes?' Mark walked around the table and opened the fridge again. She presumed, this time, it was in preparation for dinner.

'It's about the train crash,' Holly began, rooting in her bag, partly to try to find the leaflet about the meeting but also because she wanted to avoid eye contact with Mark.

She found the leaflet and put it folded on the table then went to get herself a glass of water while Mark read it. She hadn't realised that Daniel's card had fallen on to the table when she took it out.

'Who is Daniel Harrison?' Mark had picked it up and was reading the details.

'He's . . .' Holly paused, not quite sure what to say, feeling guilty for still not having told Mark about him yet. 'He's the man who stayed with me, when the train crashed.'

'Oh, I see,' Mark said, although he clearly didn't. 'When did you see him again?'

'He was on the train today,' she lied, knowing that if she told him she'd met Daniel her first day back, he'd want to know why she hadn't told him. Holly wasn't sure herself. There was nothing to hide from Mark, but for some reason she'd wanted to keep her meeting with Daniel to herself.

'And you spoke to him?' Mark said.

'We had a quick chat on the platform at Victoria.' Holly was now telling Mark what had happened when she'd first met Daniel again. 'And he gave me his card, but he was rushing to work.'

'Will he be at this meeting?' Mark asked now, picking up the leaflet.

'I don't know.' Holly felt uncomfortable being cross-questioned.

'Do you want to go?' Mark asked.

'I think so.' Holly turned on the tap. She could feel her husband looking at her, even though she had her back to him.

'I didn't think you were keen to . . .' Mark paused, as if searching for the right words '. . . go over things.'

'I just thought I might pop in and see what it was like,' Holly said, filling her glass and drinking from it.

'I could come with you.' Mark had moved over to where she was standing now and put his arm around her. She wanted to shrug him off but had no reason. He was only being thoughtful.

'No,' she said, a bit too abruptly. 'It's not worth your coming all the way up. I might change my mind and I probably won't stay long anyway. I don't want to be too late home.'

'Stay if you want to,' Mark said, taking his arm away. 'It might be helpful.'

Holly suspected he wanted her to go to the meeting for the

same reason he had wanted her to see the counsellor again. He thought she needed to talk about what had happened.

'Maybe you could go to the school meeting and report back?' Holly suggested, not wanting to talk about the survivors meeting any more in case Mark guessed that her real reason for going was because she wanted to see Daniel again and the meeting gave her an excuse.

When I got on the train today, she was sitting with him again – the man who was waiting for her at the ticket barrier. I wondered, briefly, if they were married but I don't think they are. They weren't sitting together the first time I saw her on the train, after the accident, although it's often hard to find two seats together. I rarely managed to find one next to Geoff on the occasions we both caught the same train.

But they don't look like a couple. He's much younger than her. And she's beautiful, I think, while he is quite ordinary in comparison – almost geeky looking. They don't look right together, yet they seem easy in each other's company, as if they know each other well.

They both looked up when I paused, wondering whether to sit in the vacant seat opposite. She smiled, as if she recognised me, so I sat down, wondering if she would acknowledge me further. But that was it, a brief smile when I sat down.

They'd been looking at a leaflet, which she then folded and put in her bag. There was another on my seat and I unfolded it and began reading, like a mirror opposite, about a meeting for survivors of the crash.

I wanted to ask if they were planning on going. It would have seemed perfectly normal to ask but by the time I'd plucked up the courage, a newspaper hid her and his face was obscured by a laptop screen – a barrier between us.

I wondered then what my mother would have thought about this meeting with its promise of information about where to get help with compensation claims and trauma. Nobody ever offered my mum help and she didn't seem to realise she needed it either. The sleepless nights, the flashbacks, and the inability to talk to my father about it . . . she thought that was all normal and would get better in time. It was only when she found herself standing in the bathroom with a bottle of paracetamol, intending to swallow them all, that she went to the doctor.

She said she thought then he might give her some sleeping pills or 'something to take the edge off it'. She never thought she'd be admitted to hospital; never envisaged that without her there my father would find himself unable to cope with his only daughter and send me to live with friends; never realised that her not being there made me start clinging desperately to anyone who was, as if sheer force of will would stop them disappearing too.

I thought if I loved Geoff enough he'd always be there for me, and then it all started to fall apart; first the announcement on the radio, then the waiting for further news, and finally the sickening realisation that he wasn't coming back.

I looked across the space between our seats again and wondered if the woman sitting opposite had seen Geoff on the train that day. I decided then that I'd go to the meeting. Perhaps I'd be able to introduce myself to her there, if she went too, or others who'd been on the train that day. Perhaps there'd be other meetings and a survivors group would give me the sense of purpose which I lacked without Geoff to look after.

'It could get difficult if you start talking to people who were on the train,' the voice of Helen, my former counsellor, suddenly said in my head. 'Do you see yourself as a survivor?' she added.

'Yes,' I told her, in defiance of anything she might say.

I do see myself as a survivor. That's just exactly what I'm doing right now – surviving. I'm not really living at the moment, just going through the motions, because losing Geoff is the worst thing that has ever happened to me; worse than seeing my mother in the psychiatric ward, and worse than being sent to live with Lisa, and even worse than losing the baby.

Chapter Twelve

DIMITRI AND REBECCA were hidden by the screen that surrounded her desk so Holly couldn't see them, but she heard Dimitri say, 'Stop, someone's coming.'

Then Rebecca stood up and peered over the edge of the screen. 'Oh, hi, Holly.' Did her greeting sound slightly guilty?

'Hello-o?' Holly elongated the word slightly, to sound questioning and imply that she knew something was going on.

'Morning, Hol!' Dimitri was grinning, as if he realised the game was up, whatever the game was. 'You look very glamorous this morning. Is that a new coat?'

'No.' Holly gave him a firm look to indicate that compliments were not going to put her off the scent of whatever it was she was on to.

She secretly admired Dimitri's persistent flirtatiousness. Twenty years ago she might have thought it slightly creepy – the way he never passed up an opportunity to compliment a woman if there was one in the vicinity. Now that she was older and not often on the receiving end of compliments, she liked the way he was with women.

'I've been wearing this coat every day for the past fortnight,' she said, looking at him squarely, taking in his dark good looks but feeling rather school-marmish as she did so. She imagined he came from the sort of family where you'd be letting the side down if you didn't try it on with women as a matter of course.

'How was your journey?' Rebecca asked innocently, then coloured slightly as if remembering that, with Holly, the question could be construed as loaded.

'It was fine.' She suspected Rebecca was only asking to deflect her attention from whatever it was the two of them had been doing.

'Close the page,' Rebecca hissed. It was supposed to be a whisper, audible only to Daniel, but it came out much louder.

There was something about the way Dimitri was looking at her, the resigned shrug of his shoulders, that seemed to invite Holly to ask more.

'What are you two up to?' She accepted the hint of an invitation.

'Christopher Perrin is coming in this afternoon.' Dimitri smiled, and moved his head slightly, indicating she should come round to their side of the desk.

'I know.' Holly had arranged for him to come in.

Christopher Perrin was an un-typical historian. In his mid-forties, he was good looking and energetic and, after making a series of television documentaries in which he bounded his way through the ruins of Ancient Mesopotamia, Damascus and Georgia, had become a household name.

The press were won over by his looks and energy, and their interest in him was further aroused when he married cookery writer and TV chef Rosa Martinez. She was Spanish and extremely beautiful. If you were cynical you might have thought it was her accent and cleavage that made her programmes popular, especially with men who had no intention of creating tapas in their own home.

Mark was one of those men.

'I think I might watch Rosa Martinez this evening,' he would say to Holly. 'She's doing Cantabrian cooking tonight.'

'Really?' Holly would reply. 'I wonder what she'll be wearing?'

'I won't notice.' And Mark would grin, knowing that Holly knew full well that he would.

She'd bought him Rosa's cookery book for his last birthday.

'You are a very good wife,' Mark had said, opening it and looking appreciatively at the photographs. 'Buying me porn for my birthday!'

The food was only foreground interest, the focus was always Rosa.

'I know,' Holly had laughed. 'I thought about getting you Nigel Slater but I guessed you might prefer this.'

'You guessed right!' Mark said. 'Shall I keep it by our bed?'

Holly had found the book a few weeks later by Jake's bed and presumed he shared Mark's admiration of Rosa's perfectly rounded breasts. She thought about taking it downstairs and then decided she would rather Jake thought about Rosa under his duvet than some shaven porn star he might have access to via the internet.

James Darling was also a fan of Ms Martinez.

'I met his wife once at a festival. She is a fascinating woman.' He had become all animation when, earlier in the week, Holly had suggested an interview with Christopher Perrin.

'Research notes for Darling,' Dimitri said now, touching her arm briefly as she joined them in front of the computer screen.

He and Rebecca had pulled up several images from the internet. They were of Rosa Martinez: bending revealingly over plates of steaming food, licking sauce off a spoon suggestively, and peering out seductively over mountains of vegetables.

Holly laughed.

'What are you going to do with them?' she asked, looking from Dimitri to Rebecca as they exchanged a look.

'Actually, don't tell me.' She decided to leave them to it. 'Is James in yet?'

'He was in earlier,' Rebecca confirmed. 'But he's gone out to record something at the British Museum with Natalie.'

'Oh, yes.' Holly vaguely remembered her friend saying something about being out in the morning.

She unlocked the door of her office and ignored Natalie's phone, which was ringing. She'd let it go to voicemail. This instructed people to call Holly if they needed to talk about the programme urgently.

This caller obviously did as, by the time she had taken her coat off and hung it up, her phone was ringing, too.

'Hello. Holly Holt speaking,' she said, pulling the phone across the desk so she could sit down.

'Hi, Holly, it's Guy,' Natalie's husband identified himself. 'I'm trying to get hold of Nat, do you know where she is?'

'I think she's out recording something.' Holly settled back in her chair. 'Can I help?'

'Only if you can pass yourself off as Al and Kirsty's mum.'

Guy MacDonald was a reluctant house husband. He'd started his working life as a freelance travel writer and photographer, and spent a lot of time filing copy from far-flung locations.

Natalie had met him on a press trip to the Greek Islands.

She told Holly that when she wrote her piece, she had raved about the crisp white sheets and nautical décor of her cabin, but in reality she had never actually slept there. Over the next few years she'd been increasingly absent from her own bed, using all her annual leave to join Guy wherever he was.

Now they were married, had two children, and Guy was a stay-at-home husband.

'Guy's work dried up during the credit crunch,' Natalie always said when explaining their arrangement. 'And I have a full-time job so it makes sense for him to look after the children rather than pay a nanny.'

Holly wondered whether Natalie would have stayed at home and looked after the twins if Guy's work hadn't dried up. She doubted it. Natalie loved her job and loathed domesticity.

Guy adored the children but Holly suspected he resented being with them all the time.

'Apparently she's at the British Museum with James,' Holly said to Guy now, switching her computer on as she spoke.

'She never mentioned it,' he said, sounding pissed off. 'Do you know when she'll be back?'

'Not sure.' Holly flicked through her emails as she spoke. 'She said something about it last night, but I wasn't listening properly.'

'Maybe she said something to me.' Guy sounded doubtful.

'Do you want me to give her a message?' Holly reached for a pen in readiness. 'Or you could try her on her mobile.'

'I already did,' Guy said. 'It was switched off.'

'They were probably recording. Is it important?' Holly didn't have anything terribly important to do herself but felt she ought to be getting on.

'Al's doing some sort of performance at school today,' Guy told her. 'He thinks Natalie promised she would come. I told him she was working but he seemed adamant. So I just thought I'd ask, in case she was planning to sneak off work and come and see it.'

'Well, if I speak to her before you do, I'll tell her you called.'

Holly thought it unlikely that Natalie would be able to get out of the office today but she sensed the frustration in Guy's voice, as if Natalie's not going would be an issue in the MacDonald household.

Natalie announced her arrival back at work by storming into their office, muttering about infantile behaviour.

'Have you seen what they've done?' she fumed. 'We've only got half an hour before Christopher Perrin arrives. What if James wants to chat to him in his office before we go to the studio?'

'Hang on a minute.' Holly wished Natalie were a bit less volatile sometimes. 'Who's done what?'

'Those bloody immature children!' She spat out the last word. 'Dimitri and Rebecca. Go and have a look at Darling's office for yourself.'

Holly shrugged and stood up. She was curious and didn't really want to be sharing the same air space as a fuming Natalie.

Whatever it was that had made her so cross had clearly had the opposite effect on James Darling.

Holly bumped into him as she made her way down the corridor to his office. He was roaring with laughter.

'Holly,' he cried, 'have you seen my office? It's fucking hilarious! Do you know who the decorators are?'

'Of what?' Holly thought she would decide whether to reveal her suspicions about the decorators once she had seen whatever it was they had done.

James turned round and she followed him to his office where he opened the door with a triumphant, 'Dah-dah!'

Rebecca and Dimitri had been hard at work. They had printed out all the pictures of Christopher Perrin's glamorous wife on sheets of A4 paper, and then plastered them around James Darling's office.

Rosa Martinez was everywhere: smiling coyly from the notice-board, running her tongue over her top lip from the screen of

Darling's computer, icing fairy cakes on his desk, and pouting and preening all over the walls.

It was childish but very funny, and James Darling clearly saw the joke. Holly laughed but also shared Natalie's misgivings about what Christopher Perrin might think.

'I'm going down to reception now to wait for Perrin,' James told her. He obviously felt he had the crisis under control. 'I'll go straight to the studio when he arrives. Will you tell Natalie to meet me there?'

'Sure,' Holly said, and went back to their office.

Natalie was still angry.

'It is quite funny,' Holly ventured.

'It's pathetic,' Natalie snapped. 'They're like a couple of schoolkids.'

'By the way,' Holly decided to change the subject, 'Guy called.'

'Bloody hell, that's all I need.' Natalie's response left Holly wondering if subject changing had been such a good idea after all.

She was about to tell her he'd called to remind her that Al was in some sort of performance at school when the door opened and James Darling stuck his head round.

'Nat,' he said, 'I need you.'

Natalie flounced out of the office after him.

'You're not the only one,' Holly said to their departing backs.

Chapter Thirteen

'CAN YOU SPARE any change?'

Three men were sitting drinking from beer cans on the corner of the road when Holly and Daniel emerged from the building in which the survivors group meeting had been held.

'Sorry, don't have any,' Holly mumbled out of habit.

'No worries, love.' One of them raised his beer can as if he was about to toast her meanness. 'Next time we see you, we'll have credit-card facilities.'

Holly laughed, stopped and took out her purse.

'Let's see,' she said to herself as she looked inside and discovered she had been telling the truth. She didn't have any change. A fiver was the smallest denomination she had but she felt she couldn't very well not give them anything now.

'Don't spend it all at once.' Holly handed the money to the man who'd made the credit-card remark.

'Thank you, gorgeous.' He looked surprised but grateful. 'Thank you.'

'We're going to have a loyalty card as well,' one of the others said.

Holly looked at him. He didn't look much older than Jake. She was glad now she'd given them the money. She didn't want to think about the reasons they might be there, but she knew they weren't likely to be good.

'So, next time you come, we'll stamp it for you,' the young boy said. 'Six stamps and you get . . .'

He paused and looked around, as if wondering what he could offer. His dog sat quietly next to him.

'To stroke the dog?' His tone was questioning, as if Holly needed to agree to his proposition.

'Thank you,' she said. She looked at him and smiled before walking on.

'There was something about the young one . . .' Holly looked at Daniel, wondering if he'd looked at the three men properly. 'He didn't seem much older than my son.'

'He was certainly young.' Daniel glanced back over his shoulder.

'I suppose I just felt a bit empty, after that meeting. It was all so official and businesslike.' Holly tried to explain why she'd been suddenly moved to give the man money.

'I know what you mean,' Daniel agreed. 'It felt like a planning application meeting or something, but I suppose most of the people there were only . . .'

Holly looked up at him, wondering if he was thinking the same as her.

'Like us?' she asked him. 'Not really hurt or anything.'

'I suppose the people who were really badly hurt are still recovering,' Daniel said, echoing what a man in a wheelchair had said to Holly at the meeting.

She had stood back to let him manoeuvre himself into a space and had taken in the fact he only had one leg; the other was missing from just below the knee.

'Shark attack,' the man said, in a loud cheery voice, as if he had known what she had been thinking.

'Really?' Holly presumed he was referring to his leg.

'No.' The man smiled. 'I got gangrene while I was backpacking in Indonesia, but I get bored of telling that story so I try to vary it a little. Sometimes I tell people I lost it in Vietnam, although I'm not quite old enough to have been there.'

Holly was not quite sure how to take this piece of information. It seemed in poor taste, especially given the nature of the meeting. 'I thought that maybe you'd lost it when . . .'

'In the train crash?' the American said. 'If I had, I'd still be in hospital recovering now. There's not likely to be anyone here today who was seriously hurt. Call me a sceptic but I'm pretty sure that's the only reason there's a Railtrack rep here today. He knows he won't have to face anyone who was really badly affected.'

Holly had laughed and relaxed a bit.

'Excuse me,' she heard a voice saying behind them now, as they walked up the road towards the station.

Holly turned round and saw the woman she now thought of as the make-up woman. She'd noticed her at the meeting too.

'Sorry to interrupt,' she said to them, 'but I think I saw you both at the meeting, didn't I?'

'Yes,' Daniel replied.

'Yes, you were there too, weren't you?' Holly tried to be a bit more forthcoming.

'I was. I'm Anne-Marie by the way,' she introduced herself. 'Are you heading to the station now?'

She walked with them to Victoria, telling them about herself as they went. Daniel and Holly were less forthcoming and she didn't ask what had brought them to the meeting.

'Do you want to try a Marmite chocolate bar?' A woman with long blond hair was handing out free samples in the middle of the station concourse.

'No, thanks,' Holly and Daniel both said in unison.

'Not a Marmite fan then?' he asked. 'I hate it.'

'I love it.' Holly smiled as she realised they fulfilled the Marmite you-either-love-it-or-hate-it USP. 'What about you, Anne-Marie?'

'What?' She didn't appear to have been listening.

'Marmite. Do you love it or hate it?'

'Oh, I don't mind really,' Anne-Marie replied.

'I'm just going to buy a paper.' Holly paused outside W H Smith. 'You go on and find a seat.'

'I'll wait.' There was still ten minutes before the train was due to leave and Daniel didn't seem anxious to be on board just yet.

'I think I'll go on,' Anne Marie said. 'It was nice to meet you both properly.'

'You too,' said Holly.

Daniel appeared to be examining the latest P. D. James on a bookstand, and said nothing.

'Well,' Anne-Marie hovered as if she expected them to be a little more forthcoming, 'I'll give you my card, shall I? It has my numbers on?'

'Thank you,' Daniel said, taking one of his own from his pocket and trading it.

They both looked at Holly.

'I don't have a card,' she said. 'I'll give you my number though. I'll write it on the back of Daniel's.'

She took out a pen and scrawled her direct line in the office. She didn't want to give her mobile number.

The train crash had skewed the natural order of things. Under normal circumstances commuters didn't speak to each other. Holly couldn't remember ever having seen Anne-Marie before the crash. But now she knew something about her, it was impossible not to talk to her if Anne-Marie wanted her to.

'You'd better be quick,' Daniel said, as she stood watching Anne-Marie take out her ticket and pass it though the machine.

'Oh . . . yes.' Holly wondered what he would say if she told him she didn't really want a paper but had simply not wanted to sit with Anne-Marie. Would he think her heartless and unsympathetic, after what they'd just been told?

Mark would have understood her reasons. They had more to do with safeguarding her own privacy on the train than being completely unsympathetic.

'I like our friends and everything,' he often said. 'But do they have to come to dinner?' Or, 'If we clear out the spare room, there is a very real danger than someone might come and stay!'

Mark was sociable, but he liked his own space too.

'Actually, Holly,' Daniel was shuffling his feet slightly, 'do you have to go home right now? Are you expected back?'

'Sort of.' She wondered what the alternative was. 'I mean, I told Mark I was going to this meeting and would be late. I wasn't sure what time it would end.'

'Do you want a quick drink somewhere first?' Daniel was looking at the floor as he said this, as if he wasn't quite sure if the suggestion was appropriate and couldn't quite meet her eye as he asked. 'It's just . . . I feel as if . . .'

'Yes,' Holly cut in. 'I could get the train an hour later.'

She found a quiet table in the corner of the pub while Daniel went to the bar and bought himself a pint and glass of wine for her. She texted Mark while she waited.

Meeting still going on. Can't leave easily. Will call when on train.

She told herself she would tell him later she had stopped for a drink with Daniel.

'White wine.' He put a glass down in front of her.

'That's an enormous glass.' Holly was going to have to gulp it down. 'Are you sure it's not a vase?'

'Oh, that's what the flowers were doing in it!' Daniel smiled and took a sip from his own glass. 'I needed a large drink and I reckoned you probably did too. The flowers were past their best anyway.'

'Thank you.' Holly picked it up. 'So, what did you think?'

'I was a bit anxious when we got there and the chairs were all laid out in a circle.' Daniel said exactly what Holly had decided when they'd walked into the room where the meeting was to be held. 'I thought it might be like an AA meeting and we'd all have to stand up and introduce ourselves and explain what we were doing there.'

She nodded. 'I think I'd have left if that had been the case. Although do you think Anne-Marie might have wanted that?'

'Maybe.' Daniel considered this. 'The way she spoke to us . . . It was almost as if she had come to the meeting to tell someone what happened.'

'Yes,' Holly agreed. 'I've seen her on the train before a few times and she almost invited conversation then, not quite but almost. She smiled as if she wanted to talk but knew that she couldn't.'

'What made you decide to come?' Holly had asked Anne-Marie as they walked to the station from the meeting.

'I lost my husband in the crash,' she had said quietly.

'Oh. I'm sorry . . .' Holly was at a loss for what to say next. 'What was his name?'

She wondered if she would remember it from the reports that followed the accident. Five people had been killed. Holly hadn't known any of them or even recognised the pictures they'd printed in the papers.

Anne-Marie appeared lost in thought and didn't answer immediately.

'We'd been married for a while,' she said finally. 'We wanted to start a family.'

'She seems to be coping remarkably well,' Holly said to Daniel now. 'I can't imagine that I'd be able to carry on so calmly if something like that had happened to Mark.'

'No.' Daniel took another sip of his pint, as if to fortify himself before his next question. 'Can I ask you something, Holly?'

She hated that question. It always preceded something difficult or embarrassing and, when someone asked it, she was always torn between saying 'Do you have to?' and curiosity about what it might be they wanted to ask.

Curiosity usually won out.

'What is it?' she asked Daniel.

'Well, it's not really any of my business.' He looked down as he said this. 'I don't know you well enough to ask, but does your husband . . . Does Mark . . . ? How have you been getting on since it happened?'

Holly didn't want to be disloyal to Mark. She knew she should say he'd been really supportive, was trying to look after her and had done everything he could to make things easier for her. And she should keep quiet about the fact that his solicitousness annoyed her and she didn't want to talk to him about the crash.

'It's just that,' Daniel spoke into her silence, 'things seem to have been a bit difficult between Daisy and me.'

'Same,' Holly conceded. 'With Mark, I mean. He's really looked after me and everything, but it's as if . . .'

She paused.

'The fact that Mark wasn't there seems to have created a barrier between us. Does that make sense?'

'Yes, Holly,' Daniel said, looking at her directly for the first time that evening. 'I know exactly what you mean.'

Chapter Fourteen

IT TOOK HOLLY a moment to realise the man walking up their road just ahead of her was Mark.

If he hadn't been wearing his hat, she might have walked past him. He was walking slowly, which was out of character.

Holly remembered when they had been to view their house after it came on the market. Mark had spotted the FOR SALE sign one day when he came back from work, even though Holly didn't like the area. But they'd been talking about moving somewhere bigger.

Mark had walked up the street, slowly taking in all the houses, not just the one they were going to see.

'It's the sort of street we could live in for ever,' he'd said to her then. 'I'm just taking it all in.'

The house had been owned by a vicar, whose wife had died and children had left home.

'I shall be moving somewhere smaller,' he had told them.

The viewing had been a bit like an interview and Holly had the feeling that the man wanted it to go to people he approved of.

'Will you be mother?' he had asked her after setting a tea tray down on a table in the sitting room and inviting them to sit.

She had obediently poured the tea and settled back to drink hers while Mark had charmed the vicar by being himself.

'Oh, that's you, isn't it?' he had pointed out, examining a black-and-white photo of a cricket team which hung on the wall. 'Who did you play for? I used to play for Twineham and Wineham, but then the family came along.'

And later, on, spotting a book about a yacht voyage that nearly ended in tragedy, 'Do you sail as well? I don't but I read that book. I loved it.'

The vicar, if he hadn't been delicately picking up crumbs from a floral china plate, would have been eating out of Mark's hand.

They offered a little under the asking price and their offer was accepted immediately.

'He wanted it to go to a nice family,' the estate agent had told them. 'And he said he liked you.'

'Obviously the well-read, cricket-playing family man with a wife who would be mother, went down well then,' Holly had said to Mark as they opened a bottle of wine that evening and allowed themselves a tiny celebration.

'I reckon he's a bit of a dark horse,' Mark had said. 'Cheers, Mother!'

'Why do you say that?' Holly had asked, thinking he had seemed a typical vicar to her, right down to the horn-rimmed spectacles and his fastidiousness with the tea.

'I don't know. There was just something about him . . .' Mark had said, and been proved right when they moved into the house and found a stash of exceedingly hard-core pornography and some women's underwear tucked at the back of a shelf in one of the cupboards.

'I wonder how the pervy vicar is doing?' Mark used to wonder out loud, a lot, until Holly asked him to stop.

'It makes me feel as if he is still here, watching us,' she told him once when they'd just gone to bed and sex was obviously on the agenda. 'You're putting me right off what we're about to do.'

'We don't want that,' Mark had said, kissing her and dropping the pervy vicar from his repertoire of anecdotes.

'Mark?' Holly called out now, not quite sure if she wanted him to stop and allow her to catch up with him or whether she wanted the last couple of minutes of her journey home to herself.

'Hello.' He turned and waved. 'How was it?'

'What?' Holly asked, thinking back to her drink with Daniel and wondering how Mark could possibly know about it.

'Your meeting,' he said,

'Oh, well, it was rather boring actually.' Holly looked past him, not wanting to meet his concerned expression. 'Where have you been?'

At this time of night it wasn't unusual for him to walk up the hill to the off-licence, but there were no giveaway bottles of wine about his person.

'I went to the presentation at Chloe's school,' he reminded her, as they approached their house. 'About the trip to Botswana.'

'Oh, yes,' Holly said, unlocking the door.

She wished he hadn't been to that meeting. It would only raise Chloe's hopes about going on the trip and, as they could not afford it, it seemed pointless to do so.

'Hello!' Holly called once she was inside.

There was no answer but she could see Jake and Ed, sitting at her desk looking at her laptop.

'Hello,' she said again.

'Oh, hi.' Jake did not look round.

'Hello.' Ed was a little more forthcoming. 'We're doing a homework project together.'

'I said I'd run him home after dinner,' Mark said. 'Chloe's made something.'

'Good.' Holly was hungry and knew if Chloe was cooking something it was likely to be pasta and ready soon. 'What's the project?'

'What?' Jake appeared to have heard but not understood her question.

'The homework.' She gestured towards the computer screen. 'What are you working on?'

'Oh, something for PHSE,' Ed answered for him. 'We probably don't need to do it. Mr Stone is never actually in. He just gets supply teachers to give out homework sheets on his behalf.'

'He must be in sometimes,' Holly said.

'Hardly ever.' Jake appeared to be less engrossed in the home-work than he had been when she came in, and swivelled round in his chair to face her.

'There's a sign in his room that's printed and laminated. It says, "Mr Stone is unwell and will not be in today." He obviously doesn't expect to be in much, if he has a special sign.'

Holly smiled to herself. Jake was becoming more like his father as he got older. She could see him retelling this anecdote about the teacher with the laminated absent sign, refining it as he told it again and again, adding or subtracting details depending on the response they got. She wondered if she would ever start to find him annoying.

'Oh, by the way,' he said. 'V called. I said you'd call her later.'

'Hi, Mum.' Chloe came out of the kitchen, wearing as apron which was covered in flour. 'Where's Dad?'

'He was right behind me.' Holly wondered what she was cooking. 'He must have gone upstairs.'

'Did he say anything about the trip?' Chloe asked as Mark appeared at the top of the landing and began coming down.

'It certainly looks fantastic.' Mark smiled at his daughter.

'But we can't afford it,' Holly cut in, hating herself for being the killjoy but irritated with Mark for not being firm.

'We'll talk about it after supper.' He addressed this remark to Holly. 'Is it nearly ready?'

'Just waiting for the rolls to cook,' Chloe said, and then to Holly, 'I've made an Irish stew and soda bread rolls. It's a recipe from *Masterchef*.'

'Wow!' Holly was impressed.

'It'll only be about five minutes.' Chloe seemed to have guessed that she was hungry.

'Great.' Holly smiled.

'Do you want to sit down and I'll get you a drink?' Mark asked her.

They were still hovering in the doorway to the sitting room. The boys had shut the laptop and were trying to get past.

'Going to my room,' muttered Jake.

'OK,' Holly said, wondering if Mark would guess that she'd already had one. She didn't want to drink too much on an empty stomach.

'And then you can tell me a bit about the meeting,' he said as Holly sat down and he left the room.

Holly was just finishing stacking the dishwasher when Mark got back from taking Ed home.

'Will you talk to Dad about the trip when he gets back?' Chloe had asked after he'd left.

'I will, Chloe,' Holly said. 'But to be honest, darling, even if he says it's the most fantastic trip in the world and thinks you should go on it, I really don't know where we are going to find that sort of money. I'm sorry, but that's the way it is.'

''S'all right,' Chloe mumbled and left the room.

Holly wasn't sure if she was angry or just disappointed.

Jake had stayed and helped her clear the table in companionable silence. She was thankful for both the help and the silence.

'Chloe's gone up to her room,' she told Mark when he came back. 'I think she's leaving us to talk about the school trip, although I've told her we can't afford it.'

'I've been thinking about that.' Mark, who had not drunk with dinner as he was driving Ed home, now poured himself a glass of wine. 'Want another?'

Holly shook her head and put the kettle on.

'How was your meeting?' Mark asked, conversationally, as if he'd just remembered and was asking her out of politeness.

'It was a bit weird, really,' Holly sighed. She didn't want to talk to him about it. 'Quite low-key. There wasn't anyone there who'd been seriously injured.'

'That's good,' he said.

'Why?'

'It might have been difficult.' He paused. 'For you, I mean. Were there any relatives there?'

'I don't think so.' Holly didn't want to tell him about Anne-Marie. She thought he might worry about the effect the encounter could have on her.

And she didn't want to tell him about her drink with Daniel. Not just yet anyway.

'So what were you thinking about the trip?' Holly asked, as she poured boiling water into a cup.

'I've been thinking about giving my office up,' he said.

'What?' Holly turned abruptly, and splashed herself with boiling water. 'But then you will have nowhere to work,' she said, running her hand under the cold tap.

'I could work from home.' He was fiddling with something on the side, refusing to make eye contact with her. 'The lease on the office runs out in August and I don't really need the space any more. If I wasn't paying rent every month, we could use some of that money to pay for this trip, if that's what Chloe wants to do.'

'But if you don't have an office to work from, you won't be making any money,' Holly protested.

Mark rented a small office in a block near the seafront. A few years ago he'd downsized from a large office in the same block when work started to dry up and he began shedding staff.

Holly thought giving up the office was tantamount to giving up even trying to get more work.

'I could work from home,' he said again.

'How long have you been thinking about this?' Holly thought he sounded defeatist.

'A little while.' Mark was vague. 'I know it's not ideal, but if work picked up I could rent another place. In the meantime we'd have a bit more money from what I would save.'

'I don't know,' Holly said, feeling irrationally angry towards him. He seemed to her to be throwing in the towel, relinquishing all responsibility for earning to her.

She wasn't sure if she could take it.

'"... I Nearly Died" is on, Dad.' Jake wandered into the kitchen, oblivious to the tension in the air. 'You know, that programme I was telling you about? Are you going to watch it?'

'I'll be in in a minute,' Mark said, as Jake ambled out again. 'It's a new programme with that Scottish comic we like. You know?'

Holly thought he was asking her permission to go and join Jake and felt too drained after her day to carry on the discussion they'd begun about his office.

'You'd best go and watch it then.' She sounded, to herself, as if she was talking to a naughty child.

Mark could obviously detect the displeasure in her voice.

'Why don't you come and watch it too?' he entreated.

'In a minute. I'll just finish making my tea.'

Today was the first time I've actually said it out loud to someone I didn't know: someone who hadn't already guessed, when Geoff didn't come home, what had happened.

It felt something of a relief, as if saying it gives me licence to ask what it was like to have been on the train when it was hit, and if I know, maybe it will help me understand.

I need to tread carefully, I know that, but I think Holly might be able to talk to me about it.

I know her name now because I did go to the survivors group meeting.

It felt strange and businesslike. Someone talked about compensation claims and what was being done to improve safety. There were a few questions, but the atmosphere felt like an ordinary work meeting. They could have been talking about pitching for a new contract. No one behaved as if they were discussing a momentous event, which changed people's lives.

The only reference made to the fact that it might have was when one of the speakers said that there was information about counselling and dealing with post-traumatic stress on the website, and leaflets at the back of the hall.

No one ever offered my mother or me counselling until it was too late. No one ever seemed to think that we might be affected in any way by what we'd been involved in.

Mum told me she felt responsible because she'd suggested to the security guard that he might open the doors. She told me that she could see his anxious young face, looking up at her, wondering what the right thing to do was, and later she couldn't bear to think that her face might have been the last one he ever looked at properly.

I keep hearing her saying that to me now and wondering whose faces all the people killed in the tunnel had seen before it went dark; whose expressions of boredom or insouciance would be the last things they ever noted.

I'd expected someone in the meeting to get angry or emotional but it was all very restrained. Perhaps everyone feels as I do; that they need to stay in control or they might go completely to pieces.

I screamed at the radio the other day — really screamed, like a madwoman, and afterwards I felt ashamed and hoped the neighbours weren't in and hadn't heard me through the walls.

I was working from home and I had it on as background noise. I wasn't really listening but I knew they were talking about cooking. One of the women was talking about less used vegetables; things like beetroot and artichokes and radishes. She was saying, 'It's very important to use these vegetables so that they don't get forgotten.'

She stressed the words very important and there was something in her tone of voice that really got to me. She sounded as if she meant it, that it really was very important, and if we didn't realise that we were somehow stupid.

And that's when I started shouting, 'It's not important. It's not important at all! You need to know that. You need to realise what's important before it's too late . . . before you lose it!'

Then I picked up the cup of coffee I was drinking and hurled it at the radio, but it missed and hit a photograph of Geoff and me on our wedding day, and the glass shattered, and that's when I knew I had two choices.

I could have slumped down on the floor with the broken pieces of glass and looked at the pictures and let it all out, but I didn't.

I took a deep breath and went and got the dustpan and brush from the kitchen, and I swept it all up and put it in the bin, even the photograph.

I thought perhaps if Geoff weren't sitting there on the bookcase looking at me, it would be easier.

Then I concentrated very hard on finishing the report I was writing.

I told Helen my imaginary counsellor about that and she said, 'It's OK to cry. You need an outlet for your emotions.'

But I'm not like that. I can't let it all out. I need to keep going.

I sense that Holly is like me in that respect.

She never said anything at the meeting, nor did Daniel, the man I've seen her with. They both looked as if they weren't sure if they should really be there, which was exactly how I felt.

I caught up with them walking to the station afterwards.

That's when I said it.

Holly asked, 'What made you decide to come to the meeting?'

And I took a deep breath and told her.

'I lost my husband that day,' I said. And even though they must have expected someone to say something like that at the meeting, they both looked shocked.

They didn't seem to know what to say or how to respond.

'What was his name?' Holly asked, after a while.

I thought that was a strange question to ask. She said it as if I'd been talking about a new baby or something, but I didn't mind. People don't know what to say, not at first. Nobody knew what to say to me after I lost the baby. They couldn't even ask its name, and when Mum was in hospital people just seemed to pretend that nothing was happening, that it was perfectly normal for her to be away and me to be living with Lisa and her family.

'Which hospital?' some people would occasionally ask, but then, when they realised it was the psychiatric one, they'd look awkward and say something about how it must be nice for me to be staying with Lisa and her family.

I never told them that Lisa didn't want me there; that my presence in her home had ruined our friendship, turned it from an easy teenage alliance into something altogether more claustrophobic.

I know from experience that people need time to absorb shocking information and work out their response to it.

I realised Holly needed time before she could really talk to me. That's why I went on ahead once we got to the station.

She stopped at the newsagent's to buy a paper but I said I wanted to find a seat. I don't know if she and Daniel made that train. I didn't see them later but we exchanged numbers. So now I know their names and I'm sure we'll meet up and get to talk properly.

I talked to Holly in my head on the way home.

'Geoff was in the fourth carriage,' I told her in my imagined conversation, although I didn't know this for sure. 'Where were you sitting, Holly?'

Chapter Fifteen

'I USED TO want to be an architect,' Fay told Holly, pausing to look at one of the photographs on the walls of the RIBA restaurant.

The Royal Institute of British Architects was just up the road from Broadcasting House and Holly thought the restaurant would be a good place to take her elder sister.

'Did you? I never knew that.' Fay was always guaranteed to tell Holly something she didn't know. They were only two and half years apart in age but her sister was always coming up with things which Holly either never knew or had forgotten. If Holly questioned them, Fay pulled rank and told her she must have been too young to remember.

'It was when I was going through my Lego phase,' Fay said, as she looked around, taking in the patterned marble and wood floors and vast floor-to-ceiling windows. 'I wish I had been now. Hanging out here beats the inside of a police station!'

'How old were you then?' Holly asked, wondering if it was warm enough to sit on the roof terrace.

'Six or seven, I suppose. We had a huge box that some friend of Dad's gave me. I was always making towering edifices.'

'I can see the attraction.' Holly decided against going outside but found a table by the window. 'I don't remember playing with Lego as a child but I used to love helping Jake make fire stations and airports. He used to want a job at Legoland, but now he wants to work with computers. What changed your mind?'

Fay was a forensic psychologist for Reading police.

'I'm not sure,' she answered, looking at the glass-etched doors of the restaurant. 'Though I do remember Dad saying it was a man's job. Perhaps I could have been the next Richard Rogers.'

'I don't suppose Dad thinks working with rapists and murderers is women's work either,' Holly commented.

This was how their parents described Fay's job.

While Patrick and Susan weren't very good at disguising the fact that they were not entirely happy that Fay was a lesbian, neither could they seem to help wondering if they were somehow to blame.

'Patrick thinks it's his fault because we didn't have a boy, so he taught her to play cricket and climb trees,' their mother had once said.

'Do you think the fact Fay works with so many rapists has put her off men?' was another often-asked question.

'Fay says she always knew she was gay,' Holly had told them both on many occasions, wishing they could try harder to accept her sister for what she was.

'You used to want to be a cheese-maker when you grew up,' Fay said to her now.

'Did I? How very Pythonesque.' Again, Holly had no recollection of this and wondered if it was true or a story Fay had made up to amuse her friends. 'Is that because I wanted to be blessed?'

'No, it was because you liked cheese,' Fay told her. 'Mum only ever bought Cheddar but some friends, I think it might have been

Hugh and Jean, always brought lots of "exotic" cheese when they came to stay. I thought they were disgusting but you loved them and were fascinated that they all began as milk.'

'Really?' Holly picked up the menu and looked at it.

'Anyway,' Fay added, 'you were blessed. You always led a charmed life.'

This was a frequent refrain of hers and Holly had learned to let it pass without comment. Whether it was because their parents found it hard to accept Fay's sexuality and career choice, or because of something else, she had decided that she was the second-best sibling in their eyes.

'Fay definitely thinks that I am their favourite,' Holly told Mark once when they were discussing her parents' attitude to their daughters. 'But I don't think that's true. She was always the clever one, the achiever. I think they are really proud of her, they just don't know how to show it.'

'She says it was because you were in intensive care when you were born,' Mark had replied.

Holly was two months premature and spent the first weeks of her life in a specialist baby unit.

'Fay says she was always expected to achieve things when she was little, but you just had to stay alive and your mum and dad were delighted,' he explained. 'I guess there may be some truth in that.'

Holly considered this. She didn't think her parents favoured either of them, but if Fay thought that they did she had to be sympathetic to her feelings.

'Shall we order?' she asked her sister now.

'So what brings you to London?' Holly asked, as they waited for their food.

'I had a meeting with someone at the Met about a case,' Fay

told her. 'I dealt with something similar a few years back. I can't really go into details, though.'

'You *can* tell me about the case you've already worked on.' Holly was used to her sister being secretive about her work, but she knew it wasn't always necessary.

'It wasn't very nice.' Fay leaned back, waiting while a waitress brought them cutlery and their drinks.

'It was a man who killed one of his children. He smothered him with a pillow while the child slept. But he wasn't really fit to stand trial.'

Holly pictured her own children sleeping. This was when she loved them most. They always looked so beautiful and peaceful that, even though they now closed their bedroom doors firmly at night, she couldn't resist pushing them open and watching them while they slept.

Chloe still slept with her hands up beside her head, as she had done when she was a baby, but Jake invariably had his hands down the front of his pyjamas. She knew he wouldn't forgive her if he knew she looked at him, but he was still only thirteen, still her boy.

'Why did he do it?' Holly asked Fay.

'It was very sad,' she answered. 'They had two boys and he had taken them to a festival. There was a crush near one of the main stages and the younger boy was trampled to death.'

'Oh, yes, I remember that.' Holly had heard the story in the news. 'But I don't think I heard anything else about the boy's father.'

'He was devastated obviously,' Fay told her. 'And he felt guilty because he'd been with them when it happened. He got this idea that it wasn't fair the younger one had died.'

'Is that why he killed the other?' Holly was horrified.

'Yes, but he really didn't know what he was doing,' Fay told her. 'The CPS wanted to bring a murder charge but he wasn't fit to stand trial.'

'Poor man,' Holly mused. 'And his poor wife. Are they still together?'

'I don't know,' Fay said. 'I shouldn't think so. People often split up when one of them has been through a major ordeal anyway. They often don't seem to understand each other any more.'

'One venison steak and one fillet of sea bass.' The waitress was back.

'The fish is for me,' Fay told her.

'Thank you,' Holly said, glad of the food and the chance to change the topic of conversation.

'Have you seen Mum and Dad recently?' she asked.

'We went over there last weekend actually,' Fay replied. 'It was a bit odd, though.'

'How so?' Holly began cutting her steak.

'Well, we thought we were going because it had been Lucy's birthday in the week. Mum asked us for lunch and we thought she wanted to see Lucy and give her her present but when we got there she never mentioned it,' Fay told her.

'Shit!' Holly paused, her fork halfway to her mouth. 'I forgot too. I'm really sorry.'

'You've got good reason. I told Lucy that. She doesn't mind.'

'No, I don't,' Holly protested. 'I'm her aunt. I shouldn't have forgotten. I was going to get her something from that shop in the North Laine that we went to when you last came down, but I forgot all about it. I don't have a good reason at all.'

'You've been in a train crash,' Fay said in a tone which Holly couldn't help thinking was patronising.

'And lived to tell the tale,' she replied dismissively. 'Tell her

I'm really sorry. I'll make sure I get something in the post to her this weekend.'

'You don't have to,' Fay said again.

'I do and I want to,' Holly said firmly. 'Anyway, what else was odd about lunch with Mum and Dad?'

'Well, Dad wasn't there for starters,' Fay said, flaking fish off the bone with her fish fork.

'For starters, Dad wasn't there at all?' Holly quibbled. 'Or Dad wasn't there for starters?'

'What are you on about?' Fay adopted her big sister tone. It infuriated Holly still, even though they were both grown women.

'I mean, was the first thing that was odd the fact that Dad was not there? Or was Dad absent when you ate your starter but did he turn up for the main meal?' Holly spelled it out.

'He wasn't there at all,' Fay answered. 'And we didn't have a starter. We had roast chicken, and vegetables for V.'

V was a vegetarian but their parents never acknowledged this and served her only whatever vegetables they were having anyway.

She generally had to stomach potatoes cooked with meat if she wasn't to go hungry.

'What no "nut cutlet"?' Holly used the expression her mother used to describe any vegetarian food. 'Where was Dad then?'

'He'd gone to help Jean Hayward sort though Hugh's old clothes,' Fay told her. 'Mum said Jean couldn't face it on her own.'

'I suppose her daughter can't come back from France to help.' Holly couldn't imagine their father sorting through old clothes with anyone, let alone the widow of an old friend. 'It's a long way for Dad to drive on his own, though, and I'm surprised Mum didn't go to help.'

'That's the other thing,' Fay said. 'Mum seems totally

preoccupied with learning to use her laptop. She spent most of the time we were there asking Lucy to show her how to set up a Facebook account.'

'Really?' Holly wouldn't have been surprised if Susan had decided to take the computer back. 'She did say something about keeping in touch with old friends. I don't suppose many of them are on Facebook though.'

'There were a few,' Fay told her. 'And she kept going on about making new ones too.'

'Oh, yes, she mentioned that to me. Perhaps she's having some sort of mid-life crisis.'

'Only if she's going to live to one hundred and forty,' Fay retorted.

'OK, well, a seven-eighths life crisis or something!' Holly joked. 'Three-quarter life crisis probably. Mum shows no signs of flagging.'

'No, but Dad seems older.' Fay looked concerned.

'He is older,' Holly pointed out. Patrick was five years older than Susan, although he seemed to have very little energy these days and his hearing was going, making him sometimes appear much older.

'I know.' Fay nodded. 'But he suddenly seems older and more frail somehow, and their friends seem to keep dying. I wonder if Mum has started worrying about him going and being left on her own. Perhaps he's ill and she's not telling us.'

'Maybe,' Holly said, feeling suddenly tired.

She'd been looking forward to seeing her sister but the meeting was bringing her down somehow. She kept thinking about the man who'd killed his child and was cross with herself for forgetting her niece's birthday. Now Fay had suggested something else for her to worry about.

'Mum has always been more sociable,' she said. 'Maybe she

just wants to get out a bit more while Dad sits at home doing the crossword.'

'Maybe.' Fay did not sound convinced.

'Look, it *is* Lord Rogers.' Holly nodded to a corner of the restaurant. She felt cheered by a bit of celebrity spotting. 'Isn't it?'

Chapter Sixteen

'L ET'S ALL GO for a walk on the beach and have lunch some-where,' Mark suggested at breakfast on Sunday.

Holly wondered if this was his attempt at foreplay. They hadn't had sex for a while, certainly not since the train crash. It hadn't become an issue yet, but Holly suspected it would soon.

Mark usually slept in a t-shirt and boxers but the previous evening, he'd taken all his clothes off before coming to bed and immediately slid his hand under her t-shirt. Holly had feigned sleep and Mark had got up again and gone to the bathroom. She suspected he'd sorted himself out while he was there.

'It would be nice to spend some time together,' he said now, pushing the button down on the toaster. 'We've hardly seen you this week.'

It *was* a nice idea. Working late and a couple of train delays meant Holly had been home late on several occasions in the last week. She had thought that on Saturday she might see a bit of the children, but Chloe had gone out with Ruaridh and Jake seemed to spend the entire day hunched over the computer.

'Do we have to come?' Chloe protested. She looked sidelong at Jake who was staring at the back of a cereal packet. He failed to notice his sister's none-too-subtle stare.

'It'll be nice.' Holly tried to make it sound more inviting. 'We could look at some of the stalls by the West Pier and have lunch outside. It's warm enough.'

'I was going to go into town with Megan today.' Chloe sat next to her brother and nudged him in irritation as she did so.

'I've hardly seen you all week,' Holly said, wondering if Chloe was pissed off that the Botswana trip had not been mentioned again. 'You could arrange to meet Megan afterwards.'

'Yeah.' Jake gave the impression of someone about to join in the discussion but then went back to the back of the cereal packet.

'Yeah, what?' Chloe challenged him.

'What?' Jake had only recently taken on this adolescent torpor in the mornings. It was funny to watch. He really seemed to have no idea what was going on around him.

'What are you saying yeah to?' Chloe took the cereal packet from under his nose and poured some into her bowl.

'Going for a walk with Mum.' Jake lowered his gaze from where the box had been to his cereal bowl. 'It'll be nice.'

'That's settled then.' Mark rubbed his hands together, as if he had just concluded a major business deal. It was something he did a lot around the home and, again, something Holly found increasingly irritating. It was as if there was an indirect correlation between the number of triumphs he was not having at work and the number of things he considered to be achievements elsewhere.

'That's done then!' he'd say, slapping his palms as if he'd just secured a new client, rather than changed a light bulb. Or 'Job well done!' when he'd hung the washing out. The fact that he'd hung it folded in half, so it would not dry, and Holly had had to take it down and hang it properly, seemed to escape him.

There'd been an item on the radio that morning, which she and Mark had listened to as they lay in bed, making the most of not having to get up. It was about men doing nothing around the house, not even the traditional DIY.

'That's true,' Holly had commented.

'I do things around the house.' Mark had immediately jumped to his own defence. 'I cleaned the filter on the washing machine last week.'

'OK.' Holly conceded this. 'But when was the last time you dusted the sitting room?'

'It doesn't need dusting, does it?' Mark had asked, in a show of innocence.

'Somebody needs to rebrand household chores,' Holly said, trying hard not to rise to his bait. 'If they called dusting "minute particle extraction" and there was a tool with a motor to do it with, men would be quite happy to blitz the house.'

'And I changed the light bulb in the bathroom last night.' Mark obviously still thought he did his fair share.

'Well, if I listed every single thing I had done in the house this week, we'd still be in bed at lunchtime,' Holly said, under her breath but loud enough for Mark to hear, as she pushed the duvet off and got up.

The conversation had obviously irked him and after breakfast he decided to wash the kitchen floor.

It was self-defeating.

'Has someone been painting in here?' he asked the rest of the family, as he tried to get a white mark off the tiles.

'That's from when we had the room painted after we moved in,' Holly told him.

'I've not noticed it before.'

'Really?' This didn't surprise her. They'd only lived in the house for five years.

'Slow down a bit,' Holly said to Mark, who was powering down the seafront. 'Chloe's not with us. She's probably dawdling by one of the stalls.'

Holly had just spotted Daniel, walking ahead of them, accompanied by a woman with a white-blond bob. She hadn't anticipated Mark meeting Daniel like this and didn't want him to. She wasn't ready for it. But Mark seemed keen to work up an appetite, or perhaps he was just walking too fast to discourage further discussion about his plans to give up his office. Holly had broached the subject tentatively in the morning but he had ignored her.

'No, she's up ahead.' Mark pointed. Chloe was wearing a dress that was noticeable for its bright turquoise colour and incredible shortness.

'Is that actually a dress?' Holly had asked her as they got ready to leave.

'It's a t-shirt but it's long enough to be a dress,' Chloe replied, as Holly registered that it barely covered her knickers.

It made her easy to spot and Holly could now see her, drawing level with Daniel.

'Chloe!' Mark shouted, so loud that several people stopped to look round, as if forgetting that they were not actually called that.

Holly still looked about her when anyone shouted 'Mum', even if she knew Chloe and Daniel were both at school. It was a reflex you never seemed to grow out of.

When Jake was younger, he'd realised that calling 'Mum' in a park, shopping centre or other crowded place was not particularly selective, and if he lost sight of her he used to shout 'Holly Holt!' so that she alone would react. He wouldn't call out to her in public now. That would be far too embarrassing.

Daniel was amongst those who'd reacted to Mark's shout. He turned, immediately catching sight of Holly, and looked unsure what to do as her family advanced towards him.

'Hello!' Holly feigned surprise, even though she had known he was there.

'Wait for us or we'll lose you,' Mark was saying to Chloe. Then he realised that Holly was talking to someone else.

'Hi.' Daniel took in the four of them.

Time for introductions.

'Mark, this is Daniel,' Holly said, noting the way her husband tensed slightly. 'Daniel, Mark,' she continued. 'And this is Jake and Chloe.'

'Nice to meet you all.' Daniel shook the hand Mark had extended and smiled vaguely at the children.

'This is Daisy,' he said, as the blonde woman slipped her arm though his.

She was extraordinarily pretty which, for some reason, Holly had not anticipated. Her white-blond hair looked natural and fell in an almost perfect bob around her face, which was small with two huge blue eyes, taking Holly in.

'Hi,' she said. 'Daniel's told me about you.'

Holly thought she detected a note of warning in her voice but the accompanying smile was friendly enough.

'You too,' Holly lied. Daniel had told her very little about Daisy and she'd expected someone different.

Daisy was wearing a close fitting t-shirt and tracksuit bottoms. She looked fit for purpose, as if she had just finished some gravity-defying yoga poses rather than slipped on some clothes that were comfortable.

'Good to meet you, Daniel,' Mark said. 'Enjoying the sunshine?'

'Yes. It's nice to get down to the sea,' he replied. 'Sometimes I go for weeks without seeing it.'

'Long hours?' Mark asked.

'Sometimes,' Daniel told him.

There was a pause. The small talk appeared to have run dry and Holly hoped they would mutter things about getting on and go their separate ways. But Mark seemed keen to interrogate Daniel and his wife further.

'What line of work are you in?' he asked.

Holly squirmed. She thought Mark sounded pompous but the question was one that men always seemed to ask almost immediately.

She often wondered what she would say if she didn't have a job to the frequently asked 'And what do you do?'

'I'm a systems analyst.' Daniel didn't ask what Mark did in return, but he had already moved on, to focus on the beautiful Daisy.

'What about you, Daisy?' Mark was doing his charming thing. 'What profession are you in?'

'None,' she said, exhibiting signs of the nervousness Holly thought she'd feel if she didn't work at all.

'Really?' Mark sounded extremely surprised. 'That's unusual.'

Holly couldn't believe quite how rude he was being, failing to mask his astonishment that in this day and age a woman should not have a career.

'I've trained as a fitness instructor.' Daisy appeared flustered. 'But I'm not working much at the moment.'

'Oh, I see.' Mark started laughing and they all looked on, wondering what it was that he found so funny about the exchange.

'I'm so sorry, Daisy,' he said, putting his arm over-familiarly on her shoulder. 'I misunderstood.'

Further explanation was needed.

'When you said none,' Mark wiped the tears of laughter now forming in the corners of his eyes, 'I thought you meant you were a nun!'

Now they all laughed, although Holly felt cross.

'I thought you were far too pretty to be a nun.' Mark seemed bolstered by the laughter his faux-pas had generated.

Daisy accepted the compliment, smiling, and turned the huge pools of her eyes on him.

'Julie Andrews was a pretty nun.' Jake spoke for the first time. 'In *The Sound of Music*.'

'We were all going to have lunch at the Terraces,' Mark said. The misunderstanding seemed to have relaxed him. 'Why don't you two join us?'

'I'm not sure . . .' Daniel looked at Holly.

'Daniel and Daisy probably want some time on their own together,' Holly said. 'Though of course it would be lovely if you did want to join us.'

'It's very kind but . . .' Daniel began, then Daisy interjected.

'We'd love to,' she said. 'Wouldn't we, Dan?'

He didn't answer.

'Lunch on us then,' Mark said, oblivious to the fact that both Jake and Chloe were looking at them both pleadingly, obviously not wanting to spend lunch with people they'd never met before.

'Think of it as a small thank you, Daniel,' Mark was saying. 'For what you did for Holly.'

She hoped Mark wouldn't bring up the subject of the train crash over lunch. It wasn't the right time or place. The two men were now walking slightly ahead and she could hear Mark saying, '. . . draw a line under things.'

It was as if he thought buying Daniel lunch would somehow make what he had done and Holly's friendship with him go away. She smiled uneasily at Daisy, who was walking beside her and Jake, knowing that it wouldn't.

Chapter Seventeen

'WHAT DO YOU fancy then?' said Natalie, picking up the plastic-coated menu and peering at it.

'James Cracknell for starters!' Holly had just encountered the former Olympic rower going into the lifts of Broadcasting House as she came out.

A bit of side dancing had gone on, as he and Holly had mirrored each other's getting-out-of-the-way steps and stayed in each other's way, until he had finally taken a ninety-degree turn and held out his arm, gesturing for her to pass.

She smiled a 'thank you' at him and was almost certain he'd winked at her in return.

'In the flesh he is almost unbearably gorgeous,' she said to Natalie. 'You couldn't really look at him for too long.'

'Or what?' Natalie handed the menu over to her. 'I'm having the goat's cheese salad.'

'I don't know. You'd tingle so much that you might explode or something!' Holly had already decided what she wanted to eat but she ran her eyes over the menu anyway, as if it was expected of her.

'You must be having some sort of pre-menopausal hormone rush,' Natalie said, trying to catch the waiter's eye as he walked past, but he was busying himself cleaning another table and refused to be drawn into taking orders.

Holly wondered if there was a small amount of truth in what Natalie was saying. She did seem to keep finding herself semi-attracted to all sorts of people, but put it down to finding Mark increasingly less alluring.

It was as if there was some sort of quadratic equation at play where $y = a \times b/c$, with y being a level of attraction, a being another person, b your partner and c his current desirability status.

'By the way,' Natalie added, looking at the waiter, who reluctantly came over and pulled a pad from his belt loop, 'who were you talking to on the phone before we came out?'

The waiter's presence meant Holly didn't have to answer Natalie's question. She'd been talking to Anne-Marie who'd called 'to say hello'.

Holly couldn't think who she was at first and then remembered that she was the woman they'd met at the survivors meeting. She'd asked what train Holly usually caught and if they might meet up some time. Holly had been vague in her 'Yes. Why not?' reply. She wasn't sure if she wanted to meet up with her, but it felt callous not to.

'I'd like a goat's cheese salad and a Diet Coke,' Natalie told the reluctant waiter.

'And I'll have the aubergine and mozzarella panini and a glass of water,' Holly said.

'Still or sparkling?' The waiter didn't look up as he scribbled in his pad.

'Just tap water.' Holly smiled pleasantly as he scowled at her response. 'You'd think half the waiters in London only got paid if they manage to flog a couple of bottles of mineral water with every meal,' she said to Natalie, when he'd gone, but her friend was focusing on two people sitting in the corner of the café.

'Isn't that Rebecca and Dimitri?' she asked.

'Oh, yes.' Holly twisted round to look.

'Do you think they're having an affair?' Natalie was still looking in their direction.

'No.' Holly hadn't really ever considered this before. 'I think they're just having lunch.'

'But they're very flirtatious with each other,' Natalie persisted. 'And they spend a lot of time together.'

'Well, Dimitri is very flirtatious with everyone.' Holly stated a fact. 'And he lives with his girlfriend and Rebecca is always going on about her boyfriend, so from where I'm sitting they're just colleagues who get on well.'

'They obviously fancy each other.' Natalie was still looking at them. 'They should do something about it, if they're going to, before they get married and have kids.'

'I'm sure they're perfectly happy as they are.' Holly resisted the urge to turn and look at them again. She wondered if Daniel and Daisy were happy.

'I'm sorry if Mark forced you to have lunch with us,' Holly had said as she sat down next to Daniel on the train that morning. 'I'm sure you wanted a quiet lunch with Daisy.'

Holly had thought about pretending she hadn't seen him when she spotted Daniel sitting by a window. He'd half-waved as she walked past his carriage and she wasn't sure if he was trying to attract her attention or simply acknowledging her. She suspected he might have had enough of her.

But she wanted a debrief after the weekend's seafront encounter.

'It was nice.' Daniel looked up at her. 'It was good to meet your husband and your children. They're great.'

'They're OK, when they're not moody,' Holly said.

'Well, they weren't moody yesterday.' Daniel smiled. 'Daisy said they were lovely kids.'

'They were very taken with her too.' Holly resisted adding

'all' to include Mark in the being very taken with her category. 'She's very beautiful.'

'Yes.' Daniel nodded. 'She always has been.'

'Have you known her long then?' Holly was curious as to how Daniel had met Daisy. They were so different; what her mother would have called 'an unlikely couple'.

'Since school.' He bent down to move his bag towards him when a man came to sit opposite. 'We were at the same secondary school.'

'Wow, you've been together since then?' Holly was impressed. It was unusual for people to stay together from such a young age. Sex and experimenting with other people usually got in the way.

'No,' Daniel corrected her. 'We weren't together at school. I knew who Daisy was. Everyone did. She was gorgeous and very popular. But I don't think she ever noticed me.'

'So how did you meet?' Holly found she could easily picture Daisy as young and blonde, sporty and surrounded by admirers of both sexes. She couldn't quite imagine the quieter, mousier Daniel attracting her attention.

'There was a summer holiday,' he told her. 'Nearly everyone was going on a school trip to Norway. It was a camp after GCSEs. It was optional but virtually everyone went.'

'I know the sort of thing.' Holly thought again about the Botswana trip.

A tent in Norway was more like it.

'I was supposed to go, but I fell off a wall and broke my leg the day before.' Daniel paused as if wondering how to phrase what came next. 'Daisy was supposed to go too, but her parents had caught her in bed with a boy at the weekend and banned her from going.'

'So you were the only ones left?' Holly wanted him to tell her the full story.

'Well, not quite the only ones, but we grew up in a fairly small village.' Daniel paused, remembering. 'I was sitting by the cricket pitch one day with my leg in plaster and she came and sat next to me, tapped my cast and asked if that was why I hadn't gone to Norway.'

'You had a lucky break then.' Holly only realised she'd made a very poor joke when the words were out.

'I guess so.' Daniel was polite enough to smile, at least. 'I don't think she would ever have looked at me twice if I hadn't been virtually the only person left for her to hang out with.'

'I'm sure that's not true,' Holly said, looking past him to his reflection in the window. He wasn't immediately striking but he definitely grew on you.

The train had just stopped at Haywards Heath when she suddenly saw Anne-Marie, walking down the aisle looking for a seat, reflected in the window.

'Oh, hello,' she said, stopping where they were sitting.

'Hi.' Holly smiled and Daniel turned and said, 'Hello.'

There were no empty seats where they were and she moved on a couple of rows and sat down, not within earshot but close enough for Holly to feel that she was in their space.

'It's funny that Daisy and I both have names from American classics,' she said to Daniel, recalling something Mark had said the day before.

'She is my idea of what Daisy Buchanan should have looked like. I didn't like the woman who played her in the film.' Mark had obviously been very struck by Daisy.

Daniel looked blank.

'I was named after Holly Golightly in *Breakfast at Tiffany's*,' Holly explained.

'I don't really read novels.' As he said this, Holly realised she had never seen him take out a book on the train.

'You must have seen the film?' Perhaps he hadn't. Would she have consigned every bit of it to memory if her mother hadn't been such a fan? 'And *The Great Gatsby*.'

'Not seen either of them.' He smiled. 'Which one is Daisy in?'

'*The Great Gatsby*,' Holly said. 'She's very attractive and fought over by men.'

'Sounds like Daisy,' Daniel had replied.

'Mark has decided to run the Brighton marathon,' Holly told Natalie as they waited for their food. 'Did I tell you he was thinking about it?'

'Last I heard, he was thinking of getting a sports car,' Natalie answered. 'Or was it a motorbike?'

'Both. He went off the sports car idea when he found out how much it would cost to insure,' Holly told her friend. 'And I think I put him off getting a bike by taking the piss out of his friend Tim.'

'Does he have one then?' Natalie asked.

'Yes. A great steaming beast of a machine, which he rides very slowly, with a couple of other middle-aged men on similar bikes, down to the café at Roedean where they drink tea!' Holly raised her eyebrows.

'Is that the café that was in *Quadrophenia*?' Natalie's knowledge of Brighton was taken mainly from films.

'One of them, yes.' Holly nodded. 'I don't suppose Ace Face asked for sweetener in his tea!'

Natalie laughed.

'So has Mark started training?'

'No.' Holly pulled a face. 'He hasn't actually run anywhere in years, but he keeps talking about it. And I looked at his internet history the other day and he'd been looking at shoes, so he must be serious.'

'Well, at least it will keep him busy.' Natalie moved back in her seat as the waiter returned with a Coke and a very small glass of tap water – a begrudging amount if ever Holly had seen one. 'Guy's driving me mad at the moment. He's really lethargic and never does anything that actually needs doing.'

'Neither does Mark,' Holly sympathised.

'All Guy's sentences at the moment seem to begin with, "I know I ought to know this but . . ." And then he asks where we keep the vacuum cleaner.'

'Mark's the same,' Holly agreed. 'Last night the washing machine finished its cycle, just as we were about to have dinner. He spent about ten minutes looking in the oven and fiddling with the timer to make it stop beeping. He had no idea it was the washing machine making the noise!'

The occasional lunch and coffee with Natalie was one of the few opportunities Holly got these days to air family grievances. She'd had to stop going to her book group when she started working full-time again, and missed the company of the other women.

'They never actually discuss the book,' Mark used to say of the group. 'They just drink a lot and bitch about their husbands.'

Men didn't seem to understand that women needed to vent their frustrations.

'I wish Guy had more get up and go,' Natalie sighed, as the waiter placed a plate of leaves and glistening white cheese in front of her. 'I like men who are good at their jobs. There's something sexy about that. Like . . .'

'Like James Darling?' Holly asked, wondering if this was why her sentence trailed off.

'Not necessarily.' Natalie took a mouthful of salad. 'Like Mark. I've heard you saying you catch yourself looking at him with fresh eyes when you've been to his office and seen him fielding phone calls and getting into a project.'

'That happens less and less at the moment.' Holly had told Natalie that Mark's business hadn't been doing so well since the credit crunch. 'He's talking about giving up the office altogether. I'm more likely to see him at home, trying to make himself appear useful without much success. Hence the marathon running, I think.'

'Well, I suppose running is better than zooming about in a sports car with a woman half his age. Can I pinch a tiny bit of your bread?' Natalie tore off a corner of Holly's sandwich and began to mop up oil from her plate with it.

'Yes, I suppose so,' said Holly.

Last night, Mark had said, casually, as if it were of no real importance, that perhaps *he* should have a couple of personal training sessions and get some advice on running. No prizes, thought Holly, for guessing who he had in mind to be the personal trainer.

Chapter Eighteen

DANIEL ALWAYS APPEARED to be half smiling, as if he were enjoying some private joke. He had earphones in and was staring out of the window so he didn't see Holly until she was all but sitting down next to him.

She mouthed 'Hello' as her presence caused him to look up. He took his earphones out and smiled a whole smile.

'Hello,' he replied, as if surprised. It was a much earlier train than either of them usually caught and he obviously had not expected to see her on it.

'Am I disturbing you?' Holly was still hovering, not quite sure whether to sit down or not.

'No.' Daniel patted the seat and she sat down, glad to have bumped into him unexpectedly.

'So are you skiving as well?'

It was early in the week and Holly had put in all the calls she could to possible guests for this week's programme, had had a meeting and spoken at length to James Darling. Dimitri and Rebecca were liaising with reporters. There was very little left for her actually to do, so she'd decided to leave work early.

It was only three o'clock.

'Not exactly.' Daniel suddenly looked a little thrown by her presence, as if the initial pleasure he'd felt on seeing her were being gradually wiped out by having to explain what he was doing.

'Well, it's nice to see you anyway.' Holly wriggled out of her coat, thinking the action would show she was moving on from her earlier question and there was no need for him to explain.

She felt pleased to see Daniel, which contrasted with her hope that Mark would not be at home when she got back. He'd hinted in the morning that he might go for a run after work.

'If dogs are colour-blind,' Jake had been listening to something on the radio about canine eyesight, 'how do guide dogs get people over pedestrian crossings?'

'I've no idea.' Holly had been trying to get something to eat before leaving for the station.

'They wait for a gap in the traffic.' Mark knew the answer to Jake's question. 'Then they cross.'

'Right.' Jake had appeared satisfied with the answer.

'That's why they don't have greyhounds for the blind,' Mark had joked. 'Although they could be guide dogs for very busy people.'

'What?' Jake had appeared confused.

'Because they run so fast,' Mark explained his joke. 'Their charges might not be able to keep up, and get run over.'

'Poor taste,' Holly had muttered.

'Talking of which,' he had said, ignoring her comment, 'I might go for a bit of a run myself this evening.'

'Fine.' Holly finished her cereal and put the bowl in the dishwasher. 'Good luck.'

She'd wondered if he'd ordered the running shoes he'd been looking at on the internet and was reminded of this now when a man wearing no shoes at all wandered into the carriage.

'Is this train going to Brighton?' he asked, picking up a newspaper that had been left on the seats opposite.

'Yes.' Holly tried not to stare at his bare feet.

'Anywhere else?' he asked.

'I'm sorry?' She was not quite sure what he was asking.

'Does it go anywhere else apart from Brighton?' He looked around the carriage as if it might hold the answer to his questions.

'It stops at East Croydon,' Daniel said. 'And I think it stops at Haywards Heath as well. Where did you want to go?'

'I haven't decided.' The man smiled and walked on down the corridor.

'How strange,' Holly said.

'Completely different people at a different time of day,' Daniel observed, obliquely referencing the fact that they were both going home early.

'I was at an unusual loose end at work,' Holly explained. 'So I decided to knock off early.'

'I've got a doctor's appointment . . .' Daniel was interrupted by the train announcer, telling them that the train would indeed be calling at both East Croydon and Haywards Heath. 'That gives our friend three destinations to choose from then.'

Holly laughed and wondered if Daniel's appointment was related to the crash. She'd not been sleeping very well lately and Mark had been urging her to go to the doctor. She'd assured him she didn't need to.

'Nothing serious, I hope,' she said. It was the sort of ubiquitous line you used when people said they had a hospital appointment.

'Maybe.' Daniel looked briefly around the carriage as the train pulled out of the station. He seemed to be checking that they were alone and that what he said would not be overheard by others.

Shoeless Man appeared to have gone and they seemed to be the only people in the immediate cluster of seats.

'I'm not ill or anything.' Daniel shifted awkwardly and looked out of the window before turning back to her. 'It's a bit delicate.'

'You don't have to tell me,' she said. 'It's none of my business, obviously.'

'I'd like to, though,' Daniel caught her eye directly and she returned his gaze. 'I haven't really talked to anyone about it and I feel as if I need to.'

'OK.' Holly fixed her attention on him.

'Daisy and I . . .' He paused as if unsure how to go on and scanned the carriage again. 'We've been trying to have a baby for a while, but it doesn't seem to be happening.'

'Oh.' This was not what Holly had been expecting. 'Well, it sometimes takes a while.'

'How long did it take you?' Daniel asked, shrugging as if to acknowledge that it was a somewhat personal question.

'Well, no time at all actually,' she laughed. 'But it takes most people a bit longer. I wasn't really ready to have a baby, but friends had said it had taken them a year or so to get pregnant so I thought we could start trying and it happened first time. It was rather a shock.'

'Weren't you pleased?' Daniel asked.

'Not exactly, no.' Holly still felt slightly guilty about saying this. She obviously didn't regret having Chloe, not for a minute, it was just at the time, she'd thought she'd have another couple of years working, get herself more established on the career ladder.

'I was twenty-eight when I had Chloe. It seemed an odd age,' Holly tried to explain to him. 'Everyone in my antenatal group was either sixteen or thirty-five. None of my friends had started having babies at the time. I felt a bit out on a limb.'

She remembered Natalie had barely been able to mask her horror when told the 'good' news.

'But you've only just been made a producer,' she'd said, echoing the thought that Holly was keeping to herself. It didn't feel like a good time to have a baby as far as her career was concerned, though after Chloe was born her career was the last thing on her mind.

'I didn't really feel ready,' Holly told Daniel. 'It sounds ridiculous because you ought to know what's going to happen if you start trying to have a baby, but it took me completely by surprise.'

'But you don't regret it?' he asked.

'Oh, God, no. It was the best thing that ever happened to me,' Holly said truthfully. 'All I'm saying is, maybe it's not such a bad thing, if it takes a while. It gives you more time to get used to the idea.'

'I've always wanted to have children,' Daniel told her. 'And Daisy has too. Her mother died when she was doing her A-levels. Maybe if you lose a parent when you are young, it makes you want to have children of your own sooner rather than later.'

Holly noted that having a parent die relatively young was something Daisy had in common with Mark. She wondered if they would talk about it in the training session he said he had booked with her.

'How old is she?' This was a good opportunity to find out exactly how old Daniel was too.

'She's twenty-five.' That was even younger than Holly had thought. Nearly twenty years younger than she was. Daniel looked younger than her but Holly didn't notice the age gap when she talked to him. Now that he'd said his wife was twenty-five, she suddenly felt ridiculously old.

'That's no age.' She smiled ruefully. 'There's still plenty of time.'

'I know. But it puts pressure on . . .' Daniel stopped talking and looked out of the window. Holly wasn't sure whether to ask him to go on but he did so unprompted.

'Do you remember I told you things had been a bit strained between us since . . .'

Holly nodded. Neither of them liked referring to the crash directly.

'To be honest, they were already a bit strained because of the baby thing.'

'So have you had tests?' Holly wasn't sure if she should have asked the question but the conversation had already taken a personal turn.

'That's what the appointment is about today,' he told her.

'I'm sure it will happen,' Holly reassured him. 'You're both still so young.'

'I think Daisy finds it difficult because she doesn't have a career.' Daniel looked out of the window again and carried on talking. 'Daisy's clever. She was going to go to university and do law, but after her mother died she decided to wait, then she got a job and we got together and it never happened.'

'She could go now,' Holly ventured.

'It would be difficult,' Daniel said. 'Maybe one day, but for the moment she's . . .'

'In limbo?' Holly could well imagine the frustration Daisy must feel if she was bright but going nowhere. And then, having decided to have children young, nothing was happening.

'I guess.' Daniel considered this.

'What about you?' Holly asked. 'Do you want to be a father?'

'Of course. I've always wanted kids,' he told her. 'I'd be gutted if we couldn't have them.'

Holly remembered Mark's reaction when she'd said she was pregnant with Chloe. She'd been so ambivalent about it herself that she'd wanted him to be delighted for both of them. But his reaction had been one of mustered up enthusiasm rather than pure genuine joy.

'I always thought I would have a family,' Daniel went on. 'Everything is in place. I've got a lovely wife, a good job. I can provide for them. I just can't have them . . .'

Holly said nothing. The one thing Mark had been pleased about, when she'd first got pregnant, was that it confirmed his virility.

'First time!' he'd say, with the smile of a Cheshire cat if people asked if they'd been trying long.

The fact that he could get his wife pregnant, just like that, seemed to please him more than the fact that another human being was on the way. It was another manifestation of the fact that twentieth-century man was still a caveman at heart.

It had been just as important to Mark to get her pregnant naturally, she now realised, as it had been for him to provide for the baby she had been carrying too.

'You don't have to go back to work,' he kept saying after Chloe was born and Holly couldn't bear to be parted from her. 'I can earn enough to keep us afloat.'

Daniel had echoed those sentiments when he'd talked about having a good job and being able to provide for a family.

She wondered how he would react if the tables were turned and Daisy became the main breadwinner.

Holly was beginning to realise that Mark hated this new facet of their relationship as much as he probably would have hated having to go through IVF.

'The next station is Brighton,' the train announcer interrupted her thoughts. 'Please ensure you have all your bags and belongings with you when you leave the train.'

Daniel stood up and pulled his briefcase off the overhead luggage rack.

'Between ourselves?' he said, taking his coat off the peg next to the seat.

'Of course.' Holly began putting her coat on.

'I'll have to run,' he said as the train drew into the station.

'Sure.' Holly was in no great hurry and realised he probably needed to separate himself from her to get in the right frame of mind for his doctor's appointment.

'I might see you later in the week.' Daniel leaned towards her and kissed her.

It was kiss on the cheek, a perfectly natural goodbye, but somehow it felt different, perhaps because it came after the conversation they had just had.

'I hope so,' she said.

Chapter Nineteen

Holly had paused by Rebecca's desk on her way to the meeting, then, as she was busy doing something on her computer, felt bound to wait for her.

'Facebook?' she said conversationally, catching sight of various photographs set alongside a few lines of text.

'Just checking my boyfriend's wall.' Rebecca shut the page and got up from her seat. 'OK, I'm ready.'

'Why do you do that?' Holly was only half-heartedly on Facebook. She had no details or picture on her profile and it mockingly reminded her whenever she did go on that she had only five friends and three of them were her own family.

'I want to see who he's been talking to,' Rebecca said matter-of-factly as they made their way towards the lift. 'Make sure none of his ex-girlfriends has been in touch with him.'

'Doesn't he mind you checking up on him like that?' Holly asked. 'Don't you trust him?'

'I check my wife's page.' James Darling had obviously been behind them long enough to overhear their conversation. 'Don't you ever look to see what hubby's been up to?'

'No.' Holly baulked at the word 'hubby'. 'I don't think he ever uses Facebook anyway.'

'You should have a look.' Darling pressed the button for the third floor.

'How was your day?' Daniel was asking Holly now as they managed to bag a double seat before the train began filling up.

'Fairly unproductive.' She shrugged. 'We had a programme-planning meeting, which involves a lot of going round in circles.'

'Isn't that what all meetings are like?' Daniel grinned. 'I hate them.'

'So have you been . . .' Holly paused because she had absolutely no idea what a systems analyst might do on a day-to-day basis '. . . analysing systems?'

'Yes, I have.' Daniel laughed, bending down to pick his bag off the floor as a man came to sit opposite them. 'I've been doing a job for one of the big ticketing agencies, actually.'

'The ones that sell theatre tickets?' Holly asked.

'And for sports events and music gigs – that sort of thing.' Daniel moved his legs in as another commuter paused, then thought better of commandeering the free seat opposite and moved on. 'What was your meeting about?'

'We seemed to end up talking about Facebook for rather a lot of it,' Holly said, thinking back to the conversation she'd started with Rebecca earlier in the day.

'Do you mind if I sit here?' Her thoughts were interrupted by the arrival of Anne-Marie.

Holly hadn't contacted her since the night of the meeting and hadn't thought to ask Daniel if he had.

'No!' Holly's voice was loud and abrupt. She'd intended her response to be friendly but thought the way it had come out sounded a little hostile.

'I mean, no,' she said again, more softly.

Anne-Marie hesitated as if the level of the first response was an indicator she was not actually welcome.

Her moment of hesitation cost her the seat, as another woman muttered a brief 'excuse me' and sat in it.

'I'd best go and find somewhere else then,' Anne-Marie said, and disappeared before they had time to ask her how she was.

'That was odd,' Holly mused. 'I wonder why she didn't just sit down.'

'You told her not to.' Daniel's voice had an edge to it that Holly hadn't heard before. He was looking at her curiously too.

'I didn't,' Holly protested. 'I told her she could sit here.'

'She asked if she could sit there,' Daniel persisted. 'And you said, "No!"'

'No,' Holly insisted. 'She said, "Do you *mind* if I sit here?" and I said "No", as in, "No, I don't mind. Be my guest. Have the seat."'

'I'm pretty sure she just asked if she could sit there.' Daniel looked uncomfortable.

Holly began to feel that way too.

'Oh, God, did she?' She felt mortified. 'Are you sure?'

'Pretty sure,' he said quietly.

'Oh, no.' Holly was no longer sure exactly what Anne-Marie had said. 'I'd better go and find her. I'll leave my stuff with you.' She wanted Daniel to offer her some guidance as to what she should do next.

'OK,' he said gently, as if he'd forgiven her for the rudeness he'd thought her capable of only minutes earlier. Then he touched her arm reassuringly as she stood up. 'Unless you want me to come with you?'

'No.' Holly thought she'd find it easier to talk to Anne-Marie on her own. 'But thanks.'

Holly got up and caught Daniel's eye as she did so. She couldn't quite interpret the look he gave her as he momentarily held her gaze. But it was definitely a look. Holly turned away and began walking in the direction Anne-Marie had gone.

She hadn't found a seat and was standing in the corridor between carriages.

'I wanted to apologise.' Holly came straight to the point. 'I must have seemed incredibly rude.'

Anne-Marie muttered, 'No.'

'It sounds ridiculous.' Holly wondered whether she would be believed or not. 'But I thought you asked if I *minded* if you sat opposite, so I said no, but Daniel said you just asked if you *could* sit opposite, so my answer should have been yes.'

Anne-Marie looked thoughtful and then she began laughing.

'The world is full of misunderstandings.' She smiled now.

'I suppose so.' Holly smiled back, slightly relieved. 'I hope I didn't upset you?'

'No, not really,' Anne-Marie said. 'I was a bit put out but I thought you must have your reasons.'

'Why don't you come and sit with us now?' Holly suggested. 'You can have my seat. It would be nice to talk. And I'm sorry I haven't got back to you, since you called. Things have been busy.'

'I'm OK,' Anne-Marie replied. 'Someone will get off at East Croydon and I'll take their seat. You are settled with Daniel. Another time.'

'Maybe tomorrow then?' Holly asked. 'Is this your usual train?'

'No, I usually only work in London on Wednesdays. The rest of the time I'm based in Haywards Heath,' she said.

'Oh, I see.' Holly supposed this explained why she hadn't noticed her before. 'I don't know why, I just presumed you commuted daily.'

'My husband used to,' Anne-Marie said, as if she felt the need to explain how he came to be on the train when it crashed. 'He was a regular.'

'Well, maybe next week then?' Holly suggested. 'You've got our numbers, haven't you? And we've got yours.'

She felt slightly self-conscious referring to herself and Daniel as 'we' and their respective numbers as 'ours'. 'Why don't you let us know which train you'll be on and we can try and sit together then?'

'All sorted?' Daniel asked when she returned to her seat.

'I think so.' Holly sat down. 'I said we might try and meet up with her next week. She only comes up on Wednesday, apparently. She said it was her husband who was the regular commuter.'

'Oh. I wonder if I ever saw him,' Daniel said.

The train stopped in a tunnel and Holly looked past him at his reflection in the window. She wished they would get going again and shifted nervously in her seat, unable for the moment to get the thought of Anne-Marie's husband and what had happened in the tunnel out of her head. She concentrated on her breathing and tried to think of something else.

'Well, I'm glad you sorted things out.' Daniel smiled at her and put his hand on her arm, as if he could tell what she was thinking.

'So am I.' Holly decided to revert back to the conversation they'd been having before Anne-Marie arrived.

'We might be doing something in the programme about Facebook stalking,' she told Daniel. 'People tracking down their ex's movements through their Facebook pages. Are you on Facebook?'

'No,' Daniel surprised her by saying. She thought that working with computers, he would be. 'And I'm not a stalker either. Daisy is, though.'

'A stalker?' Holly asked, half-joking.

'No,' Daniel said. 'On Facebook. She seems to use it a lot.'

Holly didn't tell him that this much she already knew.

When she'd got back to her office, after the morning meeting, Natalie had not been anxious to get on with any work.

'Are you going to have a look at Mark's Facebook site then?' she'd asked.

'I wasn't going to, no.' Holly swivelled her chair round.

'Aren't you the tiniest bit curious to see who he's friends with? Guy has hundreds of women friends. Lots of them ex-girlfriends or people he briefly dated.' Natalie paused. 'I'm sure Mark doesn't, though. I mean, you two have been together for longer than we have – less of a past to keep up with.'

'It doesn't seem right.' Holly had scruples. 'It's like going through someone's text messages.'

'Don't you do that either?' Natalie appeared flabbergasted. 'Holly, you are far too trusting.'

'I'm not sure that's true.' She considered this. 'But everything is open to misinterpretation, isn't it? I mean, even fairly innocent text messages can be misunderstood. I've probably got some texts that could be easily misinterpreted.'

'Have you?' Natalie sounded doubtful so Holly began scrolling through her phone.

'Here's one.'

Where are you, Holly? the text read. *I'm at the hotel waiting for you but you are nowhere to be seen. Are you standing me up? Darling x*

'You see, if you didn't know that James was called Darling and that I was supposed to meet him at the Cadogan Hotel to interview that American author, you might well wonder what that was all about.' She handed the phone to Natalie.

'Where were you?' Natalie asked, sounding as if she too was pissed off with Holly for not having turned up on time.

'It was the day of the train crash.' Holly adopted a jokey tone. 'I was stuck in a tunnel and there was no mobile reception.'

'Oh.' Natalie was momentarily flummoxed but she swiftly regained her composure.

'As I'm the one producing this item about Facebook stalking,' she said, 'wouldn't you like to help me with my research by checking out Mark's site?'

'OK, you win.' Holly logged into her Facebook site and was greeted by an invitation to join a group called Totally Pointless and news feed informing her that Jake had just downloaded the latest Gorillaz single and the sad fact that she only had four friends.

'I thought I had five,' she told Natalie. 'I'm sure Chloe was one of them.'

'She must have defriended you,' Natalie said, cheerily. 'Teenage girls don't want their mothers knowing what they are up to.'

'Can she do that?' Holly was not at all sure how Facebook worked.

'Easily,' Natalie told her. 'You've got a friend request though. Who's Anne-Marie Roberts?'

'She's another commuter,' Holly replied, slightly surprised at this request. She was about to confirm Anne-Marie as a friend. It seemed rude not to, although Holly wasn't sure she wanted to.

'Are we going to look at Mark or not?' Natalie asked, distracting her from replying to Anne-Marie.

Holly typed his name and was directed to his page.

'Take a look at his wall,' Natalie instructed, as Holly peered at the photographs of glamorous-looking women who had suddenly appeared alongside three-line comments.

Hey, Mark, said a Marilyn lookalike who called herself Celeste. *Great to bump into you yesterday. Let's do lunch.*

Glad that we are friends now, Mark, said a brunette, Vanessa, who Natalie pointed out tactfully was practically kissing the camera. *Must definitely have a drink when you are next in London.*

'Bloody hell! Who are all these women?' Holly had never heard Mark mention Celeste or Vanessa.

'Probably just work colleagues,' Natalie reassured her. 'I'm sure it's just all what would be normal office flirting, but posting it in public makes it look somehow worse.'

'I guess.' Holly had been distracted by another post on Mark's wall.

Looking forward to seeing you the weekend after next and hopefully get a chance to talk about how things are.

'Bloody hell,' Holly said. 'Doesn't she realise that these conversations aren't private but everyone can see what you write on someone's wall?'

'Why?' asked Natalie, looking at the post Holly was reading. 'Who is Susan Holt? Is that your mother?'

'Yessss,' Holly hissed. 'I can't believe she is talking to Mark on Facebook. It's weird.'

'I think it's funny,' Natalie laughed. 'You never use it but your seventy-something mother does.'

'It's a bit unnerving,' Holly said, clicking on her mother's profile and finding she had 23 friends.

Jake, Mark and Chloe were among them, so was Lucy, but V was not and neither was she. Holly wondered why her mother hadn't sent her a friend request and who some of the friends she had never heard of were. She was about to close the page when she noticed something.

'That's odd.'

'What?' Natalie was looking over her shoulder, taking in the information as Holly was slowly digesting.

'Who is Daisy Harrison?' Natalie asked, looking at the recent activity post, which told them that Mark and Daisy were now friends.

'She's Daniel's wife,' Holly told her.

'Daniel as in Daniel your knight in shining armour?' Natalie asked.

'Daniel from the train, yes.' Holly ignored her description of him. 'He's not even my Facebook friend.'

'No one is your Facebook friend,' Natalie pointed out.

'I suppose not,' Holly agreed. Nevertheless there was something about Mark and Daisy's virtual friendship that unsettled her.

I wonder if Lisa ever realised just how much she hurt me. I can still remember that day at school as if it were yesterday. I'd walked there with her in the morning, because by then I'd been staying with her family for nearly three weeks.

'You're like one of the family,' Mrs Granger, her mother, had remarked at breakfast, when I'd asked if I might have another piece of toast. 'No need to ask, darling. Just help yourself.'

I think it was that that annoyed Lisa more than the 24-hour, bedroom-sharing contact, which was getting on her nerves. She didn't want me overstepping the mark, getting too close to her family, not when I had one of my own, albeit one which at that moment was unable to cope with life throwing up unexpected turns of events.

We had separate lessons but usually met for lunch in the canteen, with the rest of our loosely fluctuating group of friends. There was a spare seat at the table where Lisa was already sitting as I arrived, but when I went over with my tray, she said, 'Melanie is sitting there.'

I looked around and couldn't see Melanie.

'She'll be here in a minute,' Lisa insisted, but Melanie never showed.

I asked her later, when we were doing homework on Lisa's dining-room table, why she hadn't let me sit with her at lunch, and she lowered her voice to make sure her mother, who was making us hot chocolate in the kitchen, didn't hear.

'Just because your mum's in the loony bin doesn't mean I still have to be your friend.'

I never replied because Mrs Granger came in then, with two steaming mugs of hot chocolate.

'I got some of that squirty cream today.' She beamed at us through the steam. 'I hope you like it, Anne-Marie?'

I nodded, still smarting from Lisa's earlier comment, and then she asked me if I'd got the notes we needed for Geography.

'Do you have that sheet on earthquakes?' she asked, as if nothing had happened, and I began to wonder if she had really said it.

We carried on much as before but it wasn't the same. I never felt close to her after that, and when Mum came out of hospital and I went back home, we hardly saw each other at all.

'People who don't need friends always have lots,' my mother said, after asking me why I didn't see so much of Lisa any more.

I'd told her she'd found new friends in a different crowd and didn't seem to need me. I, by comparison, needed friends but was starting to find it increasingly hard to make them.

I still do . . . need friends, that is . . . and I still seem to find it difficult to make them.

Today was a case in point.

When I got on the train this morning, I found myself looking around for two seats, thinking Geoff was with me. We used to go up together on the days when I worked in London. Not always: sometimes he had an earlier meeting or might have stayed overnight somewhere on business, but usually, if he were home, we'd go up together. As I was casting around for seats I almost believed that he was there, just for a brief moment, before the reality came flooding back to me, making me want to go back to the door of the carriage, get off and return home.

Then I spotted Holly sitting further down and I thought, If she can keep getting on, day in and day out, after what happened to her, then so can I.

She didn't see me. She was on her own, reading the paper. I wondered if she'd got my friend request on Facebook. I looked at her page, after the meeting, once I knew her name. She obviously doesn't use it very often. She only had a handful of friends and they looked to be her family. Three of them had the same name, although it was different from hers – but that's not unusual these days.

It made me wonder what I should do about my name now. I hadn't thought about it but it suddenly struck me that it will be odd going through the rest of my life, with Geoff's name but without him. At the same time, I want to keep it because that's one part of him that I can keep. If I still have his name, then something of him is still mine.

I checked to see if Holly had responded to my friend request, when I got to the office, but she hadn't and that's when I decided to unfriend Geoff.

Whenever I log on, there he is, smiling at me from a beach in Corfu at the top of my short list of friends. It was a holiday we had last year, and if I'm honest with myself it wasn't that great. Geoff was preoccupied with work and spent more time with his BlackBerry than he did with me. The picture was taken after a day when I forced him to leave his phone behind and go on a boat trip, and he relaxed a little.

It was easy to lose him. One click of the 'Remove from Friends' button and he was gone. I wish it were as easy to get him out of my mind.

When I unfriended Geoff, I had a momentary feeling of power. I've felt pretty powerless since it all happened but removing him from my Facebook friends made me feel momentarily in control of my life.

So now I have one fewer friend and I keep thinking that sooner or later Holly will respond to my request or call me. But then I saw her on the train again, after work, and she seemed almost hostile.

She was sitting with him again, Daniel, whoever he is, and there was a free seat opposite.

I asked if I could sit there and Holly said no.

I was too stunned to reply. It was like Lisa in the canteen again. I'd thought there was a kind of recognition between us. I'd thought that's why

Holly had smiled when I first saw her, before I'd introduced myself. I'd thought she could tell that we'd both been through something similar.

I couldn't think what to say so I just walked on down the train and stood in the corridor, wondering why she was behaving like that. Why is it that women who I think of as my friends can treat me so badly? I thought Holly would be different.

Then she appeared in the corridor and explained there'd been a misunderstanding. It was silly really. It made me laugh because it was so silly, and I laughed again later because I felt almost happy. She'd asked if I'd like to have a drink some time soon. And now, for the first time since it happened, I feel as if I have something to look forward to.

Chapter Twenty

'ANYONE FANCY A coffee at my place?' James Darling asked.
Holly knew he lived in Buckinghamshire in a large-sounding house called Tudor something or other.

She'd occasionally sent books or DVDs there that he needed to read or watch to prepare for the programme. She had imagined a large black-and-white edifice bought on the proceeds of the ridiculous advance he'd secured for his book. *Pretentious, Moi? A History of Perception from The Emperor's New Clothes to Tracey Emin's Bed* had sold well, though Holly had yet to meet anyone who had actually read it.

'What place?' she asked, wondering if Natalie, Dimitri and herself were expected to jump on the Metropolitan line and head out to the suburbs to take up his offer; or whether he was referring to a coffee bar he frequented so often that he claimed it as his own.

'My flat,' Darling replied, as if Holly should have known. 'It's just round the corner in Covent Garden.'

'Oh.' She had no knowledge of the flat.

There was no reason she should. James Darling's living arrangements were his own affair. A lot of the BBC presenters and correspondents did rent a pied-à-terre near work, as their hours often prevented them from getting home. Holly had imagined he would want to get back to his wife and children.

'It's in Wild Court.' Natalie's dismissive tone suggested she thought Holly would have known this.

'Well, I ought to be getting back really,' she said.

'Me too.' Dimitri wasn't letting on if he already knew Darling had a flat in the centre of town, but he didn't appear to want to go back to it.

The four of them had just been to the press night of *Je ne Sais Quoi!*, a French-Canadian variety show featuring a controversial double-amputee trampolining act. The act was good, incredible in fact, but his inclusion had sparked 'freak show' accusations. These would be discussed on *Antennae* later in the week.

'We'll say goodbye then,' said James, making no attempt at changing their minds. 'You're up for a coffee, aren't you, Nat?'

'Sure,' she concurred. 'Are you both heading towards Victoria?'

'I am,' Dimitri replied. 'Are you getting the tube, Holly?'

She nodded. She'd been on the tube now a couple of times when she'd been running late. She hadn't particularly liked it, but she hadn't panicked either.

'So,' Dimitri asked, as they began walking towards the Embankment, 'you weren't tempted by a peek at Darling's pad and some euphemistic coffee?'

'Is coffee always euphemistic?' Holly asked, turning and seeing Darling briefly put his arm around Natalie's shoulders.

'Usually is at this time of night,' Dimitri replied. 'I mean, if I suggested you got off your train at Clapham Junction and came back to my place for a coffee, what would you say?'

'I'd say I don't drink coffee,' said Holly, laughing at the very idea of the godlike Dimitri suggesting she come back to his place.

'Don't you?' Dimitri didn't sound particularly surprised. 'That fits.'

'How?' Holly wondered what part of her gave the impression that she didn't drink coffee, apart from the fact that she didn't.

'I drink tea,' she added, as if her dislike of coffee needed some sort of qualification.

'Tea is never euphemistic,' Dimitri said, smiling at her in a way which Holly suspected was indulgent.

'Never?' said Holly. 'Even if there are digestives on offer as well?'

'I suppose dunking could be a bit of a double-entendre,' he conceded, as they walked down the steps to the platform of the tube. 'But still, "Would you like to come back to my place for a cuppa?" doesn't have quite the same ring as "Shall we end the evening off with coffee?"'

'What about Horlicks?' Holly wondered. 'Could that be construed as an invitation to do anything other than fall asleep?'

Dimitri shook his head. 'I doubt it.'

'I could do with a cup of tea now.' Holly checked her watch as the underground train arrived and they took seats alongside each other; she was wondering if there was time for her to buy a cup at the station before her train was due to leave.

'There you go!' Dimitri winked at her.

'What do you mean, "There you go"?' Holly asked, noting the peculiar Englishness of the expression and how it could be used to underline a whole range of things.

'You and the not drinking coffee thing,' he said. 'It fits. You're safe.'

'What do you mean, I'm safe?' She had the feeling this was not exactly a compliment.

'Well, you know . . .' Dimitri obviously hoped he could leave it at this. 'You know', like 'there you go', could be conversational full stops but Holly put on an 'I'm waiting' expression until he elaborated.

'Well, you're married. You're Holly,' he said, as if this were an explanation in itself. 'Very married.'

'Is there such a thing as "very married"?' she queried. 'Surely you are either married or not.'

'Some people are more married than others,' Dimitri answered. 'I don't think James Darling's wife need worry if you had taken up his invitation to have "coffee".'

He made quotation marks in the air with his fingers as he said this.

'Well, obviously.' Holly inwardly baulked at the thought. 'But I could be up for euphemistic coffee with someone else.'

'Are you?'

'No.' She was failing completely to make Dimitri think she might have another side to her. 'But I could be.'

Safe indeed, she thought to herself, as the tube pulled into Victoria.

It was true, she was safe, but she would like to have given the impression that she was perhaps a little less so. Everyone around her seemed to have very specific views about her. Dimitri thought she was safe. Mark thought she was privately traumatised. The only person who seemed to assume nothing was Daniel.

'Whereas with Natalie . . .' Dimitri said as they got on to the escalator.

'Natalie what?' Holly felt a twinge of jealousy as she anticipated Dimitri saying that he thought Natalie was a bit dark horse.

'Nothing.' Dimitri had obviously thought better of whatever it was he was going to say.

'Natalie and James are old friends.' She stressed the 'friends' as they went through the barriers and on to the station concourse.

'If you say so.' Dimitri raised his eyebrows slightly.

'They are,' Holly insisted. 'I've known Natalie for years and she's worked with Darling for ages.'

'The 23.06 to Brighton, platform eighteen,' Dimitri read the departure board. 'Which also stops at Clapham Junction. I will escort you as far as there.'

'Why, thank you.' Holly smiled as they walked together to the other side of the station and passed through the barriers on to the platform.

'Are you going to get your tea then?' asked Dimitri, nodding towards the Costa coffee stall at the end of the platform.

'Have I got time?' Holly checked her watch again.

Dimitri nodded and she joined the queue, realising only as she did so that the person in front of her was Daniel.

'Hello,' she said, wondering why he was on this late train.

'Hello-o.' Daniel elongated the O slightly, as if he too was surprised to find her here at this hour. 'Can I get you a drink, as I'm here?'

'She wants a cup of tea,' said Dimitri, making his presence known.

'I would like a cup of tea.' Holly frowned at Dimitri. 'This is Dimitri, who I work with.'

'Anything?' Daniel asked him.

'No, thanks,' Dimitri said, and Daniel asked for a tea for Holly.

'We've been to a variety show on the South Bank,' Holly told Daniel once they were on the train. She felt the need to explain why she was with Dimitri and exactly when he would be leaving them too. 'Dimitri is going to Clapham Junction.'

'Oh, right.' Daniel looked slightly relieved. 'Was it good?'

'It was,' Dimitri confirmed. 'We're going to be talking about it on the programme later this week.'

Daniel nodded.

'But I imagine Natalie and Darling may have sewn up exactly what angle the discussion will take over "coffee".' He made the finger sign again. Holly shot him a warning glance.

'There's a guy with no legs doing a trampolining act in it,' she told Daniel. 'Although he was so good that you stopped noticing that he didn't have any legs.'

'Which is the point,' Dimitri said, standing up when the train slowed as it neared Clapham Junction.

'Nice to meet you.' He nodded to Daniel. 'See you tomorrow, Holly.'

'Yes, see you tomorrow.' She smiled at him.

'Unless . . .' Dimitri turned, as he was about to get off '. . . you fancy a coffee?'

'I don't drink coffee, as you know.' She laughed and felt flattered by the attention, despite knowing he was taking the piss.

'What's all that about?' asked Daniel.

Holly shook her head after Dimitri knocked on the window and mimed a coffee-drinking action through it.

'Office gossip.' She shrugged, not wanting to go into details. 'About some of our colleagues.'

'Why all the thing about coffee?' Daniel looked out of the window at Dimitri's departing back.

'One of the women I work with has just gone back to the presenter's flat, for a coffee.' Holly wondered if this would satisfy him.

She was tempted to explain how they'd discussed euphemisms and Dimitri had described her as safe. But she decided not to because, it began to dawn on her, she didn't want Daniel to think of her that way.

Chapter Twenty-One

'B LOODY HELL, WHO left those there?' Holly muttered as she tripped and nearly lost her balance coming down the stairs on her way to the kitchen.

She realised who had left them there, when she realised what they were; Mark's fairly new, but already dirty and smelly running shoes. He seemed to be taking running seriously. He'd been several times now and had a session with Daisy.

It was not yet 9 o'clock on Saturday morning. Holly had wondered where he was when she woke an hour earlier and found their bed empty. The space where he should have been was cold, as if long since vacated. Any thoughts about his whereabouts had quickly been replaced by making the most of his absence. There was no one snoring or pulling the bedclothes away from her, no half-hearted foreplay (Saturday morning had once been their preferred time to have sex). So Holly had an opportunity to enjoy a lie-in and think her own thoughts, without anyone asking what they were.

'I nearly broke my neck falling over your trainers,' she said blearily as she went into the kitchen, hoping to make herself a cup of tea and head back to bed.

'Good morning!' Mark sounded ridiculously up for this time in the day and ignored her rather grouchy greeting. 'Sleep well?'

'Have you been running?' Holly asked.

It was a rhetorical question; the trainers and the sweat-infused t-shirt gave her the answer.

'Four miles.' Mark beamed, obviously hoping she would share in his sense of achievement.

'That's great.' Holly tried to sound enthusiastic. 'You really are taking running the marathon seriously.'

She had expected him to lose interest after a few jogs around the park.

'I need to build up distance gradually,' Mark said, with the air of a seasoned pro. 'And try to improve my times as well.'

This was not the talk of someone who was about to give up.

'Where did you go?' asked a voice which sounded much lovelier and softer than Holly felt.

She looked over at the table and noticed Chloe, behind a cereal packet, looking all fresh haired and gorgeous as she poured milk on the supermarket-brand cornflakes.

'Hello, love.' Holly hoped the pronounced change in her tone when she addressed their daughter was not as noticeable to Mark as it sounded to her. 'You're up early.'

'Yeah, I'm going out.' Chloe took a mouthful of cereal.

'Already?' Holly wondered where she was off to, so early on a Saturday morning, but doubted her daughter would tell her if she asked.

Chloe nodded and Mark saved her from further interrogation by filling them in on the details of his run.

'I ran up to the golf course, round Hollingbury Fort then back via your school, Chloe.' He paused momentarily and Holly was pretty sure deliberately too, to give his next words more dramatic effect. 'Four miles!'

'Wow, that's pretty impressive.' His utterance had had the right effect on Chloe. 'You've only been running a couple of weeks.'

Holly was going to say nothing but her daughter prompted her as she filled the kettle up.

'That's good, isn't it, Mum?'

'Did you actually go through Chloe's school?' Holly decided not to play up to his mid-life posturing. 'Isn't it locked at the weekend?'

'I went round.' Mark was looking slightly disappointed that his morning feat of endurance had provoked so little reaction from his wife.

'You can cut across the playing fields at the moment,' Chloe volunteered. 'Someone's pulled down a section of the fence on Surrenden Road.'

'Don't take offence,' Mark quipped.

Holly groaned inwardly as she filled the kettle up, only apparently it was outwardly as Chloe, usually the first to point up 'terrible Dad jokes', accused her of being unfair.

'That was funny, Mum.' Her daughter was giving her an angry look as she brought her now-empty cereal bowl over to the dishwasher.

'It was funny the first time.' Holly wondered why Chloe was suddenly being so defensive of Mark. 'But I've heard it before, quite a lot.'

'Yeah well . . .' Chloe's voice trailed off as she put her spoon in the cutlery rack. 'You could laugh sometimes, just to be polite.'

Holly was about to say something about not needing to be polite when you'd been married for sixteen years, but she stopped herself. It unnerved her that her fifteen-year-old daughter appeared to be giving her marriage guidance advice. Holly had thought the subtle putdowns or simply her lack of reaction to Mark went largely unnoticed, but this was obviously not the case.

Chloe was right. She ought to make more of an effort with Mark, for Chloe and Jake's sake, if not for his.

'Do you want a croissant?' She hoped this would suffice as a peace offering.

'No, thanks,' Chloe said.

Holly switched the radio on as she busied herself with the croissants.

A husband and wife were talking about how they had met. They'd been on a climbing expedition in the Himalayas and the man had fallen and broken his leg. The weather was closing in and they needed to get down the mountain but he was slowing up the rest of the party so the woman had volunteered to stay with him, dig a snow hole for the night and start the descent again the following day. She was a doctor and had made a make-shift cast for his leg.

In the event the weather had not cleared and they'd been stuck there for several days.

'I knew that she would always stick by me,' the man was telling the radio interviewer. 'Because she stuck by me then.'

'That's really sweet,' Chloe commented, but Mark seemed cross.

'Most people would do that if they found themselves in those circumstances,' he growled. 'But not everyone does.'

'I have to go.' Chloe got up from the breakfast table.

'Do you know where she's off to?' Holly asked as their daughter breezed out of the kitchen.

'Somewhere with Scrabble Boy, I think,' Mark said.

Holly made a concerted effort to laugh now at the Scrabble Boy reference.

'Do you want a croissant?' she repeated. 'You must be hungry after a four-mile run.'

'Yes, please.' Mark hovered in the middle of the kitchen as Holly took some croissants out of a paper bag and stuck them on a baking tray. 'Oh, great – crescent ones. The best.'

'Is there a difference?' She lit the oven and stuck the tray in it. 'I mean, apart from the shape?'

'Straight ones are made with margarine, but the crescent-shaped ones are butter.' Mark was full of random information, some of it interesting. He was a one-man pub quiz trivia resource, always willing to point out that a banana plant was a shrub and not in fact a tree, and that there were three landlocked countries beginning with B on the African continent.

'Really, I never knew that?' This particular piece of information Holly did find interesting. 'It had never even occurred to me that there might be a reason for the difference in shape.'

'They are like women,' Mark said. 'Straight ones are margarine but curvy ones are butter.'

Holly, who was on the curvy side, had no idea what he meant. But as the mood seemed to have turned light and buttery, she wondered if it might be some sort of verbal foreplay.

'Well, I am going to take my tea and buttery croissant back to bed,' she told her husband. 'Do you want to come?'

She wondered what would happen if he did.

'I don't think so.' There was an edge to Mark's voice, which Holly was not quite sure how to translate. 'I'm kind of up now.' He gestured towards his t-shirt and tracksuit bottoms as if the wearing of them made it impossible for him to go back to bed. 'And I was going to have a look at the guttering this morning. It's been driving me mad, dripping every time it rains.'

'OK.' Holly knew his reluctance to follow her upstairs was partly her fault. She hadn't done much recently to prop up his flagging self-esteem, but Chloe's earlier dig had nudged her and she was trying to make amends.

'Why don't you get a man to fix the gutter?' she suggested.

'I am a man,' Mark snapped.

'I know.' Holly was slightly taken aback. 'I just meant you

could get an odd job man and not have to spend your weekend dealing with it.'

'It won't take me long.' Mark was adamant. 'And I am perfectly capable of doing it myself.'

'I know,' she said, on the defensive now. 'I just thought it might be easier to get someone in.'

'I'm perfectly capable of clearing the gutter and fixing it too, if necessary.' Mark had his hands on his hips, as if squaring up for a fight. 'I know you seem to think I'm not up to much these days, Holly, but I'm doing my best.'

'I don't know what you mean,' she faltered.

She did know what he meant. She had been treating him, not exactly badly, but dismissively. She wondered how things could seem to change so quickly. This time last year she would have described herself and Mark as happy. Now she wasn't so sure. They weren't unhappy but they were definitely coming unstuck.

'Oh, I think you do,' he said bitterly, and made towards the back door. 'I'm going to get the ladder out of the shed. You take your croissant upstairs and leave mine in the oven. I'll have it when I've finished being a man.'

Chapter Twenty-Two

Natalie appeared unusually anxious to be away from work. 'I need to leave by five-thirty today.' She looked at the clock on the wall of the meeting room. 'So, are we finished here?'

'I think so.' Katherine began gathering various bits of paper, which seemed to signal the weekly ideas meeting was at an end. 'Going anywhere nice?'

'What?' Natalie seemed unable to think why she might be going anywhere nice. Then she realised that as far as workaholic Katherine was concerned, leaving early implied something worth leaving early for.

'Me? Oh, no, just home.' Natalie's answer had the predictable effect of causing Katherine to raise her eyebrows ever so slightly. The reaction would have been barely discernible to a passer-by but those who worked with her on a daily basis were attuned to her indications of displeasure.

Natalie ignored her and picked up her things to leave, providing a cue for the rest of the team to do the same.

Holly wondered if Natalie had taken the recent discussion about house husbands personally.

It had arisen when Dimitri had suggested they interview Claire Jacobs, a detective novelist, whose books aimed at teenagers were now topping the bestseller lists.

'I don't think so,' Katherine had dismissed the idea. 'We'll leave that to *Front Row*.'

And that would have been it, if Darling had not mentioned that he'd met Claire Jacobs at a literary festival once.

'She's a bit of a witch,' he'd said.

'A bitch or a witch?' Dimitri had asked.

'Well, both,' James had told them. 'She was laying into her poor husband in his absence as if he were a complete no hoper.'

'What does her husband do?' Holly had asked.

'Well, that was her gripe,' Darling said. 'He looks after their children while she writers her bestsellers, but she seems to resent him for it.'

Holly said nothing more because she found herself sympathising with Claire Jacobs. She wondered how many women really were content with role reversal, and how many, even if they worked, would rather their partners were also eagerly pursuing their careers.

She looked up and caught Natalie's eye but looked away as Rebecca spoke up.

'I read that house husbands are five times as likely to have affairs as other men.'

'And how likely are other men to have affairs?' Dimitri had asked, winking at her as he spoke.

'I don't remember.' Rebecca smiled to herself.

'Dimitri, can I have a word?' Katherine stopped him as he headed for the door. 'It won't take a minute.'

'Wonder what that's about?' Rebecca mused as the rest of them headed towards the lift.

'Probably just making sure he doesn't try to leave before it's dark,' Darling said, raising his eyebrows in an expression no one could possibly miss. 'What are you heading home for, Natalie? Anything nice?'

'No,' she giggled. 'Twins' bath and bedtime. Guy has started going to the gym on Wednesday evenings and it's more trouble than it's worth making him miss it.'

'Fuck! That reminds me . . .' Darling's expletive caused eyebrows to be raised a third time in as many minutes by an elderly man who emerged from the lift as it arrived and the doors opened.

'Reminds you of what?' Natalie asked, as they all piled in.

'I'm supposed to get home early too,' he replied, pushing the button for the sixth floor.

Now it was Rebecca's turn to raise her eyebrows. She caught Holly's eye across the lift and moved them in a gesture that was clear enough. It implied, Natalie has to leave early, Darling has to leave early, what do we make of that then?

Holly suspected Darling had seen her face in the mirror at the back of the lift.

'Mila has a sculpting class to go to,' he said, as if in answer to Rebecca's unasked question.

'I didn't know she sculpted,' Holly said, realising she knew very little about Darling's wife other than the odd thing he threw into the general discussion, which was usually something to do with her attitude to childcare.

'Well, it's a relatively new thing,' said Darling as the lift doors opened and they began dispersing. 'She used to do a bit of stone carving but this is working with bronze or something . . .'

He reached the door of his office and began unlocking it.

'See you tomorrow then.' Natalie touched his arm briefly as she walked past, causing him to turn.

'Yes, have fun in the bath,' he said, responding to her touch by putting his hand on her shoulder and running it down her arm as far as her elbow.

'I doubt it.' Natalie smiled as she moved on towards the office she and Holly shared.

'I didn't know Mila sculpted,' Holly said, following her in.

'Yeah, she's an artist.' Natalie was beginning to gather up stuff, ready to go home. 'Or, at least, she was. She doesn't really do anything any more.'

'She does if she's going to sculpting classes.' Holly thought Natalie was being slightly dismissive of Darling's wife.

'I mean professionally,' Natalie said. 'At one stage she used to sell quite a lot of stuff. That's how they met. Have you seen my phone?'

'It's on your desk,' Holly pointed. 'How did they meet?'

'Oh, yes.' Natalie put the phone in her bag. 'They met at one of Mila's exhibitions, at a gallery in Cork Street. James was a business reporter at the time and he was doing a piece on investing in art. Mila was the hot young next big thing.'

'Really?' Holly was impressed. It was strange, she thought, how easily women were reclassified once they became mothers. She had never heard James refer to Mila as anything other than a wife and mother, and yet she must have been ... no, she corrected her thoughts, still was . . . a talented artist. 'That's really impressive.'

'Well, she doesn't do anything any more.' Natalie put Mila firmly back in her box.

'I don't suppose she has a lot of time,' Holly said. 'What with the boys and . . .'

'And what?' Natalie asked.

'And James not being around much.' Holly wondered if her friend would jump to his defence. 'I imagine his career comes first and Mila gets left with most of the childcare.'

'Their children are at school.' Natalie put the emphasis on 'are', as if these few hours a day left Mila more than enough time to get her career back on track. 'And she does write a bit. For art-history journals or something.'

'She can't have much time left to do her own work then,' Holly mused. 'Kids take up an awful lot of time when they're young.'

'I do know that,' Natalie said crossly. 'I have got two of my own, in case you'd forgotten.'

'Of course not.' Holly tried to inject some warmth into her voice while she thought to herself that Natalie didn't really know.

Natalie checked her watch, which, it occurred to Holly, was not something she often did. She hardly ever rushed to pick the twins up from nursery or get back before bedtime. She left most of that to Guy.

'I ought to be going.' She sat on the edge of her desk, showing no sign of following up her statement.

'So Guy's started going to the gym?' Holly tried to send her on her way. Her sympathies for the moment were with him. She remembered what it was like to have been at home with children all day.

Natalie nodded. 'Yes, they all seem to be at it. He started going a few weeks ago. Apparently there was some sort of deal at our local health club. I don't suppose it will last, though.'

'Why not?'

'Well, Guy keeps having these bursts of enthusiasm for various projects, but they never seem to amount to much.'

'I guess he doesn't have that much time,' Holly remarked.

'Don't start defending him. The twins go to nursery. He does fuck all a lot of the time, as far as I can tell.'

Holly decided to say nothing.

'What about Mark?' Natalie asked.

'What about him?' She didn't feel entirely comfortable talking to Natalie about Mark's current lack of direction.

'Is he still an aspiring marathon man?' Natalie asked, picking up her bag and standing up.

'He is actually. He seems to keep disappearing for the odd hour and arriving back hot and sweaty.'

'From running?' Natalie asked. Now it was her turn to raise her eyebrows.

'Well, if it's not running, it's something he does in running shoes and shorts,' Holly told her.

'Middle-aged men used to sleep with dumb blondes.' Natalie smiled. 'Now they cosy up with dumb-bells instead.'

'A good headline.' Holly could see it in *Men's Health* or one of the other magazines, which catered for middle-aged men's obsession with their bodies.

'I suppose it's better than having an affair.' Natalie appeared to concede Guy's entitlement to an evening in the gym and finally began to walk towards the door.

It was opened from the outside, before she had the chance to do it herself.

'Are we off then?' Holly heard Darling's voice, and then, as she shut the door, Natalie's reply.

'Yes. Let's go, shall we?'

Chapter Twenty-Three

'EXCUSE ME.' SUSAN had just yawned.

'Are we boring you, Gran?' Chloe asked.

'Of course not.' Susan straightened her back as if this would re-energise her. 'I just had a bit of a late night last night.'

Holly's mother and father were 'doing the rounds', spending a few days visiting friends and relatives on the South Coast before returning home to Northampton.

First stop was lunch with Holly and family, then on for a night in Chichester. The following day would be spent with an old colleague of Patrick's he insisted he had never liked, but whose wife Susan claimed as a good friend. Then they'd have a night with Fay, in Reading.

Holly knew these visits were arranged by her mother. Her father, given the choice, would happily stay at home and never see anyone at all. Patrick was five years older than Susan but sometimes it seemed liked fifteen. He seemed to get very tired and had little appetite for keeping up with old friends, never mind making new ones.

Holly looked at him closely now, as he sat at the dinner table, and wondered if he was OK or if her sister was right and he was ill. He looked quite normal to her.

'What were you doing last night?' Jake was spinning his knife around on the table while they waited for Holly to dish out their lunch.

'She went to the theatre with her new chums,' Patrick said, and Holly noticed that he reached out his hand instinctively to stop Jake playing with his cutlery. Then, as if he'd remembered this was not his child, he put it back on his lap.

'I've joined a theatre club.' Susan beamed at them all as they sat around the table. 'They do block bookings for shows, so we get discounts for whatever's on at the Playhouse and every now and then we go on a trip to London. We went to see a Japanese play with subtitles at the South Bank last night.'

'No wonder you're tired,' Jake said. 'A Japanese play would send anyone to sleep.'

'Your grandmother is tired because she got on the wrong train home,' Patrick said quietly.

'We misread the platform number.' Susan shrugged, implying that it was easy enough to do. 'Ended up getting on a train to Cambridge and having to change.'

'Do you remember when Mark went to a meeting in the wrong country?' Holly put a steaming dish of chicken casserole down at the end of the table.

'Did he?' Susan sounded surprised, although Holly was sure they must have heard this story before. At one time it had been a favourite mealtime anecdote of Mark's.

'You tell it, Mark.' She smiled at her husband, anticipating that he would relish the chance to tell one of his funnier stories.

'I'm sure they've heard it before.' He looked reluctant. 'Jake, don't do that.'

Jake had picked his fork up and was holding it to his eye, staring through the steam from the casserole at Chloe. It was a habit he'd started when he was about three and had never seemed to grow out of. Whenever there was anything that produced steam on the table, he was instantly compelled to pick up his fork and look at his sister through it.

'Yes. Stop it, Jake, you retard.' It infuriated Chloe, which was probably one of the reasons he found it hard to give up.

'Chloe!' Her grandmother instantly admonished her for her use of the word 'retard'. She'd become aware of political correctness in her later years. Patrick was mystified by the twenty-first century and its new use of language and still said things like 'Is he a queer?' and referred to black men as 'coloured chaps'.

'I don't think we've heard about your meeting in the wrong country,' Susan switched the subject back again.

'It was a long time ago.' Mark sounded slightly irritated now and got up to take some wine out of the fridge.

'It's really funny.' Chloe encouraged him to tell the story too.

'You tell them then, if everyone wants to hear it.' Mark sounded distinctly surly. Holly hoped her parents hadn't noticed.

'Dad and Chris were going to a meeting in Stockholm,' Chloe started. 'You know, Chris who he used to work with?'

'Yes, we remember,' Susan spoke for them both, although Holly suspected her father would have no memory of Chris.

He had joined Mark a year after he'd first set up his own marketing and PR Company. The work was coming in thick and fast and Mark could not cope with it all on his own. They'd soon taken on another permanent member of staff, Fiona, and contracted a couple of freelancers as business boomed.

A few years after that, Chris had left to set up his own company, taking Fiona with him and marrying her while he was at it. Mark had been gracious about letting them go but didn't mention Chris or what he was up to much these days. Holly wondered if his company was doing well and if he and Fiona were still together.

'They got a taxi from the airport and when they got to the headquarters of the company, where their meeting was, it was dead quiet and there was just one man sitting at the reception desk,' Chloe told them.

'Oh, yeah!' Jake suddenly seemed to have remembered this story too.

'They said they'd come to meet with the managing director.' Chloe paused slightly before delivering the punchline. 'And the reception guy said, "But he is in Copenhagen!"'

'They'd flown to Stockholm instead of Copenhagen,' Jake added, for the benefit of anyone who'd missed this.

'We were always flying back and forth between Sweden and Demark at the time,' Mark said defensively. 'More wine, Patrick?'

'Oh yes, please.' Patrick moved his glass a fraction across the table.

'I suppose that must have happened a lot.'

'Never,' Holly interjected. 'You asked the man on reception that, didn't you, Mark?'

She paused but he said nothing. So she continued, doing her best to put on a Scandinavian accent.

'I have worked here for fifty years and never before has this happened!'

They all laughed, except Mark. It was a good story and, in the days when he used to tell it at dinner parties, he'd done so to greater comic effect than either Chloe or Holly could muster. Today he appeared to be embarrassed by the incident.

'That was in the days before *Yuppienalle*,' Mark commented, trying to interest them all in something else.

'What?' Chloe and Jake asked in unison.

'Mobile phones,' Mark said. 'Or "yuppie teddies", as the Swedes used to call them, because they were like security blankets for yuppies, when they first came out.'

Patrick laughed.

'This is lovely.' Holly's mother sensed the subject needed

changing and switched it to the food. 'What's the sauce with the chicken?'

'Tomatoes, olives, chilies and capers,' Holly told her. 'It's a Jamie Oliver recipe.'

'I got it off the internet, Gran,' Chloe told her. 'You could look it up. It's on jamieoliver. com.'

'Oh, yeah. How's your laptop, Gran?' Jake was suddenly interested in the conversation.

'I don't know how I ever managed without it, Jake,' she said. 'There's so much you can find out so easily, and of course I can find out what you're up to by looking at Facebook.'

Holly was surprised that Chloe and Jake had accepted their gran as a friend. She had thought they would not want her to see some of the posts they put up, especially Chloe. But this generation seemed content to live their whole life in the glare of the internet and not be particularly bothered by who saw them living it. Secrets for them were virtual impossibilities.

'What have you discovered about Jake that you didn't already know?' Holly asked Susan now, but Mark cut in before she had time to answer.

'Holly never goes on Facebook, Susan. She thinks it's a waste of time.'

Holly decided not to tell him that she had been on earlier in the week and was likely to go on again soon to find out if he'd maintained Facebook contact with Daisy. Or anyone else for that matter.

'You haven't been tempted to join the digital age then, Granddad?' Jake was asking Patrick.

'He does have a mobile.' Patrick appeared not to have heard Jake, his hearing was getting worse, and so Susan answered for him. 'But he never seems to use it.'

'Really?' Jake raised his voice. 'Have you got a mobile, Granddad?'

'A yuppie teddy!' Patrick replied. 'Yes, I have. You'll be able to call me if I get lost again.'

He was referring to his long walk when they'd tried to call him on Holly's phone.

'I've tried that,' Susan said. 'When he's been out and I've been wondering where he's got to. He never answers, though.'

'Delicious!' Patrick said, bringing the subject back to the food.

'You have a Jamie Oliver restaurant in Brighton, don't you?' Susan asked. 'Have you been?'

'Yes, when it first opened. But we haven't been for a long time,' Holly told her. 'It was nice, though.'

'And I was reading about a very good vegetarian restaurant in the paper. Terra something or other.'

'Terre à Terre?' Holly said. 'I used to go a lot when I worked at Radio Sussex, but I haven't been recently. I'm told it's very good.'

'It's always very busy – apparently,' Chloe said.

'We should try that, Patrick,' Susan said enthusiastically. From where Holly was sitting, at the other end of the table, she couldn't be entirely sure but she thought she heard her father mutter, 'Must we?'

'It's really hard to get a table.' For some reason, Chloe seemed to want to steer them clear of the restaurant. 'You're better off going somewhere else.'

'Quite right,' Patrick said.

Holly suspected he was having trouble hearing everything that was being said but wanted to join in.

'So, Mark,' Patrick cleared his throat slightly, 'how's business going?'

'It's quite tough at the moment. Difficult times and all that,' Mark said quietly, trying to keep the conversation just between the two of them. 'But I might have a new client. An off-licence in Kemptown.'

'That sounds interesting,' Patrick said politely.

Holly wondered if her father remembered that, in the not-so-distant past, Mark's company had had a contract with one of the world's major drinks distributors. They'd decided to do their marketing in-house a few years ago. Holly sensed that while the off-licence in Kemptown was work that he needed, it also served as a reminder to Mark of his more illustrious client. She didn't tell her parents that he was thinking of giving up his office and working on Sean's account from the table they were sitting around now.

'No more karaoke in Taiwan then?' Patrick said, proving that he did enjoy and remember Mark's anecdotes.

'Karaoke in Taiwan?' Jake obviously didn't remember this one.

'I used to go on a lot of business trips to Taiwan,' Mark said, apparently happy to dust down this story for the benefit of the assembled company.

'It was when you were much younger, Jake. The Taiwanese were very civilised by day, but at night, when we did research trips to various bars and clubs, they were a different breed.'

'Research?' Chloe interjected.

'Yes, Chloe,' Mark continued. 'It was a hard job but someone had to do it. Anyway, my Taiwanese colleagues used to drink me under the table and I found it hard to keep up.'

'I find that hard to believe,' Jake said.

'It was rude to refuse a drink.' Mark ignored his son. 'But there were always karaoke machines everywhere. If I went to wait my turn to perform, then I could have a bit of a break from whisky. Taiwan is the only place where I have found myself jumping up and queueing to sing "I Will Survive" to a room full of businessmen!'

They all laughed.

'That's funny,' Holly said, hoping to make up for having brought up the 'meeting in the wrong country' scenario earlier.

'Holly never actually laughs any more,' Mark said. His tone was even but she suspected that had her parents not been present, he might have injected some bitterness into it. 'She just says if she thinks things are funny.'

Holly was about to protest but realised that there was some truth in what he said. She laughed at other people's jokes, but she didn't seem to find Mark funny any more. She wondered if this was just because she'd heard most of his stories before and knew his humour so well that she could predict where he was going with new ones, or if it was part of the general malaise in their marriage.

'Susan and I had lunch in a public house last week.' As a rule, Holly's father didn't like abbreviations, even ones as common as 'pub'. 'And when I asked for the menu, they gave me one for all the drinks they stocked behind the bar. We were hoping for some food, but we had to go to the restaurant for that.'

'They've started doing that in a quite a few places,' Mark told him.

'I had a quick look and one of the things they sold was whisky from the Corkney Islands!' Patrick said.

'That's funny,' Mark said, without seeming to realise he was doing what he'd just accused Holly of. 'It sounds like an island where they sent East End evacuees during the war!'

Holly laughed out loud and got up to clear the empty plates.

'Did you know Dad is going to run a marathon?' Jake asked his grandmother as Holly scraped the plates and put them in the dishwasher.

'Really? How very impressive,' Susan said.

'Well, I've only just started training. We'll see if I make it. But it's good to have a goal.'

Holly took out a strawberry pavlova from the fridge.

'What is it?' Jake asked as she put it on the table. He never wanted to try anything unless he knew exactly what it was.

'Pavlova.'

'Aren't you supposed to ring a bell before bringing it out?' quipped Mark.

'What?' Jake asked. Holly knew he'd heard the Pavlov's dog quip many times before. Mark said the thing about ringing a bell first every time they had it.

'That looks lovely,' her mother said, admiring the pudding. Then, as if it warranted an announcement, she made one.

'We have some news,' she said, looking slightly nervously at Patrick as she said this.

Holly sat down again. A slight feeling of panic came over her. She hoped neither of them was ill. Perhaps Fay had been right and there was something up with Patrick.

'You don't have to look so worried,' her mother said.

'I . . .' Holly was not quite sure what to say so she waited for her mother's news.

'I'm going to Thailand for four months,' Susan announced.

'Oh,' Holly said. 'That sounds lovely. When will you go?'

'I was planning to leave in September. Or late August, so that I'm back in December. I don't really want to leave Patrick on his own for Christmas.'

That took Holly aback, not least because Susan sounded as if she were talking about leaving a dog behind rather than her husband of forty-plus years.

'Oh,' she said again. 'Dad's not going with you then?'

'Not really my sort of thing,' Patrick said. His tone didn't give away what he felt about his wife going off on her own.

'I suppose not.' Holly was not sure exactly how to interpret this piece of information. She stuck a knife into the pavlova and wondered if her mother sometimes found her father as difficult to be with as she was finding Mark.

'But won't you be lonely, Dad?' she asked. 'And how will you manage?'

Her father hadn't cooked anything more elaborate than a boiled egg in the past forty years, and he couldn't survive on boiled eggs for four months.

'Oh, I'm sure people will rally round and cook for him,' Susan said, in a voice which hinted that she thought this conversation was at an end.

Chapter Twenty-Four

'HERE SHE IS now!' James Darling looked up from Holly's desk and told whoever he was talking to on her phone that she'd just arrived at work. 'She's just walked through the door. She looks a bit wet.'

Holly made a face and mouthed, 'Who is it?' as she took off her coat and pushed rain-soaked hair off her face.

'It's your sister Fay,' he told her, and then continued the conversation he appeared to be having quite happily with Holly's elder sibling. 'She's just de-robing, Fay. Her coat is off. Her sweater is coming off . . . Holly, stop, I can't take any more!'

Holly raised her eyebrows at Natalie who was watching Darling as he chatted to her sister. She had a plate on her lap and was picking croissant crumbs from it and putting them in her mouth.

'Give it to me!' Holly said, putting her hand out to take the phone. She didn't trust Darling not to start asking Fay all sorts of things about what she'd been like when she was little.

'Nice talking to you, Fay,' James said, holding up a finger in a 'one minute' gesture to Holly. 'Your little sister wants to take over now . . . You too. 'Bye.'

Holly took the phone and motioned to James to get off her chair too. He made a great play of the effort involved, before finally standing up and going to sit on Natalie's desk.

'Oh, and your husband called too,' he mouthed as Holly picked up the phone. 'Can you call him?'

She nodded and began talking to her sister.

'Hello, Fay?' Holly's tone was questioning because it was unusual for Fay to call during office hours. Her job was not the sort that allowed her to take or make personal calls at work. 'How are you?' Holly asked. 'Did you get on OK with Mum and Dad?'

'Who was that who answered the phone?' Fay asked now, ignoring her question about their parents.

'Oh, that was James Darling. He presents the programme.' Holly looked over to where Darling sat perched on Natalie's desk. He was fiddling with her bag and, she suspected, still half-listening to her conversation with her sister.

Natalie had her back to Holly but she appeared to sense her glance in their direction and tapped James on the leg.

'Let's go and get more coffee,' she whispered, nodding her head in Holly's direction. She obviously thought she could do with some privacy.

'Sure,' James slid off the desk, brushing briefly against Natalie as he did so.

If he'd behaved like that with Holly, she would have considered it an invasion of her space. Natalie didn't seem to mind or even notice.

'He's got a lovely voice,' Fay said. 'Very deep and masculine.'

Holly checked herself. She'd been about to say something along the lines of 'I didn't think you went in for deep masculine voices', but realised this was just the sort of thing her parents might say.

'Yes,' she replied, and paused until the door clicked firmly behind Darling and Natalie. 'It's completely at odds with the rest of his appearance.'

'Really?' Fay sounded surprised. 'He sounds as if he might look like George Clooney.'

'That is the beauty of radio,' Holly told her. 'In fact, he looks like a paler, balder, bespectacled and bearded Tom Cruise.'

'Not a very flattering picture,' Fay said.

'Quite accurate though,' Holly continued. 'Sometimes we get listeners writing in asking for signed photos of him and I worry they may stop listening when they find out what he actually looks like.'

'Do Radio Four listeners really write in for signed photos?' Fay commented.

'You'd be surprised,' Holly said. 'Do you remember Uncle George?'

George was their mother's brother-in-law. He had died when they were in their twenties and their aunt had remarried a car salesman, and left the pub in Dorset which they had run together.

'What about him?' Fay asked.

'Oh, I was just reminded of him telling me one day how he always used to close the pub and then listen to *Woman's Hour*,' Holly told her sister.

'Well, I certainly wouldn't have had him down as a *Woman's Hour* man,' Fay commented.

'Nor me.' Holly had thought it completely out of character. 'But then he told me he used to watch Jenni Murray when she presented the news on BBC South and was rather taken with her looks – and in particular her bust.'

'Bust' was not the word Uncle George had used, Holly realised, continuing. 'When she left BBC South he followed her career with great interest. And ended up hardly ever missing an episode of *Woman's Hour*!'

'That's so sexist,' Fay said, as Holly had anticipated she would.

'I know,' Holly agreed, 'but it just goes to show that not everyone is listening to Radio Four for the content.'

Lizzie Enfield

'S'pose not,' Fay agreed. 'Anyway, I didn't call to talk about radio presenters.'

'No, I thought not if you're calling from work,' Holly said. 'Did you want to talk about Mum and Dad?'

She wondered what Fay had made of the news that their mother planned to spend several months in Thailand on her own.

'No, why?' Fay sounded as if she could think of no reason why she would want to talk about their parents.

'I presume Mum told you she was off travelling?' Holly flicked her computer on as she chatted to her sister.

'Oh, yes, that,' Fay said, as if it was of no importance.

'Don't you think it's a bit odd?' Holly asked her, typing her login with one finger.

'No, not really. She just wants to do her own thing for bit,' Fay replied. 'They *are* worried about you, though. They asked me to talk to you.'

'Why are they worried about me?' Holly said, feeling defensive. She was used to them worrying about Fay. 'I cooked a nice lunch.'

'Yes, of course you did.' Both sisters knew their mother judged them largely on the basis of what they produced at mealtimes. Accordingly they did their best when their parents visited. 'It's not your culinary skills they're worried about. It's you and Mark.'

'They don't need to worry about us.' Holly hoped Fay hadn't picked up the slight defensiveness that had crept into her voice. She tried to inject a bit of light-heartedness into it.

'Dad ought to be worrying about Mum going off to Thailand, and Mum should worry about how Dad will cope if he's left on his own.'

'Seriously,' Fay said. 'Apparently Mark had a chat with Dad after dinner, when he was showing him how to send an email.'

'Really?' Holly recalled Mark telling Patrick he would show him, so that he could communicate with Susan while she was away.

'Yes,' her sister said. 'Mark told Dad he was worried about you. He said you're working really long hours and you don't talk to him any more.'

'I do talk to him,' Holly said, knowing this wasn't entirely true. She hadn't had a proper talk with her husband for a long time. But they passed the time of day.

'What did Dad say?' she asked.

'He probably asked how many days emails took to get there,' Fay joked. 'You know what he's like. He doesn't like to talk about anything remotely personal.'

'I know.' Holly recalled another phone conversation with her sister following the weekend she had told their parents she was gay.

Fay had told her, 'I went into the sitting room and said to Dad as a precursor to my news, "We don't really talk, do we, Dad?" And he said, "No," and left the room!'

Fay had then had to force her parents to sit down and listen to what she had to say.

'Mum said you looked tired as well,' she said to Holly now.

'I am tired,' Holly told her. 'It's tiring going up and down to London nearly every day. And I'm not sleeping very well at the moment. I think it's the light mornings.'

'Or you might be suffering from post-traumatic stress?' The psychologist in her sister reared her head.

'From having Mum and Dad to lunch?' Holly joked.

'No, you know what I mean.' Fay had adopted her serious elder sister tone. 'After the crash. I know you *say* you are fine and you've been carrying on, but sometimes these things affect you in different ways; like not sleeping, and not being able to have functioning relationships.'

'I have functioning relationships all over the place.' Holly began to feel angry.

'OK, fine.' Fay sounded unconvinced. 'But if Mark's worried about you, perhaps you need to reassure him. It would probably do you good to talk to someone, Holly. Though I realise that someone is probably not your interfering older sister.'

'Sorry,' Holly said, realising Fay probably didn't want to have this conversation any more than she did. 'I didn't mean to snap. It just annoys me that people assume anything slightly wrong must be down to the fact I was in a train crash. Mark's not been easy to live with since his business started having problems, you know.'

'I realise that,' Fay said sympathetically. 'I know it can't be easy for you, being the main breadwinner and doing all the family stuff as well. I don't suppose Mark does all the things you used to do when you were at home?'

'Of course not.' Holly sometimes envied her sister, living with another woman. They were the only people she knew who actually shared domestic chores equally. 'But he thinks he does.'

'It might be worth giving the counselling another go,' Fay said gently.

'It won't help make Mark do the washing up,' Holly joked, but Fay didn't react. 'Did Dad say he thought I should have counselling?'

'No, of course not!' her sister laughed. They both knew this was an unlikely scenario.

'Dad thought you seemed fine,' she conceded. 'He was just passing on Mark's concerns. To be honest . . .'

'What?' Holly challenged her to be just that.

'I thought maybe you could do with talking to someone outside the family about what happened. And about what's going on at home too.'

'There is someone I talk to,' Holly said, and wondered if the family grapevine had heard via Mark that she'd been meeting up with Daniel.

Holly remembered when she'd finished talking to Fay that she needed to call Mark too. She wasn't sure if he would have gone into his office or still be at home so she tried him on his mobile.

'Hello.' Mark sounded breathless when he picked up.

'Hello. It's me,' she identified herself.

'Yes?' Mark sounded distracted.

'Are you OK?' she asked.

'Yes, I'm just on my way somewhere. Was there something you wanted?'

'You called me earlier,' Holly told him. 'Darling said you wanted me to call you back.'

'Oh, yes.' Mark cleared his throat and Holly wondered if his slight breathlessness was because he was out running. 'Only to say that Fay called. She said she'd try you at work.'

'I've spoken to her,' Holly told him, wondering why he didn't tell her he was out running, if he was. Perhaps he thought she'd be pissed off that he wasn't at work.

'Everything OK?' Mark asked her.

'Yes. Fine.' This conversation didn't seem to be going anywhere.

'Good.' Mark sounded very distant now. 'See you later then.'

Chapter Twenty-Five

'I'M GLAD YOU arrived first.' Daniel was already nursing a pint at a table in the corner when Holly arrived at The Shakespeare's Head.

He stood up and kissed her and she was immediately glad that they'd decided to have a drink here and not just try to talk awkwardly on the train.

'Anne-Marie is coming then?' Holly asked.

'Yes. She said she might be a few minutes late. Can I get you a drink?' Daniel half stood up.

'You're all right,' Holly said, sitting down with her back to the entrance. 'I'll wait for Anne-Marie to arrive and then get us both one.'

'This feels a bit odd, doesn't it?' Daniel said what Holly was thinking. 'Arranging to meet someone we hardly know. All the rules of commuting have suddenly gone out of the window.'

'Yes, I know what you mean.' Holly lowered her voice. 'I feel desperately sorry for Anne-Marie, but at the same time I'm not really sure that I want to get involved. Does that sound selfish?'

'No.' Daniel leaned forward and touched her arm. She thought it was a gesture of understanding, then realised he was nodding his head towards the door, alerting her to Anne-Marie's arrival.

'Hello.' She approached their table and pulled the spare seat back. 'I hope I'm not too late?'

'No,' Holly said, giving what she hoped was a welcoming smile. 'I've only just got here, though Daniel is on his third pint.'

He grinned, and Anne-Marie looked confused.

'I'm joking,' Holly said, wondering if every encounter with Anne-Marie was going to be riddled with such misunderstandings. She stood up. 'But you and I do need to do some catching up. What would you like to drink?'

'It still seems quite early to be drinking.' Anne-Marie looked a little hesitant. 'I'll have a small glass of white wine, please.'

Holly went to the bar, leaving Daniel to the small talk. When she came back he was saying something about ensuring computer systems met needs. Anne-Marie must have asked what he did.

'There you are.' Holly put the glass on a beer mat in front of Anne-Marie and sat down next to Daniel. 'Cheers!'

'Cheers!' they all chorused, and then there was a moment of awkward silence.

'So . . .' began Holly, although she had not yet thought of anything to say. Anne-Marie was also saying 'So' at the same time.

They both stopped and did a bit of 'you first'-ing. Anne-Marie was more insistent and Holly had to go first.

'What made you decide to go to the meeting?' she came up with. She hadn't intended to ask this but couldn't think of anything else. 'Had you been to any others?'

'No.' Anne-Marie didn't seem put out by her probing. 'That was the first. I might go to the next one perhaps, if you are? I'd

heard there were a couple of other meetings not long after . . .
I didn't think I should go to them, because I wasn't actually on
the train myself . . .'

Her voice trailed off.

'That was my first too,' Holly said. 'I felt a bit of a fraud
because I wasn't hurt or anything. Daniel thought the same.'

She stopped, thinking she should let him speak for himself.
He'd previously implied he felt that, but she didn't really know
if this was the case.

'Are you both married?' Anne-Marie asked, looking from Holly
to Daniel.

In other circumstances, the question might have seemed out
of place but, as they knew they were only meeting now because
of the accident in which Anne-Marie had lost her husband, it
seemed perfectly natural.

Holly, however, felt slightly guilty answering in the affirma-
tive. It felt indecent to flaunt the fact they both had spouses when
Anne-Marie no longer had hers.

'Yes,' she said, tentatively.

'Yes,' Daniel answered, at the same time, with more
conviction.

'How long?' Anne-Marie asked.

'Five years,' he said.

'Sixteen years,' Holly said, wondering if that must seem like
an eternity to Daniel.

'I thought when I saw you both at the meeting that you might
be married to each other,' Anne-Marie said. 'And when I saw
you sitting on the train.'

'I'm far too old,' Holly said quickly, feeling embarrassed and
wondering if Daniel felt the same.

'So how do you know each other?'

'We met on the train,' he said, looking at Holly as if he needed her permission to say exactly how they'd come to know each other.

'We were sitting in the same carriage when the train stopped in the tunnel that day.' Holly didn't want to tell Anne-Marie what had happened but didn't really see how she could avoid it. 'I got trapped when the carriage turned over. Daniel stayed with me until the fire crews arrived.'

She didn't like being forced to recall the exact moment when the carriage was hit by the other train and the ensuing chaos.

She could feel it now, the terror she had experienced when she realised that people were trying to clamber out of the carriage and she was stuck.

'Can anyone hear me?' she remembered asking, and wondering why she didn't just yell, 'Help!'

'Are you OK?' Daniel had asked.

She hadn't been able to move. She didn't feel hurt but her leg was stuck underneath something. Her whole being was screaming at her to get out, and she couldn't, and if she didn't she had no idea what might happen.

'Where are you?' Daniel's voice had asked again, and she'd sensed a hand moving in the darkness and finding hers.

It had seemed like hours that they'd stayed like that, time in which Holly wondered at the selflessness of this man. She'd thought of Mark and Chloe and Jake and how much she wanted to see them again. He must be thinking the same about somebody, she'd thought. He must be as desperate to get out as I am, but she'd held on to him and he hadn't left.

Holly took a long sip of wine now and stared at the table. She felt upset with Anne-Marie for having made her go back to that moment, and in retaliation decided to ask her a direct question.

'Where was your husband? Was he on the same train as us, or

the one that hit us?' Her voice sounded harsh as she said it. She wasn't sure why she was so cross.

'I'm not sure exactly.' Anne-Marie sounded upset.

'How long were you married?' Daniel asked.

Holly couldn't look at him when he asked this. She didn't want him to be angry with her for asking the question she had, but when she did look up he caught her eye and smiled, as if he understood.

'Three years,' Anne-Marie said quietly. 'I thought we'd be together for ever.'

I tried to find out a bit more about Holly and Daniel before I went to meet them this evening. I Googled them both, but very little came up. Daniel was simply listed on his company's website as a systems analyst. Holly is credited with producing programmes for the BBC, but there was nothing else out there, so I tried Facebook again.

She still hasn't responded to my friend request, but I'm not going to let this bother me. She obviously hardly ever uses the site. I looked at the rest of her friends and am sure they are her family.

Jake, who must be her son, had pictures of himself with her on what looks like a family holiday. In one they are walking along a cliff top, waving at the camera. In another they are sitting with their arms around each other beside a barbecue. And there were some of Holly with her daughter Chloe, paddling in the sea. They have their arms raised and look as if they might be dancing.

Chloe's page had the locked symbol and the thing saying she only shares some profile information with people who are not friends, but Mark's was full of stuff.

Mark Constantine – he must be her husband – has 292 friends. His family include Chloe and Jake Constantine, though strangely not Holly. Perhaps I am wrong about him being her husband, but I don't think so. He's into French cinema, likes stand-up comedy and Belgian fruit beers.

It's amazing what you can find out if people will let you, and Mark Constantine will let you.

Mark's recently been to the Old Market Arts Centre in Hove and the Komedia and had lunch at the Red Roaster Coffee House. I made a note of this. I thought I might go into Brighton at the weekend. I don't really know what to do with myself at weekends any more. So I thought I might do a bit of shopping and have lunch somewhere; try to be normal. I might try the Red Roaster. It's good to have a recommendation.

A lot of Mark's friends are women. I wondered if Holly knows or minds, and then I wondered if Mark knew how much time she seems to spend with this Daniel and why.

They were already in the pub when I arrived, looking quite cosy, so I asked them, when we'd all got a drink, 'Are you both married?'

I wanted to know the answer but also to remind them that, if they are, they already have someone. They don't need each other. They don't.

He looks nice, Holly's husband, Mark Constantine. She's lucky to have him and I don't want her to lose sight of that. I think that if we become friends then I must make sure I remind her of the importance of appreciating the person you are with, making sure they know how you feel about them, before it's too late.

Holly answered 'yes', but she said it in a way that made her sound as if she wasn't quite sure.

So I asked her how long and she said 'sixteen years', and I thought that was a long time, the sort of time after which you start taking things for granted.

So I decided to tell her, to warn her, how things looked from the outside.

'I thought when I saw you both at the meeting that you might be married to each other. And when I saw you sitting on the train.'

Holly said something about her being too old. But they both looked awkward, as if maybe they had something to hide.

Then she asked me about Geoff and there was something steely about her tone, as if she was deflecting attention from herself rather than asking me because she actually wanted to know how long we'd been together.

I thought back briefly to when I'd first met Geoff, the day my mother died.

My father had already been dead a couple of years and the realisation that I was now on my own in the world hadn't quite dawned. So it was with almost perfect timing that Geoff walked into my life within hours of my mother leaving it.

I'd been carrying on in a surprisingly normal way. I'd left the hospice, after sitting with Mum, holding her hand and listening to her struggling to breathe, until she stopped struggling and her hand began to go cold. And then I'd gone home, knowing that the next few weeks would be a round of sorting and organising, and that busying myself with funeral arrangements and sorting my parents' house would delay the grief for a while.

I hadn't counted on the kindness of strangers.

I'd stopped off at the supermarket on my way home. I'd spent so much time at the hospice that I hardly had any food left. As I was walking out of the revolving doors with several bags on each arm, someone tapped me on the shoulder and I turned round and there was Geoff.

I didn't hear what he'd said at first but when I did it all came out. I burst into tears and, within minutes, they were huge, vast, heaving sobs.

'Do you want my Nectar points?' was what he'd said. 'I don't collect them. Do you want mine?'

He had a soft lilting accent, which I couldn't quite place, and he looked at me expectantly as if he wanted me to have them. And that was what got me going.

'Thank you.' I tried to choke back the tears but I couldn't, and the man who was simply offering me unwanted Nectar points found himself dealing with a woman on the edge.

Geoff didn't seem to find this odd at all.

'Here, let me take your bags,' he said, and he slung them on top of his trolley. 'Then we'll find somewhere to sit down.'

He found a low wall outside the store. We sat on it and he asked my name and what was bothering me.

'Well, Anne-Marie,' he said, after we'd chatted for a while, 'it sounds as if you've had a hell of a few weeks and I would drive you home, but I don't want you getting in a car with strange man. So I'm going to call you a taxi instead and I'll pay for it. My treat. And I'm going to give you my number. And when you get home, I want you to put this fish pie for one . . .'

He held up the pie, which he'd found in one of my bags.

'I want you to put this in the oven, pour yourself a large glass of wine and text me to let me know how you are.'

He'd fished in his pocket and gave me a card with his name and numbers on.

'And if you think that I might be able to cheer you up, rather than reducing you to tears, you could call me some time and we'll go out for a coffee or something.'

It was an inauspicious start to our relationship, but it was the start.

'Three years,' I told Holly, when she asked how long we'd been married. 'I thought we'd be together for ever,' I told her, and tried to stress the 'ever' to make her understand.

Chapter Twenty-Six

THE PROSPECT OF a new client had put Mark in an exceedingly good mood. There was an energy to the way he was darting about the kitchen which had been lacking in recent months.

'How was your day?' he greeted Holly animatedly, unable to wait for her to settle back into home before sharing his potential good news. 'I might have a new client!'

'Really?' Holly could see from the zestful way he was taking the cork out of a new bottle of wine that he was excited by whoever it was. 'Who?'

'Jimmy Finlay?' He poured wine into the two glasses he had ready and waiting.

'What? The comedian?' Representing a comic would be a new direction for Mark and Jimmy Finlay was extremely popular. 'I love him. He's brilliant. What's he doing? How do you fit in?'

'I know.' They'd both been watching him on . . . *I Nearly Died* only a few days beforehand with Jake, and had found him very funny. 'Apparently he's going to run from Inverness, around the entire coast of Scotland, to raise awareness of heart disease. He wants a big PR campaign, to make sure everyone knows he's doing it.'

'Really?' Holly wondered if she'd got the names muddled up and was thinking of the wrong man. The Jimmy Finlay she was thinking of was a young Scottish comic who didn't look as if he'd be able to run for a bus, let along the entire circumference of Scotland.

'I know what you're thinking.' Mark picked up a glass and handed it to her. 'Cheers!'

'That I've got the wrong Jimmy Finlay?' Holly asked.

'I thought you'd be thinking that Jimmy Finlay is too fat to run anywhere!' he laughed. 'I mean the Jimmy Finlay we were watching on TV the other night.'

'The one that must be at least twenty stone and incredibly unfit,' Holly pointed out.

'The very same.' Mark still seemed excited by the prospect.

Holly feared it might never happen. If Jimmy Finlay ran anywhere in his current state, she thought he would probably have a heart attack. . . . *I Nearly Died* might suddenly take on a terrible irony. She didn't say this because she didn't want to hear Mark's irony joke.

'And why does he want to run round Scotland?' Holly didn't want to spoil Mark's moment but she couldn't help sounding a note of caution. 'Or think he will be able to?'

'Ah, well, that's the thing,' Mark said, using that peculiar English explain-all phrase.

He moved over to the work surface where he'd begun preparing dinner.

'Steak,' he said, indicating four slabs of meat marinating in something herby-looking.

'Lovely.' Holly still wanted to hear more about Jimmy Finlay.

'Apparently his father died recently of a heart attack.' Mark took a steak out and began hammering it with the tool designed for the purpose. 'He was only forty-five.'

'That's terrible!' Holly was genuinely shocked, both by the fact that Jimmy Finlay's father had died at such a young age and that Jimmy Finlay had a father who only a few months ago had been the same age as Mark.

'Awful,' he agreed. 'But it's given Jimmy a bit of a wake-up call and he's decided to get fit and do something to highlight the high rate of heart disease in Scotland. He's not planning to start the run until next year so he'll have time to get in shape.'

'As long as he doesn't have a heart attack too.' Holly could suddenly see a carefully orchestrated PR campaign going horribly wrong.

'Well, we'll just have to make sure he doesn't.' Mark had finished bashing steaks and was transferring them to the grill.

'So how might you come to be involved?' Holly brought the conversation back to its starting point.

'Well, that's the thing,' Mark said again, as if this alone explained something. 'He's started going to this gym in London, to try to get fit, and someone Daisy knows works there. He told her about it and Daisy told her that I was in marketing and . . .'

'So have you actually been in touch with him directly?' Holly was slightly confused by all the 'he said, she said' and she was worried that Mark was placing too much hope on a chat that someone else had had in a gym. She imagined someone like Jimmy Finlay already had someone to handle his PR and Mark might simply be clutching at straws.

'Yes,' he said emphatically. 'Daisy got his email address and I emailed him and said I'd be interested in pitching for the campaign, and he emailed back and said he'd looked at my website and knew that I was training for a marathon too, so that was a plus, and he hasn't got anyone else in mind and wants to meet me.'

'That's great.' Holly was pleased that Mark was at least getting to meet Jimmy Finlay and had been so pro-active. He generally made a good impression face to face and Jimmy Finlay would be a good client. If Mark got him, more work was bound to stem from it.

'When are you meeting? Have you set a date?'

'Next Wednesday.' Mark picked up his glass of wine and clinked Holly's. 'Cheers!'

'Cheers,' she said, looking at him. He seemed different in a way she couldn't quite put her finger on. Perhaps it was just that he seemed happy.

Holly knew that Mark had been worried about his lack of work, but she hadn't quite realised the extent of the impact on him personally.

Now that there was the prospect of something which might excite and stimulate him on the horizon, she could see the old Mark again, the will-do, energised, man of action that she'd first met. She smiled at her own mental description of him.

'What?' Mark was looking at her too.

'What do you mean, what?'

'What are you smiling at?' he asked.

'I am allowed to smile at you if I want to,' Holly said, and smiled again, an over-the-top wide grin.

She expected Mark to return the expression with an equally stupid face, but he put his glass down and walked over to her and kissed her. Holly closed her eyes, savouring the taste of her husband's lips. She realised she hadn't kissed him for ages.

It was nice. But it didn't last long. They were interrupted by the ear-piercing beep of the smoke alarm, in response to the charred steaks which Mark had forgotten were under the grill.

'Bugger!' He pulled away from Holly and took them out.

'Language!' Jake, who had been lying on the sofa, staring at the ceiling in the living room, had been roused from his state of torpor. 'What's for dinner?'

'Steak.' Mark inspected them. 'Well done.'

'Is it ready?' Jake eyed his father suspiciously.

'It was ready about five minutes ago,' Mark replied. 'Can you go and get Chloe? I think she's in her room.'

'That was a lovely evening,' Holly said to Mark later as he got into bed.

'Right down to the burned steaks!' He switched off the bedside light.

'I like them well done.' Holly moved towards his side of the bed as he got in. 'It was a pity Chloe missed dinner.'

'She is spending a lot of time with Ruaridh at the moment.' Mark put his arm tentatively around Holly. 'But he's a nice lad.'

'Yes, I just wish she'd spend a bit more time at home.' Holly wondered how the evening was going to end.

She was tired. They had watched television waiting for Chloe, who had been to the cinema with Ruaridh, to come home. But Mark's upbeat mood had infected Holly too and she'd enjoyed just being with him, without the children. Now he was slipping his hand under the vest she wore to bed.

'We could all benefit from spending a bit more time together,' he said, running his hand across her stomach and pausing as if expecting Holly to push him away or turn over.

'Yes.' She reached out and began to caress her husband, thinking that perhaps they should try and go away for a weekend.

'Daniel said he and Daisy are going to Southwold for a couple of days.' He had mentioned this in passing at some point during the week and Holly wondered if Daisy had also told Mark.

She intended this statement to be a precursor to suggesting they should get away themselves

It had the opposite effect.

'Bloody hell!' Mark sounded angry. He rolled away from her.

'What?' Holly had no idea what had provoked this sudden mood swing.

'I thought we might be going to have sex for the first time in God knows how long,' he said. 'And then you have to go and mention Daniel.'

'I was just going to suggest that we should go away too.' Holly kept her tone neutral. She didn't think she had anything to apologise for.

'What, with Daniel and Daisy?' Mark's tone was now sarcastic.

'No, of course not,' Holly tried not to rise to the bait.

'Because from where I am standing,' Mark said as he began to get out of bed, 'it seems Daniel can do no wrong and I can do no right.'

Holly said nothing.

She began to formulate a defence in her head. Daniel was a good friend to her, and Mark's insecurities about work had nothing to do with him. She was working all hours and doing everything she could to keep the family afloat. That was why they hadn't had sex in a long time.

Plus, she thought, as she looked at Mark taking his dressing gown from the back of their bedroom door, he had spent much of their evening saying how fantastic Daisy was; how he'd never have got the introduction to Jimmy Finlay without her; how brilliant his personal training sessions with her had been; and how, if the job came off, he might try to get her involved in the campaign.

Holly was about to point this out when he opened the bedroom door.

'I'm going to get a drink,' he said, and left the room.

Chapter Twenty-Seven

H OLLY HADN'T KNOWN what time Mark had come back to bed on Friday night and, when she woke the following morning, the bed beside her was empty, though warm from having been slept in. The radio alarm said it was 8.30 and she wondered if he'd got up to go running.

She was no longer tired, or particularly worried by the altercation they'd had the night before. Looked at with fresh morning eyes, it had been a slight and stupid row. She was glad they had not made it worse by saying more when they were both tired.

She acknowledged to herself now that mentioning Daniel just as they were about to have sex had probably not been a good idea.

Holly got up, took a bathrobe off the back of the bedroom door and went downstairs. Mark was not in the kitchen and his running shoes were not in the hall. She made herself a cup of tea, and set a pot of coffee ready for him when he came back from wherever he was, and switched on the radio. The news was just finishing and a continuity announcer was giving details of the rest of the morning's programmes on BBC Radio 4.

'And on *Excess Baggage* this week,' Holly heard her saying, 'we will be talking about staying in touch on your travels. The humble postcard is a relic of the twentieth century. These days the traveller blogs, emails, Facebooks and texts. Reporter and presenter

James Darling, travel writer Mark Johnson, and founder of last-minute.com Martha Lane-Fox, will be joining John McCarthy at nine-thirty . . .'

Holly scooped ground coffee into a cafetière and wondered why Darling was on the programme. It wasn't a likely subject for him to be discussing.

'Hi, Mum,' Chloe interrupted her thoughts.

'Hello,' Holly said, looking at her daughter. Chloe had dark circles under her eyes. 'You must be tired.'

'I'm OK.' Chloe slumped down at the table, her posture suggesting this was not entirely true. 'Are you making coffee?'

'Yes, I was getting a pot ready for when Dad gets back. I think he's gone out running.' Holly took a couple of cups from the cupboard.

'Why is Dad always running?' Jake slunk into the room. 'It's like all he ever does.'

'He needs to train if he's going to run the marathon,' Holly explained, wondering if he'd keep it up if he got the job with Jimmy Finlay.

'He must be tired,' Chloe volunteered. 'I came down to get a drink at three and he was still watching telly.'

'What was he watching?' Jake asked, his interest in the general goings-on triggered by the mention of television.

'Well, he wasn't really watching anything,' Chloe told them. 'He'd fallen asleep on the sofa and the TV was still on. I woke him up and told him to go back to bed.'

Holly put the cafetière on the table and placed mugs next to it as Chloe continued to talk.

'He had his pyjamas on so he must have decided to watch the news after getting ready for bed. He always does that.'

'Often, yes.' Holly was grateful for her daughter's interpretation of events.

She opened the bread bin and took out some croissants that she'd bought on her way home from the station the previous evening.

'I thought I might go into town later. Does either of you fancy coming?' Holly knew this was a long shot. 'Or joining me for lunch somewhere?'

'Where are you going for lunch?' Chloe's interest appeared to have been stirred.

'The Red Roaster probably,' Holly answered. 'I'm cooking tonight so I'll probably just have a sandwich or something.'

'Oh, right.' Chloe looked relieved and Holly wasn't sure why. 'I'm going to meet Emma in town later so I'll probably get something with her. I don't know why you always go there, Mum. You don't even drink coffee.'

'I like it there,' Holly said.

'I think I'll stay here today.' Jake looked up. 'I've got stuff to do.'

The front door rattled and slammed. Mark panted in, sweat running down his face and his chest still heaving.

'Ten miles this morning,' he gasped, throwing himself down on the easy chair at the side of the kitchen. 'I'm knackered.'

Holly looked at him and tried to suppress an instinct to recoil as he stretched his sweaty legs across the kitchen floor. At this moment she couldn't quite imagine how she had even entertained the thought of having sex with him the night before. If that was the state Mark was usually in when Daisy spent time with him, there was no chance of her finding him a turn on.

'Do you want something to drink?' she asked, forgetting that the last communication they had had was when he'd stormed out of the bedroom.

'I think I'll take a shower.' Mark ignored her question and began getting up. 'What's everyone up to today?'

No one in the room volunteered anything so Holly answered for them.

'Chloe is off out with Emma, Jake's planning on an exciting day staying in, and I am going into town and thought I might have lunch out. Do you fancy joining me?' She hoped he would say yes and they could wipe clean the slate from the night before.

'I don't think so,' Mark said, but he did smile as he said it, so it wasn't a complete brush off. 'I've got this meeting with Jimmy Finlay on Wednesday and I want to put together a bit of a presentation. I think I'll work on that today.'

'I'll just have lunch on my own then.' Holly found she was saying it to herself as Mark was already leaping upstairs on his way to the shower and Chloe and Jake were edging towards the kitchen door.

Left on her own, she wiped croissant crumbs from the table and put coffee cups in the dishwasher then took her phone from her handbag.

There was a new message in her inbox.

Hi, Holly, it read. *Really good meeting you properly the other day. I might be in Brighton over the weekend and wondered if you fancied meeting again for a coffee or something. Hope you are OK? Anne-Marie.*

Holly was not sure what to reply so she ignored it and instead pressed the Create Message option.

Beautiful day ☺ *What does yours hold? A few chores in town for me. Don't suppose you fancy a quick coffee?*

She pressed the Send button and sent the message to Daniel.

Holly looked around for a table, feeling unnerved by having walked straight into Anne-Marie, who'd been leaving the Red Roaster.

'Hi, Holly,' she'd said, as if she had fully expected to see her there.

'Hi.' Holly tried to sound enthusiastic but didn't want to encourage her to stay. 'This isn't your neck of the woods.'

'No,' Anne-Marie replied. 'But I've been doing a bit of shopping and decided to have lunch here. It's a nice café.'

'Yes.' Holly nodded, wondering if she was going to have to ask her to stay for a coffee. 'Look. I'm sorry I did not reply to your text. I had my phone off. I was going to reply, when I sat down.'

'Do you come here a lot?' Anne-Marie asked.

'Sometimes, at the weekends. Mark's office is around the corner and he sometimes comes here if he needs to pop in at the weekend.'

'Oh.' Anne-Marie seemed unsure what to say. 'What does Mark do?'

'He works in marketing,' Holly said, looking over her shoulder to see if she could spot a free table.

If there was one she supposed she should ask Anne-Marie to join her for coffee but the café was busy and none seemed to be free.

'Are you meeting him now?' Anne-Marie asked.

'Possibly.' Holly did not want to tell her she was meeting Daniel. 'It looks busy, though. I might just call him first.'

She took her phone from her bag, which Anne-Marie took as a cue to leave.

'Well, nice to see you, Holly,' she said. 'Maybe see you in the week?'

'Yes, that would be nice.' Holly smiled as Anne-Marie set off towards the Pavilion and scanned the café again for somewhere to sit. 'I'll be in touch.'

'I'm just leaving,' a woman sitting at the table Holly was hovering by with her tray of tea said to her, and began gathering up her stuff.

'Oh, thank you.' Holly smiled at her and put her tray down on the table.

'There you go, darling,' the woman said, picking up a scarf from the back of a chair and winding it around her neck.

Only then did Holly realise that this wasn't a woman at all but the man Mark referred to as the most convincing transvestite in town.

Holly had been meeting Mark for a coffee in town a few years ago and when she'd arrived had found him chatting to a tall blonde.

Quick work, she had thought to herself, since she wasn't more than a few minutes late, hardly long enough for him to have picked up another woman.

'Oh, here she is now,' Mark said to the blonde as Holly approached the table they were both sitting at.

'Nice to meet you, Mark,' the blonde had said, getting up to make way for her.

'Interesting woman,' Mark said to Holly as she sat down, stressing the interesting, as if to underline the fact he'd only been talking to her because of that, not because she was tall and blonde.

'Very interesting, I'm sure,' Holly had said, looking at the departing figure of Mark's erstwhile companion. 'But no woman.'

'What do you mean?' Mark asked.

'A transvestite,' Holly said. 'I've seen him doing cabaret at the Komedia. I think he's called Michael something or other.'

'Are you sure?' Mark had asked. 'If you're right, he's the most convincing transvestite in town!'

They'd seen him a few times since and Mark had gradually become convinced. Strange, Holly thought now, that he was once again giving up his seat in a café for her, albeit this time it was Daniel and not Mark she was meeting.

'Sorry I'm late.' Daniel had arrived now, slightly out of breath, from walking fast. 'Can I get you anything?'

'I've already got tea.' Holly indicated the tray.

'Won't be a minute.' He went to get himself a coffee before sitting in the seat recently vacated by Michael.

'It's nice to see you.' Holly was about to make some remark about meeting on a Saturday. Most of their meetings before had been somehow linked to journeys to and from work. They were treading new ground now and Holly felt it needed alluding to.

'It's good to get out of the house,' he said, sitting down. 'Things haven't been very easy at home.'

'I'm sorry.' Holly gave what she hoped was the right response. There was a slight pause. She didn't feel she could ask him any more and Daniel seemed to be considering whether to continue.

'You know I said we were trying to have a baby?' He looked up as he stirred his coffee.

'Yes.' Holly maintained eye contact but took another sip of her tea. 'You said you were having some tests . . .'

'We got the results.' Daniel picked up a sugar packet and started fiddling with it absent-mindedly. 'And there doesn't seem to be any reason why Daisy is not getting pregnant.'

'That's good.' Holly watched his hands as he twisted the paper.

'That's what I thought, initially,' Daniel told her. 'But the doctor said something about some people being incompatible. He said we are both perfectly capable of conceiving children, but unable to conceive them with each other.'

'Can't they help?' Holly thought this was when IVF was most successful.

'Possibly.' Daniel put the packet down. 'In the end. He told us to give it a while a longer but . . .'

He stopped talking and took a sip of his coffee.

Holly thought he'd probably decided against finishing the sentence he'd begun, but she was wrong.

'There's nothing like a doctor telling you you might be incompatible to put a strain on a relationship.'

'What will you do?' Holly asked, noticing that the usual playful smile around the edges of Daniel's mouth had disappeared and the sparkle in his eyes had given way to something that looked more like tears.

'I don't know, Holly,' he said. 'I'm not sure what to do.'

Chapter Twenty-Eight

'I SN'T IT A bit late to go running?' Holly opened the door of the house, expecting everyone to be settling in for the evening, but found Mark in shorts and running shoes doing calf stretches in the hallway.

The running was starting to make him look well, she thought, as she watched him straighten up. From a distance you might think he was in his early thirties, rather than his late forties. He was still a good-looking man. His recent loss of energy and vigour had made him appear to lose some of his sparkle, but today, she thought, he looked almost the same as he had when she'd first met him.

'I like running at this time of night, when the days are long,' he said, stretching his other leg but looking up, as Holly closed the front door. 'And I've arranged to run with Daisy. Plus I'm a bit hyped up and need to work off some excess energy.'

'Why's that?' Holly asked, wondering to herself why he had arranged to run with Daisy at a time when he knew she would be home from work and everyone would want dinner. She knew, too, that she was being unreasonable.

'I had the meeting with Jimmy Finlay today,' he said, as if she might have forgotten.

'I know,' Holly retorted. 'I did leave a message, asking how it went, and I texted.'

'Did you?' Mark sounded surprised. 'What time was that?'

'Early afternoon.' Holly was sure he must have got one of her messages. 'Anyway, how did it go?'

'Really well, actually.' Mark stood up now and grinned. 'He was very funny, very easy company, and we got on well. He wants me to do it!'

'That's fantastic, Mark. Well done!' Holly put her bag down and reached up to kiss him. 'We should celebrate.'

'Thank you,' he said, looking pleased. 'We will, when I get back. I haven't told Daisy yet, and if it wasn't for her there would be no job with Jimmy Finlay. I'd better go.'

He looked at his watch, anxious to get out of the house.

'OK, see you later,' Holly said, feeling that the celebratory moment had been lost.

She closed the door behind him and wondered why, instead of feeling pleased that Mark had some decent work, she felt a bit pissed off and a little suspicious. She hadn't asked him where he was planning to run but wondered if it was along the seafront. It was a lovely evening and the summer sun was low now. The promenade would be busy with people strolling, rollerblading, skateboarding. Other runners, too. She felt suddenly jealous of Mark running with Daisy.

She remembered the one and only time she had been running with her husband, which must have been about twenty years ago. Holly didn't like running, never had. She preferred walking and swimming and used to do yoga, though no longer had the time or, if she was honest, the inclination. She could, she thought wistfully, do with a rather more toned body than the one she currently had.

Mark hadn't attempted marathons in his twenties but he did like to clock up a regular three or four miles before or after work, claiming it enabled him to eat well without putting on weight and stopped him getting tired after sitting at a desk all day.

'You should try it,' he'd said one evening when Holly had come home from work and flopped on the sofa, exhausted from having been in the office all day. 'It'll make you feel much better.'

She had allowed herself to be persuaded.

'We'll have to go very slowly.' She'd smiled at Mark as she laced up a pair of trainers, which she had no business to own. They were a relic from a time when she had thought about going to the gym, but had never got further than the sports store.

That had a been a beautiful evening too, late summer, the sun was setting and Holly had thought, as they ran along the seafront in the direction of the Marina, that her life was just about perfect. She lived in a beautiful town, with a man who seemed to think *she* was just about perfect, and she had a job that she loved. She also started to find she was enjoying the sensation of running, albeit slowing along the front, thinking her thoughts and taking in her surroundings. But that feeling had been temporary. Her legs had started to hurt and her breathing became more laboured and she'd felt hot and disinclined to run much further. So she had turned off the promenade and run down the shingle and flopped on to the pebbles by the shore. Mark had followed, mocking her for being a lightweight, and lain down beside her.

'You were doing well, for a beginner,' he'd teased her.

'I definitely prefer swimming,' Holly had said, propping herself up on her elbows and looking at the sea.

Then she'd surprised herself and Mark. This part of the beach was empty. It was out of town. It was now almost dusk and there was a slight chill in the air. She looked around then stood up and took off her trainers, t-shirt and tracksuit bottoms. She thought about diving into the sea in her bra and knickers, then threw caution and them to the wind and ran in naked. Mark laughed and stood up slowly, watching her swim out to sea. Then he slowly took off his t-shirt and shorts and underwear and joined her in the water, which had felt warmer than either of them anticipated.

'What are you thinking about?' Jake said now, sitting at the kitchen table with the computer, looking at Holly as she stood in the doorway, reminiscing. 'Are you OK, Mum?'

'Nothing.' Holly shook her head to remove the mental image she'd captured. In its place came another of Mark running along the seafront, with Daisy easily keeping pace with him, talking and laughing. She wondered if she would tell him what Daniel had told her on Saturday.

'I didn't see you there, Jakey. What are you up to?' She tried to focus her attention now on her son who had a plate of cheese and crackers on the table beside the computer and was shoving a Ritz with a large slab of Cheddar on it into his mouth.

'You are a *fresser*!' Mark had said to him earlier in the week, coming up with another word pilfered from another language. 'It's Yiddish for someone who eats too quickly.'

'Just talking to Ed on Facebook,' Jake muttered to Holly, through the mouthful. 'There's a message from Gran too. She's in Koh Samui. She says it's cool.'

'Did she actually use the word cool?' Holly couldn't keep up.

'Well, she probably said beautiful or something,' Jake conceded. 'Ed's got a ukulele.'

'We haven't seen him round here for a while,' Holly said, picking up a bit of cheese that had fallen on to the table and putting it in her mouth.

'No, I've been busy,' Jake said, as if it were true. He looked back at the computer screen and began tapping away again.

Holly decided to text Daniel, partly because she now knew Daisy would not be at home when he got there.

She hadn't been in touch since having coffee with him on Saturday.

Haven't seen you last few days. Hope you're OK. Hx

'Who are you texting?' Jake looked up.

'No one.' Holly hoped the answer would satisfy him but they were both distracted by the sound of a key turning in the door. Chloe came in.

'Hello, love,' Holly called out. 'Where have you been?'

'Hi, Mum,' Chloe said coming into the kitchen. 'I've been round at Ruaridh's. Is Dad back?'

'Back, but gone out again,' Holly told both children. 'He's gone for a run. He needed to work off some excess energy.'

She thought she'd give Chloe and Jake the same reason he'd given her.

'Oh, he had that meeting today, didn't he?' Chloe remembered. 'How did it go?'

'I haven't had time to talk to him properly but really well apparently,' Holly told her. 'He seems to have got the job.'

'Fantastic. That's really good.' Chloe seemed relieved.

'Will he get lots of money?' Jake showed signs of interest.

'I don't know.' Holly didn't. 'It's a charity run, so I don't imagine there will be much money involved. But it should be good for his company. He'll probably get other work off the back of it.'

'That's good,' Chloe said again.

Holly wondered if she thought this might mean she could go on the school trip. She hadn't mentioned it again and Holly didn't know if she'd accepted that it was unlikely she could go or whether she still harboured hopes that she would.

'Have you eaten anything?' she asked Chloe, wondering what to cook.

Jake appeared to have eaten half a pound of cheese but that

never dented his appetite, and Mark would no doubt be hungry when he came back from running.

'Not really.' Chloe's answer was ambiguous and Holly noticed that she smelled slightly of fried food. Perhaps she and Ruaridh had been to the chippy.

'Yuk!' Chloe had picked up another piece of cheese that Jake had dropped on to the table and put it in her mouth. 'What is that?' she exclaimed.

'D'oh. Cheese,' Jake told her. 'What's wrong with it?'

'Oh, in that case, nothing.' Chloe smiled and appeared to savour the food in her mouth. 'I thought it was a bit of shortbread when I picked it up, and it tasted all wrong.'

'There ought to be a word for that,' Jake commented. 'Is there, Mum?'

'Is there what?' Holly's phone had just bleeped and she was opening a message from Daniel.

'A word for when you eat something that turns out to be something else,' he said.

'I can't think of it, if there is,' Holly told him. 'It's the sort of thing Dad might know, though. Ask him when he gets back.'

She looked at the text again.

I'm OK. Felt better for talking to you at weekend. Always do.x

Holly smiled to herself and put the phone down.

She wondered if there was a word for the feeling she felt whenever she had contact with Daniel. She couldn't put it into words but she felt reassured, calmer, and less afraid of the world and all its uncertainties.

The way she used to feel when she first met Mark.

Chapter Twenty-Nine

'IT'S A WAY of perceiving things as colours.' Holly was telling Daniel about the programme she had produced that day.

There'd been a discussion about synesthesia, which had prompted a lot of calls from listeners.

'A lot of synesthetes see numbers as colours or emotions.'

'Like a blue mood?' said Daniel. 'Or being green with envy?'

'Yes,' Holly replied. 'Or just going through a yellow phase, which is what one of the guests on the programme said she was going through.'

'What's that then?' He had spotted her through the window of the train and had joined her where she was sitting.

'I couldn't say exactly.' Holly found the subject fascinating, but couldn't quite comprehend the various aspects of it. 'She just said her life had been very yellow lately.'

'I saw Anne-Marie further back,' Daniel said. 'I nearly joined her but I hoped I might find you so I moved further down the train. What colour would you say she is?'

'I don't know.' Holly considered his question. 'Purple maybe?'

'Why do you say that?' He looked at her keenly.

'Because she seems bruised,' Holly said, feeling this was an accurate summary of how she found Anne-Marie.

'A new report claims as many as one in ten people have some

Lizzie Enfield

form of the condition,' she continued. 'It causes people to perceive certain sensations in another form; like seeing numbers as colours or dates as specific places, or hearing a visual motion – like a flicker.'

'I suppose we all have a certain amount of that,' Daniel observed. 'Like being able to see if someone is unhappy. You'd think you can't, but sometimes you can.'

Holly looked at him, wondering if he was alluding to her or himself.

'The woman going through the yellow phase,' she carried on, 'said her children were green and brown and her husband was grey.'

Holly didn't say to Daniel what she had said earlier to Natalie: that she thought a lot of middle-aged women might describe their husbands that way.

'Your job sounds really interesting,' he said, considering it further. 'It must be so different every day.'

'It is.' Holly knew her job was better than most but could still moan about it at the drop of a hat. 'Although sometimes you feel as if you're just setting up interviews with the same people. They are different, but it can start feeling all a bit samey.'

'I imagine you're very good at it,' he said encouragingly.

'I'm OK.' Holly shrugged. 'Not bad enough to get rid of anyway.'

'No, I bet you *are* good at it,' he emphasised. 'You've got a very warm way with you. I imagine you can bring out the best in the people you have on the programme.'

'That's really down to the presenter,' she said, though she felt uplifted by his comment. 'But thank you.'

Daniel flipped the lid off the cup of coffee he'd brought on to the train and took a sip.

He frowned slightly then looked up at her.

'This coffee's not quite right.' He held the cup towards her for inspection. 'It tastes a bit . . . green!'

Holly looked at the drink, which looked perfectly normal to her, and realised, a beat too late, that Daniel was joking.

She laughed and shoved him slightly.

'I don't know,' she said. 'It looks pretty black to me.'

As she said this, she sensed a presence to her right, which anyone who was not a synesthete would have described as pinstripe.

She turned to find Carl, her friend Hannah's husband, in the aisle beside them.

'Hi, Holly,' he said. 'I thought that was you.'

'Hello,' she said. 'How are you?'

'Good, good.' He paused. 'How are you?'

Carl had readjusted his face slightly to show concern and spoke more quietly than he had at first.

'Fine,' Holly said, knowing what had brought about the change. It still happened a lot, this gradual dawning on people that she had been involved in the crash and therefore had to be treated differently.

'I'm fine,' she said again, to emphasise that she was really OK.

There were no spare seats, and Holly thought Carl would want to keep the conversation brief and find somewhere else to sit. But he didn't move and was looking at Daniel, as if expecting an introduction.

'This is Daniel,' she obliged. 'And this is Carl. You look very smart today,' she said, turning to Daniel and adding, 'Carl usually works from home and wears jeans and a t-shirt.'

'A client meeting,' he explained. He was an architect and, while most of his work was done from the loft of the family home, every now and then he had to leave it and go out into the big wide world. 'Chance to take the suit for an outing!'

'I hope it enjoyed it?' Holly joked.

'It had a productive day,' Carl replied. 'But now it wants to find a seat. Nice to see you, Holly.'

'You too.' She half-rose as he half-bent to kiss her. 'Send my love to Hannah. We keep trying to go the cinema together but never seem to make it.'

'I will tell her that rather nice dress you are wearing wants to see the latest Quentin Tarantino.' Carl smiled. 'We'd both like to see you properly. You and Mark should come for dinner. Nice to meet you.' He nodded in Daniel's direction.

'You too,' Daniel muttered and, when he was out of earshot, 'Who was that?'

'My friend Hannah's husband,' Holly told him. 'And also Chloe's friend Emma's dad. We met when the girls were at junior school together.'

'He's very silver!' Daniel seemed to have warmed to the synesthesia theme.

'By which do you mean very good looking?' Holly asked.

Carl was one of the best-looking men she knew.

'Oh, you think he's good looking, do you?' Daniel raised an eyebrow.

'Well, he is, by any standards,' she said. 'But he is my friend's husband so no need to raise your eyebrows.'

'You can still fancy him.' Daniel appeared to be teasing her in a way he had never done before.

Holly wondered if he was flirting. To date, he'd been affectionate and tactile but never flirtatious. She'd tried to imagine how she might appear through his eyes and could only think that she seemed old and staid, especially compared to his beautiful wife.

'The funny thing is, I actually don't. He is very nice, and what you might call devastatingly good looking, but he's very . . .'

Holly paused, trying to put her finger on what it was that stopped her from fancying Carl. 'Smooth. There's no edge to him, I suppose.'

She'd stopped short of saying he was safe, knowing how much she'd resented being described that way by Dimitri.

'Plus, of course,' she added, 'because he is my friend's husband, I know all about all his bad points and annoying habits.'

'God, do women always tell each other everything?' Daniel grimaced.

'Pretty much.' Holly lowered her voice. 'You see, I know Carl snores terribly and always hangs one leg out of the bed when he's asleep. Hannah says it trips her up every time she has to get up in the night.'

'That doesn't sound too off-putting,' Daniel said. 'I thought you meant things that were a little more intimate.'

'Oh, I know those too.' Holly smiled. 'But I couldn't tell you them. Plus all the usual moans about never doing the washing up, not knowing the children's names, barely tolerating the mother-in-law – though that's pretty standard stuff.'

'So do women tell each other this stuff to warn their friends off their husbands then?' Daniel asked. 'Is gossiping just a slightly more friendly way of saying, "Hands off, he's mine!"?'

'I hadn't thought of it like that before.' She considered Daniel's remark. 'It's an interesting theory. You should be doing my job. It's the sort of thing we might discuss on *Antennae*.'

She could imagine this. They'd find a social anthropologist, who would tell them how cavewomen used to tell their friends that their husbands grunted like mammoths during sex and were equally hairy too. This, the required expert would explain, was not because they wanted to bond with their fellow gatherers, but rather to put them off trying to lure someone else's mammoth-hunter into their cave.

'So am I right?' Daniel looked at her quizzically. 'Is bitching about your partner behind their back a way of warning others off?'

'Possibly, but it might just be a way of letting off steam,' Holly said in response to his hypothesis. 'Men can be very difficult to live with.'

'So I am told,' he sighed, a slightly weary sound that suggested someone close to him had let it be known he was difficult to live with.

Holly couldn't imagine that he was. She found him considerate and quietly funny. She could now see why the beautiful Daisy had been attracted to him over all the other Alpha-males who had pursued her.

'I . . .' Holly began to speak at the same time as Daniel also said, 'I . . .'

'You first,' she laughed.

'No, you go on,' he countered.

'I was going to say, I suppose no one is that easy to live with all of the time.' Especially not after sixteen years of marriage, Holly thought to herself. 'What were you going to say?'

'I was going to say that I'm glad you don't spend any time with Daisy,' Daniel said. 'I hate to think what she would tell you about me.'

Holly said nothing although she too was glad Daisy was not among her circle of friends. She didn't want to hear his wife's version of what Daniel was like at home because, at the moment, Holly's loyalties were with him.

'Tickets, please!' The guard was making his way down the carriage.

Holly took out her ticket and wondered, not for the first time, what Daisy and Mark told each other about her and Daniel when they were out running together.

Chapter Thirty

'I'LL SEE YOU there then, shall I?' Natalie unhooked her coat from the back of the door.

'Yes, I won't be long.' Holly glanced up briefly from her computer screen, but carried on typing an email. 'I said I'd let this guest know who else was appearing with him on the programme and give him an idea of the questions. You go ahead.'

'OK.' Natalie smiled. 'I told Guy we'd be there from six, and if he arrives and I'm not there yet, he may not stick around.'

'Of course,' Holly answered.

Natalie had told her earlier that Guy's parents were staying for the weekend and had offered to baby-sit, so that they could go out together.

Holly wasn't sure if they realised that going out together constituted Guy coming along to the pub with Natalie and her colleagues, who were celebrating a minor professional success.

Antennae had won a Sony award. Holly had overheard Dimitri telling his mother it was the radio equivalent of an Oscar, on a long-distance call to Athens. The award was for Best Radio Feature, for a piece they had done about kidney donors, broadcast during National Organ Donation Week.

James Darling had interviewed a mother who had donated a kidney to her daughter, then developed a serious infection in her remaining good organ and needed a donor herself. He'd also spoken to a newly married man who had previously had a kidney transplant where the donor had been his brother. This organ had just failed and his new wife wanted to donate hers.

Darling had been praised by the Sony judges for his sensitive and compassionate treatment of the guests while at the same time managing to ask probing and thoughtful questions. The piece had prompted a debate about the ethics of organ donation, which had been picked up by other media and had run for several days.

'We all deserve a celebration,' Katherine announced after she and James returned from the awards ceremony. 'I'll put some money behind the bar of The Adam and Eve next Friday evening. Partners are invited too.'

'Is your husband coming?' Rebecca asked when Holly joined her and Dimitri, who were waiting by the lift.

'No.' she shook her head. 'He'd have to come up from Brighton specially.'

Holly didn't tell them that she hadn't even asked Mark. She didn't think he'd have been interested if she had, and she would have resented his disinterest.

She'd told him that the drinks were taking place and that she'd be home late. He hadn't seemed bothered, only said something about how he planned to run in the evening anyway and that Chloe wanted to cook dinner. The implication seemed to be that Holly would not be missed.

'Your boyfriend?' she asked Rebecca as the lift arrived and they filed inside.

'He might,' Rebecca said as she caught sight of her reflection in the mirror of the lift and adjusted her hair slightly. 'He wasn't sure what time he would finish work.'

'Yours?' Holly directed this question to Dimitri.

'I don't have a boyfriend, Holly.' He winked at her.

'You know what I meant,' she said ruefully.

'My girlfriend's waiting in reception,' he told them.

Rebecca checked her appearance in the mirror again as the doors opened to reveal the reception area.

Holly was curious to see what the Greek god's girlfriend looked like. She imagined Rebecca was too. She pictured a female version of Dimitri; someone beautiful, with dark exotic good looks, but petite and slender in contrast to tall, powerful Dimitri.

The only person waiting in reception was the exact opposite, but she was standing up and walking towards him. The word Amazonian sprang to Holly's mind, as she watched her colleague kissing a tall pale woman with shoulder-length reddish-blond hair. There was a squareness to her jaw which was almost masculine, and, while she was attractive, she wasn't the beauty Holly had been expecting.

'This is Anna,' Dimitri introduced her. 'Anna, this is Holly.'

Holly shook her hand while Rebecca mumbled a, 'Hi, Anna.' Holly wondered if they had met before.

'Please to meet you, Holly,' Anna said, and Holly detected an accent which she could not immediately place. She thought it might be German.

The four of them began walking towards The Adam and Eve. The pavements were crowded. There was not room for them all to walk abreast of each other. Rebecca and Holly found themselves falling behind.

'Have you met Anna before?' Holly asked.

'A couple of times,' Rebecca murmured, non-committally.

'She's not what I imagined,' Holly told her. 'Where is she from?'

'Berlin,' Rebecca confirmed her intuition about the accent, then changed the subject. 'Did you speak to the man who's on Monday's programme?'

★

Natalie and James were squashed on a bench seat behind a table, at the head of which Katherine was sitting. There were three bottles of champagne on the table and an array of glasses. They looked up as the newcomers walked over to join them.

'Anna, this is Katherine the boss, James the talent, and Natalie,' Dimitri said, introducing his girlfriend.

'What does that make me then, Dimitri?' Natalie raised her eyebrows. 'We have the boss, the talent, and then just me.'

'Natalie is the office pin-up,' he said, and she raised her eyebrows and smiled at Anna.

'Nice to meet you at long last,' Natalie said as Anna took the spare seat next to her. 'I don't know how you put up with him. Champagne?'

'Thank you,' Anna replied, nodding her head slightly.

'Pass the bottle, Darling.' Natalie nudged James's elbow.

'Oh, where are my manners?' he responded, picking up the bottle and pouring all round.

'Are you two married?' Anna asked.

'No,' Natalie laughed. 'I mean, we are married, but not to each other.'

Holly was vaguely aware of a presence behind her as Natalie said this and turned round to see Guy hovering beside the table, not quite sure how to announce his presence.

'Guy!' Natalie said. 'Great. You're here.'

'I'm here,' he confirmed.

'Shove up,' Natalie said to James, and he shuffled further along the bench, making room for Natalie's husband.

'She's married to me,' Guy said, sitting down and introducing himself to Anna. 'I'm Guy.'

'Anna,' she said, looking confused. 'I am with Dimitri.'

'Anna overheard your wife calling our illustrious presenter

Darling.' Dimitri extended his hand across the table to Guy. 'I'm Dimitri. I think we met briefly in the office once before.'

'Yes, I remember,' Guy said.

'James's surname is Darling,' Dimitri explained to Anna.

'Oh.' She paused to consider this and then her face lit up as she realised her mistake. 'I see!'

Holly briefly thought back to the evening when she and Daniel had met Anne-Marie. She had asked if they were married. What was it, she wondered now, that had given that impression?

Anna began laughing at her mistake and the rest of them joined in.

'Have I missed a good joke?'

They all turned to look at the indisputably beautiful woman who was pulling up a spare chair.

'Hello, Darling,' she said. 'I hope I'm not late.'

James's wife Mila was as unlike him as Anna was from Dimitri. She was tall and slim, with thick dark hair and sparkling green eyes. There was a grace to her movements that made you want to stop and simply watch her as she dragged a stool closer to the table and leaned across it to kiss her husband.

'I can't remember who's met Mila and who hasn't,' he said. 'You know Natalie, and Katherine. Have you met Holly and Rebecca . . . or Dimitri? We've only just met Anna. Anna, this is Mila and Guy. Mila, this is Guy.'

'Hello.' Mila smiled and gave a slight wave to where Anna and Guy were sitting. She was too far away from them to shake hands.

'Who is she?' Anna whispered to Guy.

'James's wife, I think,' he said to her. 'She was probably using his surname as an actual term of endearment!'

Anna smiled, as if glad of a fellow outsider to feel slightly conspiratorial with.

'Hello, Natalie.' Mila had extended her hand across the table to her.

Natalie took it with what Holly thought was slight reluctance.

'Good you could come,' she said. 'Who's looking after the children?'

'They are with friends,' Mila said matter-of-factly. 'Who is looking after yours?'

'Guy's mother.' Natalie nodded towards her husband.

Holly wasn't sure if she was imagining a coldness in this exchange. If there was she put it down to the suspicion with which working and non-working mothers tended to treat each other.

She'd seen similar exchanges take place numerous times between women who worked full-time and those who had stopped altogether. Because, for the time being, they had no common ground, their conversations often seemed obliquely to challenge each other's life decisions.

Natalie and Mila's brief exchange ended when Katherine clapped her hands.

'Before we all get too drunk,' she joked, 'I'd just like to say a few words.'

Katherine did indeed keep her words to a minimum, reminding them all why they were celebrating, congratulating the team on a wonderful programme, among many other wonderful programmes, and giving Darling a special mention on account of the quality of his interviewing technique.

'Congratulations!' Katherine raised her glass and there was a graduated murmur in response.

'What was the programme about?' Anna asked.

Dimitri had obviously not filled her in on the details. So Natalie did the honours.

'It was one of those interviews which raised lots of questions. James handled it perfectly,' she concluded.

'Humph,' Guy grunted.

'What do you do, Anna?' Natalie asked, ignoring him.

'I'm a photographer.'

'Really? Guy used to be a photographer too. Didn't you?'

'I still am,' he said through gritted teeth.

'Oh, well, I didn't mean . . .' Natalie trailed off.

Holly imagined Guy would have perceived the remark as a putdown. She knew he wasn't working at the moment. His plans to go back to doing some of the things he used to do, now that the twins had started school, didn't seem to be bearing any fruit.

Guy drained his glass and glowered at his wife who reached across the table for a bottle but found it empty.

'I'll get another,' she said, to no one in particular, and got up to go the bar.

'I'll help you,' Holly offered. 'I'm just going to go to the Ladies first.'

'I'll get a couple more bottles. There's still money behind the bar,' Natalie said as Holly rounded the corner to where the Ladies were.

When she came out a small group of men in suits were blocking her path back to the body of the pub. She hovered, wondering if she could squeeze past without having to say a loud 'excuse me' and, as she waited, heard Natalie and Guy talking in agitated, hushed voices.

'Why do you always put me down like that in front of your colleagues?' he hissed.

'I don't know what you mean.' Natalie sounded placatory.

'Yes, you do. Saying I used to be a photographer,' Guy returned.

'I just meant you are looking after the children at the moment,' she told him.

'Our children.' Guy sounded cross.

'Yes, our children, obviously.' Natalie was beginning to sound pissed off.

'You go on about what a wonderful interviewer James fucking Darling is, and in the next breath you say I'm an old has-been.' Guy was clearly rattled.

'That's not what I said.' Natalie sounded as if she were talking to a small child. 'Just calm down, will you? This is my evening.'

'Fuck you, Natalie,' he said. 'I'm going home. Tell your precious colleagues there's a childcare crisis, which your neutered husband has to deal with.'

'Excuse me.' Holly tapped one of the men in suits on the elbow and they moved aside. She walked past and saw Natalie crossing the bar with two bottles as Guy stomped towards the door.

'Is everything OK?' Holly asked her before they reached the others.

'Don't ask.' Natalie pulled a face and glanced over at Guy, now smiling at Mila who also appeared to be leaving the party.

'Mila's gone to have a cigarette,' James explained her absence when they rejoined the group.

'She doesn't look like a smoker,' Katherine said. 'Her skin is far too good.'

'She only smokes occasionally.' He smiled, as if accepting the compliment on his wife's behalf. 'She gets a bit stressed when she's with people she doesn't know that well.'

He glanced over to where she stood chatting to Guy.

'So does Guy,' said Natalie.

Chapter Thirty-One

'OH, CONGRATULATIONS,' NATALIE said, as Holly came into the office on Monday morning.

She'd been about to remark on Natalie's new haircut and wondered what she was being congratulated for.

'What for?' Holly felt momentary panic that she might have been promoted or moved to another programme. She was not sure she could cope with the added stress that either involved.

'Your new husband,' Natalie said, indicating her computer screen.

Holly looked over Natalie's shoulder, and saw she was looking at her Facebook page. Natalie hit a few keys and Mark's profile appeared.

'Look at this.' Natalie pointed to a heart icon which flashed and announced, 'Just married!'

'What's all that about?' Holly wondered if Mark had had some virtual Facebook wedding without telling her. 'Why is it saying that?'

'Don't look so worried,' Natalie soothed. 'He must have just updated his profile over the weekend. I've seen this happen before. If you set up with only sketchy details then go back to change it, the site flags all the new stuff up.'

'I see.' Holly was not sure that she did.

'Mark must have added that he's married and has children,' Natalie told Holly. 'Then Facebook puts out a "just married" alert!'

'Oh, you had me slightly worried for a bit.'

She knew, obviously, that Mark had not gone out and married anyone real over the weekend but she was relieved he hadn't had a virtual wedding either.

Both Mark and Jake had been locked on to their computers when she came home after her office pub outing. Jake had been non-committal when she'd asked what he was up to and Mark had said he was working on the logistics of Jimmy Finlay's run.

He'd run twelve miles himself on Saturday morning and disappeared to the office in the afternoon. On Sunday, Holly had suggested that if he was going to go into the office, which he no longer seemed to be giving up, then perhaps they could meet for a coffee in town.

'OK,' Mark had acquiesced. 'How about two-thirty? There's a new Spanish deli down the road. I'll need something to eat by then.'

Holly wasn't sure if he'd agreed to meet so he wouldn't have to eat alone or if he actually liked the idea of spending a bit of time with her away from home.

In the event, he was with her in body but not in spirit. He had his phone on the table between them and kept checking it for messages and looking as if he wanted to get going again.

Mark had ordered a Spanish omelette and Holly asked for a pot of tea and something which looked like a custard tart, which the waitress said was called a *nata*.

'So I'm going to have a cuppa and a natter then,' Holly had joked but Mark had looked at her blankly.

'I can't stay too long,' he replied. 'I want to finish planning the itinerary by Monday.'

'It's OK, I was making a joke,' Holly said, unable to keep the irritation from creeping into her voice.

'What?' he asked, but was looking at the waitress as if willing her to bring their food quickly.

'A pun,' Holly replied, but decided the joke wasn't worth making again. 'Oh, it doesn't matter.'

Mark wolfed his omelette down and left her to have her tea and *nata* on her own.

He'd obviously done some updating of his Facebook page while he was back in the office.

'Now you come to mention it,' Holly said to Natalie, 'I do remember him saying something about using Facebook more. It was something to do with this Jimmy Finlay thing he's doing, I think.'

'Well, there you go then,' said Natalie. 'You should have a look at some of the messages he's been getting. They're quite funny.'

'I think I'll just get a coffee.' Holly desperately needed one. 'Want one?'

'I'm all right,' Natalie replied. 'Darling's just gone to get me one. He should be back in a minute.'

'OK.' Holly took her coat off and hung it on the back of the door, feeling slightly irritated that whenever Darling was in, working on the programme, he seemed to prefer their office to the one he'd been allocated.

'I'll see you in a bit then.' She took her purse from her bag and headed towards the canteen.

'Here's the blushing bride!' James Darling had rolled Holly's chair over to Natalie's side of the office and was looking at Mark's Facebook page with her. 'Your husband has three hundred and fifty-two friends.'

'Thank goodness he doesn't invite them all round for dinner.' Holly chose to ignore his bride joke. 'By the way, Natalie, I like your hair.'

'Oh, God, it's hideous, I look like Richard the Second,' she said.

Her hair, which had been long-ish, was now cut in a short bob.

'I think it's nice,' Darling said, reaching across and playing with the newly cut ends. 'It suits you.'

'Nice if you like Plantagenet hair!' Natalie laughed.

'I do like Plantagenet hair,' Darling said, looking at her closely. 'I like it a lot.'

Holly felt as if she ought not to be here, as if she was intruding in some way, but it was partly her office after all. She cleared her throat and James looked away from Natalie's hair and back to the computer screen.

'Not many of your husband's friends seem to know you,' he commented, and began reading aloud from the screen.

'*Congratulations, Mark, anyone we know? . . . You're a dark horse, who's the lucky woman?* And look at this one. *Congrats, Mark. Was it a wedding or a civil partnership?*'

'Let me see.' Holly crossed to Natalie's side of the office and James got up so she could sit where he had been.

'Some of these names are familiar.' Holly began scrolling down the messages and paused when she reached a comment from a sender she thought she knew.

'A lot of them are probably work contacts,' Natalie said.

'Noel. Mark used to do a lot of work with him in Hong Kong . . . and Ted.' Holly read out the postings from names she recognised, although they belonged to people she had never actually met.

'*Congratulations, Mark. Let us know the name of your new wife. Where are you living now?*'

'I can't believe he spent years going back and forth to Hong Kong, doing business with these guys, and never once mentioned he had a wife.' She looked at Natalie for reassurance.

'They're probably just treading carefully,' Natalie said. 'If Mark hasn't been in touch with them for a while, they might think you two got divorced or something.'

'Well, listen to this one.' Holly read out another. '*Good news, Mark. Presume you finally married Holly? Better late than never. Neil Somerset.* Neil Somerset was at our wedding!'

'Think of it as a compliment,' James told her, sitting on the edge of Natalie's desk.

'How so?' Holly looked up at him.

'Well, perhaps not a compliment exactly.' He paused to reconsider. 'But testament to the strength of your marriage. You've been married so long that even people who came to your wedding find it hard to believe you still are.'

'That's an interesting way of putting it,' Natalie interjected. 'But it's true. You and Mark have been married longer than anyone else I know, which is quite an achievement in this age of divorce.'

'Mmm.' Holly was only giving Natalie a small portion of her attention.

Mark had a new Facebook friend. It was Anne-Marie, which was decidedly odd. He didn't even know her. She must have seen that he was friends with Holly and sent him a request, but Holly wondered why and why Mark had confirmed it.

Then she was distracted by a new posting from Daisy.

'*Better to wait and marry late than marry young and green.*'

'Is that a famous quote?' She pointed at the on-screen message and Natalie leaned in and read it.

'It might be.' She didn't sound convinced.

'What do you think she means?' Holly asked.

'Maybe something about knowing the person you are

marrying?' Natalie suggested. 'Rather than marrying when you are young and not quite sure what you're letting yourself in for.'

'Best not to know,' Darling said. He was now reading a newspaper article but obviously still keeping abreast of their conversation. 'You'd never do it if you knew what you were letting yourself in for.'

'Oh, I don't know.' Natalie looked at him. 'I think it becomes harder to accommodate another person as you get older.'

Holly wondered if she was talking about herself and Guy. She was curious as to whether they'd continued the argument she'd overheard in the pub back home – and whether they'd resolved it or not.

Holly got up, moved her chair back to her desk and switched on her computer.

Darling shifted his position on the edge of Natalie's desk a bit, moving slightly closer to her. Holly would have found this annoying but Natalie didn't seem to mind. They had certainly known each other long enough to accommodate each other at work.

'Coincidentally,' Darling said, shaking out the paper he was reading, 'Katherine gave me this when I passed her office this morning. Thought it would make a good discussion.'

'Let's have a look.' Natalie put out her hand to take the paper from him and began to read out the headline. '*Till the Main Meal Do Us Part – Is Marriage for Life or Just for Starters?*'

Natalie carried on reading to herself, then handed the paper over to Holly.

'What do you think?' she asked.

'"You may set out thinking marriage is for life, yet all too often it can be a brief affair, especially amongst twenty-somethings. Should starter marriages, which end after a few years, often without children, be seen as failed relationships or a trial run for a lasting, more fulfilling, long-term second marriage?"'

'Maybe,' Holly said out loud. 'Though it smacks a bit of some charlatan having coined the term "starter marriages".'

'Yes, we'd have to get a charlatan to take part in the discussion,' Darling nodded, as if in agreement with her.

'And we'd need to find someone with a brief failed marriage,' Natalie mused, 'and then preferably a longer, more successful one.'

'It seems a bit like doing a *Hello!* though,' Holly said. 'Inviting people to talk about their long and happy marriages.'

'I've always been fascinated by childhood sweethearts,' said Darling. 'They seem to fall into a category of their own. Every now and then you read about people who have known each other since they were at school and then get married. I wonder if their marriages last as far as dessert?'

'*Ikabaebae,*' Holly said, finding something that Mark had told her had suddenly floated to the top of her mind.

'What?' said Darling and Natalie together.

'*Ikabaebae,*' Holly repeated. 'It means to be engaged from childhood in some Pacific island language.'

'Know anyone who falls into that category?' Natalie asked both Holly and James.

'William and Kate,' James suggested. 'Although I suppose they met at university. Still, good going.'

Holly kept quiet.

The only person she could think of who fell into that category was Daniel, and she wasn't about to volunteer this information to her colleagues.

Chapter Thirty-Two

HOLLY WANTED SOMEONE to be nice to her and hoped she might find Daniel on the train.

She felt unnerved after Mark's reaction to the posting she'd made on his Facebook wall and his refusal to tell the virtual world who his actual wife was.

Congratulations, Mark, she'd written. *I think you might have forgotten to divorce me first . . . wife no. 1.*

Holly had intended this to be a joke but Mark had not found it funny. He'd phoned her at work, saying it made him look stupid.

'I updated my page because I'm expecting more people to look at it, thanks to Jimmy's run.' He sounded very pompous.

'Well, it leaves me out altogether,' she retorted. 'Half your Facebook friends don't even seem to realise that I exist.'

'Now you know what it feels like,' Mark had muttered, but refused to be drawn when Holly had asked what he meant by this.

Their marital tiff had been cut short when she had to go to the studio to record an interview. She'd thought about calling Mark back later, but decided to save whatever 'discussion' they might need to have until she got home. Too often, lately, she seemed to be having minor tiffs with him that ended unresolved and with accusations unspoken.

At the moment he was making Holly feel that she was not a very nice person, that everything she said or did was somehow wrong, but she always felt reassured by Daniel. There was something in his manner and his attitude towards her that made her feel that what she was doing was right.

As Holly reached the middle of the train, she saw him sitting next to a window, facing backwards but with an empty seat next to him. She smiled to herself, pleased that she would be able to sit there.

Daniel looked up and saw her.

'Hello,' she said, approaching the space where he was sitting. 'Mind if I sit here?'

'Please do.' Daniel stressed the *do*. 'Which way do you want to face?'

Holly had registered, as she approached the seat, that there was someone already sitting opposite him, but not who it was. Now she turned and saw that it was Anne-Marie.

'Oh, hello,' she said, hoping she sounded convincingly pleased to see her.

Holly had been hoping to have some time with Daniel on her own, if she discounted the other people in the carriage, which she did. Anne-Marie made Holly feel edgy and unnerved, partly because of the way she seemed to keep appearing: on the train, in John Lewis, at the meeting, in Brighton at the weekend, and now on Mark's Facebook page too. It didn't seem like pure coincidence.

'Hello, Holly,' Anne-Marie said, not sounding too pleased to see her either. Her tone was positively dejected.

'How are you?' Holly forced herself to sound cheery and decided, against her inclination, to sit down next to Anne-Marie.

'Not great,' she replied, and Holly's heart sank.

She wished now she'd grabbed a seat at the back of the train.

She didn't like herself for wishing this. She could only imagine what Anne-Marie must be going through and knew she ought to be sympathetic. For some reason she felt anything but.

'Bad day?' Holly said, imagining that for her some must be worse than others.

'It's her wedding anniversary today,' Daniel explained, filling Holly in on the detail Anne-Marie had already shared with him.

'Oh.' Holly cursed herself for her attitude to Anne-Marie. What, she wondered, had made her become so hard-hearted?

'I'm sorry,' she said. 'How long were you . . . would you have been married, I mean?'

'This would have been our third wedding anniversary,' Anne-Marie told her. 'We were married on the fifteenth of June three years ago.'

That wasn't long, Holly thought to herself, although she knew this wasn't relevant. She wondered which was worse: losing your husband in the early stages of a marriage, when you were still madly in love and had plans for a future, or when you'd been together for years?

'Did you not want to take the day off?' Holly couldn't quite think of what else to say.

'I thought about it, but I decided it was best to carry on,' Anne-Marie told her.

As she was speaking, it occurred to Holly that, if Anne-Marie would have been married for three years on 15 June that meant she herself had been married for seventeen years on 8 June. Both she and Mark had forgotten their anniversary.

'Oh, no!' she said. 'That means I forgot our wedding anniversary. It was last week.'

She realised, as soon as she said this, that it was not tactful.

'Sorry,' she said to Anne-Marie. 'I know that sounds terrible. Especially when . . .'

'How long have you been married, Holly?' Anne-Marie interrupted.

'Seventeen years,' Holly said, feeling as if she should also apologise for this to Anne-Marie. It seemed to her somehow indecent to have been married so long when Anne-Marie's marriage had been cut short.

'And you, Daniel?' Anne-Marie turned to him, a touch of the inquisitor about her.

'Five,' he said. 'We got married when I was twenty-three.'

Holly wondered if Anne-Marie had forgotten that she had asked them both how long they'd been married when they'd met in the pub. Holly remembered the conversation but it seemed to have slipped Anne-Marie's mind.

'That's young,' she commented.

'We were at school together,' Daniel, said, as if having known each other from a young age made twenty-three not so young to get married at all.

Holly thought about telling them about the discussion they were having on her programme but knew this would also mean saying that statistically his marriage only had a certain chance of lasting.

Instead she decided to keep quiet and send what she hoped would be a conciliatory text to Mark.

Happy Wedding Anniversary, Mark. Sorry I forgot . . . Long-standing wife xx

'Seventeen years is quite an achievement,' Anne-Marie said.

'You're telling me,' Holly laughed, but sensed that Anne-Marie was not in the mood for joking. 'It seemed to come round very quickly, though. It doesn't feel like seventeen years, except when I stop to think how much has happened over that time. I guess, before we know it, we'll have been married another seventeen.'

'You're very lucky, Holly,' she said. 'Not everyone is as committed as your husband obviously is.'

Holly wasn't quite sure what she meant by this remark or why she'd singled Mark out as the committed half of the marriage when obviously it took two to stay together.

She was saved from having to reply by a text from Mark.

Happy Anniversary to you, long-standing, long-suffering wife. I am sorry about my own Alzheimer's. Must have forgotten with all the excitement of recent wedding! Sorry, Hol. Will make up xx

Holly smiled.

'Forgiven?' Daniel said, as if he knew the text had been from Mark.

'I think so,' she said, putting her phone away.

'Can you imagine having been married seventeen years?' Anne-Marie asked Daniel, looking at him directly. There was something challenging in the way she put it.

'I suppose so.' He began to take his laptop out of his bag. 'I've imagined certain things in the future. But you can never be quite sure what will happen, can you?'

His answer was oblique and Holly wondered how Anne-Marie might interpret it. Would she think he was alluding to the accident that had ended her own brief marriage? Holly wondered if he was referring to the children he seemed unable to conceive with Daisy, or to something else.

She looked at him and, as he opened his laptop, he glanced up and held her eye briefly. Holly wondered if Anne-Marie had noticed.

'Must finish a presentation.' He nodded at his flickering screen.

'And I have some papers to read.' Anne-Marie fished in her bag and the three of them fell into companionable silence, until the train neared Haywards Heath and Anne-Marie began preparing to get off.

'Have a good evening. I hope . . .' Holly stopped mid-sentence, then continued, 'I mean, I hope it's not too hard, going home alone tonight.'

'I know what you mean,' Anne-Marie said flatly. 'I hope you have a good evening, too, if you ever get round to celebrating your wedding anniversary.'

'Bye then,' Daniel said, as she got off the train. And then, to Holly, 'Did she seem a bit off to you? Perhaps she was upset.'

'Yes,' Holly agreed. 'And that's understandable. I thought she was pissed off with me too, though. Did I interrupt something when I arrived?'

'Not really. We were just chatting,' Daniel told her. 'She'd told me it would have been her wedding anniversary so she was feeling a bit down.'

'This may sound daft, but I felt she was cross with me for forgetting my wedding anniversary,' Holly said. 'As if I ought to appreciate what I have more. But we've never really made a big thing out of anniversaries anyway.'

'Will you celebrate it, now that you've remembered?' Daniel asked.

'I don't know,' Holly said, wondering if going out to mark the occasion might be just what she and Mark needed, or whether it would be best to let it pass this year.

I'm not sure who I am missing most today, Geoff or the baby that we never had.

I had a conversation in my head with Holly this morning. I imagined that rather than ignoring my text at the weekend and meeting up with Daniel, she had replied and agreed to meet me.

'Call me whenever you need to talk,' I would have said to her when we left together, instead of my walking out of the café on my own and bumping into her, then waiting a while and seeing Daniel turn up.

'And you call me too, if you need, any time,' I put the words into her mouth. 'Really, any time at all.'

I would have called her this morning, before I left for work, because I knew today would be hard.

'Are you sure you're up to going to London?' Holly would have asked. And I would have told her that life goes on.

People keep saying that to me, as if they don't know what else to say. 'Life goes on,' they say, and it does go on but it's not the same, is it?

I would have told her that it was our wedding anniversary today, or rather it would have been, and that we would have been married for three years. Then I would have told her about the baby, who would be two and a half years old.

'So you were pregnant when you got married?' she'd have asked.

'Just a couple of months,' I'd explain. 'I didn't want to be too huge

266

walking down the aisle. We were going to get married anyway. But the baby made us decide to do it sooner rather then later.'

This isn't entirely true.

We might never have got married if I hadn't got pregnant. Geoff made that very clear last year, on our wedding anniversary. It was a registry office affair, not the big white wedding I'd imagined when I was younger. But I no longer wanted that anyway, not with Mum and Dad both dead.

There weren't that many people I would have wanted to invite, so a small intimate affair seemed more appropriate. And that was easier to organise quickly too. There was no rush on Horsham registry office on a Wednesday afternoon or the restaurant where we all went for a meal afterwards. It was a quiet family affair, with Geoff's mum and dad and sisters.

But it was still the best day of my life, because suddenly things seemed to be moving forward for me. I was going to be with Geoff and we were going to have a baby.

He'd been stunned at first, when I told him I was pregnant, because I was on the pill. But I'd had an upset stomach the week before so it probably hadn't absorbed properly.

He was angry initially, that I hadn't told him this, but then he apologised because he knew that I was upset and said it would be wonderful for us to have a baby, it was just the shock of finding out that made him react that way.

I hadn't expected him to ask me to marry him, but of course I accepted when he did. I couldn't believe my luck. I was so happy. Looking back on it, those few weeks leading up to the wedding were probably the happiest of my life.

'Are you sure you want to do it so soon?' Geoff's mum had asked. 'You might not be feeling so good, Anne-Marie. I was sick with Geoff for nearly four months.'

'I feel great,' I told her.

I did. I'd felt really tired and nauseous at first, although I wasn't ever *sick, but once I was past six weeks I felt fine – full of energy, in fact, which I put down to thinking about the wedding and our future. I never imagined for a moment how soon it would all start to go wrong.*

That's why I thought I'd find it hard today; not because this time last year it had all been champagne and roses, but because it had been awful.

Geoff hadn't planned to do anything to celebrate our anniversary last year and that upset me. He said because it was midweek he was too tired to go out, but I really wanted to do something and we ended up going to an Italian in town.

I wished I hadn't insisted, as Geoff obviously didn't want to be there. He hardly spoke all evening and kept checking his phone.

I asked him if he couldn't forget about work or whatever it was that was bothering him and enjoy the evening.

That was when he said it.

'Let's face it, Anne-Marie,' he said. 'We'd never have got married if it hadn't been for the baby.'

That made me think back to the awful moment when we went for the scan. It felt like a bad joke on the part of the ultrasound operator.

I remembered her putting the gel on my stomach and Geoff holding my hand and both of us looking expectantly at the monitor, waiting for a grainy image of the baby to appear.

'There's nothing there,' the operator said.

'What do you mean, nothing?' Geoff asked. I was too stunned to speak.

'I mean, there's no baby. I'm afraid your wife's not pregnant,' she said gently.

'But I am.' I half-sat up, half-turned to look at the monitor, to make sure she hadn't missed anything. 'I took four tests. I've got a slight bump. My breasts are bigger. You must have made a mistake.'

'I am sure you were pregnant, Anne-Marie,' she said to me. 'Sometimes people conceive but the baby doesn't develop very far and the body simply reabsorbs the foetus rather than miscarrying. It's called a phantom pregnancy. I'm very sorry.'

It wasn't just the baby I lost that day, I realise now, it was my hopes for the future. Geoff was angry that I hadn't known I wasn't pregnant any more. He behaved as if he thought I'd tricked him into getting married with some fantasy I'd made up. We started arguing. We'd probably have argued again today, on our wedding anniversary, if he'd been here. And I'd have wondered, for the umpteenth time, if I hadn't lost the baby, would everything have been different?

Chapter Thirty-Three

'I'M OFF,' HOLLY said to Dimitri, as she walked past his desk on her way out.

'Why is everyone sloping off early today?' He looked up from his computer.

'It's not early.' Holly resisted the temptation to check her watch. She knew it was only 5.30 and she could also see from where she was standing that Dimitri was on Facebook.

He might still be in the office but he wasn't actually doing any work.

He was probably waiting for Rebecca, who was still in the studio, recording an interview for later in the week, so that they could slope off wherever it was they seemed to slope off to after work.

'I guess not,' Dimitri conceded her right to leave the office. Then, qualifying his earlier statement, added, 'Natalie left just after lunch.'

'I think you must have had a late lunch,' Holly told him. 'She left just before five.' She did this regularly on a Wednesday, as it was Guy's day for going to the gym.

'You'll miss your train if you stand here arguing with me.' Dimitri leaned back in his chair and smiled at her.

'Actually, I don't have a train to catch just yet,' Holly laughed. 'I'm meeting my dad for dinner.'

Her phone beeped as she spoke and she took it out of her pocket and was surprised to find a text message from her father. *Train just in. CU L8r.*

When and where, Holly wondered, had her dad learned to send a text message and use text speak while he was at it? She no longer entirely recognised her parents.

'I thought your parents were in Thailand doing yoga?' Dimitri said, underlining what she was just thinking.

Holly had forgotten that she'd mentioned her mother was in Thailand, when they were talking about protests at Bangkok airport earlier in the day.

'My mum is there,' she explained. 'My dad is usually in Northampton, but he's booked himself a theatre break and is taking me out to dinner before he goes to see the Danish Ballet with an old friend.'

'Oh, right,' Dimitri replied. 'So your parents are divorced?'

'No, they just aren't joined at the hip.' Holly echoed what her mother had said when she had elaborated on her plans to travel alone for four months.

She didn't understand her parents' relationship quite well enough herself to explain it to anyone else. They appeared to get on well when they were together and yet they seemed to spend increasing amounts of time apart.

'I've spent the last thirty years with him,' her mother had said when Holly mentioned this to her. 'Don't you think I'm entitled to do my own thing?'

Holly hadn't wanted to argue with her, and as her father seemed to be perfectly happy with the arrangement, she'd not questioned it further.

'Right, well, have a nice evening.' Dimitri tapped his keyboard and closed his computer down as Rebecca came into the office.

He looked at her and inclined his head slightly towards the door, as if to say, Shall we be off?

Her father was already sitting at a table in the Australian brasserie in Exmouth Market when Holly arrived. Natalie and Guy lived not far from here and Natalie had recommended the place when Holly had asked if she knew of somewhere she could meet her dad that was near Sadler's Wells.

'Are you meeting someone?' an Aussie waiter asked as soon as she set foot inside.

'My dad.' Holly nodded towards her father who was watching the world go by, but hadn't seen her. His mind appeared to be elsewhere.

'Ah, right, you'll be going with him to the Danish Ballet then?' the waiter asked. He'd obviously already had a chat with her dad.

'No.' Holly walked over to join him. 'Just having dinner with him first. Hello, Dad.'

'Holly!' Her father pushed his chair back and stood up to kiss her, then waited for her to sit down before he sat himself. 'How are you?'

'Fine.' She sat down and the waiter handed her a menu.

'Everybody here seems to be Australian,' said her dad, as the waiter retreated to the bar. 'That young man has recently arrived from Sumatra. I have never before met anyone who has been to Sumatra. What would you like to eat?'

Holly picked up the menu. It was fairly typical of her father to fall into conversation with strangers. He generally found them easier to talk to than members of his own family. But she also wondered if he'd started quizzing the waiter because he was lonely. Her mother had been gone for nearly a month and his days were spent largely on his own.

'Have you heard from Mum this week?' Holly thought her

father's mention of Sumatra provided a natural segue to the subject of someone who was in Thailand. They were both in the Indian Ocean and, Holly was pretty sure, on the same fault line.

'She sent an electronic message last Friday.' He had reluctantly started to use email, forced to by Susan's use of it, but emphasised his reluctance by refusing to call it by its abbreviated name.

'She was about to take a train up into the mountains, but I've not had time to go to the public library and see if she has sent any more letters this week.'

'And are you getting on OK at home?' Holly and her sister had both been copied in to the email that her mum had sent on Friday.

She knew about the trip to the mountains but had hoped her mother would have sent her father his own, more personal email. Unless there was one waiting for him on the computer terminal at the local library, it seemed she had not.

'Pretty well,' her dad answered. 'I've been reading a biography of Stanley Baldwin. It's very good. Have you read it?'

'No.' Holly smiled to herself, thinking that her dad seemed quite happy to fill her mother's absence with a weighty tome and the odd trip to London. 'So who are you going to the theatre with tonight?'

'Jean Hayward,' her father said, as the waiter came back to take their order. 'She doesn't get out much these days, without Hugh around.'

Jean and Hugh used to travel a lot themselves and Holly wondered if Jean would start travelling on her own again or if the fact that Hugh had died after having a stroke on their trip to Petra would put her off.

'How is she?' Holly asked.

If she'd asked this question to someone of her generation, Holly thought, they would probably have answered that Jean was generally OK but rather lonely, having lost her partner of forty-plus years and not having any children nearby to keep an eye on her.

'She's very well,' her father maintained.

He was now looking up at the waiter who was standing expectantly with pen poised over notepad.

'Shall we order?'

Patrick ordered pork belly and white bean stew, and Holly asked for the gilt-head sea bream.

'I wonder what it was feeling guilty about?' she quipped as the waiter left, but her dad appeared not to have heard.

'What have you been up to?' he asked. Perhaps he thought she'd said something about feeling guilty herself for leaving work early or not going home.

Over dinner, Holly told him that she'd interviewed a man who had held up a bank with a Toilet Duck. Held under his jacket, the staff thought it was a gun. She talked about Jake settling into secondary school and Chloe becoming so independent that they hardly saw her any more.

'And Mark's got some work with a Scottish comedian.' Holly didn't imagine his name would mean anything to her dad. 'Jimmy Finlay.'

'Oh, I love him!' he said, surprising her. 'He's the one on that dot dot dot *I Nearly Died* programme, isn't he?'

'Yes, I didn't think that was the sort of thing you watched?' Holly replied.

'I've been watching a lot of rubbish since your mother has been away.' Holly noted that her dad hardly ever referred to Susan by name, always as her mother. 'But I like that programme. Good for Mark. What's he doing?'

Holly told him briefly about the run and what she knew of his involvement in it.

'He's organising the run itself, plotting the itinerary and organising hotels and a back-up team,' she repeated some of what Mark had told her. 'And then he's trying to arrange a big press launch in a few weeks and more press coverage throughout.'

'It sounds like a lot of work,' her father commented, and Holly nodded and decided not to say that, what with one thing and another, she'd hardly seen him since he landed the job. 'And is he still running himself?'

'Yes,' Holly said. 'When he's not working on Jimmy Finlay's run.'

If she had been having dinner with her mother, Susan might have asked if she'd managed to see Mark at all in between all this running and working. Her father did not.

'I'd better get the bill,' he said, when they'd finished eating. 'I said I would meet Jean outside Sadler's Wells at seven forty-five. Are you going to come and say hello?'

Holly wasn't sure if her father wanted her to come and greet an old family friend or if he was simply unsure how to get rid of her. She suspected the latter.

'I should probably start heading home actually, Dad,' she said apologetically. 'There's a train in forty minutes, which I could probably make if I rush.'

'Jolly good,' he said, signalling to the waiter.

He paid the bill in cash and asked for his coat.

'I might just go to the cloakroom before we leave,' Holly said. 'So I'll say goodbye now.'

'Yes.' Her father was putting his coat on. 'Well, goodbye. Nice to see you. I'm glad everything's OK.'

Holly wondered, as he said this, if meeting up had been his idea or whether her mother had urged him to see her.

'Yes,' said Holly, kissing her father on both cheeks, although she suspected he would prefer just to shake hands. 'Say hello to

Jean from me, and send Mum my love when you hear from her next.'

'Yes,' he said, holding his hand up in a royal wave as he walked towards the door.

Holly waved back and looked about her.

'Downstairs,' the waiter said, interpreting her scanning of the room correctly.

'Thanks,' Holly said, and went downstairs.

When she came up, she noticed a table tucked around the corner. It wasn't visible from the main part of the restaurant and even now she could only see it reflected in the mirror on the stairs. If that hadn't been there, she wouldn't have noticed the table at all, or the two people sitting at it, holding hands.

She stopped on the stairs, unsure what to do next. If she walked up quickly, could she go past and pretend she hadn't seen them? Too late. They'd seen her and had quickly unclasped their hands and sat back, too far back, in their chairs, creating a yawning space between them.

'Oh, hi.' Holly tried to sound casual, as if it was quite normal to bump into a friend's husband holding hands in a restaurant with the wife of the presenter of the programme she worked on.

'Hi, Holly.' Guy stood up and kissed her, as if he too thought their meeting like this was quite normal. 'What are you doing in this neck of the woods?'

'I've just had dinner with my dad.' She nodded in the direction where they had been seated and Guy looked, obviously expecting to see him.

'He's gone to meet someone at the theatre now,' Holly explained. 'I was just on my way home.'

'You know Mila, don't you?' Guy motioned towards James Darling's wife, who was wiping the edges of her mouth with a napkin.

'We've met a couple of times.' Holly smiled, unsure whether to shake her hand or kiss her or just leave out any sort of greeting altogether.

'Hi.' Mila glanced briefly in her direction but didn't make eye contact.

'Well, I'd best get going.' Holly looked at her watch to under-line this fact. 'I've got a train to catch.'

Chapter Thirty-Four

'D<small>O YOU HAVE</small> a number for Guy?' Mark asked, as Holly buttered a slice of toast. She'd overslept, was running late and would have to eat it on her walk to the station.

'No, why?' Holly picked up the toast and took a bite.

She'd been through the list of contacts on her phone last night, wondering if at any point Natalie had given her Guy's mobile number. But Gina and Giles were the only Gs.

She hadn't known exactly what she would have done with the number had she found it. Texted him and asked what he was doing with James Darling's wife? Unlikely. Called him and asked if Natalie knew where he'd been? She knew Natalie thought he was at the gym. Holly had no idea what to do about having caught him having dinner with Mila.

She'd wondered whether to tell Mark that she'd seen them together, but decided not to. This was partly because he was uncommunicative when she got home and partly because she kept telling herself there must be an innocent explanation.

For the time being doing nothing seemed the best option.

'He's a photographer, isn't he?' Mark said, pouring himself some coffee. 'Jimmy wants an official photographer to document his run. He asked if I knew of any.'

'Would that mean going to Scotland for the duration?' Holly

asked, glancing at the kitchen clock and noting that she should have left by now.

'I guess.' Mark sloshed some milk into his drink.

'He *is* a photographer,' Holly said. 'But he looks after the twins these days. I don't know if he'd be able to do it.'

Jake appeared in his school uniform and nodded before taking a box of cornflakes from the cupboard and pouring what looked like almost the entire contents into a bowl

'Surely that's up to him.' Mark looked at her accusingly, although Holly was not sure what she was being accused of. 'He can probably work something out.'

'I suppose so,' Holly said, although she knew it would be difficult. In the days when Mark's business had been booming and he was almost always busy, it had not always been easy to sort out their childcare.

'We'll work something out' had always been Mark's verbal solution to any problem. In reality this meant 'I'm too busy to look after the kids. See if you can find someone else'.

'I'll ask Natalie for his number.' Holly grabbed her keys off the work surface. 'Got to go now.'

'OK. See you later.' Mark was making himself more coffee and giving the task his full attention. Holly noted that he seemed to have stopped kissing her goodbye in the mornings.

''Bye, Jake,' she said, kissing the top of his head.

He grunted and took a mouthful of cereal. The food seemed to trigger part of his brain.

'How was Granddad?' he asked. 'Is he missing Grandma?'

'He was fine,' she told him.

She wasn't sure what the correct answer to the second part of his question was.

★

'How was your dad?' Natalie asked the same question when she got into the office.

'Fine,' Holly said again.

'Did you have a nice meal?' Natalie enquired, looking up from her computer screen.

Holly wondered if she was just being polite or if she might have found a receipt from the restaurant in Guy's pocket and was asking Holly this to find out if she'd seen him there.

'Very good, actually.' Holly sifted though a pile of papers on her desk to avoid making eye contact with Natalie as she said this. She decided to say nothing, and then wondered if Guy might have mentioned seeing her there.

'Thanks for the recommendation. Have you and Guy been there often?'

'Neither of us has ever been.' Natalie's answer put paid to the possibility that he might have come clean. 'But our next-door neighbours have been several times.'

'Oh.' Holly was unsure what else to say.

'They don't have kids.' Natalie seemed to think an explanation of her next-door neighbours' eating habits was in order. 'So they eat out quite a lot.'

'Well, it was good. You should go,' Holly said, wondering how Guy would manage to keep up the pretence of never having been if he went again with Natalie.

'By the way,' Holly added, 'Mark is looking for a photographer to do some work. He was wondering if Guy might be interested?'

'Well, I'd be interested in Guy doing some work,' Natalie replied enthusiastically.

'Don't you need him to look after the twins?' Holly repeated the reservation she'd voiced to Mark earlier that morning.

'They're at nursery during the day,' Natalie said, 'and he doesn't seem to do anything useful while they're there. It would be great if he had some work.'

'Right.' Holly didn't feel like explaining that the work might involve his going away. 'Can you let me know his email or mobile number?' She tried to sound casual, knowing that once she had them she would most likely contact Guy herself as well. 'So that Mark can talk to him about it.'

'Yes.' Natalie began writing Guy's details down on a Post-it note, then looked up.

'That's odd actually,' she said. 'He was asking what your mobile number was this morning. Are you two having some sort of secret affair or something?'

'Nat . . .' Holly was saved from having to answer by James Darling sticking his head in at the door of their office. 'Are we in the studio this morning?'

'Yes,' said Natalie, looking up and smiling at him. 'I'll be down in ten minutes. Do you have the interview script?'

'Right here.' He waved it at her, noticing Holly sitting at her desk. 'Morning, Miss Golightly.'

'Morning, Darling.' Holly smiled. She wondered when it had dawned on him that her name was taken from *Breakfast At Tiffany's*.

'Shall I get you a coffee on the way down?' James was addressing Natalie again.

'Oh, thank you, Darling!' She smiled at him. 'I'll be down in a sec.'

Holly looked at Natalie as she finished what she was writing on the yellow square of paper.

'There you go.' She handed over the email address and mobile number to Holly. 'Mark's probably best emailing him first off. He never seems to answer his phone. Not to me anyway.'

She picked up a script from her desk and walked out of the door with Darling.

'I tried to call Guy several times when he was the at gym last night,' Holly overheard her saying to James. 'Kirsty was coughing terribly and I wanted to know if he'd given her any medicine already. But he never answered once.'

'You were lost in thought.'

Holly looked up and smiled as Daniel slid into the seat next to her.

She had been staring out of the window and, as he rightly pointed out, lost in thought. She hadn't noticed him approaching.

'Hello,' she greeted him.

'Or were you just considering whether to change your broadband provider?' Daniel indicated the poster outside the window, which had Holly been taking in her surroundings she might have noticed.

'No, you were right the first time,' she told him. 'I find myself with a bit of a conundrum.'

'A conundrum?' he said, questioningly.

'I went out for dinner with my dad last night,' she began.

'That's nice,' Daniel commented. 'Where did you go?'

'Oh, an Australian place near Sadler's Wells. He was going to a show later.' Holly tried to skim through the details of their meeting.

'So what is the conundrum?' Daniel asked.

'Well, someone I work with . . .' Holly decided not to divulge Natalie's name '. . . she and another colleague get on very well. They've worked together for years and they are good friends.'

'And?' Daniel prompted.

'Well, a lot of people at work make comments about them behind their back.'

'What sort of comments?' Daniel seemed unsure where she was going with this.

'Oh, you know,' Holly said vaguely. 'That there might be something going on between them. That sort of thing.'

'And is there?' Daniel asked.

'I used not to think so,' Holly said, truthfully. 'I thought they were just very good friends. I don't really like the man, to be honest, and the woman's husband is lovely, so why she might like someone else is beyond me.'

'So you're not sure?' he asked.

'I'm pretty sure they're not,' Holly said. 'But then last night, when I was having dinner with Dad . . .'

'Did you see them having a candlestine dinner?' Daniel guessed. 'I mean . . . What's the word?'

'Clandestine!' Holly smiled. 'But I like candlestine. It's a good word for a clandestine candlelit dinner!'

'And did you catch them having one?' he persisted.

'Not them,' Holly told him. 'But their spouses. They were in a quiet corner and I didn't see them until I went to the Ladies. His wife was sitting with her husband. They looked very cosy.'

'Maybe there's an innocent explanation?' Daniel suggested.

'I hope so,' Holly said. 'But it puts me in a difficult position.'

She'd sent Guy an email earlier in the day, outlining briefly why Mark wanted to get in touch and giving him both Mark's and her mobile number. She hadn't referred to the night before but he had her email address and her mobile number now. The ball was in his court.

And he'd batted it back almost immediately with a text message.

Hi, Holly. Mark's job sounds interesting. Will email him next. Btw I know how it must have looked last night. But not what you think. Hope to see you soon – maybe we can have a quick coffee later in the week? Guy x

That was a textbook cop out, 'not what you think', and Holly wasn't sure she believed him.

'As far as I know,' she said to Daniel now, 'they'd never met, until we all had a drink after work last week.'

'What if the boot was on the other foot?' Daniel looked at her closely as he asked this, making her feel slightly flustered. 'What if your colleague had seen us having a drink and talking? What do you think she would have thought?'

'I don't know.' Holly looked away as she spoke.

'She might have wondered what you were doing in a pub with me, and you'd have told her there was a perfectly innocent explanation.'

Daniel lowered his voice as he said this. The passengers seated opposite both had earphones plugged in but he didn't seem to want them to hear what he was saying.

'Yes,' Holly agreed, though she couldn't think what the innocent explanation for Guy and Mila being together and holding hands might be.

'Sometimes two people can look very cosy together,' Daniel said. 'In fact, they can be very comfortable together. But that doesn't necessarily mean there is "anything going on".'

He made quotation marks in the air as he said this.

'Does it?' He looked directly at her again.

Chapter Thirty-Five

'I LIKE IT here.' Holly looked around at the solid wooden shelves that lined the walls, all groaning under the weight of jars of olives and tapenade. 'When did it open? Didn't there used to be a charity shop here?'

'I think it used to be the Alzheimer's shop,' Mark said, pouring her a glass from a carafe of Rioja. 'But I can't remember.'

'I don't remember there being an Alzheimer's shop here,' Holly began, then realised that Mark was probably joking. In the spirit of their conciliatory wedding anniversary dinner, she laughed.

'Mind you, I haven't been to the North Laine in ages. I just rush past on my way to and from the station.'

'Perhaps work will pick up for me, if this thing with Jimmy Finlay goes well.' Mark lifted his menu. 'Then you won't have to rush past quite so much.'

'Oh, well, no . . . I just meant . . .' Holly stuttered, thinking that even her throwaway comment could be construed by Mark as criticism for his not having enough work. 'I meant I hadn't noticed how many of the shops have changed. Anyway, this is nice.'

She smiled at her husband, who looked up from the menu and smiled in return, not just a reflex facial tic or a quick curving of the mouth but a slow, spreading, proper smile, as if he were taking Holly in properly, and thinking of all the reasons he had to smile at her.

She hadn't given him many of late; Holly admitted that much to herself. But she wasn't entirely to blame for what seemed like the increasing distance between them.

'Happy Wedding Anniversary, Holly.' Mark put the menu down and raised his glass. 'Here's to you.'

'Happy Wedding Anniversary to us!' she said, and tapped his glass with hers. She was already beginning to sense that the job for Jimmy Finlay was re-energising her husband and making him feel more positive about everything. 'How did you hear about this place?'

'Chloe told me about it actually,' he said. 'I was wondering whether we should go to Terre à Terre, after the conversation we had with your parents, but she said it's always busy and you can't book. She said she'd heard this place was good.'

'Since when did our daughter become so knowledgeable about restaurants?' Holly took a sip of her wine. 'She's not really a child any more, is she?'

'No,' Mark agreed. 'She's quite a woman about town these days. She certainly seems to know more about what's going on than I do!'

'I know.' Holly began studying the menu as she spoke. 'Do you think she's OK? She does seem to go out a lot these days and she gets very tired. I never went out when I was her age.'

'It's not as if she's doing anything her friends aren't,' he said. 'And school's fine. She deserves to go out and have some fun too.'

'I suppose.' Holly was not entirely convinced, but Mark was right about Chloe doing well at school. They didn't really have any reason to stop her going out, just because things were different when they were young.

'What about her and Ruaridh?' Holly asked.

'What about them?' Mark was studying the menu.

Holly had been about to ask if he thought they were sleeping together and if this might account for Chloe's tiredness, but then she decided not to. She couldn't quite face the subject of sex, as she and Mark had not had any for several months. Perhaps tonight, she thought to herself, smiling up at Mark and muttering 'nothing' in relation to Chloe and Ruaridh.

'So what do you fancy?' He picked up the menu again. 'I like the look of the pork and artichoke hearts . . . and would it put you off if I had the rabbit?'

'No.' Holly was not going to get sentimental about rabbits. 'I quite fancy the squid. Do you think that's what they've got?'

Mark looked in the direction of the table Holly had just nodded towards. A young couple were forking up rings from a plate of deep purple ink.

Mark nodded. 'It certainly looks like squid. Do you remember that restaurant we went to in Andalucia, before we were married?'

'That's just what I was thinking!' Holly presumed they were thinking of the same restaurant. 'The one in Ronda? With the waiter . . .'

'And the squid!' Mark sat back, laughing at the memory, and Holly felt a huge surge of warmth for her husband and their shared life. She was glad they had come out and were forgetting the strains of the last year; remembering, instead, some of the highlights from their past.

'I don't suppose the same thing will happen here,' she said, looking at the waiter who was approaching to take their food order.

'I don't know.' Mark sat back and looked at her while she asked the waiter about the squid.

The Andalucian incident they'd both been reminded of had

happened not long after Holly and Mark met. The company he worked for at the time was doing the marketing for a firm of olive-oil importers. They had sent him to Andalucia to see where their products originated. Mark had told Holly she could come with him.

'They will pay for everything,' he'd said, but she'd discovered a credit-card bill, when they returned, and found Mark had bought her flights and paid for most of the meals they'd had too. He'd never told her because he'd thought she'd insist on paying for herself or else might not come. She would have gone, no matter what.

'I think he's thinking about it,' Mark said, when the waiter had taken their order for a selection of tapas and left them to chat again.

'What?' Holly had lost the thread of their former conversation.

'Finding a flagon somewhere.' Mark raised his eyebrows, referring again to the incident in Andalucia.

They'd been out for dinner on their last evening to a fairly rustic, rough-hewn restaurant with pots, pans and plates all over the walls. The waiter there had been a very intense individual; dark and brooding, with a rasping voice when he told them exactly what they would be eating. He hadn't wanted to know what they might choose for themselves. For Mark it had been a very dark, purple, smoky octopus and for Holly roast suckling pig.

The waiter had been so sycophantic towards her it was comical and, at the end of the evening, had marched over and rasped that he wanted to pay homage to her beauty. He then reached for a flagon of wine, announced that his next gesture was for her, and poured it all over his face, so that it ran down his cheeks and chin and spilled on to his chest. It was the most extraordinary gesture, very erotic, and the sort of thing you would never encounter in England, but had seemed quite natural in Spain.

Mark, who was beginning to suffer from the hallucinogenic effects of the octopus ink, had sat back, not entirely sure if this was really happening.

'I doubt it,' Holly said, remembering that, when they'd returned to their hotel at the end of the evening, they'd abandoned the slightly polite, considerate sex which they'd been having with each other to date and replaced it with something much more wild, abandoned and passionate. She wondered if Mark remembered this too.

'I've become invisible with middle age,' she told him now.

'No, you haven't.' Mark studied her. 'You're still a very beautiful woman, Holly. People still look at you.'

'Not sexy young waiters.' She smiled, appreciating his compliment but never quite able to accept one with grace. 'I'm way too old for him.'

'No, you're not. As I said, you're a very beautiful woman. I'm sure a lot of people find you very attractive.' He took a sip of his wine.

'Thank you.' She tried to find the grace that had eluded her earlier, then decided to change the subject.

'So, how's this thing with Jimmy Finlay shaping up?' she asked. Mark had told her what he'd been planning but she hadn't asked him much about it for a while.

'Well, I think. It all seems to be going ahead,' Mark said as the waiter returned with the first of their dishes.

'How far have you got with the planning then?' Holly asked, eyeing up the artichoke hearts.

'The route is more or less planned,' Mark told her. 'But I still need to arrange press coverage and I'm trying to get a hotel chain to sponsor it which will help with the accommodation en route.'

'If he's doing it all for charity, who pays *you*?' she asked, hoping not to dampen Mark's enthusiasm by voicing the thing that had been nagging at her since he first got the job.

'Jimmy's paying me out of his own pocket.' Mark did not seem to mind the question. 'He really wants to do it, because of his dad, and he's single and has no family. He must earn quite a lot from . . . *I Nearly Died*. That's what he wants to do with it.'

'He sounds like a nice man,' she said.

She was pleased Mark had this job. It could be just what he needed to kick-start the business, although she was slightly worried about how they would manage the family between them if he became busy again.

'Will you have to go to Scotland when he's actually doing the run?' she asked, thinking that she would miss him if he did. She'd been taking his presence for granted recently, and finding it irritating at the same time. Now she found herself thinking it would be lonely coming home to a house without him in it, especially if he went for the duration.

'I might go up every now and then, but not all the time,' Mark reassured her. 'He needs a team to accompany him though; a backup vehicle and driver plus a photographer and a PA. Do you want some of this?'

He pushed a dish of fried chorizo towards Holly who spooned some of it on to her plate.

'I had a chat with Guy about the photography but he's not sure he can do it.'

'It would be difficult for him to get away.' Holly reiterated what she'd said before.

'I said I might have a coffee with him, next time I'm in London,' Mark told her. 'Discuss it anyway.'

'Right.' Holly tried to sound disinterested. She'd arranged to have coffee with Guy herself the day after next.

She liked Guy but she wasn't looking forward to this meeting. She'd been going over and over in her mind what reason he could have to be eating out with Mila and couldn't think of one, except for the obvious. She didn't want to be asked to keep that a secret.

'I thought I might ask Daisy to do the PA-ing,' Mark said, as Holly took a mouthful and was momentarily unable to comment.

'Daisy? Daniel's Daisy?' she asked, forgetting immediately about Guy and Mila. 'But she's not a PA . . . and anyway, does she want to go away for that length of time?'

'I don't know.' Mark moved some of the dishes on the table to make way for a plate of rabbit which the waiter had brought.

'I won't know until I ask her. She worked as a PA before, in HR at BT.'

'That sounds like something to do with the menopause,' Holly remarked.

'Human Resources for BT. She said she hated the job because it was mostly sacking people, so she took voluntary redundancy herself,' Mark explained. 'She's bright and efficient, I'm sure she'd be great. Jimmy wants someone with him to deal with admin stuff, and it would be useful if that person were a personal trainer too. She could help with the running.'

'But it's a long time to be away from home.' Holly knew the run would take at least six weeks.

She wondered if Mark knew that Daisy and Daniel were trying to have a child.

'Well, that's up to her, isn't it? I thought I'd ask her if she wants to work on the press launch, which will be in a few weeks,' he said, spearing a piece of rabbit as he did so. 'Then she can see if she wants to do the actual run. Do you think it will be a problem with Daniel?'

'I don't know,' Holly said quickly. 'Is the rabbit good?'

'Try some.' Mark pushed the plate towards her. 'How often do you see Daniel anyway?'

'Not that often.' Holly avoided looking directly at him and concentrated on getting the rabbit from the dish to her plate. 'I bump into him on the train every now and then. Just to say hello to.'

She wondered if Mark would accept what she said or if he guessed that it wasn't entirely true. She wasn't sure why but she didn't want him to know just how much time she spent talking to Daniel, any more than she wanted him to have another reason to spend more time with Daisy.

Chapter Thirty-Six

HOLLY FELT THE need to put some physical distance between herself and Guy and Natalie. She wanted to be out of London and on her way home but the departure boards weren't showing any trains to Brighton.

She'd met Guy for a coffee in a shop off Tottenham Court Road at midday. She'd told Natalie that she was going to look for some web-studio software that Jake wanted. He did want some web-design software, and it gave her just the excuse to head out of the office in that direction for half an hour.

She hadn't liked lying to Natalie but couldn't very well tell her she was meeting her husband.

Cuppa Coffee was an unusually homely affair for this part of town. Faux-suede sofas strewn with embroidered cushions were parked around coffee tables, creating the impression of a front room rather than a café. It seemed to be frequented entirely by mothers with young children and infants.

'Hello,' Holly said, spotting Guy sitting in an armchair in a corner. 'We should have a baby!'

She indicated the mothers and babies.

'It's too soon,' Guy said, grinning as he got up to kiss her.

Holly laughed, despite feeling that laughter wasn't entirely appropriate given their reason for meeting up.

'And I don't really want any more babies,' he added, catching the eye of the waitress who was approaching them. 'I don't think I could bear to go back to the early years again. What will you have, Holly?'

'A cup of tea, please,' she said to the waitress. 'English Breakfast.'

'I'll have an Americano, please,' Guy said, settling back into his chair as the waitress left with their order.

'So . . .' Holly was not sure how to start this conversation. 'You spoke to Mark about this Jimmy Finlay run?'

'Yes, it was good of him to consider me,' Guy replied. 'And previously I'd have jumped at the chance, but it's difficult. I mentioned it to Nat and she said it was impossible. Her career seems to have to come first.'

'It's not the sort of job you can leave behind at the end of the day.' Holly detected the note of pique in his voice.

'Look, I know what you're probably thinking,' Guy said, coming to the point. 'I know things looked bad the other night.'

'I don't know what to think,' Holly told him. 'But you two certainly seemed very cosy.'

'It's the first time I've met Mila,' Guy said. 'Well, obviously, I met her at the do for the programme, but that's the first and only time I've met up with her alone.'

Holly said nothing.

'The thing is . . .' Guy paused as the waitress came back and put their drinks on the table between them '. . . I had a bit of a chat with her then when I went to have a cigarette, about being at home with young children and how you don't have time to do anything for yourself.'

'It goes with the territory,' Holly pointed out.

'I know.' Guy took a sip of his coffee. 'Anyway we just got chatting about what we used to do, my photography and stuff. She's a sculptor but hardly gets time for it any more.'

'I know,' Holly said.

'Well, anyway, we exchanged numbers and I said we should meet and talk about ways of doing our own work.' He paused. 'But that's not really why I wanted to meet.'

'No?'

'I wanted to find out if she gets as rattled about the way Natalie is with James as I do.' A frown started to crease Guy's face. 'Because, from where I'm sitting, Holly, they are more than just colleagues. Natalie denies that there is anything going on but I don't know whether to believe her or not.'

'Why wouldn't you believe her?' Holly asked, thinking of the idle office speculation that there already was about James and Natalie and wondering if he had any firmer evidence.

'Because he just seems to take precedence in our lives,' Guy said. 'She's always on the phone to him, ostensibly talking about something for the programme, or going to functions with him, and just generally dropping his name into the conversation. It drives me mad.'

Holly shrugged. 'They do work together every day.'

'But you don't phone him every evening, do you?' Guy challenged.

She shook her head.

'Anyway, I met up with Mila. I wanted to ask how she found things.'

'What did she say?' Holly was curious to hear how Mila viewed her husband's relationship with Natalie.

'She said, "I don't consider Natalie to be a threat,"' Guy mimicked her accent. 'There was something condescending in the way she said it, as if Natalie wasn't worthy of fucking James Darling.'

'And is *she* a threat to Natalie?' Holly asked. She knew Guy knew she had seen them holding hands.

'Oh, God, no,' he laughed. 'I think she thinks I'm rather pathetic. What you saw . . . she was treating me like a child, Holly. She put her hand over mine and talked to me as if I was a four year old . . .

'"I do not think you need to worry, Guy."' He did a good imitation of Mila's voice again. '"You should stop worrying about your wife and do something to feel better about yourself. Do something you enjoy."'

'That's probably good advice.' Holly decided to choose to believe what he had told her, for the moment at least. 'Natalie said you'd been going to the gym, is that something you enjoy?'

'Yes.' Guy looked away, a bit shiftily, Holly thought. 'I used to stay fit just lugging cameras around the world, but I need to do a bit more these days. What about Mark? He said he was going to run a marathon?'

'So he says.' Holly was wondering how much of anything anyone said was to be believed.

She'd found it hard not saying anything to Natalie about Guy when she got back to the office and was relieved when it was time to go home, although now the trains seemed to be conspiring against her getting there.

'What's going on?' Daniel stood next to her as she scanned the train departure boards at Victoria.

'I've no idea,' she answered, surprised at just how often they managed to bump into each other, given the number of possible trains they might both choose to catch. 'All the trains to Brighton are coming up as cancelled but there's no more information.'

'I'll ask someone.' Daniel began walking towards the guard who was manning the ticket barrier. He turned and smiled at Holly just before he got there and she felt a surge of intense feeling that she told herself was contentment.

'A body on the line at Hassocks.' Daniel grimaced as he returned with the news. 'No trains to Brighton until they've dealt with it.'

'What about Hove?' Holly bit back the temptation to say something about the selfishness of killing yourself on this stretch of track. Didn't whoever it was know that people who hadn't wanted to end their lives had only recently died on this line? She took a deep breath, trying to calm herself.

'No, same stretch of track.' Daniel began scanning the boards again. 'We could take that train to Lewes. Then get the coastway service back to Brighton. It will probably be quicker than waiting to see what happens.'

'Good idea.' Holly checked the platform number. 'I'd rather be on the move anyway.'

'I used to live in Lewes,' Daniel said as the train pulled out of the station.

'Did you?' Holly couldn't quite see him in Lewes.

She took her phone out. It had just bleeped in her bag and she checked her messages, half-expecting, half-hoping it was Mark, asking when she'd be home.

It was from Anne-Marie.

Hi, Holly. No trains going home. Just wondered if you were at station and fancied a drink while we wait?

Holly put the phone away, deciding not to show it to Daniel.

'We lived there briefly, when we first moved out of London,' he was saying. 'We rented a flat in Southover to see if we liked it, but Daisy preferred Brighton.'

'And do you?' Holly couldn't quite work out if it was Daisy who had driven the move to the sea.

'I liked Lewes but I'm happy in Brighton too.' Daniel didn't seem particularly bothered about where he lived.

'Mark's over the moon about this work he's got with Jimmy Finlay.' Holly presumed Daniel knew about the run. 'And he's hoping Daisy will work on it with him.'

'She said he had asked if she wanted to help set up a press launch too.' Daniel didn't give away how he felt about this.

'I knew he was thinking of that, yes,' Holly said, wondering if Daniel knew that Mark also wanted her to accompany Jimmy Finlay on the run for six weeks. 'Do you mind?'

'No,' he replied. 'She'll probably enjoy working on something like that. She never really set out to do personal training and she gets a bit bored with it. It will be good for her to do something more challenging for a few weeks.'

'Yes.' Holly decided not to mention that Mark had Daisy in mind for a role which might last longer than that.

'Do you ever go to Lewes any more?' she asked as the train began nearing the town.

'Every now and then, for a wander and meal in The Snowdrop,' Daniel replied.

'The Snowdrop?' Holly sounded surprised.

'Yes. Have you been there?' Daniel asked.

'I don't think I've been for nearly twenty years.' She realised this made her sound very old.

'It's changed hands a few times,' Daniel said. 'And been done up. It's decked out like an old canal boat, and the food is great.'

'Then it has changed quite a bit.'

Holly remembered being sent there when she was a local radio reporter, to interview a retired policeman. He'd worked on a case involving the murder of two young children and been so affected he'd taken early retirement, spending his days in the pub which then, if not exactly spit and sawdust, most definitely didn't scream gastropub.

'I'll have to go some time,' she remarked.

'We could have a quick drink now,' Daniel suggested, looking at his watch, then at her. 'If you don't need to rush back.'

'Not really . . .' Holly hesitated slightly.

She had told Mark she would try and get back by 7. He was going for a twelve-mile run and she'd promised to make dinner.

But the weather was warm and the idea of a drink with Daniel, in a pub by the river, was appealing. The trains to Brighton had all been cancelled. She had the perfect excuse for being late.

'That's a lovely idea.' She smiled at Daniel. 'I'll text Mark and let him know what's going on.'

'You're right.' Holly looked around her, taking in the décor. 'It is much nicer than when I last came!'

'What are you having?' The pub was busy but Daniel had homed in on a free barman, with a skill she rather admired.

'I'll have a white wine spritzer,' Holly said. 'Shall I go and get us somewhere to sit?'

'A white wine spritzer and a pint of Harvey's,' Daniel said to the barman. Then to Holly, 'Do you want to sit outside?'

'That would be good.' She went to find a table in the beer garden.

There were plenty free, despite the sunshine. She watched Daniel coming out, his pace slower than usual as he carried the drinks across the uneven terrain. It was funny, she thought to herself. Before the crash she would have recognised Daniel if she'd seen him somewhere out of context, but she wouldn't have thought he was attractive.

She wasn't even sure she would have thought this a few weeks ago either. But now, as he put their two glasses down on the table, she definitely did. She frowned slightly, wondering what had changed and why.

'Penny for your thoughts,' he said.

'I was wondering why the pub was called The Snowdrop?' Holly said, looking up and spotting the sign.

It gave her something to say even though she was thinking something quite different.

'Why do you think?' Daniel's tone was questioning, rather than dismissive, and he nodded towards the sign which had prompted her question in the first place.

'I'm not sure.' Holly looked at it, taking it in properly.

When she'd looked the first time, she'd seen a landscape scene and expected, if she looked more closely, it would be dotted with clusters of snowdrops.

It wasn't. There was a row of houses, tiny beneath the vast chalky cliff – not a snowdrop in sight.

'Do the river banks here have a lot of snowdrops?' she asked.

'Appalling guess!' Daniel laughed. 'I thought you would know, having been a local journalist.'

'Go on then, tell me!' Holly gave his hand a playful shove because he was teasing her. Daniel caught her eye as she did so. Again, he seemed to hold her look, and Holly felt slightly uncomfortable. 'Why is it called The Snowdrop then?'

'It's the site of the UK's biggest ever avalanche,' Daniel told her.

'Really?' Holly looked around them. The gentle undulating curves of the South Downs provided an impressive backdrop, but these were hills not mountains. Surely you needed those for an avalanche. 'But where did the snow come from?'

'From that cliff.' Daniel nodded up towards it. 'There'd been heavy snow and wind, and a huge drift built up over days at the top of it. When it eventually came down, it covered the row of workers' cottages here. About fifteen people were buried and quite a few died.'

'When was that?' Holly shivered involuntarily. The thought

of people trapped under a vast quantity of snow made her feel suddenly cold.

'It was just after Christmas, sometime in the early nineteenth century.' Daniel noticed that she was shivering. 'Are you OK?'

'Yes, it's just . . .' She paused and pulled her cardigan more tightly around her. 'I had a sudden feeling of déjà vu almost. It's the thought of all those people being trapped, in the cold and dark, waiting . . . not knowing if they would get out alive or not.'

'I didn't think.' Daniel reached out his hand across the table, took hers and held it.

He didn't say anything else. He didn't need to. Holly knew that he knew he had revived memories for her. She squeezed his hand, as he had squeezed hers when he'd stayed with her, waiting for the emergency services to arrive.

'I don't know how I'd have got through it without you,' she said.

'I just happened to be there.' He shrugged. 'Anyone else would have done the same.'

'I don't just mean then.' Holly held his gaze. 'I mean afterwards too. These last few months. I don't quite know how to say this but . . .'

'It's OK.' Daniel was stroking her hand as he continued to hold it. 'You don't have to say anything, Holly. I understand. I feel the same way too.'

Chapter Thirty-Seven

JAKE WAS SITTING at the kitchen table with Mark's laptop. It was Sunday afternoon and he had opted to set himself up in the kitchen, largely because he was about to undertake a homework assignment and from the table there would be able to enlist help from both his parents.

'What's a palindrome?' he'd asked as he finished off his English homework.

'It's a word or phrase that reads the same forwards and backwards,' Holly told him.

'Like Anna?' Jake asked.

'Well, yes. A man, a plan, a canal, Panama is a good one.' She wondered if Jake had to come up with examples.

'What's Panama?' he asked.

'A very famous canal.' Holly felt sure he must know this. 'Don't they teach you anything in geography?'

'I've got geography homework too,' he told her. 'We don't learn where anywhere is, though.'

'Never odd or even, no lemon no melon.' It didn't surprise Holly that Mark had a whole lot of palindromes up his sleeve. 'God's dog.'

'Isn't that blasphemy?' Jake queried.

'Ma is a nun, as I am.' Mark ignored him and continued running off palindromes.

'A good one for Daisy,' Holly commented, wanting to remind him of the gaffe he'd made when he first met her.

He ignored her, turning his attention to Jake.

'What's your geography homework about then?'

'It's about natural disasters. I've got to think of three different types of natural disaster and then write about the causes and effects.'

'That sounds fairly straightforward.' Mark was reading the Sunday papers at the other of the table. 'You only have to pick up the paper to find something about a volcano or an earthquake.'

'Yeah, I might do the Icelandic volcano.' Jake leaned back in his seat and played with the mouse pad. ''Cos then I can write something about us getting stuck in Italy.'

'Oh, yes.' Holly recalled the extra week's holiday they'd had, courtesy of an Italian drinks company.

Mark had been working on a contract for Italian firewater and had had meetings and site visits in Tuscany. The brief was to see where the drink was sold in Italy and who drank it.

'It's a research trip,' he'd said when he told Holly about it.

'It's a pub crawl,' she had teased him. 'You get paid to do what most people have to spend their hard-earned cash doing. Groups of men, moving round bars, drinking. It's a pub crawl!'

'The thing about this particular pub crawl,' Mark had said, putting his arm around her waist and pulling her close to him, 'is that they want to know if I want to bring my family. And I have to be sure my wife won't be rude about my job if I do.'

'It's a very important research trip, obviously!' she had replied, and kissed him.

The trip was supposed to last a week but the Icelandic volcano erupted and their flight home was cancelled. Usually, Mark would have been stressed about not being able to get home, but he had imbibed a lot of Italian *gioia vivere* and, when one of his clients invited them to stay at his home for another week, quickly accepted.

The research trip turned into an idyllic holiday, being wined and dined by the most hospitable Italians. They had played tennis with Jake, flirted with Holly, and allowed their teenage sons to flirt with the just-pubescent Chloe so much that she never wanted to come home. Mark had been in his element, happy to be working but proud to have his wife and family there.

'I want to find something a bit unusual too.' Jake brought Holly's thoughts back to the present. 'Some sort of natural disaster that no one knows much about.'

'Oh, I've got a good one.' Holly had a sudden burst of enthusiasm for Jake's project. 'Did you know that the biggest ever avalanche in the UK was in Lewes?'

'That can't be right.' Mark was quick to dismiss her input. 'There are no mountains in Lewes, and you need mountains for avalanches.'

'That's what I thought.' Holly tried to be patient. 'But it was caused when a huge snowdrift built up on the cliff and then it collapsed on to a row of cottages in South Street.'

'Was anyone killed?' There had to be deaths for Jake to be interested.

'Yes, about fifteen people who lived in the cottages,' Holly told him. 'There's a pub there now, called The Snowdrop.'

'Oh, that's perfect!' Jake was pleased with this bit of information.

Mark was not.

'How do you know that?' He sounded cross and Holly was

not sure if it was because he suspected her of having been to The Snowdrop, without telling him, or because she had an interesting bit of information to pass on which he hadn't known himself. He liked to think of interesting facts as his preserve.

'I don't know.' She decided to sound vague. 'Someone told me.'

'Who?' Mark was pressing her for more details.

'I can't remember who.' Holly continued with the deliberately vague tack. 'Or maybe I read it somewhere.'

'I never knew that.' Mark said this as if his not knowing might make the information wrong. He did have a capacity for soaking up and retaining information. Mention a small African country and he seemed to know its history and the make-up of its government. He was a good person to have on a pub quiz team, the person you would want for your phone-a-friend . . . although if you phoned him and he didn't know the answer, he would probably find fault with the question.

'There's something about it here.' Jake had Googled the Lewes avalanche and was looking at a Wikipedia article. 'It must have been awful, being stuck in the snow like that.' He looked up at Holly questioningly, as if asking about her own experience.

Holly looked at Mark, who was reading the paper and not meeting her eyes. She smiled at Jake, attempting to reassure him. 'It's OK, Jakey. It was bad but I don't go there any more. I'm OK.'

'It's a grotty pub,' Mark said grumpily.

'Apparently it's changed hands a few times since we last went,' Holly said, and almost immediately wished she hadn't.

'And the same mysterious source who told you its history told you that too?'

Holly shrugged and wondered if perhaps he already knew that she'd been to the pub with Daniel on her way home. There was only one way he could. Daisy must have told him. But that seemed unlikely because Daisy could only have known if Daniel had told her.

'When did you tell Mark you'd be back?' Daniel had asked in the pub on Friday evening. 'Have you got time for another drink?'

'I didn't give him a time,' Holly said. She hadn't told Mark she was finding an alternative route. 'I just said there were no trains to Brighton and I'd be late back.'

'Daisy's not expecting me.' Daniel began to get up, as if to make for the bar. 'She's doing a training session this evening.'

'I'll get these.' Holly stood up herself and began picking up their empty glasses. 'Same again?'

Daniel nodded as she went back inside. She wondered as she stood at the bar whether he knew Daisy's training session was with Mark or if he minded the time they were spending together. There was no reason why he should. It was her job after all. But if Daisy was going to work on the Jimmy Finlay job, they would be spending even more time together.

Every now and then it crossed Holly's mind that Mark might be using his personal training sessions as an opportunity to try to make a move on Daisy. But even if he did, she was fairly confident he would not succeed. Daisy could do better, she thought, and as she did realised it was not a particularly pleasant thing to think about your own husband.

'Here you are.' She handed Daniel another pint and sat down. Now that they were here, away from their different worlds, she wanted to talk to him. 'Do you ever get flashbacks?'

'Sometimes.' Daniel did not seem surprised by her question, as if he had been waiting for her to ask it for some time.

'It was the dark that scared me more than anything,' Holly

told him. 'It was so total. Every now and then something happens that brings it back to me.'

'I find it happens when I'm least expecting it,' Daniel confided. 'I'll be with a client in a meeting, having a perfectly normal conversation, and suddenly I can hear people screaming. I just have to keep talking and focus on the job and it usually recedes.'

'I find it comes back in quieter moments,' Holly told him. 'Mark thinks I should see a counsellor but most of the time I'm fine. I don't want to keep going over stuff, I'd rather just get on with life and try to forget it.'

'I'm the same.' Daniel sipped his pint and considered what she'd said. 'I mean, if someone like Anne-Marie can carry on and get the train regularly, what have I got to complain about? I wasn't hurt. I didn't lose anyone. We spent half an hour stuck on the train . . . that's all, really.'

'Anne-Marie does seem very angry,' Holly ventured.

'Well, she's got good reason to be.' Daniel was pushing some spilled beer around the tabletop. 'I'm sure she has bad days.'

'Do you have bad days?' Holly asked.

'Sometimes.' He looked up at her. 'But talking to you helps.'

'Perhaps we should talk more?' she suggested. In response Daniel put his hand over hers but said nothing.

A barmaid had come into the garden, looking for empties to clear away. She approached Holly and Daniel and peered briefly at the half-empty glasses between which they were holding hands.

Holly wondered what she made of them. Did they look like any couple having a drink on a Friday night or did they look different? Would the barmaid go inside and comment that they didn't look right together, but she wasn't quite sure why?

'The thing I find hardest,' Daniel said, after a few moments' silence, 'is connecting with everyone around me. I can go through the motions . . . I can have conversations . . . I can walk along the seafront with Daisy . . . but I feel slightly apart from them.'

'I know what you mean.' Holly felt like this, even with Chloe and Jake. 'I feel as if my friends and family don't understand me.' She paused and took a sip of her drink then corrected herself. 'Can't understand me.'

'The only person I think might understand me is you,' Daniel told her.

Then his phone had rung, and he'd picked up because it was Daisy, and although he turned away from her slightly as he reassured his wife that he would be back soon, Holly could still see enough of his face to notice it soften into the expression people use when they're talking to someone they are close to.

'I ought to be getting back,' she said, as soon as he had finished his call.

'OK, I'm going to do the avalanche, the tsunami and an earthquake.' Jake had decided the direction his geography project would take.

'We were in the tsunami.' Mark looked up from the travel section. 'Don't you remember?'

'No!' Now it was Jake's turn to express disbelief. 'I think I would have remembered.'

'Not exactly in it,' Holly said. 'Only the shallow end anyway.'

'It was still the tsunami though.' Mark addressed this to Jake. 'We were on holiday in the north of Thailand. It was our tenth wedding anniversary, wasn't it, Hol?'

'Yes.' She'd forgotten they'd decided to mark this milestone by all going to Thailand for a couple of weeks.

'And there was one day we were on the beach,' he continued, 'and it was suddenly covered in water.'

'It wasn't deep,' Holly joined in the recollections. 'Not more than an inch really, was it?'

'No,' Mark agreed. 'We thought it was quite fun at the time. We didn't know then what devastation it was wreaking elsewhere.'

'We were lucky then,' Jake said.

'And we've been in an earthquake too.' As she said this Holly suddenly realised her life seemed to be a series of minor involvements in major incidents.

'Oh, yes, on our honeymoon,' Mark told Jake. 'We were in Chile and there was an earthquake in another part of the country. We just felt a small tremor where we were. Do you remember, Hol?'

'I remember the earth moving!' Holly smiled, feeling some of the old warmth between them revived by this spontaneous bout of reminiscing.

'Oh, pl-ease.' Jake grimaced. 'I just want to hear about the earthquake.'

'Don't worry, Jakey,' Mark said, suddenly serious again. 'There's no earth moving around your mother any more.'

Holly shot him a furious look.

'I'm going to make a phone call,' she said, and left the room.

Chapter Thirty-Eight

Holly slowed her pace, not sure if she wanted to talk to Anne-Marie. She was pretty sure that was the person Daniel was chatting to. Holly had a slightly awkward conversation with her earlier in the day and didn't want to repeat it.

'We're doing something in the programme next week about Survivor's Syndrome,' the producer who'd introduced herself as Melanie had said. Her voice was quiet and concerned, and Holly wondered if she'd adopted that tone, specially to talk to her.

'Right . . .' Holly waited for her to say more.

'I hope you don't mind my call?' Melanie went on. 'But someone told me that you were on the train which crashed near East Croydon earlier this year, and I wondered if you thought it might be something you could talk about?'

'I'm not sure,' Holly said, but she was. 'To be honest, I don't think I'm a particularly good example. I wasn't hurt in the crash and I don't know anyone who was.'

'It doesn't have to be anyone who was hurt. Sufferers from Survivor's Syndrome often feel guilty about having escaped.'

Holly felt lucky to have escaped unharmed. She didn't want to be pigeonholed as a survivor.

'I don't want to do it,' she told Melanie firmly.

'I also wondered if you might know of anyone else?' Melanie asked tentatively.

'There is someone.' Holly had thought of Anne-Marie. 'But I'll have to speak to her first.'

Holly took out her season ticket and passed it through the barrier. She could see Anne-Marie saying goodbye to Daniel and heading for the exit alongside W H Smith. He went the opposite way into the mini M&S on the opposite side of the station.

Suddenly an instant meal seemed like a very good idea.

'Fancy meeting you here.' Holly surprised him as he plucked a steak-and-kidney pie from the chiller cabinet.

'Hello.' He stood up and grinned, brandishing the pie. 'One meal for one! What are you here for?'

'Another meal for one.' Holly started looking in the chiller cabinet herself.

'No one cooking for you?' Daniel glanced at her sideways.

'No.' She tried to concentrate on the food. 'Mark's out running tonight and both the children are out, too. What about you?'

'Daisy has a few training sessions this evening,' he said. 'I think one of them is with Mark actually.'

Holly nodded as if she knew this, although she didn't. Mark must be seeing an awful lot of her at the moment. She'd also begun working on the Jimmy Finlay project. He wouldn't actually start his run until much later in the year, he needed to get a lot fitter first, but Mark was talking of setting up a press conference in a couple of weeks. Daisy was helping with that.

'Do you fancy a quick drink before your date with the microwave?' Daniel asked, as they stood in the checkout queue.

'Yes,' Holly said, emphatically. 'Did I see you talking to Anne-Marie?' she asked, giving away the fact that she had spotted him before he hit M&S.

'Yes, I bumped into her when I got off the train.'

'Did she say anything about talking to me today?' Holly asked, as they walked the short distance from the station to The Battle of Trafalgar.

'No, why?' Daniel said quizzically as they went into the pub. 'What are you having?'

'I'll get them.' Holly took out her purse. 'It's my turn, I'm sure.'

'A pint of Sussex Best then, thank you,' he said. 'What did Anne-Marie want then?'

'Oh, well, I called her.' Holly ordered the drinks and they carried them into the beer garden at the back. 'It was a bit awkward, really.'

'Why?' Daniel took a sip of his pint and looked around. Holly wasn't sure if he was taking in their surroundings or looking to see if there was anyone he knew there.

'A producer from *Woman's Hour* called me. Someone at work must have given them my name.' Holly followed the direction of Daniel's gaze.

The garden was fairly empty. A couple of gay men sat in the corner holding hands and an elderly woman sat by herself, pulling a bright orange cardigan tight around her, even though it was warm, as she nursed what was left of a pint.

'They are doing a programme about Survivor's Syndrome,' she told Daniel. 'They wanted to know if I would talk to them, but I said I didn't have much to say and suggested Anne-Marie.'

'What is Survivor's Syndrome?' he asked.

'A mental condition that occurs when a person thinks they've done wrong surviving a traumatic event.' Holly parroted what Melanie had told her.

'And do you think Anne-Marie has it?' He looked sceptical.

'I don't know,' Holly said. 'I was just trying to fob off the producer with someone else, really. I know that's a terrible thing to do. But I suppose I also thought Anne-Marie probably does have mixed emotions about the fact that she wasn't on the train and her husband was.'

'What did she say when you called her?' Daniel asked.

'She was angry.' Holly hadn't given much advance thought to how Anne-Marie might react. 'She was really cross. Said I didn't understand anything about her and I had no right to go talking to journalists about her behind her back. Although she took the producer's number.'

Daniel put his arm around her in a brief gesture of reassurance.

'It was probably just a spur-of-the-moment reaction. She seemed happy enough when I spoke to her.'

'I hope so.' Holly smiled at him gratefully.

'I haven't been here for a while,' he said, looking round the beer garden again.

'Me neither.' Holly couldn't think when the last time was. 'Mark and I used to come here a lot when we first met. He had a flat near here.'

She thought back to the early days, when she had first met him and had gone to visit him in the flat he had moved into by himself, not long after meeting her.

'It will give us more space together,' he'd said, as if he needed to justify moving out of the shared flat above her colleague from work. 'I don't want Tim getting in the way every time you come round.'

'He doesn't,' she'd laughed, but was flattered that, so early in their relationship, he was wanting to spend more time alone with her. Not long after he'd taken on the new flat, he'd asked her to move in with him.

'Isn't it a bit too soon?' she'd asked, worried that he seemed to be rushing things and might have second thoughts. But Mark had looked her in the eye and said, 'Why? I know I want to be with you. Why wait?'

Holly felt sad now, thinking back to those early heady days. She'd known the intensity of her relationship with him would not last, that it would become more settled and predictable, but she'd never imagined that they would start becoming strangers to each other, living side by side but failing to connect.

'You don't come here any more then?' Daniel asked, as if he could sense what she was thinking. 'With Mark? Or does he come with friends?'

'No, I don't think so.' Holly had never really thought about this. Perhaps Mark did still come here sometimes.

'Once the children came along, we stopped going out as much,' she said. 'We haven't really started again.'

She looked up and smiled. A cheerful smile that she hoped would pull her out of her slightly melancholy mood.

'Make the most of the time you have before the children arrive,' she said.

'If that ever happens.' Daniel stared into his pint and Holly wished she hadn't said it.

'No news then?' she asked.

'No.' He looked up at her. 'The consultant said to give it more time, but to be honest . . .'

He paused and Holly didn't say anything, unsure if he wanted to continue this line of conversation.

'We haven't really been getting on that well recently,' he said, looking at Holly again and holding the look. 'It's a bit of an issue and Daisy won't talk about it.'

'That's probably natural.' Holly felt slightly flustered. 'A lot of couples say it puts enormous pressure on them, trying for a baby.'

She wondered if Daniel had the same misgivings she'd had about Daisy and Mark working together so closely.

'It's not just that . . .' He looked away.

Holly felt her phone vibrating in her bag, which was on the floor against her leg. She ignored it. She couldn't very well answer it now.

'The thing is . . .' said Daniel, then he appeared to be searching for the right words to communicate whatever it was he had to say.

'What is it?' Holly asked, looking at him again, which was when Daniel leaned forward and kissed her.

It was something of a relief when his phone rang. The ringtone was loud, which made it hard to ignore.

There'd been an awkwardness to the finishing of their drinks, the polite enquiries about whether they wanted another, the starting to ask questions at the same time and the 'you first', before saying something other than what they had meant to say.

Holly was reminded of an Ingrid Bergman quote: 'A kiss is a lovely trick designed by nature to stop speech when words become superfluous.' And she was tempted to kiss Daniel again because it had been nice, kissing him, very nice, but somehow not quite right. Not as in morally 'we are both married to other people so we shouldn't be kissing', but not what she'd expected.

She wondered, if she kissed him a second time, if it would feel different, and where it might lead. They were awkward with each other now; the kiss had done away with the old easy familiarity.

Holly drained her drink and smiled to herself, wondering what Dimitri would think if he'd seen her kissing Daniel in the beer garden of The Battle of Trafalgar.

She could imagine him teasing her. 'Nice try, Holly, but it was still a pretty safe kiss.'

'What's funny?' Daniel asked.

'I was just thinking of something a colleague said.' She left it at that.

'Listen, Holly, I . . .' Daniel paused as his phone began to ring. He took it out of his pocket and looked at the caller ID.

'It's Daisy,' he said, apologetically. 'I'd better get it.'

Holly nodded and watched him.

'Hello,' he said.

There was something beautiful about his face, she thought as she watched him now. Something she'd only come to appreciate having got to know him.

'Is everything OK?' Daniel was saying to his wife, and a look of anxiety crossed his face as he glanced up and caught Holly looking at him.

She looked away quickly, embarrassed.

'No, I'm just having a quick drink,' she heard him saying as she studied the grain of the wood on the table instead of his face. 'I thought you were out for the evening?'

Holly ran her finger around the contours of a large knot, concentrating on this so as to try not to listen to his conversation with his wife.

'Yes, she is with me,' she heard him say. 'We just bumped into each other, coming out of the station.'

Holly caught his eye and felt alarm. Did Daisy suspect there was something going on between her and Daniel? She felt panic beginning to mount at the prospect of a confrontation, even though, apart from their one brief kiss, there was nothing really to confront anyone about. Or was there? She was confused.

'I guess she must have it switched off,' Daniel was saying, but he was still looking at Holly, no longer tuning in to his conversation with his wife.

Holly reached for the phone that was in her bag, remembering someone had been trying to reach her just before she had begun kissing Daniel.

She checked the call log and found she had one missed call. But it was from a number she did not recognise.

'Do you want to speak to her?' Daniel's face had gone pale and Holly felt the colour beginning to drain from hers too. Why would Daisy want to speak to her? Had Mark said something to her while they were training this evening?

She took a deep breath and held on to the edge of the table now, wondering what she would say to Daisy, but Daniel was still talking to her.

'OK, yes. Of course,' he was saying.

Holly strained to hear what Daisy was saying at the other end of the line.

'I'll tell her,' he said. 'And get a taxi from the station.'

Daniel was obviously being summoned somewhere, quickly. Holly breathed a small sigh of relief that Daisy no longer wanted to talk to her. Perhaps she would later.

She raised her eyebrows questioningly, in a way she hoped would convey 'Is everything OK?' and elicit a reassuring 'Yes, everything's fine' nod. But Daniel's face remained impassive.

'OK, see you in a bit.' He started to wind up the phone

conversation. 'Daisy,' he said, as if she'd been about to hang up and he wanted to keep her on the line a moment longer.

'Yes?' Holly heard her reply.

'I'll see you in a bit.' Daniel had already said this. He had obviously been about to say something else to her, but had thought better of it in front of Holly.

'Is everything OK?' she asked, now that he was slowly putting the phone back in his pocket.

'Holly,' Daniel began. 'Something's happened.'

Chapter Thirty-Nine

'**A**RE YOU A relative?' The receptionist at A & E had an air of suspicion about her, as if people who weren't relatives turned up all the time, trying to gain access to Accident and Emergency patients.

'Yes, I'm his wife,' Holly said, which had the effect of making the receptionist transfer her suspicions to Daniel.

'And you?' she asked.

'I'm a friend,' he told her coolly. 'And my wife brought him in.'

If Holly's emotions hadn't been in the heightened state they were, she might have noticed that the receptionist raised her eyebrows ever so slightly. Fortunately she didn't.

'He's been transferred to the Albion and Lewes ward,' the woman revealed, after typing Mark's name into her computer. 'Take the lift to the eighth floor and let the staff there know who you are.'

'Thank you.' Holly began looking around for the lifts.

'You can go up with her, if you want,' the receptionist told Daniel grudgingly.

'I've no intention of doing anything else,' he muttered, as they made their way through the walking wounded to the lifts.

Holly had once been very familiar with A & E and didn't need to look around to know that there would be a few drunks, passed out or brought in by the police, some anxious parents thinking their child may have meningitis, and a couple of older people, waiting patiently, not wanting to trouble the doctors, even though they may have broken a hip falling several hours ago.

A few years back she and Mark had been the anxious parents, sitting with Jake on various occasions: after he'd stepped on a rusty nail and got blood poisoning; jumped from the roof of the shed and broken several toes; and fallen off his skateboard and cracked a rib.

Holly remembered how the woman who'd been living next-door when he was born had told her she'd get used to coming into Casualty. The neighbour had three boys and was wondering whether to keep trying for a girl.

'Boys injure themselves all the time,' she'd said cheerily as Holly cradled her day-old son and thought to herself that she would do all she could to protect him.

The neighbour had been right, though. A few months down the line, Jake had stuffed a Lego figure so far up his nose it required a surgeon's skill to remove it. Since then A & E had become a regular haunt. Holly had expected to be back there at some point, and frequently envisaged a scenario where a car knocked down Jake while he was walking to school, his hearing impaired by an iPod and his sight blinkered by the cowl of his hoody.

She hadn't expected to be here because Mark had had a heart attack.

She could feel her own heart racing as they emerged from the lift and was surprised by how pleased she felt to see Daisy as they crossed the newly disinfected floor to the nurses' desk.

'Holly,' she said, touching her arm. 'He's going to be OK.'

Holly managed a half-smile as Daisy told the nurse that this was Mark's wife.

'Can I see him?' she asked.

'Of course.' The nurse at the desk had picked up more of a beside manner than her colleague downstairs. She stood up and nodded to a young uniformed man. 'Ashwin, this is Mrs Constantine.'

Mark was lying on a bed with an oxygen mask over his face and a drip in his arm. He was wearing a hospital gown.

'Hello,' she said gently, not sure how much of his surroundings he was taking in.

'Holly,' Mark said, lifting the mask from his face and speaking with some effort. His skin looked grey. 'You were right about the marathon being a ridiculous idea!'

'Oh, Mark.' Holly bent down to kiss him. 'What happened?'

Ashwin spoke for him.

'He's had a minor heart attack.' He confirmed what Daisy had already relayed via Daniel. 'We are going to operate to unblock one of his arteries. He's going to need a local anaesthetic and we're just waiting for the cardiologist.'

'Who's that?' Holly asked because she felt she needed to ask questions and wasn't sure what else to ask.

'Dr Parkinson,' the nurse told her. 'He's very experienced.'

'I hope he doesn't . . .' Mark was lifting his oxygen mask again and trying to speak.

'Doesn't what?' Holly asked.

'Have Parkinson's!' Mark said, smiling despite the effort and letting the mask fall over his face again.

Holly smiled back, wondering whether hospital etiquette allowed emergency patients to joke about their condition.

'No, his hands are perfectly steady,' the nurse laughed. 'He's a bit of a comedian, your husband, isn't he? Apparently he made the paramedics laugh in the ambulance too. I keep telling him he should be trying to relax.'

'He can't help himself.' Holly sniffed, finding that she was now beginning to cry. She took Mark's hand and squeezed it.

'I was trying to make you laugh,' he said through the mask.

'You did,' she said, stroking his hand and feeling overawed that despite the fact he was lying on a hospital trolley, waiting to have a heart operation, he had not lost his sense of humour. She wondered now how she could ever have found his relentless jokiness irritating. He was naturally funny, and how much better a man who tried to use his humour to get through the difficult times than one who just allowed himself to become depressed.

'You do.' She emphasised the *do* and bent down to kiss him.

'Ready for Mr Constantine,' announced a man in scrubs. He had heavily tattooed arms, was chewing gum, and would have looked more at home backstage at a heavy metal convention than in a hospital corridor.

Oh, God, don't let him be the surgeon, Holly thought, slightly ashamed of her innate prejudice against multiple tattoos.

'The porter will take him up for his operation,' Ashwin put her mind at rest. 'You'll have to wait here.'

'Yes.' Holly had watched enough episodes of *Casualty* to know this much.

'I love you,' she whispered to Mark.

He didn't reply and she wasn't sure if he'd heard her. He looked scared now and so was Holly – scared that the future she'd always thought she would have with him might be in jeopardy.

Daniel and Daisy were sitting side by side on plastic chairs in the reception area. They looked up at Holly with a mixture of sympathy and query as she walked towards them.

'Has he gone in?' Daisy asked.

Holly nodded.

'So what do you do now?' Daniel enquired.

'They suggested I go home and get him some clothes and stuff.' Holly looked at them both, seeking their approval for this course of action.

It seemed to her somehow callous and uncaring to leave the building while Mark was being operated on, but she could see that it might be better to do something practical rather than pace around Reception, feeling slightly sick.

'I can take you.' Daisy seemed to decide for her.

'Thank you.' Holly accepted the offer and, for the first time since Daniel had taken Daisy's call in the pub, realised she had not let the children know anything was amiss.

She'd thought about calling them as she sat in the taxi on her way to the hospital with Daniel, but had decided to find out exactly what was happening with Mark first.

'I need to let the children know what's going on.' She looked from Daniel to Daisy, wondering what Daisy would think if she'd known that an hour or so ago Holly had been kissing her husband in a pub garden. She wished it had never happened.

'I called them after I called you. I hope you don't mind?' Daisy said. 'Mark said Jake had been going for a sleepover but it was cancelled so he'd be at home. And he said Chloe was out but she'd want to know too.'

'Thank you.' Holly was grateful to her again. She hadn't wanted to call them out of the blue and tell them the news. She didn't know exactly what Daisy had told them but, whatever it had been, it would make it easier for her to call them now.

'I told them Mark had been taken ill while running.' Daisy appeared to read her thoughts and filled her in. 'And that he was going to hospital to be checked over. I didn't want to tell them any more than that.'

'You seem to have done everything absolutely right,' Holly said, thinking that Daniel and Daisy were well suited to one other. They both seemed to know instinctively what to do in a crisis.

'Shall I take you home then?' Daisy asked. 'The car's on a double yellow line around the corner. At least, I hope it's still there.'

'Shall I wait here?' Daniel suddenly seemed set apart from the unfolding drama, unsure what to do.

'I've got a Smart car,' Daisy said, to explain why he would not be coming with them.

'I could wait until you get back.' Daniel sat down again, as if this was what he'd decided to do, and again Holly realised it was the right thing. She felt better leaving Mark knowing there was someone else in the building, someone who could contact her if necessary, someone who would be there, looking familiar, when she walked back in.

'Thank you,' she said to him.

'See you in a bit then.' He stood up a little awkwardly as if wondering whether he should make any sort of parting gesture, but Daisy was already guiding Holly towards the lift.

'Are you OK?' she asked as they got in.

'No,' Holly answered.

She was anything but all right. She felt sick, brought up short by the sight of Mark and the shock of what was happening to him. She felt guilty for being in the pub with Daniel when her husband was suddenly seized by overwhelming pain, and she felt powerless to do anything to help him.

'He'll be OK,' Daisy said, looking at Holly as if she knew exactly what she was thinking. 'I'm sure you'll both be OK, Holly.'

Chapter Forty

JAKE CLOSED THE computer hurriedly when Holly walked into the sitting room. He seemed furtive and, even in her emotional state, she made a mental note that she and Mark really must check what he did on it. She suspected he might be looking at porn, but her suspicions were based only on the general impression that that was what all teenagers were doing these days.

'Oh, hi Mum.' Jake got up from the sofa and put the laptop back on the desk.

Then he walked over and hugged her, burying his head in her chest as he used to do every morning when he woke up, until about a year ago when a new set of hormones kicked in and told him that all physical contact with your mother should be avoided.

'Is Dad OK?' he said, raising his head and seeing Daisy hovering in the corridor behind Holly. The sight of her caused him to spring away from Holly as if he'd been caught in a clinch with someone who was not his mother.

'Not really, Jakey.' Holly wished Jake was still holding her but she knew the teenage psyche was like a yo-yo on high-grade elastic. 'Shall we sit down?' She motioned towards the sofa and Jake obediently ambled over and sat.

'Shall I make you a cup of tea?' Daisy was the one now hovering in the doorway.

'Oh, yes, please.' Holly realised this was just what she needed.

'Jake?' Daisy asked.

'OK.' He was graceless in accepting her offer.

'Do you want sugar?' This was addressed to Holly again, and although Holly didn't take sugar, she realised that she wanted it.

She nodded, and as she listened to the footsteps going down the corridor to the kitchen she wondered if Daisy was going to be looking for the kettle and the tea and the cups, and having difficulty finding them, or whether she was already completely au fait with the layout of their kitchen.

'Dad's not very well,' Holly said, sitting down next to Jake on the sofa. 'I don't want you to be too alarmed, because it sounds worse than it is, but he had a minor heart attack while he was running. He's going to be OK though.'

'Oh, right.' Jake's reply was characteristically nonchalant.

Holly had expected this news might provoke an atypical reaction.

'Our headmaster had a heart attack when he was running,' Jake said, as if hearing about middle-aged men having heart attacks was something he was very used to. 'He had three months off last year.'

'And is he OK now?' Holly wondered why Jake had never mentioned this at the time, and why the school had never told them. Perhaps they'd sent a note which had never made it out of the depths of Jake's bag or, if it had, only as far as Mark's hands, not hers.

'Yeah, he's fine,' Jake told her. 'He was a fat bastard before but he looks much better now. Some of the girls think he's really fit.'

'Do they?' Holly wondered if this was his way of trying to reassure her. She found the image of the girls that Jake knew lusting after the headmaster somewhat unsettling.

'They say he looks like Richard Gere, but he looks more like a grey-haired David Cameron to me. His skin's all shiny too.' Jake began laughing, nervously at first, and then when Holly laughed too, more wholeheartedly.

Holly was reminded of a time when she'd been away for a few days when he was six years old. She'd gone with a group of other mothers for a long weekend in Lisbon. Mark said the kids had been fine while she was away, but when she came back Jake had sat on her lap and laughed so hard that he almost cried. Holly had thought then that he probably wanted to cry because he had missed her while she was away, but had turned the tears into laughter instead.

She thought the same was probably true now and put her arm around him, trying to reassure and comfort him, even though he wasn't showing visible signs of distress.

'Declan's dad had a heart attack too,' Jake said, when he'd stopped laughing.

For someone in his early teens, he certainly seemed to know a lot of people with heart problems. 'Or was it heart failure? He has to take pills every day now.'

'Dad's having an operation.' Holly admired his easy acceptance of the situation but suspected he was using it to cover more mixed emotions. 'He's in hospital now. One of the tubes that goes into his heart got blocked and they are going to do something to make it bigger so that doesn't happen again.'

'Angioplasty?' Jake asked, a question Holly had not thought to ask when the procedure was being explained to her at the hospital.

'Yes. Do you do this in biology or something?' She wondered at her son's apparent knowledge, which certainly seemed to be more extensive than hers.

'No, I read about it on the internet,' he told her. 'I was looking into . . .'

He stopped as if he was revealing too much, Holly was not sure why.

'Tea.' Daisy came in and put two steaming mugs on the table in front of them.

'How are you, Jake?' she asked. 'I liked your pictures of your shadow friends.'

'Thank you,' Holly said, referring to the tea and wondering what Daisy was talking about. Who were Jake's shadow friends?

'Thanks.' Jake looked momentarily animated. 'Mr Bannister says I should enter them for this competition.'

'You should,' Daisy agreed. 'They're really good.'

Mr Bannister was Jake's art teacher, this much Holly knew, but he hadn't shown her the pictures which Daisy seemed to know all about. Holly wondered how she knew, and how she'd been able to find the sugar, which was fairly well hidden as no one normally took it.

'I saw the pictures on Jake's Facebook page,' Daisy commented, as if realising that her knowledge of Holly's son's life needed some explanation. 'We're friends.'

'Ah.' Holly should have guessed.

'By the way, Gran says to let her know about Dad,' Jake said.

'Did she call?' Holly wondered if super-efficient Daisy had somehow also got word to her mother's yoga camp in Koh Samui that Mark had been taken to hospital. She was beginning to understand why Mark had put her forward for being Jimmy Finlay's PA.

'No, I was Facebooking her earlier,' Jake said. 'She's always online around five o'clock. It's when she catches up with everyone.'

Except me and my dad, Holly thought to herself.

She took a sip of her tea and for a moment almost forgot that this cuppa was only a brief interlude before she went back to the hospital where her husband was currently undergoing heart surgery.

She shivered at the thought and Jake put his arm around her, as if he knew what was going through her mind.

'He'll be OK, Mum,' he said. 'Are you?'

Holly smiled at him, thinking she was the one who should be reassuring him.

'I'm just going to pack a few things for Dad,' she told him. 'He might need to stay in overnight. Then we'll go back to the hospital. Do you know where Chloe is?'

'She's out somewhere.' Jake was typically vague. 'But she called. She said she'd meet us there. Are we driving?'

'I'm not sure I'm up to driving,' Holly said. 'We could get a taxi.'

'We won't all fit in my car,' Daisy said. 'Shall I call a cab while you're packing, Holly?'

'I'll do it,' Jake said, and Holly suddenly thought how like Mark he was, better able to cope with a situation if he was actually doing something.

'I'll be off then,' Daisy said. 'If you're OK? Daniel said he'd make his own way home after you got back. Let me know how Mark is, won't you?'

'Of course,' Holly said, wondering how imperative it was that Daisy knew how the operation had gone. Did she want to know because she was a friend or was she more than that?

'Are you sure you'll be OK?' she asked.

'No,' Holly said, laughing in the way that people do when they are trying not to cry. 'But I'm going to try to be.'

She went upstairs and could hear Daisy saying goodbye to Jake and telling him to look after his mother. She opened the door of their bedroom and surveyed the unmade bed and dirty clothes strewn across the floor. Mark usually tidied up a bit before she got home.

He knew it annoyed her to find the bed still unmade and yesterday's clothes where they'd landed. This evening, though, in Mark's absence, Holly felt comforted by the mess. The discarded shirt in the doorway provided evidence of his existence in the way his mess had done when she first met him.

Back then, when they had shuffled between their respective flats, Holly had delighted in seeing Mark's stuff strewn around her bedroom when he was not there. It had been a reminder that she had a gorgeous new boyfriend, rather than evidence of a husband who never tidied up.

She picked his shirt up off the floor and held it to her face, breathing in the smell of Mark and washing powder. She put it on the bed, thinking she might use it as a comforter that evening, if he was kept in overnight. She hoped he would not stay in for longer than that. She wanted him home as soon as possible.

Holly pulled an overnight bag from the top of the wardrobe in their room and opened the drawer under their bed, where Mark kept his underwear and t-shirts. Today the drawer seemed to hold more than just clean clothes. Like the rest of the room it held reminders of Mark, and rather than just pulling a few clean t-shirts from near the front of the drawer, Holly found herself sitting down and staring at its contents.

Nearest to her was the bottle green t-shirt that he usually wore while out running. He must have been wearing a different one today. Holly began leafing through the folded tops, much as someone would flick through files in a filing cabinet, briefly conjuring up images of the last time she had seen her husband in a particular shirt. She wasn't being maudlin. She had just realised, sitting here now, with Mark in hospital, how little attention she had been paying him recently and how much she regretted that.

Holly reached to the back of the drawer and pulled out a pale blue garment she had not seen him wear for years. She hadn't even realised he still had it. It was a nondescript t-shirt but she remembered it because it had been the one he was wearing at the party where they'd first met. It probably didn't even fit him any more and she wondered why Mark had kept it. Was it for sentimental reasons?

She pulled it out of the drawer, to look at it, not to pack it, and as she shook it out a white envelope fell out and into her lap.

'Holly' was written on the front, in Mark's writing. She turned it over but the flap at the back was stuck down. She wasn't sure what to do. The letter was addressed to her, but hidden. She obviously wasn't meant to find it. She thought she should probably wrap it up in the t-shirt and put it back, pretend she'd never disturbed it.

But lately, she hadn't been doing many of things she ought to do.

Chapter Forty-One

Dear Holly,

I don't know if I will ever give you this letter. I am writing it because, right now, I am not sure what else to do. There are so many things I want to say, that I feel I need to say to you, but it may be better if some of those things are left unsaid. Perhaps what I am feeling at the moment is just me, now, and in a few weeks or months it will have passed. By then, I may breathe a sigh of relief that I never actually aired what I am about to write.

Or perhaps I will still feel the same, and I will give you this letter, or sit down and tell you exactly how I am feeling. I don't know. All I know is that now I am not happy and I need to do something. I know that writing you a letter I may never give you is not very pro-active, but I hope it will at least make me feel better without damaging us more than we already seem to be.

A lot has happened to us over the past couple of years, Holly, and I feel as if we are gradually coming unstuck. People talk about the glue that holds a marriage together but to me that always suggests that the marriage was something a bit broken in the first place. Glue is usually used to fix things that someone has dropped on the floor (in our house anyway). I think of marriage more as two people being joined together like links in a chain, and I used to think that you and I were a very strong chain. I'm no longer so sure. I feel as if someone has prised open a link and, while we are still together, it may take only a small swerve or sudden jolt to force us apart.

You used to joke, when we first met, that I was always doing something. I think it used to annoy you that I could never just sit in the garden of that first flat that we rented together, but would always be cutting something back or putting something up. It's true I do like to do things, it makes me feel more in control in this out-of-control world, as if by cutting back a bit of honeysuckle I am maintaining control over my life.

I feel I am losing that control now. There have been too many things beyond it, conspiring to change my life, and it scares me to feel so powerless over my own destiny.

I thought that knowing me, as no one else does, you would realise how vulnerable losing contracts at work and struggling to keep my business going would make me feel. I thought you would support me, as you always have done, and that I would be able to get through a difficult patch with you behind me. But you seemed to think the only thing to do was take everything on yourself, and you seemed to despise me for my failure at work.

Or perhaps despise is too strong? I know, Holly, that I am no longer the strong, capable, outgoing, funny man you first fell in love with – not to you anyway.

I know it's not supposed to be this way any more, but not being the main breadwinner makes me feel completely emasculated. When my company began to suffer and you went back to work full-time, I felt like a failure. I know that lots of women are the main bread-winners and there are plenty of men left holding the fort. You see, I can't quite bear to admit to being responsible for domestic affairs. I have to refer to our home as the fort! Anyway, who am I kidding? You'd done the bulk of the strenuous childcare by the time you went back to work. Jake and Chloe pretty much look after themselves. Being in when the internet shopping arrives and cooking dinner hardly compares to what you did for the kids when they were little.

I am full of admiration for you, Holly, but at the same time it scares me how competent you are. My role in the family seems to be becoming more and more redundant. To be honest, I started to feel quite depressed about this but I tried not to let it get me down. That's why I started running, not in some mid-life crisis quest to retain what's left of my youthful looks and body (I know when age is winning), but so that I was doing something. Oh, we're back to the need to do something again.

But I do enjoy running (well, not actually the running bit but the feeling slightly better for having done it bit) and it has led me via Daisy to Jimmy Finlay, and I feel positive about that. If we pull this off, it may be just the boost my company needs, but it will also take me away from home and I'm scared how that will affect us.

In the past I hated leaving you for weeks at a time, to sell whisky to the Japanese, because I missed you so much, but I never worried that the time spent apart would damage our relationship. Now I worry that if I go to Scotland for a week or so, I may return and find there is even more distance between us.

I know things were a bit difficult already, but the

thought keeps occurring to me that the train was not the only thing that came uncoupled when it did. We started to unlink as well.

This is a terrible thing to say, and I wish more than anything that you'd caught a later train that day and not had to endure what you did, but a small selfish part of me hoped that the accident would bring us closer. I thought you'd be shaken and scared and that you would need me again, in a way you have not seemed to need me recently. But the opposite was true.

I still worry that you went back to work too soon and that you protest too much that you are fine. It's incredible the way you have carried on, as if nothing at all happened, but something did happen, Holly. It shook me. I wonder what it really did to you. I wish you'd tell me but you don't want to talk – not to me anyway.

I don't know why I am trying to stop myself from sounding petulant and jealous, as I will probably delete this letter once it is written, but I hate to admit that the thing I most resent about the train crash is that Daniel was there and not me. If you'd been sitting somewhere else or been on another train, you and he might never have been thrown together.

Of course, I am glad that there was someone there who was big enough to stay with you, while you waited for the fire brigade to cut you free. At first, I was also pleased that you could talk to him about what happened. But the more time you seem to spend together, the more jealous I am of him.

I can hear you now, saying, 'Don't be ridiculous. He's half my age,' although that would make you fifty-six. I know I'm bad at remembering birthdays and dates of birth but I'm pretty sure neither of us is quite there yet!

Anyway, if in this hypothetical conversation you mean I am ridiculous to suggest that there is anything sexual between the two of you, that is not what I am suggesting. In fact, I think I might find it easier to deal with if there were. I would be jealous and devastated, of course, but I think we could put an affair behind us. It's the sudden emotional closeness you have with Daniel that I can't stand, but can't really do anything about.

What sort of a man would I be if I stopped you talking to the man who was there for you when you most needed someone? But, as time goes on, I fear you are growing ever closer to Daniel, and that inevitably means further away from me.

We used to share all the details of our lives. You used to come home and, even when you were tired after two hours on the train and ten hours in the office, tell me something about the programme or something funny that had happened on your journey, enough to allow me to imagine you in that world. You tell me nothing these days and the lack of detail in our daily lives is leaving our marriage a shell.

I know that Daisy is worried about Daniel and their future together too. I like Daisy, she's a lovely woman, and I don't like seeing her unhappy, any more than I like seeing you becoming closer to someone else.

I bumped into someone I used to work with many years ago the other day, who told me he'd just split up with his wife. He said they'd been living separate lives for some time and only stayed together for the sake of the children. Now the kids had left home, he said, there was no reason to stay together any more.

You hear people say things like that a lot. But that was the first time hearing it ever made me wonder if that could be me. I felt as if someone had punched me in the stomach and I started to panic.

I had to dart into the nearest public toilet to splash water on my face. When I looked up in the mirror, I wondered if I was looking at a man who was biding his time with a wife who no longer loved him, waiting for the children to leave home before they went their separate ways.

I love you, Holly. I think you still love me too, but you don't seem to respect me any more or need me. I'll always love you but I'm not sure if this is enough any more, for you – or for me.

Bloody hell! Writing this has worn me out! I feel I have run an emotional marathon. Perhaps this will help me get some of those pent-up feelings out of my system. I hope so.

Mark xxx

Chapter Forty-Two

'DO YOU WANT to come too?' Holly asked Jake who was pouring chocolate-flavoured cereal into a bowl, absent-mindedly, so that the small puffs of whatever it was before it got turned into sugar overflowed on to the table.

It was only just 7 in the morning, early for Jake to be up, let alone having breakfast, and even earlier for him to be already dressed in his school uniform. Chloe was still fast asleep but Jake had obviously found it as hard to stay in bed as Holly had.

She'd kept checking the clock at regular intervals. The last time she consciously remembered looking it was 4 a.m. and she was pretty sure she hadn't slept at all up to that point. Then it was 6.30 and she decided to get up and make a cup of tea.

When Jake appeared, looking to all intents and purposes (or 'all in tents with porpoises' as Mark usually said when using this particular phrase) as if he was planning on going to school at the crack of dawn, Holly asked if he wouldn't rather have the day off. She would be going to see Mark, when visiting hours began.

'No, I need to go to school today,' Jake said, grabbing handfuls of excess cereal and shoving them back in the box. 'They're doing trials for the rugby team. I won't get in if I'm not there.'

Holly hadn't even been aware that he wanted to get into the rugby team, and wasn't sure she wanted him to. With Mark lying in hospital, it suddenly seemed a dangerous sport for her son to be playing. Given his track record of injuring himself at every possible opportunity, she didn't see how he would escape breaking his neck, if surrounded by a group of bulky teenagers. But she didn't say anything. She suspected the rugby trials were a cover for simply not wanting to go back to the hospital.

Jake had seemed distinctly uncomfortable there last night even though Mark had been surprisingly upbeat, when the two of them had gone to deliver his overnight things.

'Hello,' Holly had said tentatively when they found him lying in bed, surrounded by monitors and with tubes attached to various parts of him. A doctor was in attendance. 'How are you?'

'Fine.' Mark looked sideways at her and Jake, who shuffled awkwardly by the bed. He needed somewhere to sit, ideally with a computer in front of him, to feel comfortable. 'Am I in Devon?'

The doctor looked up abruptly, sensing something was amiss.

'No, you're in hospital in Brighton,' he said sternly, and then to Holly, 'I might have to ask you to leave for a moment, Mrs Constantine. Your husband seems a little disorientated.'

'It's a joke,' Holly told him.

'I feel like I've died and gone to Devon,' Mark explained, and the doctor laughed.

'Oh, yes,' he said. 'Wasn't there an advertising campaign for Devon that used that slogan a few years ago?'

'That was one of mine,' Mark said.

Holly wondered if he had already told the doctor enough about his work for him to understand from this that Mark's company had once had a contract to rebrand Devon. His brief had been to make it appear as appealing as the Caribbean and his 'Feels like I've died and gone to Devon' slogan had been a success. Off the back of it, he'd secured a contract with the Czech

Republic. But neither Paignton nor Prague needed his help any more.

'Really?' The doctor sounded suitably interested and looked at Mark's notes once more before introducing himself to Holly.

'Mrs Constantine,' he said, extending his hand to her. 'I'm Dr Grant. I'm looking after your husband while he is in coronary care.'

'How's he doing?' A man in a striped shirt appeared on the scene then. His sleeves were rolled up and he had a general air of authority about him.

Holly wondered if this was the cardiologist. She remembered doing a piece on the programme a couple of years back about hospital doctors being stopped from wearing white coats in order to prevent the spread of MRSA. Experts had recommended the change because they thought regular clothes were washed more often than white coats. They had also banned ties and said sleeves must be worn rolled up as well. The move seemed sensible to Holly but had prompted more letters to the *British Medical Journal* than almost any other issue. The doctors were up in arms about the changes, which they said were unnecessary. The proposers said they just didn't like being told what to do, or being made to look like everyone else on the ward.

But this man cut a swathe through the place as he walked into it. There was no mistaking that he was in charge.

'Are you his wife?' he asked Holly now.

'This is Dr Parkinson,' Dr Grant introduced the newcomer. 'He operated on your husband.'

'Thank you.' Holly took the hand he had proffered and found herself noting how steady it was.

She could think of nothing to say or ask him, even though there should have been a million things about the operation, Mark's condition and his future prognosis. Instead, she found herself asking a question which sounded ridiculous to her as she asked it.

'Why is it that surgeons never call themselves doctors?' she heard herself saying, wondering as she said it why, if he'd operated on Mark, he was a doctor and not a surgeon.

'Your husband just asked me the very same question.' Dr Parkinson didn't seem to think it was out of place. 'It's because until the mid-nineteenth century surgeons didn't have to have any medical training. They just served an apprenticeship with another surgeon. Of course, that's all changed, but the title remains the same.'

'I see,' Holly said.

'Your husband's operation was straightforward enough to be done by a cardiologist,' Dr Parkinson added, answering her unasked question.

Holly looked at Mark and smiled, feeling a certain relief that, despite the letter she'd just found, they still seemed to be on a shared wavelength when it came to talking to doctors.

She felt sick every time she thought of that letter.

'So how did the operation go?' she continued, suddenly finding there were a lot of questions she wanted answers to. 'How long will it take him to recover? When will he be able to come home?'

'It was a success,' the doctor said, raising his hand like a traffic policeman to stem the flow of questions. 'But we'll be keeping him in overnight for observation.'

He paused and looked up as the door opened. A quizzical, slightly bemused expression crossed his face but he smiled as if he was pleased to see whoever it was who had come into the room.

'Did one of you order a takeaway?' he asked.

Holly turned and took in Chloe wearing some sort of uniform that was not her school one and carrying several bags, which did indeed look like takeaway food.

Lizzie Enfield

'Chloe?' She knew her daughter would infer that she wanted to know what the uniform was and why the food, from the upward inflexion given to her name alone.

'I was at work and I didn't pick up your message till I had my break.' Her daughter shrugged. 'The manager said I should bring some food. He said hospital food is crap. Is Dad OK?'

Chloe looked apologetically at Dr Parkinson as she said this.

'He's going to be fine,' he reassured her, smiling as he spoke. 'And your manager is right. The food is crap, and your dad needs to eat something. Where do you work?'

'Yes,' Holly pitched in. 'Where *do* you work, Chloe?'

'Terre à Terre,' she mumbled, putting the food down.

'I didn't know you had a job after school. Is that where you've been all the time?'

Chloe nodded.

'Did you know about this, Mark?' Holly could hear that her tone was slightly accusing, as if he had been keeping secrets from her.

The surgeon noticed too.

'Now is probably not the time,' he warned gently, as Mark shook his head.

'Yes, of course.' Holly was duly chastised.

'Do you want some toast?' she asked Jake now as she watched him slurp up the last of his cereal.

She hoped he did. Making it would give her something to do.

'Yeah, OK.' His answer implied he knew he was doing her a favour by having it.

'So when are the rugby trials?' she asked.

'Lunchtime,' he said non-committally.

'And will you be back after school?' It was always like trying to get blood out of a stone, trying to extract words from Jake in the mornings, but Holly pressed on.

'Yeah.' He pushed his empty bowl to one side. 'When will Dad be back?'

'Hopefully I'll bring him home this morning,' Holly said, jumping slightly as the toaster popped and her mobile phone beeped at the same time.

'I'll come straight back then,' he said.

Holly took the toast out and buttered it. There was something reassuring about the action of doing this. Normally Jake would get his own toast, or if she was making some anyway, she'd stick it on a plate and leave it to him to spread, but it felt surprisingly soothing.

'How much butter are you going to put on that toast?' Jake stopped her in her reverie. 'You're doing it the way Gran does.'

'Sorry.' Holly stopped buttering and passed the toast to Jake, thinking about her mother as she put the plate on the table.

Susan did have a lot of butter on her toast. She claimed it was having grown up with rationing that made her lather it on. When butter was still rationed, she told them she used to eat most of her toast unbuttered and save her entire ration for one corner, savouring the taste of the butter melting right into the bread. Now that she could have as much as she wanted, she tried to create the same effect with the whole piece of toast.

Her cholesterol levels ought to be sky high, Holly thought, yet she seemed incredibly fit and healthy for her age.

Holly wished her mother were here now. She wanted someone else to be the responsible adult; to make breakfast and go through the motions of normality so that she could stop trying to keep everything and everyone together.

Holly shook her head to stop herself feeling maudlin and checked her phone while Jake appeared to be concentrating on the shape left after he took each mouthful of toast.

There were three messages.

The first was from Anne-Marie.

Sorry I was short with you on the phone the other day, it said. *Would like to talk to you. Could you call me? AM x*

The next was from Daniel and the other was from a number that was not in her phone book. She opened that next.

Hi, Holly, it read. *Hope you managed to get some sleep last night. Let us know how Mark is. Daisy x*

She wondered if they had both texted at the same time and were aware that the other was doing so as they did. Daniel's read: *Are you OK? Hardly slept wondering how you were. Let me know. D xx*

'I'm going to go in early.' Jake scraped his chair back, making her shiver with the noise of metal on the stone floor.

'Are you sure you don't want to take the day off and come to the hospital to get Dad?' Holly asked him again.

'I'll see him after school,' Jake said, putting his plate and bowl in the dishwasher, which Holly suspected was a gesture of appeasement for preferring lessons in one institution to waiting around in another.

Holly wasn't surprised he would prefer to go to school rather than come to see Mark in hospital. She wanted him to come with her because she felt uncomfortable about seeing her husband alone. She'd only read it once, but she had all but memorised the contents of Mark's letter to her and kept going over it in her mind.

She wanted Jake to go with her for moral support. But she could understand why he wanted to carry on as if everything was normal, the way she'd been trying to carry on for the past few months, apparently without success.

Chapter Forty-Three

'WOULD YOU LIKE a cup of tea? Or something to eat?' Holly felt as if she was talking to a new acquaintance she had just brought back to her house for the first time, not her husband of seventeen years.

Mark, for all his chirpiness in the hospital, was still weak from the operation. When she'd arrived to take him home, he'd been chatting to a doctor about his work and Jimmy Finlay's run around Scotland.

'He wants to raise awareness of heart disease,' Mark was telling the surgeon. 'It would have been better for me if he'd done it last year, then I might not be lying here now.'

'Ironic,' said the doctor, scrutinising the clipboard at the end of Mark's bed as Holly came into the room.

'And I always thought that was getting your newly ironed shirt crumpled when you tried to fold the ironing board,' Mark said.

'What?' the doctor said, as the joke, which Holly had heard several times before, slowly dawned on him. 'Oh, I see. That's very good.'

Holly had been surprised by how normal Mark seemed, but now as he got out of the car he had the gait of a much older man, and seemed to struggle as he walked up the steps to their front door, refusing her arm when it was offered, saying he needed to do it on his own.

'A cup of tea and maybe a piece of toast, please,' Mark said, sitting down on the sofa in the living room, looking unsure what he should do next. No wonder he felt like a stranger to her, Holly thought, looking at him. He must feel like a stranger to himself too.

He was not someone you would expect to have had a heart attack. He was fit and healthy and increasingly active. He must have felt completely floored by yet another unexpected turn of events.

'I'll take your bag upstairs and then go and make some,' Holly said tentatively.

She was scared of leaving him. He had seemed fine in the hospital and the doctor had signed him off to go home, but she felt as she had when she first brought Chloe home as a baby, frightened that something might happen to her precious charge now there were no doctors or nurses on call.

She didn't feel entirely confident that she would do the right thing if Mark had chest pains or collapsed again. And, realising now how he had been feeling about their relationship, she didn't quite know how she should behave around him.

Mark nodded, as if to dismiss her, and she went to the kitchen, rubbing her eyes as she walked down the hallway from the living room.

Holly had felt the empty space in their bed where Mark should have been acutely during the night, and had held one of his shirts close to her chest as she'd begun to wonder if emptiness might become a regular feature in their bedroom.

Suddenly just getting on with things and keeping going no longer seemed enough. She'd realised she needed to do more to get her life back on track, but she wasn't sure what.

There didn't appear to be any simple solutions. Holly had held Mark's discarded shirt to her face, breathing in the scent of him, and begun to cry. She'd wished she could get up and climb into bed with Jake, but suspected the teenager he was turning into would be horrified by the idea.

She missed now the disturbed nights when she would wake to see him standing by the bedroom door, looking at her and Mark in bed to see if they were awake or else waiting until his mere presence caused them to wake, before reporting that he'd had a bad dream or wet the bed or couldn't sleep because his room was too dark. Then she would either tell him to come and sleep with them and curl around him until he decided they were 'too squashy' and went back to his own bed, or get up and change his sheets then climb into bed with him until he went back to sleep or decided she alone was 'too squashy' and dismissed her back to her own bed.

Chloe had gained her night-time independence much earlier than Jake, sleeping with the lights off from a very early age, getting up to take herself to the toilet in the night almost as soon as she could walk, and barely ever seeking reassurance from her parents. Holly remembered one occasion when, aged six, she'd gone to bed complaining of feeling sick and Holly had told her to get some sleep but to come and find her if she felt ill in the night. When Holly woke in the morning she presumed Chloe's sickness had gone and she'd slept right through, but Chloe informed them she'd thrown up twice during the night. She'd taken the waste bin from the bathroom, in case she didn't make it to the toilet, and gone back to bed without disturbing anyone.

Holly wondered if this independence was a residual character trait or one foisted upon her because she was the oldest and had had to look after herself more when the needier, more demanding Jake arrived on the scene.

Because she'd always seemed independent, it shouldn't really have come as a surprise to Holly that Chloe had decided to go out and get herself a job.

'How long have you been working at Terre à Terre?' she'd said when they got home from the hospital.

'A few weeks,' Chloe had replied. 'I'm only a kitchen assistant. It's just stock checking and sorting salad leaves, and sometimes I get to help the *pâtissier*. But the people are nice.'

'Why didn't you tell us?' Holly wasn't cross but she was put out that their daughter felt she'd had to keep her job from them.

'I was trying to help,' Chloe told her. 'I know things have been difficult, with Dad's business not doing well and you having to work such long hours. I didn't want to keep asking for money, and one of Ruaridh's older brothers works as a waiter in Terre à Terre and he said they were looking for kitchen assistants. So I applied.'

'Oh, Chloe.' Holly exhaled. 'It's good that you've got a job. But you don't have to worry about money. Things aren't that bad. Is this because of the school trip?'

'Sort of,' she said.

'What do you mean?'

'I'm not really that bothered about the school trip. It just made me realise,' Chloe's voice became quieter and Holly had to strain to hear her, 'it's difficult for you at the moment. Dad not having much work seems to make things strained. I wanted to do something to try and make things better.'

She was like her father, Holly thought proudly, realising she had stopped thinking of Mark with any pride recently.

'Do things seem that bad?' She'd asked her daughter gently.

'Kind of,' Chloe muttered, looking away from her. 'You and Dad haven't been the same.'

Holly tried to formulate a reply that would reassure her but Chloe spoke first.

'Megan's parents are getting separated,' she said, staring hard at the floor, avoiding all eye contact.

'That's very sad for them all,' Holly said. 'But it might not be permanent. Sometimes couples go through a patch where they are not as close as they once were, but they can get over it.'

She hoped this would give Chloe the reassurance she appeared to need but was not going to ask for, and hoped this would be true for herself and Mark.

'Will Dad be OK?' Chloe asked.

'Yes,' Holly had said. 'And we'll be OK too.'

She'd replayed the conversation in her head several times during the night, as she lay in her bed alone, unable to sleep.

'Are you OK?' Holly said now to Mark as she passed the sitting room after taking his bag upstairs.

She popped her head in at the door and saw he was on his BlackBerry.

'I just need to let someone know something,' he said, looking up. 'There are a few things I should be doing today . . .'

'You don't need to do anything today,' Holly reprimanded him. 'You are to take it easy. You heard what the doctor said.'

'I know.' Mark gave a guilty shrug and looked down at his phone again. 'Sent now! Where's that tea and toast you promised me?'

'I'm just going to make it,' she said. 'But I have to keep making sure you are behaving yourself!'

'Sorry, miss.' Mark put his phone on the table next to the sofa. 'But the press conference is in a couple of weeks. There are people I need to let know what's happened.'

'I could do it for you,' she volunteered.

'It's done now,' he said, getting up. 'I'm just going to the loo before my tea and toast.'

'Can you manage?' Holly wondered if would be OK with the stairs.

'It's my heart, not my bladder, that's been giving me trouble,' Mark said, walking slowly towards the door.

'I'll take that as a yes then,' Holly said to herself as she went into the kitchen, listening to him taking the stairs slowly, one at a time, and shuffling across the landing to the bathroom.

She put the kettle on and took a jar of coffee out of the cupboard. She wasn't usually a coffee drinker but felt she needed something slightly stronger than tea to keep her going. It was too early for a drink. The doctor had said that Mark wasn't allowed coffee. He'd also told Holly he must take it easy for a few weeks.

'And leave it a couple of weeks before having sex,' the surgeon had added. 'It puts an enormous strain on the heart. You were lucky your husband collapsed while running. You'd be surprised how many men of his age come in having had a heart attack in flagrante.'

Holly laughed, because she thought he was trying to amuse her. But his comments only served to remind her that she and Mark had not had sex for months. As she was laughing, an image of Daisy crossed her mind. It was not one she wanted to see but one which began to make her wonder if Mark had actually been running when he'd had the heart attack.

He was taking his time in the bathroom and Holly checked her phone for messages before taking the tea and toast into the sitting room.

Another from Anne-Marie.

Worried by your silence, please call. AM x

Holly knew she ought to call her but couldn't face it so she put her phone down, picked up the tray and carried Mark's food and drink to the living room. She put it on the table just as his phone began vibrating to alert him to an incoming message.

Holly could see that the sender was Daisy. The temptation to read it was great but she knew she couldn't do so without Mark knowing. She could, she realised, read the message he had sent before he went upstairs though.

Back home feeling as if the last few days were all a dream. Have you spoken to Daniel yet? You have to tell him. Speak soon. M xx

Chapter Forty-Four

'WHEN DID YOU get back?' Holly looked across the kitchen table at her mother.

Susan looked different but Holly could not quite pinpoint how. It wasn't just the tan and the slightly longer hair, which she'd pinned up with a souvenir mother-of-pearl clasp. She looked freer, Holly thought, somehow less encumbered. Although, now that she thought about it, her mother had not been looking particularly burdened in the first place.

Holly regarded Susan as having led a fairly easy life. She'd worked for a few years, as a secretary, until she met Patrick and they'd been married the same year.

'We couldn't wait,' had been her breezy explanation of the speed at which they'd tied the knot. Holly didn't like to ask what it was they couldn't wait for. They met in the sixties so she didn't imagine they were waiting for sex, but didn't like to give this too much thought. She had wondered vaguely if her mother had been pregnant and examined the few black-and-white wedding photos carefully for any signs of a tell-tale bump, but there was nothing and her sister Fay had not been born until two years later. Of course, it was possible her mother had lost a baby.

As soon as she became pregnant with Fay, she gave up work. 'People did in those days,' she'd told Holly, and she'd only started working again, part-time as a PA in a local restaurant, when Holly had started secondary school.

'For pin money,' Patrick had said dismissively, as if he wasn't entirely happy with his wife dirtying her hands in the world of work. But Holly had remembered her mother seeming happy at the time, making friends with the other restaurant staff, buying herself new clothes with her 'pin money' and generally coming alive.

She'd lost her job when the restaurant went into liquidation. Susan had said this was not because it was losing money but because the owner had been sleeping with the pastry chef. He'd wanted to get divorced but did not want his wife to get her hands on his hard-earned profits. Holly couldn't remember the ins and outs of it. She did remember that her mother had been at a bit of a loss when the restaurant closed down but had told her there was no point in looking for another job. She was too old and Patrick would be retiring in a few years' time so they'd want to be doing things together.

Holly's father had duly retired but they'd actually seemed to spend more time apart then, if anything, he on the golf course, she at a succession of Adult Education classes: flirting with Spanish and Per, the Bolivian teacher, book-keeping because she thought she might want to do a bit of work one day, and latterly yoga and Thailand.

Had something happened in Thailand, Holly wondered, to make her mother look different? Perhaps she had had an affair with a Thai yoga teacher. Again, she didn't want to dwell on this. The idea of your mother having sex with a young Thai man, who could hook his left foot behind his ear, was not something she wanted to think about, any more than she wanted to think of her parents having sex before or after their marriage.

'I flew back in on Monday,' Susan said, rousing Holly from

her contemplation of her parents' sex life. 'I've been a bit jet-lagged for the past couple of days, but I seem to be back on track again now.'

'You look well.' Holly began pouring tea for them both. 'But you came home earlier than planned?'

'Thailand was wonderful,' her mother answered the question that hung in the air even though Holly had not actually asked it. 'But I'd had enough of travelling. I'm too old to be on the move all the time. And when I heard about Mark, I wanted to come back and see you.'

'You didn't need to come home on my account,' Holly said, pushing a cup of tea across the table and taking the lid off the biscuit tin. 'Biscuit?'

'I know.' Susan poured milk into the cup. 'But I wanted to see you anyway. I felt a long way away in Thailand. They say modern communication makes everything closer, but it doesn't really. If anything had happened, I would still be on the other side of the world. I know you were there for Mark, but what if anything had happened to your father?'

'Dad's OK, isn't he?' Holly thought back to what Fay had said, about their mother being worried about him dying before her.

'Yes, he's fine.' Her mother stirred her tea. She looked as if she was thinking about something else.

'I think he missed you while you were away.' Holly appreciated her having come home. She felt better for simply knowing that she was in the country. Even though she was forty-four, and often found her mother difficult, she liked her to be there.

Feeling well disposed towards her now, Holly wondered if Susan might tell her a little more about her reasons for having gone in the first place.

'Dad phoned more often than he usually does while you were away, and wanted to meet up with me and Fay more too.' Holly paused then decided to say out loud the thing that had been worrying her slightly about her father. 'Jean Hayward seemed to be keeping him company quite a lot.'

Her mother looked up sharply. Holly expected her to say 'nonsense' the way she usually did if she disagreed with anything that was said.

'Well, that had started before I went,' Susan surprised her by saying. 'That's partly why I did.'

Holly said nothing; she wasn't used to this sort of discussion with her mother. She rarely talked to either of her parents openly.

They just about did tea and sympathy but definitely not cappuccinos and counselling.

Holly had thought the amount of time her father seemed to be spending with Jean was a bit odd but put it down to loneliness on both their parts. Jean had recently lost her husband and Susan had gone off to Thailand. They were simply keeping each other company, she reasoned to herself. Although, if she allowed herself to think about it, there were other women who, at times, her father had seemed suddenly to be spending a lot of time with.

As if she could tell what Holly was thinking, her mother carried on talking.

'Your father likes a project,' she said. 'And he was at a bit of a loose end when he retired. When Jean's husband died, I think it made him feel useful, being able to help her out a bit. And to be honest, it got him out from under my feet. I'd been used to having the place to myself.'

She paused and took another sip of her tea.

'Well, you probably don't want to listen to me going on.'

Holly filled up her mother's cup, saying nothing, and Susan carried on.

'Like I said,' her mother looked up, but not at Holly, 'he started going over to Jean's house quite a lot before I went away. I knew people were talking, but I don't think there's anything going on between them.'

'And it doesn't bother you?' Holly asked, cautiously. 'Dad spending so much time with her?'

'Yes.' This time her mother looked directly at her. 'It does bother me, but what can I do? He's being good to a mutual and old friend of ours. I don't think they're having an affair or anything.'

Holly looked down. The idea of her father having an affair embarrassed her even at her age.

'But they're close?' she ventured.

'Yes,' Susan said quietly. 'It happens sometimes. I'm sure it will pass. I've been there myself.'

'Mum?' Holly waited for her to go on.

'Do you remember there was an awful car crash when you'd just started secondary school?'

Holly nodded. It was one of the few things she did remember about starting secondary school. She could recall quite clearly, even now, her father taking a phone call one evening, then saying he needed to speak to Susan. They'd gone into another room and closed the door. When they came out they'd said nothing but their mood had changed completely.

The next day her mother had told Holly and Fay that there'd been a car crash and Pat, a woman who lived a few streets from them, had been killed along with her two sons. Her husband, David, never really got over it. Holly knew the family slightly, but Susan knew Pat and David from the Parish Council.

'We all tried to do what we could for David afterwards,' Holly's mother said now. 'I used to take him meals, and after a while he started asking me to stay and eat them with him. He was lonely. He wanted company.'

Holly had begun dunking a digestive into her cup of tea but

forgotten to take it out again. She cursed inwardly when the soggy biscuit broke off from the dry half and sank to the bottom of her cup. But she carried on listening to her mother.

'I thought I was being a good neighbour,' her mother told her. 'But it all got a bit out of hand. David said he'd fallen in love with me. I'm sure he hadn't really, he was confused and grieving, but it made things difficult.'

'So what happened?' Holly realised how little she really knew about her parents.

'I stopped going round to him after I came home one day and found your father breaking up the garden table.' She said this as if it explained everything. But Holly needed more.

'I don't understand?'

'Patrick knew what was happening. He was worried he might lose me, but said he'd not wanted to say anything in case it made things worse. He broke up the table because he was so angry and frustrated, he needed to take it out on something.'

'That doesn't sound like Dad.' Holly thought of the mild-mannered man she knew, who rarely raised his voice or lost his temper and never resorted to physical violence.

'It wasn't,' Susan said. 'But he said he couldn't think of anything else to do. I had no idea how he was feeling. To be honest, I wasn't really thinking about him at all, Holly. I was concerned for David and didn't stop to think how that might be affecting your dad.'

Holly began scooping the soggy biscuit from her cup of tea and tried to take this all in.

'But if that was how Dad felt then, Mum,' she said, 'doesn't he realise how you must feel about him spending time with Jean?'

'Probably,' Susan said quietly. 'But I didn't want to stop him being a friend to her. Anyway, I know where his priorities lie. As soon as he heard about Mark, he called the retreat where I was and we had a long talk. He was worried about you both. It's you and Fay and me he really cares about. I know that, even if at times it might seem otherwise.'

'I had no idea, Mum.' Holly looked at her mother and saw her in a slightly different light.

'Anyway . . .' Susan signalled a change in the direction of the conversation. 'I didn't come here to talk about me. I came to see how you are, and Mark of course?'

'He's pretty well, considering.' Holly wondered if what her mother had just told her would ever be mentioned again.

As she'd sat listening to her reveal details of her marriage, which were news to Holly, she'd wondered if Susan was telling her because she could see her former situation mirrored in her daughter's. Did she know that Holly had allowed herself to drift closer to a man who was not her husband, and taken her eye off her own family in the process?

'Mark's a bit more tired than usual and he's been told to take it easy. But he's anxious to get back to work. He should be down in a minute,' she said.

Mark was upstairs 'resting', though she suspected he was probably checking emails and giving her space to talk to her mother. He'd taken a call on his mobile earlier from Daisy and gone upstairs to speak to her. When he came down again, he said they'd been talking about the press launch.

'We need to get interest going before he actually starts the run,' Mark had said, and Holly had nodded.

She'd wondered why calls from Daisy had to be taken in a separate room and if they'd yet discussed whatever it was that Mark had asked her if she'd told Daniel, in the text he'd sent her on first coming out of hospital. Holly had read a few more of his texts in the past week, too. Some of them appeared to be genuinely work-related. Others were more ambiguous and raised questions to which Holly could only think of answers she didn't want to contemplate.

How did Daniel take the news? one had read. Mark must have deleted the texts leading up to this as it didn't make sense in isolation. *Are you OK?*

She'd not found a reply from Daisy. Although she had a text of her own from Daniel later that day.

When are you back at work, Holly? How are things at home? Not so good here. Would be good to see you but realise you are needed there. D x

'I can see why you want to fix it up soon for Jimmy,' Holly had said about the press conference to Mark. 'But it might be too soon for you, don't you think?'

She was worried that, although he seemed fine, he was not taking things easy enough.

'If I was on my own, yes,' Mark agreed. 'But with Daisy helping me, it should be fine. It'll be in Edinburgh and I'll probably have to stay up there for a night or so . . .'

'Good. I'm looking forward to seeing him,' Susan was saying with a smile. 'I missed you all while I was away.'

Holly forced herself to smile back. She'd been making the comparison between herself and Mark and her parents, and it suddenly struck her that perhaps instead of taking himself off out of the country, so he could turn a blind eye to herself and Daniel, Mark might have taken himself off to be with Daisy.

'I nearly forgot,' her mother said, fumbling in her bag, 'I brought you something.'

It was a hand-sized carved wooden elephant, intricate in all its detail, right down to the wrinkles and sagging folds of skin on its legs.

'It's an elephant,' Susan said, unnecessarily. 'I got one for your father too. I thought it might give you and Mark something to talk about.'

'Sometimes people find it helps to talk about these things,' Caroline, the radio reporter, said to me. 'Or others might find that hearing what you have to say might help them.'

I'd been going to say no, to insist that I wouldn't do the interview and tell her that Holly should never have given my number to her in the first place.

'It wouldn't be live,' she said. 'We'd pre-record the interview beforehand.'

'OK,' I said, suddenly realising that what she said might be true. 'When would you like me to come in?'

It occurred to me that if perhaps it could help others, and if I couldn't talk to Holly about it first, perhaps the only thing to do was to go ahead and do the interview.

I haven't seen Holly for over a week, or Daniel either, and she hasn't returned my texts. I sent one a week ago, to apologise for being angry with her on the phone, but she never replied.

So I sent another. Not immediately, I didn't want to appear to be hassling her, but a couple of days later, saying I hadn't heard from her for a while and that I hoped she was OK. She didn't reply to that one either.

Then I let her know I was going to do the interview. I thought she might be pleased that I'd agreed, and that, as I would be going to her office, we might meet for lunch or something. Again no reply, which worried me.

'Radio silence,' as Geoff used to say.

I never really stopped to think exactly what radio silence meant, so I asked Caroline as we walked to the studio to do the interview.

'It's when a station stops transmitting,' she said, opening a huge baize-covered door. 'We're in here.'

The room was empty but for a table with several microphones arranged around it and a few chairs. On the other side of a large glass window was a much busier room, full of stuff and several people.

Caroline sat on one of the chairs and pressed a button, which allowed her to talk them.

'This is Anne-Marie,' she said, nodding towards me. They all smiled. 'We're just going to have a bit of chat before we start recording.'

They smiled some more and began shuffling papers, as if they were minding their own business, although I knew they'd be listening to every word I said.

I felt slightly intimidated by this but I'd rehearsed in my head what I was going to say and, like a politician, planned to stick to the script, no matter what Caroline asked me.

'I asked you about radio silence earlier,' I said, when she asked how I was managing now, without Geoff. 'Well, it's like that, really. I still keep expecting Geoff to be there, to be home when I get there, or on the other end of the phone if I call him, or to get a text or email in reply to one I've sent. But all I get is radio silence.'

'That's wonderful, Anne-Marie, thank you,' Caroline said, then told the gathering behind the glass to stop recording.

'Thank you so much for coming in,' she said as we walked to the lift which would take us back to Reception. 'It was a really moving interview.'

Another woman appeared, just as the lift doors were opening, and got in with us.

'I was wondering,' I said to Caroline, 'could I pop in and say hello to Holly, as I'm here?'

'Holly?' Caroline queried. *She didn't seem to know who I was talking about.*

'Holly's a friend who works here,' I explained. 'She commutes as well. It was her who gave you my number. Holly Holt.'

'Oh, I work with Holly,' the other occupant of the lift piped up. 'But she's not in. She's been away all week.'

'Oh,' I said. 'Is she on holiday?'

That might have explained her not returning my texts.

'Not exactly.' The woman looked slightly flustered now, as if she might be about to give something away. 'It's more of a personal matter.'

'Oh, yes.' I tried to give the impression that I knew all about it. 'Do you know when she'll be back?'

'I'm not sure,' she replied. Then the lift stopped at the ground floor and Caroline gestured for me to get out, putting a stop to any further questioning of this woman who worked with Holly.

Chapter Forty-Five

'WELL, IT'S LUCKY you're back, Holly, as we seem to be rather depleted this morning.' Katherine looked around the table in the meeting room.

This, Holly thought to herself, was her editor's way of not saying, 'Hello, Holly. Nice to have you back. How is your husband? I do hope he's all right now. You must have had a terrible shock. Are you sure you were quite ready to come back to work?'

It was unlikely Katherine would ever say that but Holly would have appreciated her at least acknowledging the reason for her absence over the past week, rather than just treating it as an annoyance. It was like the way she had behaved after the train crash, although Holly had been glad that she'd ignored that.

'Right . . .' Katherine took a pen out of her bag. 'Before we talk about this week's programme, I do have something I need to tell you all.'

'Are we not waiting for the others?' Holly asked.

There were only five of them around the table: Katherine, herself, Dimitri, Rebecca and a man called Andy, who Katherine had told her, as they walked into the meeting room, would be 'helping out'.

The meeting was when they tried to set the agenda for that

week's programme, and unless he had a more pressing news assignment, it was almost always attended by James Darling, and, of course, Natalie.

Holly caught Dimitri and Rebecca exchanging a look. They seemed to exchange a lot of looks these days, so she did not regard it as particularly significant.

'Natalie and James are not with us for the moment,' Katherine said. 'For personal reasons.'

Holly looked at her boss who smiled a closed smile, giving nothing away.

Rebecca raised her eyebrows and mouthed something, which Holly presumed to be 'Later'. Now, the look which she had just given Dimitri seemed to take on more significance.

'It's unlikely James will be back,' Katherine said, surveying the assembled company to see what reaction her statement produced.

Holly was surprised but tried hard not to give Katherine the satisfaction of showing it.

'And I hope Natalie will be back soon,' she continued. 'In the meantime, Dimitri will continue acting up as senior producer.'

Holly noted the word 'continue' and presumed this arrangement must have begun last week, when she was at home looking after Mark.

He always joked about the BBC term 'acting up', used to describe someone temporarily doing a more senior job. He imagined all the researchers, temporarily working as producers, and the producers working as senior producers, running around like over-excited children, shouting and doing everything they could to get themselves noticed. This was not, Holly told him, an inaccurate description.

'And Andy is an extra pair of hands,' Dimitri piped up, keen to show his acting seniority. 'He's worked with Dylan a lot in the past.'

'Dylan?' Holly had only been off for a week, admittedly a week during which she hadn't bothered to check her emails, but nevertheless, she hadn't expected to come back to work and find so much had changed.

'Dylan Williams,' Katherine said, adopting the tone a mother might use to calm a child who was acting up. 'He stepped in at the last minute to present the programme in James's absence. He will be presenting for the next few weeks as well.'

Holly knew Dylan Williams. He had gone to work as a reporter at Radio Sussex not long after she'd left and, by all accounts, was very driven. He'd begun acting up almost immediately and was news editor within a few months of joining the station.

Holly only felt she'd been working in London a few months before Dylan Williams followed her up there to work as a reporter on the *Today* programme. In less than the time it took her to get a cup of coffee in the morning, he'd become the presenter of the lunchtime news. So it wasn't exactly a surprise that if anyone was going to fill James Darling's size 12 shoes, it was Dylan Williams.

'I produce Dylan on the one o'clock.' Andy spoke for the first time in the meeting. 'I know how he works.'

Holly looked at him more closely and decided, for no particular reason, that she didn't like Andy and wasn't looking forward to working with him.

'Anyway,' Katherine held up her pen, commanding an end to banal chitter chatter, 'as I said earlier, before we start to discuss this week's programme, I do have something I need to tell you all.'

They looked dutifully in her direction, silenced by the brandished pen which, Holly noticed, had been filched from a Hilton Hotel.

'The listening figures for the programme are in and I am afraid they are not good.' Katherine paused, allowing her words to sink in.

The listening figures for programmes were the stuff of numerous management meetings. The producers were never over-concerned with them. They just carried on making programmes and didn't worry too much if anyone was listening to them or not. But analysing and discussing listening figures was the stuff which justified huge management salaries.

'As you all know, *Antennae* is a relatively new programme,' she continued. 'And we had hoped it would attract a new audience, but over the past year the figures actually seem to have diminished.'

'Whereas audience figures for the same slot on other stations have increased.' Andy spoke again. He seemed to be enjoying their pain, not that Holly was feeling particularly pained. She was listening but wishing that Katherine would hurry up with her precious announcement and get the meeting over with, so that she could call Natalie and find out the cause of her mysterious absence.

'*Antennae* was a bold experiment,' Katherine said.

'Boldly going . . .' Dimitri was acting up again, but Katherine silenced him with an angry look.

'But the audience seemed to find it too serendipitous.' This was a word she often ascribed to the programme. Holly preferred to describe it as a mish-mash of items, but she could see that serendipitous was more elegant.

'There's no easy way to say this . . .' Katherine paused again, underlining just how hard it was for her even to reach the end of a sentence. Holly suspected she was loving every second of the delay. 'The department has decided to replace the programme from the end of the month.'

'What's it going to be replaced with?' Holly asked, paraphrasing the question she wanted to ask which was, What's going to happen to all of us then?

'An obituary programme,' Katherine told them, and answered the question in Holly's mind with her next sentence. 'It's the idea of a producer in the Arts Unit who will be making it with a fairly small team.'

'Well, that's apt,' Dimitri commented on the irony of the situation. 'I suppose we will all be asked to contribute to its first episode?'

'I don't see why . . .' Katherine said slowly as it dawned on her Dimitri was definitely acting up in a childish way rather than a senior producer-ish way. 'Oh, I see. Very funny. But perhaps not very appropriate, Dimitri.'

'Who's going to present?' he asked, rubbing his wrist as he spoke, as if he had actually been slapped rather than just verbally admonished.

'Gus O'Hagan,' Katherine told them.

Gus O'Hagan was the elderly editor of *Down But Not Out* – a periodical aimed at the over-fifties. It ran far more obituaries than any other publication and Holly imagined most of them were about people Gus had personally known. She supposed he was a good choice to present. Management, she thought to herself, had obviously done an about-turn on attracting younger listeners and decided to try and pander more to their existing ones.

'Can't see him lasting long,' Dimitri said, and then, as if he had only meant to think this and realised he had said it out loud, 'Oops, sorry!'

'Anyway,' Katherine continued, 'I know this has come as a shock to all of you and I will talk to you individually about your futures. In the meantime, I don't want the two final episodes of *Antennae* to suffer in any way. So, does anyone have any ideas for this week's programme?'

'Before we try and think of some,' Dimitri spoke again, 'I have some news of my own. I was hoping Darling and Natalie would be here too, but as you're not sure when they're coming back, I might as well tell the rest of you.'

Chapter Forty-Six

HOLLY FELT AS if she was deserting the sinking ship by sneaking out at lunchtime, but Andy seemed keen to show everyone that he was more than capable of producing the entire programme on his own. He'd come up with a hundred and one suggestions in the meeting, compared to the combined one that the rest of the usual team had managed.

Holly suspected Andy might well be lining himself up to work on the new obituaries programme. It was fortuitous for him that *Antennae*'s deputy editor and presenter were both absent, giving him an opportunity to jump at.

As it was her first day back, after a week's compassionate leave, Holly had thought she needed at least to look as if she was pulling her weight. She'd envisaged a sandwich at her desk, rather than swanning off out to lunch, but felt as if she hadn't really had any time to herself in the past week. She wanted to get out and think her own thoughts without family or colleagues in the background.

Now she thought she'd buy a sandwich and walk up to Regent's Park.

Holly had called Natalie, as soon as she'd left the meeting, to ask if everything was OK.

'Not really. Not at all,' her friend had said. 'Have you got time for a drink after work, Holly? I could do with a talk.'

'I'm sorry.' She had felt bad about not making the time for her friend, but she'd promised to get home early. She felt she needed to be around in the evening, to monitor Mark both in terms of his health and his attitude to her.

'Later in the week?' Natalie had asked. 'I need to get out of the house.'

Holly sensed that something was up. And she knew she could do with talking to a friend too. The events of the past week were preoccupying most of her thoughts and she felt she needed to get some of them out in the open. Airing them seemed like one way of making things clearer for herself.

Holly wondered if Natalie already knew that their programme was being axed. She definitely sounded preoccupied. As she put the phone down, she realised her friend hadn't even asked how she and Mark were. There must be something wrong.

She had called Mark after speaking to Natalie, to ask how he was and tell him about the programme being axed, but he'd sounded distracted so she'd decided to save the news until later.

'I think we're going to have the press conference next week,' he'd said to her on the phone. 'That's right, isn't it?'

She couldn't tell, down the line, if he was asking the question of himself or whether Daisy was with him and he was asking her.

Holly knew she had to sit down with Mark and talk to him, soon. Until she did, she felt everything about their life seemed unreal. They appeared to be operating in different spheres at the moment and she knew that something needed at least to get them overlapping again. But Mark was busy with the press launch for Jimmy Finlay and Holly was wary of upsetting him, lest it put undue strain on his heart. He already seemed to be putting enough pressure on himself with the organisation of the run.

The Ladies' toilets on the fifth floor of Broadcasting House were usually empty. Just off the stairwell, they were tucked away behind the new library, which was almost entirely staffed by men. Holly usually used them on her way out, knowing there was unlikely to be a queue.

Today, a woman wearing a familiar-looking tunic was bending over the washbasin, splashing her face with water. She didn't look up as the door closed behind Holly, but turned the tap off and picked up a paper towel and began drying her face.

'Rebecca?' Holly knew it was her but there was something about her being here and the way she was dabbing her face with the towel that seemed not quite right.

'Oh, Holly, hi.' Rebecca stopped patting her face with the towel and blew her nose on it.

'Are you OK?' Holly didn't think she looked it.

'Yes.' Rebecca sniffed decisively. 'I'm fine.'

'Are you sure?' Holly thought she looked as if she'd been crying and might be about to cry again. She suspected she'd come down to the fifth floor to cry in privacy, not expecting anyone she knew to use these backwater toilets or Holly to be on her way out.

'I think so.' Rebecca sounded less certain this time. 'It just came as a bit of a shock, that's all.'

'You'll be OK,' Holly reassured her. 'They'll move you on to another programme, somewhere in the department. It can only be a better one. You won't be out of a job.'

Holly had worked for the BBC long enough to know that these sudden changes in programming were unsettling, but that everyone who wanted one usually ended up finding a new home somewhere.

'Oh, I know. It's not that.' Rebecca unzipped a make-up bag that was on the ledge by the sink, and took out a tube of foundation. She began dotting some around her slightly reddened eyes.

'I don't want to pry,' Holly said, and went into the nearby toilet cubicle, giving Rebecca the opportunity to confide what was bothering her, if she wanted, or to put her make-up on and run if she didn't.

'I've obviously completely misunderstood the situation,' Holly heard Rebecca say as she closed the door.

'I'm not with you?' Holly raised her voice to be heard though the door and tried to wee as quickly as she could.

'May I ask you a question, Holly?' Rebecca called.

Holly felt the slight dread she always felt when anyone asked that.

'You can ask, but I might not answer,' she said, coming out of the cubicle and starting to wash her hands.

'Did you ever think there might be anything between Dimitri and me?' Rebecca looked at Holly's reflection in the mirror, rather than directly at her.

'Why? Was there? Is there?' Holly answered Rebecca's reflection with more questions. It was odd, she thought, addressing each other indirectly in this way. It gave the impression that what was said between them now could be forgotten about later.

'I thought you were good friends,' she said slowly, realising that she was probably getting herself into a conversation that was not going to be quick.

The news that Dimitri had brought to the more than usually eventful morning meeting was that he was getting married.

They'd all been suitably congratulatory. Even Andy who'd only just met him had stood up and shaken his hand a bit too vigorously. Dimitri had made a face at Holly over his shoulder and shaken his arm gingerly when Andy wasn't looking.

Rebecca, now that Holly thought back to the scene, had been

slightly more reticent in coming forward and congratulating her friend. Holly had presumed this was because he'd probably already told her his news and she was just going through the motions along with everyone else.

'We are,' Rebecca said, looking at Holly directly this time. 'Very good friends. Dimitri is really good company and I can talk to him about everything.'

'Yes?' Holly looked back at her and waited.

'He talked to me about things too.' Rebecca looked down again, as if concerned she might be breaking a confidence. 'About Anna and their life together. He said she was thinking about moving back to Germany and he wasn't sure what to do about it. I thought . . .'

Holly took a paper towel and began slowly drying her hands.

'I thought he was going to split up with her,' Rebecca concluded.

'Is that what you wanted?' Holly asked.

'I thought that's what he wanted too.' Rebecca paused and looked at herself in the mirror again. 'There'd been a bit of . . . well, you know, a couple of things had happened . . .'

Rebecca wiped something Holly couldn't see from her face and then took a deep breath as if she was either going to let it all out or change the subject.

Holly was slightly relieved that it was the latter. She didn't want to know if Rebecca and Dimitri had been sleeping together. If true, it was the sort of thing that was best kept between them.

'Anyway, it doesn't matter now. He's getting married and we'll be working on different programmes,' Rebecca said. 'Life goes on.'

She zipped up her make-up bag. Holly thought this was the best way for the conversation to end. She didn't want Rebecca to tell her too much about her feelings for Dimitri and whatever it was they had shared together. She suspected her colleague might regret it in a few days, when she was less raw from the shock of hearing that he was going to marry someone else.

But Holly didn't want to appear insensitive either. She took a step closer to Rebecca and gave her a big hug.

'Sometimes,' Holly said, speaking aloud some of the thoughts which had been circulating in her head for some time, 'it's almost impossible to tell what another person is thinking, and all too easy to misinterpret the way they feel about you.'

'Thanks, Holly,' Rebecca said quietly, then picked up her bag and went towards the door. 'I'll see you later.'

'And sometimes,' Holly said to herself in the mirror, 'you're not even sure yourself how you feel about someone.'

Chapter Forty-Seven

'Sorry I'm late.' Holly didn't think she was but Natalie appeared to have been here for some time, judging by the near-empty glass in front of her. She was sitting alone, in the corner of the pub, with a gin and tonic, most of which had already been drunk.

'You weren't really.' She didn't seem to mind that she'd been kept waiting. 'I was early. I had to get out of the house.'

'Are you OK?' Holly knew the answer was going to be negative. Natalie didn't look it. She looked awful; pale, tired and thin. She had all the signs of someone who'd been going through something and Holly knew she was about to find out what.

'No, I'm bloody awful.' Natalie drained what was left of her drink.

Holly wondered how long she'd been sitting there and how many she'd had already. This wasn't like Natalie at all. Even when they went for drinks after work, she usually held back, citing early mornings or key interviews to be recorded the next day as her reason for staying relatively sober.

'Shall I get you another drink?' Holly asked, wondering if this was wise but knowing she was gong to need one herself.

'A large gin and tonic,' Natalie pushed her empty glass across the table to Holly and shrugged, as if acknowledging she was drinking too much but wasn't sure what else to do.

Holly went to the bar and texted Mark while she was waiting.

Natalie not good. Might be a bit later than I thought. Hope you OK xxx

She had asked him if it was all right for her to go for a drink after work with her friend this evening. She'd told him that Natalie had been away from work for a few days and had called, asking to meet.

'I guess you two need to discuss your futures,' Mark had said. He seemed to think the programme being axed was a good thing.

'Perhaps you can work part-time again?' he'd suggested, and Holly had bitten back the urge to say that his doing one job for Jimmy Finlay did not mean they didn't need her to contribute any more.

Under normal circumstances, she would have gone ahead and made an arrangement with Natalie without consulting her husband. But at the moment, she felt she had to ask Mark's permission. This was because she knew he was supposed to be taking it easy and she ought to get home in time to cook dinner, although Chloe had done a lot of the cooking in the past week and was also doing a rather better job of looking after Mark than Holly was.

She still hadn't talked to him properly. She'd been putting it off, using the doctor's admonition that he needed to avoid stressful situations as her excuse for doing so.

For the first time in her life Holly was unsure of Mark's feelings towards her and scared of what he might say if she asked him. She'd never felt like this before. He had always been such a constant man. Even when they'd had major arguments about things, which now seemed silly, she'd never for a moment doubted his feelings for her.

'Sure,' Mark had said, when she'd asked. 'No problem.'

Holly had wondered if this response was because he genuinely didn't mind her being back late from work or because it gave him more time with Daisy. She knew they were meeting up today, not because he'd told her but because she'd looked through his emails and found several from Daisy. They were all warm and jokey in tone, ostensibly to do with Jimmy Finlay's run and organising the press conference, but Holly couldn't help wondering if there was more to *See you tomorrow x* than the fact that Daisy would be seeing Mark tomorrow!

Holly hadn't seen Daniel since that day at the hospital. She wondered if he was having the same misgivings as she was.

Allowing Natalie to unburden herself wasn't going to help her own state of mind. But what choice did Holly have? Natalie was her friend and something was obviously very wrong. That much she could tell just by looking.

'A small white wine and a gin and tonic, please,' Holly said to the barman, who looked suspiciously in Natalie's direction. Holly avoided eye contact as he got the drinks ready. She feared that if she made it, he might say something about the length of time Natalie had already spent in her corner and the amount of gin she'd already downed. It wasn't for him to pass judgement.

Instead she read Mark's reply when her phone beeped a message alert.

OK. Send her my love. All fine here. Later x

Mark's texts seemed to lack their customary warmth these days, but perhaps Holly was just trying to read too much into them. That was the trouble with texting. It was far too easy to misinterpret a smiley face or a kiss or the lack of either. She wanted his text to reassure her that he didn't mind her staying up in London later than usual, but that he'd look forward to seeing her when she got home. What she read in those few brief words was that she wasn't really needed at home; they could all manage quite well without her.

At least there is a kiss, she thought to herself, although she knew that Mark invariably ended all his texts with a kiss and, on the occasions she'd snooped, had seen he sent more than one to Daisy.

She gave the barman the best part of a tenner for the drinks and took them over to the corner.

'Here you are,' she said, putting Natalie's down on a beer mat, which appropriately (or perhaps inappropriately) was advertising a certain brand of gin.

'Thanks.' She took a sip. 'And thanks for coming too. I know you've not been having an easy time. How is Mark?'

'He seems OK,' Holly said. 'Quite normal, considering. Thanks for the flowers, by the way.'

Natalie had sent him some flowers when he came out of hospital. *That confirms my suspicion that exercise is bad for you. Look after yourself. Nat x* the card had read. Mark had laughed when he read it, and been genuinely cheered by the flowers.

'Oh, that's all right.' Natalie put her drink down on the table, picked up the beer mat and began fiddling with it.

'What's up?' Holly asked. Then, thinking that it was often easier to talk about something difficult if you began by talking about something else, added, 'The office is like the *Marie-Celeste*. Darling's not been in all week either.'

'Really?' Natalie seemed genuinely surprised. Holly had thought she probably already knew. They were usually in more or less daily contact. 'I suppose the rumour mill has gone into overdrive then?'

'You know what people are like.' Holly wished now she hadn't brought up the subject of Darling. It was true that there was much speculation about why Natalie and James were both off at the same time.

Rather than the absences being regarded as coincidence, they seemed to confirm people's suspicions that the two of them were having an affair. Holly herself thought that James, being the slippery character he was, had probably got wind of the fact the programme was going to be axed and jumped ship straight away. He wouldn't want to tarnish his career by having to present a programme that everyone now knew was to be taken off air in a couple of weeks.

'Does everyone think he and I are having an affair?' Natalie looked directly at Holly, her look implying she wanted an honest answer.

'Well, I don't. I know you are close and people do gossip about you, but I never believed it. Why would you, when you've got Guy and the twins?'

Holly didn't air her private thoughts about James Darling. But she wondered why a liaison with someone arrogant, short and with the perfect face for radio was worth having, when, for Natalie, it would mean risking losing a tall, good-looking, charming husband.

Moreover Holly knew what it was like to have young children and a job. It didn't leave much time for hair-washing, let alone anything else.

'Guy thinks that I am,' Natalie said. 'Or at least he did. He thought . . . he thinks . . .'

She stopped talking and Holly thought she was going to cry, but she took a deep breath and carried on.

'He thinks it's been going on for years, since before I met him.'

She took another swig of her drink and began talking again before Holly had quite taken in what she was saying.

'And he thinks that because he believes I've been having an affair with Darling all along, that vindicates him for going on dates with a string of women he's been meeting on the internet.'

'What?' Holly couldn't quite believe what Natalie was telling her.

She knew about his meeting with Mila, obviously, and she'd decided to believe the explanation he'd given her when they'd met for coffee, but now she wondered if she'd chosen to believe him because his explanation was credible or simply because she wanted it to be true. If there were other women, Guy hadn't exactly told her the whole truth.

'I opened a credit-card bill,' Natalie said. 'I didn't mean to. It was in a pile with a load of bills. I wonder if Guy actually wanted me to find it. He left it there with the gas and the electricity and all the other stuff he says he never has time to deal with, despite being at home all day.'

'I can't believe he meant you to find it,' Holly began. 'And anyway, perhaps there was a reason for whatever you found on the bills.'

'Don't defend him,' Natalie said abruptly. 'There were payments for restaurants, and sometimes hotels, and a website which I looked up. Every Wednesday, when I thought he was going to the gym, he was having a quick drink with some woman he'd met on an internet site for bored married people, and if he liked them they'd go off to a hotel and have sex.'

'Are you sure?' Holly felt sick just listening to her.

'Yes, I'm sure.' Natalie started to cry now. 'I asked him outright and he admitted it. He didn't even seem sorry. He said I was as much to blame as he was.'

'How did he work that one out?' Holly felt the familiar feeling of anger she'd experienced on previous occasions when friends had told her they'd found a partner had cheated on them.

'He said it was common knowledge that I was having an affair with James Darling.' Natalie was getting angry now. 'He went and slept with other women because of a fucking rumour, Holly! Can you believe it?'

'No.' She took her friend's hand and held it, at a loss for words and unsure what to believe.

'And do you know what makes it worse?'

Holly shook her head. She couldn't think of anything much worse than discovering your husband had been having brief affairs with virtual strangers.

'He said it didn't really make any difference if I wasn't actually having sex with James or not. He said he was cuckolded by my relationship with him anyway.' Natalie took another sip of her drink. 'He said my loyalties were with James and he couldn't take it any more. I suppose he thought screwing other women would help mend his precious hurt ego.'

'Natalie . . .' Holly could think of no good way to phrase this so she just asked it. 'Is there anything between you and Darling?'

'No,' she said emphatically. 'We are good friends, you know that. We go back a long way and I really respect him. He's great at his job . . . unlike Guy, who is turning out to be a complete waster.'

'Sorry,' Holly apologised for asking. 'I never really thought there was anything more than that.'

But I can see that Guy might have, she thought to herself. And look what's happened. She could hear Mark's voice in her head now, saying what he'd said in the letter she'd read about her closeness to Daniel, leaving their marriage a shell.

'What will you do now?' she asked Natalie, wondering if the answer would help her too decide what she should do herself.

Chapter Forty-Eight

MARK WAS LYING on the sofa chatting to someone on the phone and laughing when Holly got home. He appeared to be enjoying the conversation so much that he didn't hear her opening the door or come into the sitting room.

'Oh, that's great,' he was saying. 'You're brilliant! That's perfect.'

Holly stood by the door, feeling as if she was eavesdropping on something but not sure what.

'And how are you feeling?' Mark's tone became more serious suddenly and he sat up slightly, hunching over the phone, apparently unaware still that Holly was watching him. 'Are you OK? Are things really bad?'

Holly froze, almost sure now that he was talking to Daisy and wondering why things might be bad. She suspected it had to do with Daniel; he'd insinuated as much to her by text.

Holly had no idea what it was all about but felt uneasy about the cosy concerned way Mark was talking to Daisy now.

Ironically, her freezing seemed to alert him to her presence and he sat up suddenly, looking round at Holly angrily, as if she had been spying.

'Got to go now,' he said into the phone. 'I'll speak to you in the morning.'

'You frightened the life out of me,' he said. 'How long have you been standing there?'

'I've only just come in.' She was defensive in reaction to his slightly accusatory tone. 'Who were you talking to?'

'Daisy,' he said. 'She's found the perfect venue for the press conference. It's a café in Princes Street Gardens. So Jimmy can talk and then do a bit of running round the park for a photo call.'

'Next week?' Holly asked. 'Will you be strong enough to go?'

'Yes,' Mark dismissed her concern. 'I've got a check-up with the doctor later this week, but I feel fine. It's only for a night.'

'Are you sure?' Holly felt apprehensive about the prospect of him spending a night away from home, especially if he was going to have company. 'Where will you stay?'

'We're staying at the Scotsman,' Mark replied. 'And I'll be fine. Don't worry. It's just a meeting to give Daisy a chance to spend a bit of time with Jimmy. If she's going to be his PA and trainer when he does the run, they'll need to get on reasonably well. I am sure they will. Daisy's very easy to be with, but it'll give them a chance to get to know each other.'

'Right,' said Holly, wondering if it was Jimmy who wanted the chance to get to know Daisy or Mark himself.

'How was Natalie?' he asked, getting up. 'Do you want a cup of tea or something?'

'Yes, please.' She followed him into the kitchen. 'Natalie wasn't good actually. The planets must be out of sync at the moment, everyone seems to be having some sort of crisis.'

Mark had his back turned to her as he filled the kettle up. He said nothing.

'Mark,' she ventured, 'can we talk?'

She hoped he would realise that she meant a proper sit-down serious talk.

Lizzie Enfield

'Yep.' His reply sounded casual. 'I'll just make the tea.'

'Where are the kids?' Holly asked, wondering if they would be uninterrupted.

'Chloe has gone to the cinema with Ruaridh,' Mark said. 'His dad is going to bring her home later. And Jake is in his room.'

'Has he gone to bed?' Holly asked. It was nearly ten and she would have preferred Chloe to be home by now. She had school tomorrow. But at the same time Holly was glad she was out enjoying herself instead of working.

'No, I think he's on the computer.'

'I'll go and say hello while you make the tea,' Holly said, putting her bag on the chair and walking upstairs.

When she came back down again Mark had made a pot of tea and was sitting at the kitchen table, as if he had heeded her request and was ready and waiting.

'So what's up with Natalie?' he asked, which seemed as good a way into the conversation as any.

'Guy's been screwing around,' Holly said. She didn't really like the word 'screwing' but it was the only way she could think of to describe what he had been up to. She'd thought about it on the train on the way home and wondered if it would have been better or worse if he had been having an affair.

The fallout would have been different, and perhaps harder to deal with if he'd formed an attachment to someone else. If, that is, he was telling the truth to Natalie, and had told Holly the truth about his meeting with Mila as well.

'In what way?' Mark poured her a cup of tea but had none himself.

Holly knew he was being careful, watching his caffeine intake – she just hoped he wasn't indulging in anything else that might stimulate his heart.

'The usual way. The seeing other women way.' She looked at

Mark to see if he reacted at all to this, whether he would give away something that would make her suspect Guy wasn't the only one. His face remained impassive so she continued.

'He'd started going to the gym . . . except he wasn't going there at all, he was meeting up with women he'd contacted on the internet. Sometimes he'd just meet them for a drink, and sometimes if he liked them they'd go to a hotel. Natalie found his credit-card statements and it all came out.'

'Bloody hell!' Mark looked genuinely shocked. 'Poor Natalie. How long had this been going on?'

'Not long, which I suppose is something,' Holly said. 'But long enough to have a devastating effect on her. She's in bits. She's been off work for the past week or so. I can't see her coming back any time soon, not the state she was in.'

'I'm sure it helped, being able to talk to you.' Mark smiled at Holly and put his hand briefly over hers.

It was a small gesture but something he hadn't done spontaneously for so long that she found herself immediately questioning its significance.

'The thing is, there's something else.' She looked up at him as Mark took his hand away again. 'I'm not sure how good a friend I'm being because I know something else that Natalie doesn't, and I don't know whether to tell her or not.'

'What's that?' Mark was leaning back in his chair now, looking at her curiously.

'When I went for dinner with my dad that night, Guy was in the restaurant with James Darling's wife,'

'What – the presenter?'

'Yes.' Holly couldn't remember how much she had told Mark about the gossip that surrounded Natalie and Darling or if he'd even taken it in. 'Natalie and James are very good friends, but people at work insinuate that they are more than that.'

'And are they?' Mark wasn't usually interested in office gossip but he looked interested now.

'Natalie says not,' Holly told him. 'And I believe her. For one thing, Darling is a creep, although she seems to like him. But that was one of the reasons Guy cited for seeing these other women. He told Natalie he felt cuckolded by their friendship, even if it was innocent.'

'I can understand that,' Mark said, looking at Holly and holding her gaze for a moment as if to impart extra significance to what he'd just said. 'What do you think he was doing with James Darling's wife?'

'They'd met before at some drinks after work,' Holly said, remembering she'd not invited him to come. 'Guy was very jumpy when I saw them and asked to meet me a couple of days later. I haven't told Natalie any of this.'

'And what did he tell you then?' Mark asked.

'He said they'd just met to talk.' Holly wondered if her husband was bothered that she hadn't shared any of this with him at the time. 'He told me Mila was quite dismissive, condescending even towards him, treating the very suggestion that her husband might want anything to do with someone like Natalie as ridiculous.'

'I'd have thought it would be the other way round,' Mark commented. 'Surely she's more of a catch than James Darling.'

'You'd think so, wouldn't you? But his wife is this incredibly beautiful sculptress. I was amazed myself when I met her. Darling obviously has some very well-hidden qualities which make him attractive to some women.'

'Or perhaps the circumstances in which they met had some bearing.' Mark was looking hard at her again.

Holly could feel the conversation heading towards the topic she'd wanted to raise with him, but now she felt anxious and unsure.

'Anyway . . .' She carried on talking about Natalie and James to put off the moment when they might start talking about her and Daniel. And Mark and Daisy. 'Later I wondered if Guy had really met her because he was hoping that Mila . . .'

'. . . might be tempted back to one of his hotels?' Mark said what she had been about to say. 'Redress the balance by sleeping with the wife of the person he thought was taking all his wife's time and attention?'

'I suppose so.' Holly swallowed hard, wondering if Mark was saying what she thought he might be saying to her. 'But from what Guy told me, she seemed to treat him as if he was rather pathetic.'

She was going to say 'which he is', but decided not to until she'd heard Mark's response.

'He wouldn't be the first man to try it on with an attractive woman, and I'm sure he won't be the last.' Mark was looking at her again. 'I'm not making excuses for Guy, but sometimes if you're not feeling great about your own relationship and find yourself in the company of another woman who seems to like you, you think it's worth a try. Men do anyway. Sometimes, I suppose, the women respond, but I'm sure most of the time they treat the very sugges-tion as ridiculous.'

'Do you think I should tell Natalie?' Holly asked, while mentally mulling over what Mark had just said and wondering if he was talking about Guy and Mila, or himself and Daisy, or if he had somehow got wind of the fact that she had kissed Daniel? 'I'm sure it's bound to come out and then she'll be angry with me for keeping it from her.'

'If I were you,' Mark said, looking straight into her eyes and holding her gaze as he spoke, 'I would keep quiet. If what you say is right and nothing happened between Guy and Mila, talking about it might make everyone say things that would be best left unsaid. Don't you think?'

'Maybe. If they are things that don't really matter in the long run.' Holly looked back at him, wondering what the subtext of his remarks was.

'Did you say anything to Natalie at all?' he asked, shifting in his seat and looking away as if it had been decided that they wouldn't talk about themselves, not now.

'I asked if she knew that James Darling had been off work,' Holly told him, feeling relieved that the conversation appeared to have been averted for the time being at least. 'The rumour mill at work had noted they were both off at the same time.'

'And did she know?' Mark asked.

'Yes, she did. That's the thing about Natalie and James. They seem to know more about each other than anyone else does, and Natalie seems to know more about what he's up to than her own husband.'

'So where is he?'

'He'd gone to cover a story about gay rights in Belgrade. That's where Mila, his wife, is from. Apparently he'd got wind that the correspondent there might be moving to Kiev and thought he'd make his face known.'

Mark picked up the elephant Holly's mother had brought them from Thailand and began fiddling with it absent-mindedly.

'It's very realistic, isn't it?' he said.

'Yes, very.'

'The elephant in the room. I wonder if that's why your mother gave it to us.'

'What?' Holly asked.

Then it dawned on her what he meant, and what her mother had meant when she gave it to her.

'I'm starving. Is there anything to eat?' Jake wandered into the kitchen and asked, oblivious to the fact that his parents were deep in conversation.

'There's some leftover stew in the fridge,' Mark said, getting up as if the conversation were over. 'You can heat it up if you want, Jake. I'm off to bed. I'm absolutely exhausted.'

'I'll be up in a minute,' Holly said, needing a pause to go back over the conversation and try to work out what exactly had been said about their situation.

Jake had gone for buttering half a loaf of bread over heating up leftover stew, and taken it in front of the TV to eat.

'You ought to go to bed soon,' Holly said to him, and he nodded before disappearing, giving her a moment to text Daniel.

Chapter Forty-Nine

'I'M SORRY IF it makes things difficult for you.' Anne-Marie was looking nervously around the café, afraid to meet Holly's eye.

'It doesn't,' Holly tried to reassure her. She looked like a frightened rabbit and Holly half-expected her to jump up at any minute and make a bolt for the door. 'Do you want some tea? Or coffee? And maybe some cake?'

Holly thought that her mother would be proud of her, sitting here pretending everything was perfectly normal in a peculiarly British way, talking about tea and cake.

She'd called Anne-Marie on her mobile as soon as the producer from *Woman's Hour* had left earlier that morning. Holly had thought when she looked up and saw the familiar face appear in her office that perhaps *Woman's Hour* was her fate once *Antennae* came off air. It wasn't Melanie who had called her before to ask about Survivor's Syndrome, but a more senior producer, Helen Clark, who had come to see her.

Holly had worked on *Woman's Hour* before she'd had Chloe. She had loved it, but as the programme was on air daily there was never any down time and she wasn't sure she could cope with that right now.

She hadn't for a moment imagined the conversation Helen was about to have with her would give her another major headache, at a time when her head already felt as if it would explode with the number of worries, secrets and problems she was carrying around in it.

'May I have a word?' Helen had asked, before sitting in the seat usually occupied by Natalie.

'Did anything ever come of the woman from the train? The one I put Melanie in touch with?' Holly asked, wondering if Anne-Marie had agreed to talk to them despite her concerns.

'That's what I wanted to talk to you about. I just wondered how well you know her?'

'Not that well.' Holly began to feel guilty as she nearly always did when the subject of Anne-Marie came up. She still couldn't quite put her finger on what it was about Anne-Marie that made her feel uneasy.

She seemed a perfectly nice woman and Holly wished she could feel a bit more warm and friendly towards her, but she always made her feel slightly uncomfortable. Daniel didn't seem to feel the same, or if he did he'd never said anything. She felt herself flinching slightly at the way things had been left with Daniel too.

She hadn't seen him to talk to for a few weeks. He'd texted her a couple of times, asking how Mark was and suggesting 'catching up for a quick chat'. She knew she needed to talk to him but was not sure what she wanted to say, so she avoided it. There were too many other people needing to talk to her right now. One of them was sitting in her office.

'I met her at a meeting after the train crash,' Holly told Helen. 'And we went for a drink a few weeks after. I bump into her on the train from time to time.'

'So you're not exactly friends?' she asked.

'To be honest, I feel bad about her,' Holly confessed. 'She sort of latched on to me and another man I know who commutes.'

'Did you know her by sight before you met?'

'No.' Holly remembered thinking it odd that she'd never seen Anne-Marie on the train before, but then she'd explained that she was an infrequent commuter. 'I don't think I'd seen her before. She doesn't go on the train that often. Maybe that's why she talks to us. She doesn't understand the etiquette.'

'What etiquette?' Helen looked confused.

'Oh, you know,' Holly said, although she clearly didn't. 'The "you don't speak to people you see on the train every day or you might just end up talking to them every day for the rest of your life" rule!'

'But Anne-Marie did?'

'Yes,' Holly answered. 'She seemed keen to meet up. I didn't really want to but then I felt a bit mean. She's lost her husband and she seems to be coping really well. I felt as if I ought at least to talk to her. You know how it is?'

'The thing is,' Helen said, 'she really does need to talk to someone and I was hoping you might be able to have a chat with her first off.'

'Do you take sugar?' Holly asked Anne-Marie, pouring from the pot of tea for two they'd asked for and eyeing up the cake she'd ordered. Anne-Marie had said she was not hungry.

'No,' Anne-Marie said, taking the cup and holding it close to her, like a comforter. 'So what happens now?' she asked.

'Nothing happens. I just wanted to see if you were OK,' Holly said, trying to reassure her again. Holly had always thought she was in her early thirties. She looked about thirteen now, like a schoolgirl who had been caught stealing from her parents and knew there would be trouble, even if the offence didn't carry a custodial sentence.

'The interview you did won't go out, and the bit that went

out in the trailer was only a few seconds. I don't suppose anyone noticed.'

'Except him,' said Anne-Marie, looking up and meeting her eye for the first time.

'Except him,' Holly agreed, thinking that things could have gone a whole lot worse for Anne-Marie if he hadn't.

She didn't fully understand why but she did feel sorry for Anne-Marie now, who was looking as if her world was about to crumble.

'I didn't mean for this to happen,' she said quietly.

'I'm sure you didn't.' Holly put her hand across the table and took Anne-Marie's and held it. She felt quite comfortable with her now that she knew her misgivings had not been entirely unfounded.

She could empathise with her too. Both she and Anne-Marie had been through something that day and allowed themselves to be swept up in the ripple of repercussions without ever stopping to think how it would all turn out.

Now they were both trying to sort out the resulting mess.

'Caroline Mills arranged to interview her,' the *Woman's Hour* producer had told Holly back in her office. 'She can be very persuasive.'

'Really?' Holly had heard Caroline Mills on air but didn't know her personally. She knew Anne-Marie had been reluctant to be interviewed. Perhaps that persuasiveness explained why she'd agreed.

'I heard her on the phone, setting it up,' Helen went on. 'I could tell whoever was at the other end of the line was hesitant, to say the least, but Caroline always brings people round.'

'Always?' Holly asked.

'Well, almost always,' Helen told her. 'She told Anne-Marie

it would be more of a chat really. Said they'd talk about every-thing first and then, only if she was happy, they'd record a bit of what she had to say. She told Anne-Marie her contribution was only going to be a small part of a bigger piece about the subject. You know how it works.'

'Yes.' Holly had spent long enough working in radio to know that the desperation of a producer with empty air space to fill often outweighed the reluctance of a potential interviewee to talk about something deeply personal.

'Well, anyway,' Helen told her, 'Anne Marie agreed to meet her and they recorded the interview.'

She paused and looked around the office, as if to make sure no one else was listening. The door was shut.

'Between you and me,' Helen adopted a confidential tone, 'Caroline does tend to put words into people's mouths a bit. I edited an interview she'd done once and there was a lot of "why don't you just tell me" . . . Then she'd tell them more or less exactly what to say.'

'So what did Anne-Marie say?' Holly was getting a little wary of the slightly conspiratorial nature of this meeting.

'She said more or less what we thought she would say,' Helen continued. 'She said she hadn't been on the train that day but that she'd lost her husband in the crash. She didn't go into detail about what actually happened to him and, for once, Caroline was sensitive enough not to probe.'

Holly kept quiet, waiting for Helen to reveal whatever it was she thought she needed to tell Holly, the reason she thought Holly needed to speak to Anne-Marie.

'It was a good interview. There were a few clips that worked well with the rest of the piece,' Helen told her. 'Anne-Marie seemed to have had an almost text-book experience.'

'So what was the problem?' Holly asked, urging her to get to the point.

'We used a clip of her in a trailer for the programme. It went out at the weekend,' Helen told her. 'By Monday morning, there were several messages on the answerphone in our office. They were from her husband.'

It wasn't how I first imagined meeting up with Holly for coffee would be. I thought once we'd met and exchanged numbers she'd contact me, or reply to one of my texts and we'd meet for lunch one day and talk openly about our different experiences of events that day. I thought out of our shared experiences a friendship would grow.

Instead we seemed to get off on a series of misunderstandings, and by the time I realised this, I didn't know how to put things right. If Holly had ever replied and agreed to meet me, I could have tried. But she never did. Now I know she had good reason, but at the time I thought she was just ignoring me and that made me determined to press on.

So I never envisaged sitting nervously, waiting for her to arrive, dreading what she was going to say to me, and hating myself for having misled her.

I could tell when she called that she knew. Her voice sounded different, not cross but perplexed and a bit disappointed.

'Hi, Holly,' I said, when I heard it was her on the other end of the line. 'I haven't seen you for a while.'

'No,' she replied, sounding strained. 'I've been away.'

But I already knew that.

Then she said, 'I think we ought to meet, don't you?'

And I knew then that she would want an explanation; that I owed her one.

I thought she would be angry, but she wasn't.

She looked tired, when she arrived, and I wondered where she'd been. She didn't look as if she'd had a holiday. She wasn't tanned or relaxed, rather stressed and exhausted looking, and I wanted to reach out and take her hand and ask if she was OK. I wanted to be a friend to her, which is all that I'd ever wanted really, but now everything was a mess.

I'd misled her and I feared she'd not forgive me, but she was surprisingly kind and understanding, even before I'd explained everything.

Holly said she'd listened to the interview. Caroline had played it to her in her office and she thought I came across well, especially the part about my mother and the store stampede.

'*That must have been very traumatic,*' *she said to me.* '*Did you have nightmares afterwards?*'

'*I don't remember,*' *I said, honestly. I don't remember the immediate aftermath; I only really started thinking about it in hindsight when Mum got ill.*

'*It must have been hard, your mother being in hospital and having to go and live with friends,*' *Holly continued, and she talked as if she could understand that.* '*Did you realise it was bothering her, even before it became obvious?*'

'*Perhaps.*' *I thought about this. My mother and I had always been close, and afterwards she did seem a little distant, but if I ever thought about it I'd supposed it was because I was growing up, getting older and more private, wanting my own space.*

It wasn't until she went into hospital that I realised how much I missed that closeness.

'*Geoff always said I was too clingy,*' *I said, knowing we needed to broach the subject sooner or later.* '*He said I used to suffocate him because I was too needy, and I think now maybe that's why.*'

'*That's a very harsh thing to say,*' *Holly said gently, as if she understood.* '*I mean for Geoff to say — that you suffocated him.*'

'*I don't think he thought that at first,*' *I said, because I know he didn't. I am sure we were happy when we started out.*

'Things are different when you start a relationship,' Holly said. 'People want to be . . .'

She paused and looked down at the table, trying to think of the right way to put whatever it was she meant to say.

'There's a fine line between suffocation and being completely wrapped up in another person,' she continued. 'When you first meet someone, you want to be wrapped up in them and vice versa. You want to be needed by the other person because you want to be with them. You want them to be unable to live without you really, don't you? So that they want to commit to you?'

'I'd never thought of it like that,' I said, stirring my tea and thinking that Holly was just like I thought she would be: kind and understanding.

'But then, when you've been with someone a long time, sometimes one of you starts reasserting their independence, and if the other's not ready for that . . .' Holly was staring at the table again and she never finished her sentence.

'Geoff once said that I didn't really love him,' I told her, looking around the coffee shop to see if anyone could hear us.

It felt strange to be telling all this to a virtual stranger in a public place, but I also felt relieved at the same time.

'He said I wanted someone to love so I put all my energy into loving the first person who happened to come along, without really considering if I did love him or not.' I paused and Holly looked at me. 'But I did love him, Holly. I really did. And I thought he loved me too.'

'I'm sure he did,' she said, and then she put her hand across the table and over mine, saying, 'Tell me what happened, Anne-Marie. I want to know.'

That's when I started crying, because I'd wanted to talk to someone for so long but I'd been holding it all in. Now that Holly was sitting there, asking me to tell her, the emotions I'd been keeping in check started to flood out.

I knew that people were looking at us but I didn't care, and Holly didn't seem to mind either.

'I'm sorry, Holly,' I said when I'd finished. 'I didn't mean for it to turn out like this.'

'There's no need to apologise,' she said, and I realised her hand was still over mine, she hadn't taken it away all the time I'd been talking, telling her about everything: about Mum and Dad and living with Lisa, about meeting Geoff and the baby, and then Julia.

All the time she was stroking my hand gently with hers, smiling like the friend I had hoped she might become.

'I've wanted to talk to you ever since I saw you on the news,' I sobbed.

She stopped stroking my hand then and took hers away, ostensibly to have a drink of water but she didn't put it back.

'You were being carried out of the tunnel on a stretcher,' I told her. 'I was watching the news because I didn't know what else to do after I heard, and I saw you and I wanted to talk to you.'

'Why?' Holly asked, taking small sips from her glass.

'I can't really explain,' I said, but I tried. 'There was just something about the look on your face that made me think you might understand. I thought I could talk to you. I thought you might be able to help me.'

I hadn't meant to say this. I hadn't meant to say that I needed help. I knew I was finding it difficult, obviously, but I thought I could get through it one way or another.

'I think you probably need to talk to someone else, Anne-Marie,' Holly said, looking at me. 'I'd like to be able to help you, really I would, but there are things I need to sort out in my own life first.'

Chapter Fifty

'Holly, it's really good to see you!' Daniel stood up and gave her a hug, which she felt lasted slightly too long.

He seemed reluctant to release her from his embrace and allow her to sit down and Holly wasn't sure if the hug was one of sympathy, because her husband had had a heart attack, or given because the last time she had seen him they had kissed.

Are you around at all? she had texted him earlier in the week. *There's something I need to tell you.*

Working from home this week. Are you in London every day? I really want to see you, D x

Wednesday? she had suggested.

Antennae was still on air until the end of the month but the production team were unenthusiastic and no one seemed to mind about their presence in the office any more.

Wednesday was the day before Mark and Daisy were due to fly to Edinburgh for the press conference. They'd be spending the night there.

Holly didn't recognise Daniel at first when she looked around Brown's, not only because he was in t-shirt and jeans, but also because he looked older, more tired and resigned.

'Holly,' he'd called out as she walked right past the table he was sitting at. She'd focused and seen him, looking what she could only describe as crushed.

'How are you?' she asked, thinking that if he said fine, he would be lying.

'Fine,' he said.

Holly laughed, feeling some of the awkwardness she had felt disappear.

'What's funny?' Daniel asked.

'You don't look fine,' she told him.

'Is that funny?' He raised his eyebrows questioningly and a hint of the expression of permanent half-amusement that she usually associated with him returned to his face.

'No,' Holly agreed. 'I think that's why someone came up with the expression "you've got to laugh" – for precisely those moments when laughter is entirely inappropriate. To explain away its inappropriateness.'

'So you don't actually find the fact that I am not fine funny?' He was smiling now.

'You said you were fine,' she reminded him.

'Well, I'm not.' Daniel was serious again. 'Do you want something to eat or drink?'

Holly noticed that he already had a beer and a plate of steak and fries, which was hardly touched.

'I'll have a cup of tea.' She wondered how long he had already been there. 'And I might nick a few of your chips, if you're not eating them?'

'No, I'm not hungry,' he said, pushing his plate slightly towards her.

'So what's made you lose your appetite?' she asked, taking a chip and dipping it in a swirl of mayonnaise.

'I'll tell you in a bit.' Daniel signalled to the waitress who was clearing a nearby table. 'You said there was something you needed to tell me, when you texted?'

'Well, yes, something's happened,' Holly told him as the waitress approached. 'Could I get a pot of tea and a glass of water, please? Do you want anything else, Daniel?'

When he said he didn't, the waitress left.

'Is Mark OK?' Daniel asked. 'Daisy seems completely wrapped up in this press conference, but I thought Mark was supposed to take things easy?'

'He's been busy too but he seems to be OK,' Holly answered, wondering if Daniel knew something she didn't.

'I met Anne-Marie earlier in the week.' This was the reason Holly had needed to talk to him. 'She wasn't in a good way.'

Holly stopped talking when the waitress came back and put a large pot of tea and a glass of water on the table.

'Thank you,' she said, as she unloaded a cup and a jug of milk.

'Did you just bump into her on the train, or arrange to meet?' Daniel asked.

'We arranged to meet.' Holly poured some milk into the bottom of her cup. 'Do you remember I told you I'd put someone from *Woman's Hour* in touch with her?'

'Yes.' He nodded. 'You said you thought she was angry at the time.'

'I did,' Holly told him. 'But apparently she agreed to do the interview anyway. I didn't know about it. I was off work for a week, after Mark . . .'

Daniel reached out and put his hand on hers as her voice trailed off. She pulled it back and put it on her lap, finding this physical contact slightly oppressive, in the same way she had found the hug he'd given her earlier slightly claustrophobic.

'When I got back to work, the producer came and told me

he'd done the interview. She said it was good and they'd used a small part of it to trail the programme over the weekend.'

'Trail?' Daniel asked.

'To advertise the programme before it goes out,' Holly told him. 'If you'd tuned in to Radio Four over the weekend, you might have heard Anne-Marie talking about losing her husband the day the train crashed.'

'So did it stir things up for her?' he asked. 'You said you thought she was coping too well, didn't you?'

'I did.' Holly nodded. 'I didn't know why, but I always thought there was something not quite right about Anne-Marie. And, it turns out, I was right.'

'What was it then?' Daniel was looking at her expectantly.

'It seems her husband didn't die in the crash that day at all,' she told him. 'He was on the train but got out and walked out through the tunnel, alive and unharmed.'

'So why did she say that he died?' Daniel's expression was incredulous. 'I don't understand.'

'The funny thing is, she never actually did say that he died,' Holly tried to explain. 'That was one of the things that struck me as odd about Anne-Marie, the way she said things. Even when she recorded this interview for *Woman's Hour*, she never actually said that he'd died. She said that she'd lost him.'

'Same difference surely?' Daniel asked.

'Not to her.' Holly tried to explain some of what Anne-Marie had told her when they'd met. 'She knew he was on that train, and she heard on the news in the morning that it had crashed and there were likely to be casualties.'

Holly screwed up her face as she said the word. She didn't like this euphemism for deaths but she couldn't quite bring herself to say the word either.

'Anne-Marie told me she tried to contact him but the mobile

phone lines were down. She was at home, waiting for news. Holly paused then.

When Anne-Marie had described the waiting to her, it had forced her to consider what it must have been like for Mark waiting to find out if his wife was all right.

Anne-Marie had told her the waiting was agonising. That she'd jumped every time someone walked past the house, and sat by the phone willing it to ring with positive news. Mark had been at home, alone when he was waiting for news, but Anne-Marie had had company.

Holly concentrated on these facts as Anne-Marie spoke to her and tried not to think where she had been while Anne-Marie was sitting at home.

'She told me her best friend came round, after she'd heard the news on the radio, and sat with her. She was thankful for the company. She said having someone else to wait with her broke the silence of the phone not ringing.'

'Go on,' Daniel urged her.

Holly thought back to the afternoon she'd spent with Anne-Marie.

'It was eerie,' Anne-Marie had told her. 'Usually I get lots of calls from people selling life insurance, or debt management services, or trying to make me switch electricity providers. But in that hour no one at all called until . . .'

She'd paused and looked up at Holly, her eyes filling with tears as she did so. Then she'd drunk a whole glass of water and afterwards carried on.

'Julia seemed more agitated than I was.' Anne-Marie described how her best friend kept getting up and sitting down again, and had eventually gone into the garden to have a cigarette. 'She'd given up a few years ago but she still had the occasional one.'

'When she was in the garden her phone started ringing inside her bag,' Anne-Marie told Holly. 'I took it out. I took it out and then I noticed that the number calling was Geoff's.'

'Did you answer?' Holly asked her.

'No,' she said. 'I froze. I thought that someone else must have his phone and be calling from it. I thought maybe they were going through the contacts, trying to find out who his wife was. It didn't occur to me at the time that of course I am one of the first names on the list.'

'So who was it, calling Julia?' Holly asked her.

'It was Geoff. He left a message and I listened to it while Julia was still smoking at the bottom of the garden. He was calling to tell her he was OK. He said he wanted to let her know that he was all right. Then he said he had to go because he ought to call me.'

'But I still don't understand?' Daniel said, looking to Holly for further explanation.

'They'd been having an affair.' Holly hadn't needed Anne-Marie to spell it out for her. 'Geoff had been seeing her best friend for months, apparently. That's why she'd come round – not to look after Anne-Marie, but because she too was desperate to find out if Geoff was alive.'

Daniel took a sip of his drink but said nothing as he took this all in.

'If he hadn't been on that train, the affair might have gone on much longer without Anne-Marie knowing,' Holly said. 'He told her that evening he'd been planning to leave her but hadn't worked out how to tell her. Then he packed his bags and left.'

'So that's why she said she lost her husband that day?' Daniel was beginning to understand.

'Yes.' Holly nodded. 'She lost her best friend as well. The ultimate betrayal.'

'How was she when you saw her?' Daniel asked, picking up a paper napkin and absent-mindedly shredding it as he talked.

'Not good, obviously. She was mortified that she'd misled us. She said she never meant to. It was just that we assumed that he'd died, and she said she found it easier to let us believe that than to tell us what had really happened.'

'But why did she go to the meeting? I still don't really understand,' Daniel said. 'And why did she agree to do the radio interview?'

'She said she went to the meeting because her husband had ceased all contact with her. She wanted to get some sense of what had happened and who else had been on the train,' Holly told him. 'She told me that, even after what he'd done to her, she hoped they might have a future and thought his decision to leave her might have been affected by his having been in the crash.'

'And the radio?' Daniel asked.

'She didn't want to do it at first,' Holly told him. 'But the reporter who called her was very persuasive. And she hadn't been able to speak to Geoff since. When she said she'd lost him, she really had. He hadn't returned her calls. He'd refused to meet or talk to her. She told me she thought that if she did the interview, it would force his hand.'

'It worked then, didn't it?' Daniel commented.

'It makes sense now,' Holly said. 'All the things she said, the way she was with us and even the fact that she said she had lost him. He may not have died that day but what she went through was like a bereavement. I can't imagine how she must have been feeling.'

'I can imagine, Holly,' Daniel said, looking straight at her. 'I know how she must have felt. That's why I'm not at work. That's why I needed to talk to you. I know what it feels like to find out that your partner doesn't want to be with you any more.'

Chapter Fifty-One

'Do you know where Dad is?' Holly had knocked and put her head tentatively round the door of Jake's room.

He didn't like her walking in unannounced any more. Gone were the days when she could stand by the door and watch him, so completely absorbed in a Lego construction that he didn't even notice she was there, and then, when he did, beam at her presence and show her the beginnings of a complex battleship, or whatever it was he was making.

'Don't know.' Jake had been sitting at his desk, doing something on a laptop. He closed it hurriedly as soon as he saw his mother. 'He said he might be late back, though.'

'Did he say how late?' Holly asked, wondering why he had closed the computer so fast

'He's all right,' Mark would say, when she told him she didn't like the amount of time Jake spent on it. 'That's what boys do.'

'But what if he's doing stuff he shouldn't?' she would press him.

'My parents used to worry about me listening to punk music.' Mark often used this line of reasoning. 'Thought it would turn me into a juvenile delinquent, but I turned out all right.'

As if to prove his point, Jake got up and came over to where Holly was standing near the radiator. He sat down on the edge of his bed opposite her and smiled.

'Dad said he might be late because he needed to make sure he had everything ready before he goes to Edinburgh tomorrow.' Jake appeared to be in chatty mode.

Tomorrow was the official press launch for the Jimmy Finlay run. Mark had been working hard on it ever since he'd come out of hospital. Too hard, Holly thought, since he was supposed to be taking things easy. He was flying up to Edinburgh first thing in the morning, with Daisy. They needed to be at the airport early. Holly had presumed he'd get home at a reasonable hour before that and not burn the candle at both ends.

'Where've you been anyway? I thought you were working from home today.'

'Well, I didn't really feel like working, so I bunked off and went for a wander round town.' Holly didn't like lying to Jake. She found it much more difficult than lying to Mark, but she wasn't sure he'd understand her reasons for seeing Daniel today and she didn't want him to ask about their meeting now.

'Do you know what you'll be doing yet, when *Antennae* goes off air?' Jake asked.

'Not yet.' Holly wondered if he was worried that she might be out of a job. 'I'm sure they have something in mind but have chosen not to share it with me yet.'

'Are you all right, Mum?' Jake eased himself back on his bed and lay down so that he was looking at the ceiling as he asked her this.

'Yes, I'm fine, darling.' She tried to sound reassuring, though she was anything but fine.

'But why?' Holly had asked Daniel, when he'd told her Daisy wanted to leave him. 'When did this happen? Where will she go? What will you do?'

The world suddenly seemed to be falling apart. Everywhere she turned couples were coming unstuck. Holly didn't want them to come unstuck, not just because she cared about the people involved but because it meant it could happen to her too.

'The day Mark went into hospital.' Daniel chose to answer the when part of her question first. 'When we got home, Daisy said she needed to talk.'

'Yes,' Holly said, feeling suddenly nauseous. She remembered reading the text Mark had sent Daisy, when he came out of hospital the following day. *Have you told Daniel?* it had read, and Holly had told herself it was probably work-related and tried, unsuccessfully, to dismiss any thought of what else it might be about from her head.

She took a deep breath, trying to calm herself in anticipation of Daniel now telling her something she didn't want to hear.

'She'd been a bit off earlier in the week,' he said. 'I thought there was something wrong but I wasn't sure what and I didn't ask her. I thought it would probably pass.'

'But it didn't?' Holly asked, not wanting to ask what it was that had been wrong.

'No.' Daniel had taken a deep breath himself and then explained, 'Daisy had had a miscarriage the week before. I didn't even know she was pregnant. She hadn't told me.'

'How pregnant was she?' Holly asked, wondering why Daisy would keep news like that from her husband.

'Only a couple of weeks. She'd only been sure she was pregnant for a few days before she miscarried.'

'And she didn't tell you?' Holly was thinking to herself that a few days was an eternity in which not to tell your husband you were pregnant, especially when you had been trying for a while.

'No.' He looked incredibly sad. 'Not until it was over.'

'But why?' Holly asked. She could only think of one reason why you wouldn't tell your husband that you were having a baby – and that was if it was someone else's.

'She said that when she found out she was pregnant she realised it was not what she wanted.' Daniel looked at Holly then as if perhaps she could explain this to him.

'You don't always feel as you think you should feel.' She thought back to when she'd discovered she was expecting Chloe. She'd thought in advance that she would be delighted, but found she felt strangely detached from the whole process yet terrified at the same time.

'I was really scared when I was pregnant with Chloe. I didn't feel blooming and expectant. I was scared of what it would be like having a baby . . . of what I would be like as a mother. I didn't think I'd be able to do it. But it worked out all right in the end.'

'We'll never find out now.' Daniel stared at the table.

'At least it means you know she can get pregnant,' Holly tried to comfort him. 'People often miscarry their first child. It's quite common. So if it's happened once, it can happen again.'

'It won't happen again though, Holly.' He looked up at her and his expression was one of abject resignation. 'Because Daisy doesn't want to get pregnant again, not soon and not with me anyway.'

'She can't be sure of that,' Holly tried to reassure him, and herself in the process. She couldn't get the thought out of her head that Daisy hadn't wanted the baby because it wasn't Daniel's. And if it wasn't Daniel's, whose was it? She tried to recall the exact wording of some of the texts to and from Mark that she had read. Did he know about this? She thought that he must.

'She's just been pregnant for the first time and then lost the baby,' Holly continued. 'Her hormones will be all over the place, and her emotions too. Wait a while, I'm sure she will see things differently, Daniel.'

'She was adamant,' he insisted. 'And to be honest, Holly, I'm beginning to wonder if she ever really wanted to try for a baby. I really wanted one and I thought she did too. But I'm beginning to think I misinterpreted things.'

Holly said nothing, waiting for him to explain further.

'I was the one who suggested we start trying. Daisy said she wasn't sure if it was the right time.'

'There never seems to be a right time,' Holly said.

'I should have listened to her then,' Daniel said. 'I shouldn't have let things go this far . . .'

'What things?' Holly asked.

'When Daisy got pregnant, she told me it made her realise that this wasn't what she wanted.' Daniel paused.

'A baby?' Holly asked.

'And the rest,' he said slowly. 'She said she didn't tell me she was pregnant because it had made her realise that she didn't want the life she has now. She said she didn't want to be married and living off my earnings, and she didn't want to be stuck at home with a child. She said doing this work for Mark had made her realise what she'd been missing out on, and she didn't feel ready to start settling down.'

'I can understand why she felt like that.' Holly hoped this would reassure Daniel. 'It can seem as if life, as you know it, is over when you're expecting a child, and no amount of people telling you it's only just beginning will make you believe that's true. It's a major change. It makes you run scared.'

'But Daisy said she was already running scared.' Daniel slumped back in his chair. 'She said she felt we'd married too young, and that I'm making her lead a life she doesn't want to lead. She really wants this job with Jimmy Finlay. I think she was relieved she lost the baby, Holly, because it means she can go off and do whatever it is she wants to do.'

'Perhaps it will work out for the best.' Holly wondered how

much of this Mark knew and why he hadn't mentioned anything to her. 'Perhaps she can do the job for a while, and in a year or so she may feel ready to try for another baby.'

'I've been through all of this with her,' Daniel sighed. 'We've been going round and round in circles, talking about what we both want — and it's not the same thing.'

'I'm sorry.' Holly didn't know what else to say.

'The thing is,' Daniel carried on talking, 'I could never quite believe it when Daisy agreed to marry me. I never thought someone like her would want to settle down with someone like me. It seemed too good to be true. And now it turns out I was right all along.'

'That sounds like Dad.' Jake sat up on his bed, listening to the sound of a key being turned in the door.

'Mark?' Holly called out, without moving.

'Hello,' his familiar voice came up the stairs. 'Where are you?'

'In Jake's room,' she called back, hearing the exchange as if she were not taking part in it. 'I'll be down in a moment.'

It all sounded completely normal, this exchange between husband and wife, but Holly was no longer sure if everything was normal or if this was just an illusion.

Chapter Fifty-Two

'How was your day?' Holly studied Mark's face closely for signs that anything might be amiss.

'Good.' He sounded upbeat but turned away to hang his coat on the hook in the hall so she could only see his profile. 'Everything seems to be ready for tomorrow. I'm really excited about it.'

'What time are you leaving?' Holly asked, wondering when she would find time to sit him down and talk.

'The flight's not till nine but we need to be there by seven-thirty.' Holly noted how casually Mark managed to make the 'we' that meant himself and Daisy sound. 'I'll book a cab for six-thirty and pick up Daisy on the way.'

'Right.' Holly wasn't sure what else to say, but the silence was filled by Chloe opening the front door.

'Hello!' She sounded cheery too.

Holly wondered if her family were really all in buoyant mood or whether they just appeared more up in contrast to the way she felt.

'Hello, darling,' she said to Chloe. 'What have you been doing since school finished?'

'I've been at Ruaridh's house.' She smiled at her mother. 'And stopped at the Open Market on the way back. I thought I'd cook dinner tonight, as Dad's going away tomorrow morning.'

'That's very kind,' Holly said. 'Are you sure you have time? You don't have any homework or anything to do?'

'I did it at Ruaridh's house,' Chloe answered, heading for the kitchen with a plastic bag that appeared to be bursting with vegetables.

Holly had nothing in mind for dinner, so was glad not to have to dream up something from whatever she could find. Nevertheless she felt a bit redundant. They didn't really seem to need her here, any of them.

As she thought this, Holly realised this was exactly what Mark must have been thinking for the past year.

'Can you come up to my room?' Jake stood at the top of the stairs, making this unusual request. His room was usually the last place he wanted either of his parents.

'Me or Dad?' she asked.

'Well, Dad, but both of you,' Jake answered.

'Yes, both of you,' Chloe said, as if she already knew what this was about.

'OK.' Holly started going up the stairs and could feel Mark following her.

'I need to pack for tomorrow,' he said, apparently unperturbed by the novelty of Jake inviting them both into his room.

'Do you want to sit on my bed?' he asked, sitting on the swivel chair by his desk.

Holly felt unnerved by the way he was behaving. He was obviously about to tell them something and she had no idea what. But she wasn't sure if she could take any more surprises.

'I'm really sorry,' Holly said to Daniel as they walked down an alleyway connecting the street the brasserie was in to the one that ran parallel.

'What for?' The alley was too narrow for them to walk abreast

Uncoupled

of each other. Daniel had been ahead of her but stopped now and turned to face her.

'I feel partly responsible,' Holly said. 'Because of Mark putting her up for the job with Jimmy Finlay.'

'It was Daisy who put Mark in touch with him,' Daniel reminded her.

'Oh, yes.' Holly had forgotten this. 'Still, I feel bad. Is there . . . ?'

She wanted to start walking again. She felt she could ask the question she wanted to ask more easily if they were in motion, but Daniel was blocking the way.

'Is there someone else?' Holly looked down at the pavement as she asked it.

'She says not.' He seemed momentarily rooted to the spot.

'And you don't think there is?' Holly could not get out of her head the thought that there might be, and that it might be Mark.

'I don't think there is anyone else,' Daniel said slowly, looking straight at her. 'Not for Daisy anyway.'

'What do you mean?' Holly wondered if Daisy had told him something about Mark and someone else. Was Daniel going to be the bearer of bad tidings?

He didn't answer.

Instead, he took a step closer to Holly, took hold of her and began kissing her, more passionately than the last time, more urgently too, and pushing her so that her back was against the wall of the alley and his hand was on her breast but moving down towards the top of her skirt.

Holly tried to wriggle away and say 'no', but he was kissing her too hard for her to speak, forcing her mouth open with his tongue and pushing her hand between her legs.

Holly was trying to force him away but it appeared to be having little effect. Daniel was much stronger than he looked.

He was pressing himself against her now and Holly could feel herself becoming aroused although she knew this was definitely not what she wanted. She squirmed again, putting her free hand up and pulling sharply on Daniel's hair.

He stopped kissing her and moved his face away far enough for her to speak.

'What's wrong?' he asked.

'This is wrong,' Holly said. 'This isn't going to help.'

'I thought it was what you wanted, Holly.' Daniel moved back slightly but he was still too close for her to move.

'It's not.' She tried to edge sideways and put some space between them. 'It's not what I want at all.'

'I'm sorry.' He stepped back abruptly, as if suddenly realising what he'd been doing, then turned away and began walking fast down the alley.

'Wait!' Holly called after him. 'Daniel, wait.'

But he carried on walking, too fast for her to catch up without running, and she didn't want to run after him. As he turned out of the alleyway he turned back briefly and said to her, as she gained ground, 'What do you want, Holly?'

His voice was raised but she didn't think it was in anger, just so she could hear across the distance.

She stopped as she neared the end of the alley and said quietly, so that he wouldn't hear, but out loud, as if saying it might make it happen: 'I want things back the way they were.'

Mark sat next to her on the bed, but not right next to her. There was a time when he would automatically have sat close, with his arm around her, or they would both have squeezed into bed with Jake, giving him a cuddle before he went to sleep. Now Mark's preferred position was about a foot away. Whatever news it was Jake was about to deliver, it wasn't going to be received together.

Holly and Mark were going to react separately to it from different ends of his bed.

'What is it you wanted to tell us, Jake?' Holly looked across the room to where he was sitting at his desk, now fiddling with the laptop. She dreaded hearing what he might be going to say. Was he in trouble at school? Worried about things at home? Was he going to tell them he thought he was gay, or was there something on the computer he was going to show them?

The latter seemed the most likely as he was saying 'hang on a sec' and tapping away at the keyboard.

'Take a look at this,' he said, nervously, as if they might be angry with what they saw.

'What is it, Jake?' Holly asked, feeling she needed to prepare herself for whatever it was he was going to show them.

'Have a look, Mum.' Jake was smiling now. He still looked apprehensive but not scared of what their reaction might be.

Mark got up first and peered over his shoulder.

'Oh my god!' he said, sounding surprised. 'That's amazing, Jakey. Incredible, in fact. When did you do that?'

'Have a look, Dad,' Jake encouraged him. 'Enter the site.'

'I don't know what to say.' Mark was tooling around with the mouse. Holly wondered what site Jake had discovered that could be so incredible it merited inviting both his parents up to his room to have a look at it.

'Look at this, Holly.' Mark swung his head in her direction. She got up and looked over Jake's other shoulder.

'Oh, Jake,' she said, putting her arms around him. 'Did you do that?'

Chapter Fifty-Three

Holly saw Daniel immediately, through the window of the carriage, even though she was trying to walk past without looking and without being seen. She didn't know what she would say to him when she next saw him. He hadn't called or texted her after leaving her in the alleyway, and she hadn't contacted him. So it was still there, hanging in the air, whatever it was that had happened.

She got on the train further down, feeling slightly nervous not just about her life but about the journey. Why now? she asked herself. You've done it scores of times, since the crash. But she still felt a slight feeling of dread. A week ago, Daniel's presence on the train would have made her feel safe. Now it had the opposite effect. She realised she'd been stupid, thinking he could carry on looking after her the way he had done in the immediate aftermath of the crash. He wasn't the person she needed, it was Mark.

Holly checked her watch. It was just before 8. Mark would be at the airport now, with Daisy. Holly wondered what they would be doing. Would they be having a coffee and something to eat somewhere? Or filling time separately in the airport shops? Or would they be waiting at the departure gates together? Holly had a sudden vivid mental picture of the latter. Mark and Daisy were holding hands in the transit lounge, knowing that there, airside, they were unlikely to be seen by anyone they knew.

Holly shook her head to try and remove the image from her mind, but she also cursed herself for not having found the right time to sit down and have a proper talk with her husband during the past couple of weeks. It should have been easy but initially she'd shied away from any confrontation, knowing that Mark was supposed to be taking things easy. Then, when they both went back to work, they never seemed to be in the same space at the same time, or if they were the children were always there too. And when they did find themselves together, Holly became suddenly unsure what it was she needed to talk to him about.

Last night she'd been clear what she needed to say to Mark and that she needed to say it before he went away to Edinburgh with Daisy, but then the evening took a new direction and she couldn't bring herself to spoil the mood.

She thought back now, as the train began inching out of the station, to the look on Mark's face when Jake had opened the laptop. He had been amazed and delighted and incredibly proud. And so was she.

All those hours Jake had spent on the computer, when she'd thought he'd been chatting to friends on Facebook or suspected he might be looking at porn, he'd been developing a new website for Mark.

'It's incredible, Jake, really incredible,' his father told him. 'I should have done something myself really, but I never got round to it.'

'I reckoned a lot of Jimmy Finlay fans will want to follow the run, so you needed something on your site before it started.' Jake sounded like a professional who'd been consulted about this, rather than a thirteen year old, who'd done it all off his own bat.

'If you click on the map, you'll be able to see where Jimmy

is.' He carried on showing them round the site. 'And get daily updates, which you or Daisy can add in. I did talk to Daisy about it a bit.'

He said this a little sheepishly, as if he had somehow been going behind their backs, but Mark didn't seem to notice.

'Well, I don't know what to say, Jakey.' Mark sounded almost tearful.

'It's really good, isn't it?' Chloe had come upstairs and the smell of something delicious, cooking downstairs, followed her.

'Did you know about this?' Holly asked her.

'Well, yes,' Chloe admitted. 'I've seen it. He's really clever, isn't he? By the way, dinner's ready.'

'You're both incredible,' Holly had said, amazed that they had each found a way of helping out the family.

Holly had been wrong to worry about what they were both up to when they were out or in their rooms. They'd simply being trying to help in whatever way they could. She'd thought they were off elsewhere, Chloe in body and Jake in spirit, when in fact they'd both been focused on their family.

She was the one who'd been elsewhere and she wanted to be back now, but wasn't quite sure how to get there.

'The kids are amazing, aren't they?' Mark said when they went to bed that night.

The evening had become celebratory. Chloe had produced a wonderful dinner and Mark had opened a bottle of sparkling wine and toasted both children. Then Chloe had wished him luck with Jimmy Finlay's press conference. It felt as if everyone was moving forward, excited about the future for the first time in a long while. Only Holly felt scared about what the next few weeks might bring.

Mark cuddled up to her after he got into bed, and when he put his arm around her and began stroking her back in circular motions, she wondered if they might end up having sex. His caress wasn't exactly foreplay but it was more physical contact than they'd had in months.

She found his face in the dark and kissed him, but Mark sat up suddenly.

'Damn, I forgot!' He broke whatever mood there had been. 'I need to text Daisy the time the cab is coming.'

He got out of bed and reached for his dressing gown, which hung on the back of the bedroom door.

'Sorry,' he said, cheerily. 'I won't be long.'

He wasn't. But long enough for Holly to wonder why her kissing him had reminded him he needed to text Daisy. And long enough for him to want to go straight to sleep when he came back.

'Better get some rest,' he said, climbing into bed. It sounded like a warning to Holly not to get any ideas about coming on to him now.

'Yes.' She felt like someone watching a film of her own life.

The actress in it was waiting for direction. Should she accuse her husband of something she had no real grounds to accuse him of, or keep quiet and let him go off to Edinburgh with a woman she knew no longer wanted to be with her own husband?

The imaginary director asked her to keep quiet for the moment, but to lean over and kiss Mark.

'I love you, Mark,' she said quietly.

'You too,' he said, rearranging his pillows and turning his back on her.

Holly took out her book and began reading but she wasn't taking anything in. The train was moving incredibly slowly and seemed to take forever to get to Preston Park, which was only two minutes away.

She decided to text Mark, feeling that if he was going to be away for a few days, she had to maintain contact.

My train is crawling. Hope you are on your way and that today goes really well. Am sure it will be a great success. Love you. Holly x

She sent the message just before the train entered a short tunnel on the outskirts of Brighton. When it came out again her phone showed she had a reply.

Flight delayed too! Waiting for gate to come up. Will speak to you later. Mark xx

Holly felt like a teenager, trying to analyse the true meaning of the few liquid-crystal words. He hadn't said he loved her, but he had put two kisses. Was the omission because he didn't think it needed to be said? Was it implied with the kisses, or were they simply habit?

The train picked up a little speed before slowing again as it entered the tunnel which ran under the Downs. It crept along slowly until the carriage was in the dark void and then stopped.

People began sighing and looking at their watches and phones, as if the very act of staring at their timepieces would make the train go again.

It didn't. An hour and a few gratuitous announcements by the guard later, they were still sitting there, unsure what was causing the delay or when they would get going again. Then the lights went out and they were plunged into darkness, alleviated only by the LED displays from mobile phones and laptop screens.

Holly experienced a huge wave of nausea and found she was having trouble drawing the deep breath she needed to take to quell it. She could hear herself taking short, sharp, rasping breaths. She sounded as if she was having an asthma attack but knew she was having a panic attack.

'Are you OK?' the woman sitting next to her asked.

Holly shook her head, although she knew the woman wouldn't be able to see the movement in the dark.

Holly could feel herself getting hotter and thought she might be about to faint.

'I have to get out,' she said, so quietly she wasn't sure if anyone could hear her, but her travelling companion did.

Holly felt her hand being taken.

'It's OK,' the woman tried to reassure her. 'We'll get going again soon. You just have to try and relax for a few minutes.'

'What's wrong with her?' another male voice asked.

Holly was aware of a male outline but could only think that she had to get out of the carriage. She couldn't just sit here waiting in the dark. It might happen again. She might not be so lucky this time. She couldn't just sit here waiting.

'No, I have to get out,' she said, struggling to her feet.

'You can't get out, love. We're in the middle of the tunnel,' the male voice said. 'Sit down.'

'Yes, sit next to me.' The woman's voice was more soothing, as if she was used to dealing with this sort of thing. She was still holding her hand and pulled Holly gently back into her seat.

'Take a deep breath,' she said as the train spluttered back to life, the lights came on and it moved through the tunnel and out again.

Several people were looking at her curiously now as the train gathered speed.

'Are you OK?' the woman sitting next to her said again. Holly saw that she was young, smart in a suit, and very pretty.

'I think so.' Holly smiled, trying to deflect the unwanted attention. 'I think I'll just splash my face with water.'

She picked up her bag and began walking out of the carriage. She wondered if the woman would follow her, but found she was on her own, stumbling slightly in the corridor as the train gathered speed before slowing again to stop at Haywards Heath.

The platform there was crowded with the backlog of commuters that had built up while they sat in the tunnel. Holly knew that they would all try to cram into the carriage and it would become unbearably crowded.

She stood by the doors, waiting for them to open, anticipating the crush as people pushed by to make sure they were not left behind.

There was only a couple of seconds' delay between the train stopping and the doors opening but it felt like an eternity. She fought against the flow of passengers, making her way to a bench, where she sat down and wondered what she was going to do next.

I feel better today than I have done for weeks . . . years if I am honest. In fact, I almost feel ready to stop writing things down and put these pages up in the attic, with the diary I stopped writing after Mum came out of hospital.

The last few months have felt strange but I think things are starting to get better. At least, I'm beginning to see how things are and how they were more clearly.

Geoff knocked on the door a few nights ago, the same day I'd met Holly and told her what really happened. It was early evening but I wasn't expecting anyone. I never am. I thought it would be someone trying to sell something. So I opened the door reluctantly, and there was Geoff.

'Can I come in, A–M?' he asked.

He looked tired, older too, a lot greyer than he was the last time I saw him, and thinner. He didn't look happy. I'd tried not to picture him because I didn't want to think of him somewhere else, with someone else, enjoying his life without me. But when I failed to shut out the images of what his life might be like now, he was happy, fatter, wearing new clothes, a new man. He wasn't the one standing on the doorstep now, the old Geoff but looking beaten.

'Of course,' I said, because even just seeing him there, without knowing what he was going to say to me or how we would go from here, made me feel hopeful.

'How are you?' he said, stepping inside and then waiting for me to tell him where to go.

'Fine,' I said, although I knew he knew that wasn't true. We were being very polite with each other. 'Shall we go into the sitting room? How's Julia?'

I asked this, as he sat down, casually, as if it was of no importance to me.

'I haven't seen her since,' Geoff surprised me by saying.

I sat down too.

'But I thought you'd been with her?' I said. 'I thought that's where you went.'

'I've been at my mum's,' he told me. 'Trying to sort my head out.'

'And have you?' I asked him.

'Not completely.' He looked at me and smiled then. 'It's very muddled up, my head. It's not easy to sort.'

'Mine's a complete and utter mess,' I said, and saying it made me start laughing.

Then the laughter turned to tears, and before I knew it I was sitting there bawling and Geoff had come over and put his arms round me. 'I'm sorry. I'm so so sorry. I never meant for any of this to happen,' he said.

'It did happen though, didn't it?' I answered. Then, taking a deep breath, ready to talk, 'Why did you let it happen, Geoff?'

'I don't know,' he replied, sitting up. 'I just felt I needed an escape. I know that sounds pathetic and I'm not blaming you because I know that none of this is your fault. I know that I've behaved really badly but I felt there seemed to be so much that had gone wrong in your life and you wanted me to make it all better. But I couldn't, could I? I couldn't turn the clock back. I couldn't make any of the things that had happened to you and around you go away. I felt you wanted too much from me, so I started backing off.'

'And then there was Julia?' I said this as a question.

'Julia was just there,' he said. 'She was around and she was willing and so I started sleeping with her as an escape. But it wasn't an escape, I realised that when the train got hit.'

'What happened to you then?' I asked because I still didn't know.

'I was fine,' Geoff said. 'I was in the carriage in the tunnel, but I got up and walked out. I can't have been in there more than five or ten minutes but it was like a huge wake-up call. I realised I could have died, but I didn't, and I realised that I had to sort my life out. I had to stop seeing Julia and I had to work out what I wanted with you.'

I didn't know what to say, so I said nothing and Geoff continued.

'And it also made me understand, just a little bit, some of what you must have gone through in your life,' he continued. 'I know you'd told me all this stuff, but it always felt as if you weren't really involved because you were one step removed. Then when I walked off that train, scot-free, I felt as if I had been involved in something major, something awful, but I didn't feel I had the right to say that, not really.'

I nodded.

'Can we try again, A–M?' he asked. 'Because I do love you. I just don't think I can be everything that you want me to be.'

'No,' I said, agreeing with a negative that I realised might confuse him. 'I mean, no, you can't be everything to me, I'm beginning to realise that now. I need to talk to someone, someone qualified, and then maybe we can talk too, about us?'

I had the first session with a counsellor yesterday. She's quite old, much older than Helen was, and I told her about the sessions I had with her and why I stopped going. Then we talked about everything: the department store, Mum, Lisa, Geoff, the baby, the crash and Julia. And I told her about Holly and Daniel, and the whole mess of misunderstandings that I seem to have created throughout my life.

By the end of the session I was beginning to feel that I was actually starting to sort things out properly for the first time. I felt better for that.

But Holly, when I saw her this morning, looked a whole lot worse.

She was getting off the train as I got on but she didn't see me. I tried to smile and ask why she was getting off at Haywards Heath but she just pushed past me, as if she couldn't wait to get off the train. She looked drained, like she did when we met the other day and she told me she had stuff to sort out. But she looked worse today, paler and more tired.

I knew the train had been delayed because of a power failure and the way Holly looked, it was as if it had all come back to her, as if she couldn't face being on the train any more. I thought about turning round and going after her, missing my train so I could talk to her but I wasn't sure I would be of any help. Instead, I got on the train and walked up it, looking for Daniel.

He was there, and he looked tired and down as well. I didn't ask why I told him about Holly and he said he didn't know what to do. So I told him what to do.

'Do you know how to get hold of her husband?' I asked, and he nodded.

Chapter Fifty-Four

H OLLY WASN'T SURE how long she'd been sitting on the bench but she knew it was long enough for the early crowds of commuters to have thinned. The platform was no longer crowded, people were no longer cramming themselves into trains like sardines, and the early morning chill had given way to warm sunshine.

Holly stared ahead of her, only dimly aware of her surroundings. She could hear her phone ringing from inside her bag and knew she ought to answer it but didn't want to. She needed to focus on what she was going to do now and she didn't seem able to, so she carried on looking into the middle distance, letting the world go on around her, as if she had no place in it.

Then something caught her attention. She didn't look but she sensed someone bounding up the steps to the platform and striding purposefully towards her. The energy of whoever it was roused her from her torpor and she turned her head and saw a tall dark-haired man approaching her. There was something about him which made her realise that everything was going to be all right. The way he was walking towards her with such clear intent made her think that whoever this was would know what she should do. Only when he sat down next to her on the bench did she realise it was Mark.

'Holly.' He put his arms around her and she found the feel and smell of him made her start sobbing uncontrollably.

Mark tightened his grip on her, saying nothing but holding her so close that Holly felt as if she was absorbing some of his strength and calm. Gradually her sobs subsided and Mark began stroking her hair and talking to her.

'It's OK,' he said. 'Everything will be OK, Holly, I promise.'

'What are you doing here?' She looked up at him, remembering that he had been on his way to Edinburgh. 'How did you know I was here?'

'Daniel saw you get off the train. He called Daisy,' Mark told her, taking her hand and stroking it gently while he talked. 'I was still in transit. I got a cab from the airport.'

'But you need to go to Scotland,' she said. 'It's the start of the run. Jimmy Finlay needs you to be there.'

'Daisy's on her way,' Mark told her. 'She can deal with everything. I need to be with you.'

'But it's your big day. You've been working up to this,' Holly protested, but Mark raised his fingers to her lips to silence her.

'I want to be with you, Holly.' He took his fingers away and kissed her gently, clasping her hand in his as he did so.

Holly felt so relieved at the familiarity of Mark's touch that she began to cry again, but this time the tears were quieter and gentler.

'I'm so sorry,' she said quietly.

'You've got nothing to be sorry for,' he said. 'I'm the one who should be sorry.'

'What for?' Holly asked, and hoped against hope that he wasn't going to tell her anything she didn't want to hear.

'For not realising how you really were,' Mark said, squeezing her hand. 'I thought you were OK, Holly. I thought you didn't need me. You've always been so strong, I thought you were coping with the crash and going back to work full-time. I should have been this coming.'

'How could you?' She squeezed his hand this time, trying to reassure him. 'How could you have known that anything was wrong when I didn't realise it myself?'

Chapter Fifty-Five

'DO YOU REMEMBER when we went to that gig at Wembley and missed the last train home?' Mark asked.

They had been sitting on the bench together talking for almost an hour now.

'I'd forgotten but I remember it now.' Mark had his arm around her and Holly was resting her head against his chest. She didn't want to move. It felt right now, being here with Mark, sitting like this, talking. She wanted to stay like this for as long as possible.

'We ended up going to Gatwick and sitting on a bench there for half the night,' he reminisced. 'Until the mail train to Brighton arrived. I remember thinking then, when we sat on that bench talking, that I wanted to be with you for the rest of my life.'

'What made you decide then?' Holly asked, thinking that she had thought this about him on the very first night they'd met.

'It was cold and rainy and we had a three-hour wait ahead of us,' he continued. 'I remember thinking that if I'd been with anyone else, I'd have been really pissed off. But I'd have happily sat there for ever, as long as I was with you.'

'There was another thing about that evening.' Holly smiled at her husband. 'We didn't go to the gig together. We met there, do you remember?'

'Vaguely.' He raised his eyebrows.

'You'd been to meet a client in London or something, and we'd arranged to meet outside the tube station at Wembley.' Holly could recall the evening clearly now. 'When we made that arrangement, I thought I'd be the only person there and you'd come out of the tube and look around and see me, but when I arrived there were so many people, all milling around, that I thought we'd never find each other.'

'That was before mobile phones, I suppose, wasn't it?' he queried.

'Yes. There was no way I could contact you if we didn't bump into each other.' Holly remembered the waiting and thinking she'd never find him, not in that crowd.

'Then I saw someone pushing their way through a huge mass of people and making their way towards me.'

'Me?' Mark obviously didn't remember this part of the night the way that Holly did.

'Yes, it was you,' she told him. 'And I asked you how you'd managed to see me, through all those people. Do you remember what you said?'

'That I was "looking for you in the world".' Mark smiled, clearly remembering the moment too. 'It was a D. H. Lawrence quote and I'm sure I patronised you with my sketchy knowledge of his late poetry!'

'You told me it was from one of his poems, yes.' Holly smiled. 'And I remember thinking then how perfectly that summed up what a long-term relationship is about, having someone who looks for you in the world.'

Mark said nothing but looked directly at Holly now, holding her eyes and excluding the rest of the world.

'I could hear you saying that again when you walked towards me along the platform earlier,' she told him. 'I didn't even know it was you until you sat down. You didn't stop to look around. It was as if you knew exactly where I was.'

'Maybe after so long together, Holly,' he said slowly, 'I don't have to look for you in the world any more. I know where to find you.'

'Except I haven't been in the right place for a while.' She looked down, unable to meet his gaze any longer.

'And maybe I wasn't looking hard enough.' Mark tilted her chin up with his hand so that she was forced to look at him again. 'But I have always been looking for you in the world, Holly. You and Chloe and Jake. No one else.'

'I know,' she said, believing him and thinking now that all her fears about Daisy were unfounded. 'Sometimes other people look out for you because they happen to be there, but they're not really looking for you.'

Holly could see clearly now, as if the past few months were in the distant past, that Daniel was someone who just happened to be there and get caught up in her life at a certain time. But Mark, she realised, was the one who was there and always would be.

'Do you mean Daniel?' he said, gently. He appeared to be asking, not accusing her of anything.

'Yes.' Holly looked down at her lap, feeling embarrassed now at how she'd let Daniel take precedence in her thoughts. 'I know it sounds ridiculous, Mark, but he somehow made me feel safe. I felt that if he was around, everything would be OK. Does that sound ridiculous?'

'No, not entirely,' Mark said, taking her hand. 'He was there for you then, wasn't he? He could understand something that I couldn't.'

'I'm sure you could have, if I'd let you,' Holly said softly. 'I know I blocked you out. It was my way of dealing with things.'

'It doesn't matter now.' He squeezed her hand. 'I was preoccupied with work and then the running. I was trying to prove something to you, but I should have been more supportive. It was the least I could have done.'

'It's hard to be supportive if the person you are trying to support won't let you.' Holly looked at him and was struck by how handsome he was, how kind and strong his face was, and how much she loved him.

How could she have lost sight of this, she wondered, and how much damage had she done in the process?

'I have to ask you this, Mark,' she said, looking directly at him. 'I don't want you to be angry, but I have to ask you.'

'You want to know if there is anything going on between me and Daisy?' Mark seemed to know her better than she knew herself.

She nodded.

'There isn't,' he answered his own question. 'Although . . .'

'What?' Holly began to feel cold again, wondering what 'although' preceded.

'I did try to kiss her once.' Mark shrugged and smiled as he said this.

It wasn't a smile of self-satisfaction, more one of mild embarrassment.

'She pushed me away with a firm "I don't think so", as if the very idea were ridiculous. Which it was.'

'It's not that ridiculous.' Holly laughed, now feeling slightly offended that Daisy had thought kissing Mark was out of the question. 'I would have wanted to kiss you, if I'd been her.'

'Thank you.' He smiled. 'But I can see myself though her eyes. Some overweight, middle-aged man who kept going on about his wife not respecting him any more.'

435

Lizzie Enfield

'That's not true,' Holly cut in.

Mark carried on talking. 'I kissed her because she was young and pretty but, to be honest, I was relieved she didn't respond. It wasn't what I wanted. I was just feeling lonely and Daisy seemed to need looking after. She's not very happy, Holly. I have talked to her about you, while we were running, and she's told me stuff about her and Daniel too.'

'I saw him yesterday,' Holly confessed now. 'He told me she'd had a miscarriage and that she didn't want to be with him any more. Did you know?'

'Yes.' Mark nodded. 'She'd told me about the miscarriage. I should have told you, but I promised her I wouldn't. From what she said, I think she feels too young to settle down and have a baby.'

'Daniel's devastated,' Holly said. She decided not to tell him the rest, not yet anyway.

'I think Daniel and I are probably the same, and Guy too.' Mark considered what he was saying before carrying on. 'We all have some Darwinian desire to be the great male protector, but we're all with strong independent women and don't seem to be very good at dealing with that.'

Holly wondered if she should tell him that Daniel had kissed her, but Mark prevented her from doing so by leaning forward and kissing her himself. She felt herself becoming lost in the moment, forgetting everyone else and everything that had happened, wanting nothing more than to stay here for as long as possible.

It was the arrival of a train travelling south towards Brighton which signalled the end of their kiss.

'We should probably think about going home now,' Mark said gently.

'I'm not sure I want to get on another train.' Holly didn't move. 'I don't think I can face it. Not just now, Mark, not yet.'

'I know,' he said, getting to his feet and putting his hand out to her. 'We'll get a taxi or . . .'

He stopped talking and looked down at her feet. Holly was wearing sandals. Her feet had been cold when she'd set off in the morning but she'd known the temperature would rise by midday and she'd have been hot in London.

'Or?' she asked Mark.

'Can you walk in those shoes?'

'Yes.' Holly was not sure what he had in mind.

'We'll walk home then,' Mark said decisively as he stood up and put his hand out to her.

'Are you sure?' It was a long way home and she had no idea how long it would take them. 'It's quite a distance, and you are supposed to be taking it easy still.'

'I feel fine,' he said. 'Let's go.'

He was his old self again, the decisive man of action who could sweep people along with his good-humoured conviction. Or perhaps, Holly thought to herself, he had never been anything other than his old self. It was she who had changed and stopped seeing him properly

'We don't need to rush. We'll stop for lunch somewhere on the way back,' he said, as they walked towards the station exit. 'It doesn't really matter how long it takes, as long as we're together.'

Holly wasn't sure if he was talking about the walk home or more than that. She put her arm around his waist and felt the familiar fit of him as they walked out of the station.

'OK?' Mark asked, folding his arm around her shoulder.

A tannoy announcement made it difficult for her to answer.

'Please stand clear of the train about to arrive on platform four,' a voice coming from a speaker directly above boomed out. 'This is the southbound train from London Victoria. The front eight carriages will be going to Lewes and Eastbourne. The rear four coaches are for Hove and Littlehampton. Please stand clear of the platform while the train is divided.'

Holly didn't answer Mark, just tightened her arm around his waist as they set off towards Brighton.

Acknowledgements

Thanks to all who were positive and encouraging about my first book. You stopped me getting so anxious and paranoid that I could not finish this one!

To my writers group and other writers for keeping me going and being generous and supportive, when I am sure you were inclined to be otherwise, especially Steve who was at both the conception and birth of my last book and helped me keep pushing all the way until it was out.

Thanks also to all my friends who have continued to talk to me, even though they know that by doing so they risk their best anecdotes being fictionalised. You know who you are. So do my family.

To Ruth and Nigel for their medical advice and Caroline and Amanda for the lowdown on restaurants.

Thank you also to Peter Straus and Jenny Hewson at RCW and everyone at Headline, most especially my editor, Imogen Taylor, for nagging me, in the nicest possible way, until I got here.

Now you can buy any of these other bestselling
books from your bookshop
or *direct from the publisher*.

FREE P&P AND UK DELIVERY
(Overseas and Ireland £3.50 per book)

To the Moon and Back	Jill Mansell	£7.99
The Thread	Victoria Hislop	£7.99
The Hand That First Held Mine	Maggie O'Farrell	£7.99
Destiny	Louise Bagshawe	£6.99
The Angel at No. 33	Polly Williams	£6.99
Marrying Up	Wendy Holden	£6.99
The First Wife	Emily Barr	£7.99

TO ORDER SIMPLY CALL THIS NUMBER

01235 400 414

or visit our website: www.headline.co.uk

Prices and availability subject to change without notice.